Rachel Nickerson

Luna

THE EEL GRASS GIRLS MYSTERIES
BOOK 2

The Haunting of Captain Snow

RACHEL NICKERSON LUNA

Emma Howard Books

NEW YORK CITY

THE EEL GRASS GIRLS MYSTERIES
Book 2
The Haunting of Captain Snow
By Rachel Nickerson Luna

© 2003 Rachel Nickerson Luna
Emma Howard Books, New York
Post Office Box 385, Planetarium Station
New York, New York 10024-0385

ISBN 1-886551-08-1
LOCCN: 2002096694

The trademark names *Marshmallow Fluff* and *Fluffernutter*
are used with permission of Durkee-Mower, Inc.

Manufactured in the United States of America

Cover Illustration Armando Luna

Kiki Black, Copy Editor
Book Design by Ian Luna
Typeset in Mrs. Eaves Roman
Printing by
Patterson Printing
Benton Harbor, MI

In Memory of Tia Adamo
1991 — 2001
A young sailor who has safely arrived at
home port ahead of us.

Special thanks to

Leah Bennett
Meira Bennett
Sylvia Doyle
Sophia Griscom
Sara Leschen
Elizabeth Leschen
Antonio Luna
Moraiah Luna
Cody Parker
Alexa Rosenthall
Lucinda Kent Smith
Jane West

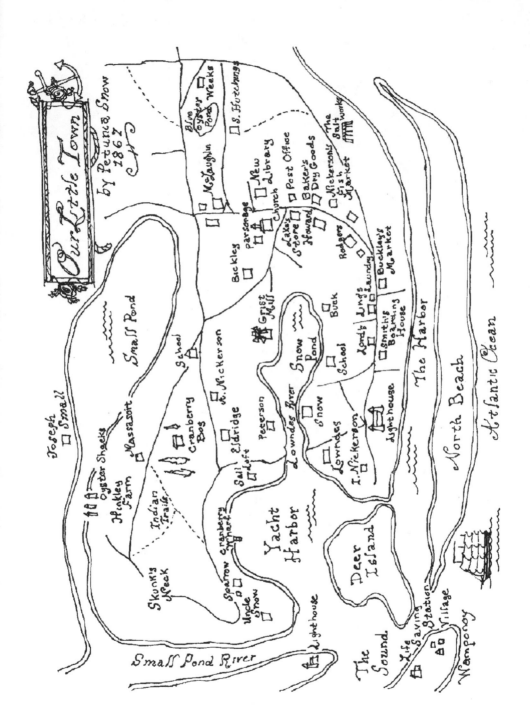

Chapter One

"Tell us about the haunted house," Abigail said to Mollie.

My friends and I sat on the bank of Lowndes River, eating ice cream cones and enjoying our summer on the Cape. Lowndes River flowed under the bridge from Snow Pond out to the harbor, then to the ocean. Sailboats and motorboats filled the waterways on this bright summer day. We had just finished solving a mystery—the murder aboard the *California Girl* fishing boat. We felt fantastic about that, but after almost getting killed a couple of times, we were looking forward to a lazy, normal continuation of our summer vacation.

I was searching the grass for four-leaf clovers. I don't believe in "good luck," but I wanted to find one for my collection of pressed leaves and flowers. I like to preserve flowers, putting them between the pages of books. When I come across the pressed plants in the middle of winter, it fills me with joy. The flowers remind me of warm summer days. I like flowers and nature. My friends call me "Nature Girl."

By the way, I'm Laura Sparrow. I live here in this Cape town all year-round. I say this because my Eel Grass Girl friends Muffy, Abigail, and Mollie come to the Cape only for their summer vacations. The rest of the year they live in other places—other states, to be exact. The four of us met at Yacht Harbor Sailing School where we formed a mystery club called the "Eel Grass Girls." Our motto is "Do the right thing." It isn't easy, though. We found that out when we solved the *California Girl* mystery!

While we were stretched out on the grass next to the "Clam Bar," our favorite snack shop, I didn't feel ready for another mystery. I had to admit, though, a haunted house sounded very interesting. Our relaxed mood changed to excitement at the mention of it!

"I don't believe in ghosts!" Muffy declared. "I don't think there is any such thing as a haunted house."

"Wait 'til you hear what happened to me and Louie Stello!" exclaimed Mollie.

"Who's Louie?" asked Abigail, looking up from her ice cream.

"Louie's in my class at school and he picks his nose," I informed them. Louie lives in town all year-round too. He isn't one of my favorite people.

"I know, but you don't really know him. He's really cool," Mollie insisted. "He knows everything about this town, like Indian trails in the woods, paths leading to mysterious old barns, pieces of shipwrecks on the beach, *haunted houses*."

Then Mollie told us the whole story. "Yesterday afternoon, I saw Louie down at the beach catching minnows—where the stream flows to the beach in front of my house. He wanted to use the minnows for bait. He asked me if I wanted to go fishing with him at Snow Pond."

"You went fishing with him?" I was shocked. We didn't usually have anything to do with boys, except for Billy Jones, but I'll tell you about him later.

"No—I just stood around talking to him while he scooped up the minnows with his net and dumped them into his bucket," answered Mollie. "When he had enough bait, we rode our bikes over the bridge here and down that dirt road up on the left there, to a shortcut he knows to Snow Pond. On the way we heard a horrible wailing, moaning sound!"

"Was it an animal?" asked Abigail, in suspense.

"No! There was no one there. No animal. No person. Nothing. We followed a narrow path to a big old falling-down captain's house. The sound was coming from there, so we crept closer—up to a window—and peeked in."

"And?" asked Muffy, breathlessly.

"No one was there either, but suddenly the door flew open, and a cold gush of air blasted right into our faces! Then the door slammed shut! We didn't hear anything else because we got out of there so fast Louie dropped his bucket! We had to go back and scoop up the minnows before we ran down to Snow Pond!"

Mollie's eyes were as big as quahog shells. She trembled just remembering it!

"There must be a logical explanation," I reasoned, though I couldn't imagine what it could be.

"Remember, I'm 'Miss Logical,'" Mollie reminded us. "Do you think I would believe it was a ghost if there were any other logical explanation?"

"What did Louie think?" asked Muffy.

"Louie said the house was haunted, but everyone says that ghosts don't come out in the daytime. That's why he wasn't afraid to cut through the yard on the way to the pond in the middle of the day. Have you ever heard about that haunted house, Laura?"

"No, but the kids say that every rickety old house in town is haunted," I replied. This kind of talk was nothing new to me. But I never took the stories seriously before.

"Want to check it out?" asked Mollie.

"Sure!" we said in unison. It seemed the "logical" thing to do. I have to admit that I was curious. Something strange had happened to Mollie and Louie. It was a good reason to investigate a haunted house. And it was something I had never done before.

Chapter Two

We finished our ice cream cones. I slung my backpack over my shoulder as we headed for our bicycles, which were leaning against the gray shingles of the snack bar. I couldn't find a four-leaf clover anyway, but I wished that I had. Even though I didn't believe in luck, I felt we needed something—something special for this new mystery. Somehow I had a bad feeling about it.

We rode our bikes across the street and along the dirt road Mollie had told us about. We left our bikes in the bushes. Before us lay a narrow path through towering weeds and brush, choking what was left of an old driveway. Cautiously, we made our way toward the haunted house.

When we approached a clearing, the old captain's house came into view. Was it really haunted? The dark curtainless windows and peeling paint made us think so. Who had lived here? And what had happened to them? The house must have been so beautiful when it was built, but what tragedy had driven the owners away? Why had the mansion been left to rot?

As we crept closer, I noticed a lovely antique rose vine growing up around the columns of the sagging porch. The tiny white petals were tinged with pale pink. My mom had told me how rare these old roses were. You won't find them anywhere except around old houses like this one. The little blossoms were so delicate and alive, not at all like the neglect and decay surrounding the old house.

"It doesn't look haunted to me," Abigail observed. "It looks like any other old house. But it does feel kind of creepy here."

It did feel creepy, but not only creepy. What was it?

"It feels lonely and sad," Muffy said.

"You're right," I agreed. "But it's creepy, too."

"Did Louie tell you how the house became haunted?" Abigail asked Mollie.

"He told me it was owned by Captain Snow," explained Mollie. "Snow Pond was named after him. They say his wife died when she heard he was lost at sea. It was winter and she went up to the widow's walk, that little balcony up on the roof there, and she looked for him, day and night. She wouldn't give up. They found her up there one morning, frozen stiff."

"How horrible!" shivered Abigail.

"Yikes! My mom tells me lots of weird stories," exclaimed Muffy, whose mother had grown up in town. "But she never told me that one! An old woman freezing to death! I'll have to ask her..."

"What was that?" I interrupted.

"What was what?" asked the others, jumping back and clinging to me.

"I just saw something pass by the window," I said, moving forward to get a better look.

"No! Don't go!" pleaded Abigail, grabbing my arm to hold me back.

"I want to see who it is." I pulled away from her and crossed the rotting porch to a window. The big empty room before me looked dismal even with bright sunlight pouring in through its dusty windows. It had once been filled with life and laughter. But now absolutely nothing—no one—was in the room, though I was sure I had seen a white figure pass by the window!

"I know I saw something. Didn't any of you see it?"

"No," they answered, wondering what I might do next.

"Let's get out of here," whined Abigail.

"No," said Mollie, firmly. "Let's find out what's going on. I want to know why this house is being haunted. It's our new mystery, don't you see? There must be more to the story of Captain Snow. Let's go in and look around. Maybe we can find some clues."

"What did you see, Laura?" asked Abigail, trembling.

"It looked like a figure quickly passing by the window. The window is so dusty that it looked white." It seemed logical.

"Sounds like a ghost to me." Abigail's voice shook. "And it's against the law to enter someone's house when they're not home."

"Well, Miss 'Lawyer's Daughter,' they *are* home," said Mollie. We didn't understand what she meant.

"What do you mean?" asked Muffy, quizzically.

"The ghosts!" Mollie explained. "Don't you get it? They live here. This is their house and they're crying out for help. They're trying to communicate with us. They want us to find out who killed them. It's Captain Snow and his wife!"

"But they weren't killed!" I protested. "You said yourself that the Captain was lost at sea and his wife froze to death. No one killed anyone."

"Someone must have been killed or there wouldn't be any ghosts," persisted Mollie. "Come on!"

"What if you fall through the floor and get hurt?" Abigail asked with concern.

"It doesn't look that bad," I concluded, peeking through the window again. "The porch is broken, but see inside? The floor in there looks solid enough. I'm going in. Who's coming with me?" I was surprised that I was more curious than afraid. I suspected it was one of the local kids playing a trick on us.

"I'll go with you," offered Mollie. "Muffy, you and Abigail stay outside."

"No way," Muffy protested. "I'm going too."

"You're not leaving me out here all alone," Abigail announced. So the four of us approached the four-paneled wooden door with its two "bull's-eye" glass windows at the top and carefully pushed it open on its creaking hinges.

The large room we entered was empty. No ghosts. But it seemed strange not to see any footprints on the dusty floor! There was no evidence of anyone having been in that room for at least a hundred years! If some local kids were in the house, they must be floating on air!

As we looked around, we saw cobwebs hanging from every corner. A musty, moldy smell filled the air. The room we had entered had probably been the parlor, the room used for weddings and funerals. The bright sunlight coming in through the big windows and French doors filled the room but could not dispel the gloomy feeling. Just like the musty smell, the gloom was getting to me. I really didn't like it. I wanted to leave.

As I looked around, I couldn't help but notice the decorative molding lining the ceilings, so beautiful even under the layers of dust. My dad is a carpenter and his specialty is restoring old homes, so he's taught me a lot about them. From the style of the architecture, I guessed that this house was built around 1850, not long before the Civil War. At the back of the parlor we discovered a hallway leading to a sitting room, library, kitchen, and stairway.

We headed to the back to investigate the library first. All the furniture and draperies in the house were long gone, yet oddly enough, books still lined the library shelves. And to our surprise, the books appeared to be in good condition. I reached for a volume to see if it held any clues. When I extended my hand, the room turned ice cold! We all felt it and looked at each other in horror.

"Is it cold in here or what?" asked Mollie, looking around to see from which direction the cold air was coming.

"I don't like this," began Abigail.

Before we could say anything more, something even scarier happened! My hand was still stretched out for the book when I felt a strong, rough grip on mine, preventing my hand from moving! I couldn't SEE anything, but I sure could FEEL it!

"*What's going on?*" I cried.

"What's the matter?" asked the Girls, staring at my hand frozen in midair.

"I can't move my hand! Somebody's got my hand! It's the ghost!" My expression of sheer terror convinced my friends I wasn't joking. Muffy was the first to help me. She grabbed my collar and pulled me out of the room. Invisible icy fingers stroked my cheek! I screamed and screamed! Muffy kept pulling. The hand gripping mine wouldn't let go! The other Girls helped her, pushing and pulling me through the parlor until we were out the front door on the porch. The coldness followed us onto the front step. The hand let go of me as the coldness faded. I was free! Then the door slammed shut in our faces!

"Let's get out of here!" I sobbed as I stumbled through the overgrowth to the dirt road. The Girls ran close behind me. We grabbed our bikes out of the bushes and pedaled out onto the street.

"To the yacht club!" Muffy shouted as we raced down the road, startling the tourists fishing on the bridge.

Chapter Three

We pedaled hard until we reached the club, where we tossed our bikes into the blackberry bushes and rushed inside the clubhouse. Panting for breath, we threw ourselves down into the wooden captain's chairs surrounding the long varnished table. I was shaking and pale as were the other Eel Grass Girls. No one else was in the clubhouse, but we felt safe. It was comforting to be in familiar surroundings. The older kids were out racing in the harbor and all the instructors were with them.

"What just happened back there?" asked Abigail. We were too stunned to fully comprehend it. Mollie was the first to answer.

"It was the ghost! There's no other explanation."

"The ghost didn't want me to take any of the books from the library shelf! Its hand clutched mine so tightly I couldn't move! Then it touched my cheek with its icy fingers! Oooh! Those hands were so cold and rough and strong!" I exclaimed with a shiver.

"It must have been Old Lady Snow," surmised Mollie. "She froze to death so it's her spirit haunting the house. She can't rest because her husband died and never returned."

"But my mom says that when a person dies, they go either to heaven or hell," Muffy informed us. "Isn't that what you believe, Laura?"

"I did believe that until today. Now I'm not so sure. All I know is that something grabbed me, something—or someone—I couldn't see." I stammered. "Maybe Mrs. Snow has come back from the grave."

"If it wasn't a ghost, then what was it?" Mollie asked Muffy.

"I don't know, but I'm going to find out," Muffy assured us.

"My grandmother told me that a ghost is the spirit of someone who was murdered," Mollie informed us. "They can't get to heaven because the murderer has never been found out. They can't rest until they tell someone, someone who's alive. That's the reason why they stay around, haunting houses. We have to discover what really happened to Captain Snow. Then Mrs. Snow can rest."

"It's not even Halloween!" Muffy noted, trying to get a laugh. It didn't work. We were all too spooked to appreciate her joke. I had just had a supernatural encounter. It wasn't funny.

We sat there, somber and shaking. Our world had been turned upside down, just as it had been when we found that dead body on the fishing boat a few weeks earlier. We had stumbled upon a new mystery, but would this mystery be dangerous as well? Last time we had investigated real flesh and blood fishermen.

Now we were facing someone who was invisible! And she or he seemed to be just as evil!

"What are we going to do now?" asked Abigail.

"I'm going to tell Louie what happened and see if he knows anything more about the Snows," said Mollie "He might know something he hasn't told me yet."

"I'll talk to my parents," I said. "They might have heard about the Snows. And my grandparents! They're pretty old. We visit them every Sunday. They might remember something about the story from the past. I'll ask them when I see them on Sunday."

"Muffy, you could ask your mom," Abigail suggested. "She grew up in town. She knows everyone so she might be able to think of an older person you could ask about the Snows. Maybe someone has heard rumors or stories about that old house. Anything would help us with our case."

"O.K. And I'll stop by the library on my way home to research Captain Snow," suggested Muffy. She just loved the library.

"There's old Mrs. Wiggins," remembered Mollie. "She lives down the road from me in that little rose-covered cottage. She's lived here all her life and she's really old. I bet she knows something. I'll stop by on my way home."

A warm gentle breeze blew in through the open doors of the clubhouse, unlike the cold rush of wind we had felt at Captain Snow's. The familiar dark wooden walls and benches along their sides, cluttered with ropes, soggy life pre-servers, and discarded articles of salt-encrusted clothing, made us feel secure. We could hear Mr. Prince, our sailing master, shouting orders to the older kids as they sailed in from their races and stowed the 420s (the sleek, fast, fiberglass sailboats) on the dock.

As we sat there not talking, I began thinking. Ours was a charming little town with beaches, fishing boats, lighthouses, and a windmill. I had lived here my whole life, but I had never dreamed that so many scary things went on all around us. Our last mystery had involved a murder. Now we had encountered ghosts!

"What can I do?" asked Abigail, breaking the silence. "I don't know anyone to ask about the mystery."

"Isn't Slim H. your grammy's gardener?" asked Mollie.

"Yes," responded Abigail.

"Well, ask him," suggested Mollie. "He's a local yokel."

"Mollie, don't use that expression!" Muffy scolded her.

"You know what I mean," Mollie defended herself.

"Yes, I do. That's why I don't want you to use it! Just because you weren't born here doesn't make you better than Slim H. You can't imagine how it feels to hear that kind of talk!" She sounded really hurt.

"You were born in New York City, so what do you care?" Mollie countered.

"My mother was born here and so was Laura and her parents. It seems that some 'summer people' have an attitude. You think you're so sophisticated compared to them. Maybe you are, but that doesn't make you better. Just because Slim H. has lived here his whole life doesn't make him inferior."

I agreed with Muffy, but I don't like to argue with people or tell them how I really feel inside. I'm too shy, I guess, but I admired Muffy for speaking up.

"I'm sorry," pouted Mollie.

"Next time, leave off the 'yokel,'" Muffy reprimanded her. "You can say 'locals,' but that's it."

"K," said Mollie, hanging her head.

We forgave her, but we still sat there brooding. First we were scared to death by invisible spirits and now we were fighting each other! We had to get a hold of ourselves! We didn't feel like moving along with any of our plans. We didn't feel like doing anything.

"What's this? Another mystery being solved?" We were startled out of our misery by Mr. Prince, our sailing master, who had just come up from the beach with a few instructors and some of the older sailors. "We need this table for a protest meeting."

Mr. Prince had known all about our first mystery. He had been there to pull us out of the water when one of the bad guys tried to kill us by bashing his motorboat into our sailboat. But we were going to keep this mystery a secret—for now, anyway. The sailors sat down for their meeting, trying to figure out who had violated which sailing rule during their race. Whoever was in the wrong would be thrown out of the race completely. It was serious business if you were out to win a trophy for the season.

Moving out to the deck overlooking the harbor, we plopped down on the gray, weathered benches, which were warm from the summer sun. Down below, the rest of the sailors rolled up their sails and stowed them away in bins lining the pier. Boats paraded by the club dock. Sightseeing cruises were leaving from the town pier to the port—I mean the left—of us. Out on the water, starboard means right and port is left. The assistant harbormaster was on duty, patrolling the harbor. Working fishing boats were bringing in their catch.

I watched pairs of butterflies dance over wild roses and blackberry bushes stretching from the clubhouse down to the shore. The little insects seemed so happy and free. I wished I could feel that way, but for now we had to stop fighting and get to work. The Eel Grass Girls had a job to do!

"At least no one's dead," muttered Muffy.

"You mean they all died a long time ago," corrected Mollie.

Abigail spoke almost in a whisper, "Maybe Mrs. Snow didn't freeze to death. Maybe she was murdered. That's why she's haunting us!"

15

"Maybe it's Captain Snow. The cold feeling doesn't mean the ghost is Mrs Snow," Mollie reasoned. "He could have been murdered and that's why he never came home from his voyage." We sat there wondering about our ghostly encounter while the older sailors climbed up the wooden stairs to the clubhouse.

"My dad is having one of his famous cookouts tonight," I told the Girls. "Why don't you all come over for dinner? We'll have a sleepover. Bring your sleeping bags. We can sleep out on the patio. We'll do our research now and then discuss what we find out when we get together tonight. K.?"

"What about the band concert?" asked Abigail. It was our routine to meet at the evening concert held at the gazebo every Friday night.

"We have a serious mystery to solve and cookout goodies to eat. Maybe we could skip it for one week," suggested Mollie. We agreed.

"But we'll go back to our schedule next week?" asked Abigail. We said we would. Now we were sounding more like the Eel Grass Girls!

We would get to work. Abigail rode to her grandmother's house where she stayed for the summer. It was near the lighthouse and Coast Guard station. Muffy rode down Yacht Harbor Road to the library on Main Street. Mollie and I lived almost next door to each other so we would ride home together along the harbor.

"Hey, wait a minute!" I called to Mollie as I ran back into the clubhouse. I had left my backpack lying on the bench. A few female instructors were still hanging around. When I came out, I noticed that the sky had become overcast. We travelled along the road which followed the shore. Little wisps of fog blew in from over the water. I turned into my driveway. "See you later!" I called to Mollie as she rode on to her house, a little further down the road.

Chapter Four

When I pedaled up to the house, I saw Mom out back hanging laundry on the clothesline, which runs from the back of the house to a pole stuck out in the yard.

"Hi Mom!" I greeted her. I had come around the house after putting my bike in the barn.

"How's my Mystery Girl?" she asked, smiling at me as she shook out an undershirt.

"May the Girls sleep over tonight?" I asked, smiling back at her.

"You know your dad is planning a cookout," she reminded me.

"I know. That's why I invited them."

"You already invited them?" she asked in surprise.

"Pleeeeease?" I begged.

"You know your dad will have more than enough food! All right," she consented, with a laugh.

"We have another mystery," I informed her. Then I nonchalantly asked, "What are ghosts?"

"Is this a ghost mystery? Something to do with a haunted house maybe?" she asked.

"How did you know?" I was startled. But I guess it was obvious.

"Ghosts like to live in houses the same way we do. They have to live somewhere," she joked.

"To be serious," she added, seeing that I wasn't amused, "I don't think they really are ghosts but evil spirits. Whenever someone visits an abandoned house, they suddenly appear. They like to scare us for some reason."

"Don't they sometimes show up in houses where people are living too?" I asked.

"Yes, that's true, but I think it's always a house where someone has died in unusual circumstances. The spirit appears in the form of the dead person, though I don't believe the spirit really is the dead person," Mom added.

"Your explanation is confusing!" I complained. "How can the ghost be a spirit but not the spirit of the dead person? Whose spirit is it then?"

"Well," began Mom. "The spirit is a demon who has taken on the appearance of the dead person."

"Why?" I asked. It didn't make sense! But it sounded scary. It seemed worse for it to be a demon haunting the house than old Mrs. Snow!

"What better way to scare four little girls?" asked Mom, though it seemed more like a statement than a question. She didn't seem to be taking me very seriously.

"What's your mystery?" she asked.

"The Captain Snow house on Snow Pond. Did you ever hear about it or go there when you were young?" I asked.

"No. I never went there, but now that you mention it, I do remember hearing about the house when I was a child. I haven't thought about it in years! They said Mrs. Snow froze to death while waiting for Captain Snow to return from a voyage. She went up to her widow's walk on top of the roof, day and night, all year-round. As I remember, the kids used to sneak into the house. They said that Mrs. Snow's ghost would grab them with her cold, bony fingers and exhale her freezing breath in their faces."

"That's just what happened to me!" I exclaimed.

"You were in Captain Snow's house?" Mom suddenly changed her tone of voice.

"Yes," I confessed. "Mollie and her friend went there yesterday and heard moaning. They peeked in the window. The freezing air blew out of the door right onto them. The Girls and I went over today to check it out and we went in."

"That's private property! You know you shouldn't go into someone's house like that." While she scolded me she was wringing out some of my underwear and other laundry before attaching it to the clothesline with wooden clothespins. It was an effective way of getting her point across.

"But the house is abandoned!" I protested. "If the owner cared about it, he would fix it up."

"You don't know what reasons he has for not taking care of it. I want you to stay away from that house. You might get hurt falling through a rotten floorboard or it might collapse on top of you."

"But Mom," I whined. "We have a mystery to solve!" Why had I told her about the house? If I'd kept it to myself, she wouldn't have forbidden me to go back. I wouldn't have to feel guilty when I disobeyed her later. Because I knew we'd go back there again.

"What if I find out who owns the house and get permission?" I asked her.

"All right," she replied very smugly, thinking I would never be able to do that. As she continued hanging the clothes, I marched into the house, got out the phone book, and called the town offices. There had to be a way of finding out who owned that property. The town clerk connected me to the tax collector who told me that the house belonged to Alfred Snow of Cleveland, Ohio. I then looked up the area code for Cleveland and called information to get his number. Fortunately there was only one Alfred Snow in the city. And he just happened to be at home.

"Uh, Mr. Snow?"

"Yes," he answered. He sounded old but dignified and cultured, the sort of grandson Captain Snow would have been proud of had he ever lived to know him. Or maybe it was his great-grandson. He paused, waiting for me to continue.

"This is Laura Sparrow from the Cape, in Massachusetts. I'm calling about your house here. The one that belonged to Captain Snow."

"Yes?" He waited for me to go on.

"My friends and I would like permission to go in the house so we can solve a mystery," I blurted out, immediately regretting that I had mentioned the word "mystery."

"What sort of mystery?" he asked suspiciously. I told him about Mollie and Louie's adventure, the story of our encounter with the ghost, and what my mom had said about evil spirits.

"Let me tell you the real story, my dear. There is no mystery at all, except why my family has been silent for so many years about what happened. Captain Snow was my great-grandfather," Alfred Snow began. "It was partly as you said: Captain Snow was reported lost at sea and his wife, Susanna Bickly Snow, was found frozen to death on the rooftop. But that is only a small portion of the story. There is much, much more." Mr. Snow took a deep breath and continued.

"My grandfather was 20 years old when his parents died. Grandfather said that the house was always cold after his mother passed on. He and his sisters sensed that the house was haunted, so they wouldn't stay there. Grandfather traveled to Boston to study, then moved out here to Cleveland. His sisters went to live with relatives in Milton, near Boston. They never returned to the house again."

"They must have sold all the furniture," I interjected. "Nothing's left except the books in the library,"

"That's strange," mused Mr. Snow. "I would have thought that everything would have been cleared out. If not by Grandfather and his sisters before they moved, then by vandals."

"But that's the point," I urged. "The ghost won't let anyone touch the books. I told you that she caught my hand and held onto me when I tried to take a book from the shelf."

"Well, I don't know about that," said Mr. Snow. He hesitated. "You said 'she.' Do you think that the ghost is my great-grandmother?"

"I'm not sure. Both your great-grandparents died, but only your great-grandmother died in the house, so she's probably the one who's haunting it."

"Yes, yes," muttered Mr. Snow. "But let me finish the story. Wait a minute. Just how old *are* you? You don't sound old enough to solve a mystery."

"We've already solved one mystery. We even worked with the local police and the United States Coast Guard," I bragged, evading his question. "Please tell me everything."

"Well, never mind your age. Captain Elkinah Snow was a good sea captain," Mr. Snow explained. "He showed great concern for his sailors and took good care of the ships he sailed. At the time of his death, he was sailing a schooner called the *Agnes* owned by two prominent local townsfolk, Mr. Lowndes and Mr.

McLaughlin. My great-grandfather had always spent the rainy season at port in China. It was safer to travel home after the monsoons had past. But no! Mr. Lowndes and Mr. McLaughlin insisted on a schedule that would force him to return with his cargo of Oriental silks and spices during the most dangerous period of storms. If he didn't, he would lose his job and reputation. He had to return on their schedule, or else!"

"But why?" I asked. "Wouldn't they have wanted to wait so the ship could sail home safely? They wouldn't want the boat to sink and lose all their cargo!"

"Ah! That is the irony of it!" Mr. Snow's voice was grave. "Mr. McLaughlin had the *Agnes* was insured to the hilt. He wouldn't lose a dime whether the ship came home or not. In fact, my great-grandmother found out from her nephew, who happened to be McLaughlin's bookkeeper, that the old scoundrels would stand to make *more* money if the ship *did* sink! Her nephew also told her McLaughlin had tremendous gambling debts. He needed that extra money. He would collect a bundle of cash if the ship was lost at sea. That piece of information alone could have killed the poor woman!"

"With all that evidence, couldn't your great-grandmother have brought a case against Mr. McLaughlin?" I asked.

"Not with Lowndes being the local judge! No, she just went up to her widow's walk that frosty winter night and never came down again—alive that is."

What a horrible story! It made me shiver just to hear it. Yet, it was not really a mystery, as Mr. Snow had said. He had all the facts and details of what had taken place all those years ago. It was more of a tragedy. Only one question remained: Why was Mrs. Snow haunting the house?

"My great-grandmother's spirit wants justice!" he thundered in my ear, as if he could read my mind. "My grandfather, my father, and I have done nothing about it. We have never gone back to the old home. We have stayed away from it and from her. We have blocked our eyes and ears and hearts to the cries of her soul pleading day and night for justice! Mr. McLaughlin and Mr. Lowndes must be convicted for their crimes! Then and only then can my dear great-grandmother's soul sleep in peace." He wasn't really making sense.

"Aren't those men dead by now?" I asked, wondering what he was talking about.

"Yes, of course they are, but no one ever accused them. They died without a spot on their reputations, yet they were murderers! They killed my great-grandparents, destroyed my grandfather's happy home, drove us all away, ruined our lives. The public must learn what they did. Yes! You, Laura Sparrow—that is your name, isn't it? You must bring this case to the media. Expose "Lowndes & McLaughlin" for who they really were. I will even pay you. After the truth is known, my great-grandmother will be able to rest in peace. Why have I never thought of this before?

"I'll do what I can, Mr. Snow," I told him. I hung up the phone. Yikes! What a story! We now had permission to go into Captain Snow's house, but there was no mystery to solve. Mr. Snow wanted us to tell the world that it was the evil shipowners who were responsible for the *Agnes* sinking and for the death of his great-grandparents. But what I couldn't understand was why the ghost wasn't helping us! Why was she keeping us from reading the old books in her library? It just didn't make sense.

Chapter Five

"Still thinking about that haunted house?" asked Mom. We were in the kitchen, preparing for the cookout.

"It was really frightening," I confessed.

"I'm sorry I didn't take you seriously at first. Would you like to talk to your dad about what happened?"

"Yes. I'd like to know if he remembers that old house and any stories he heard about the Snows." I didn't share my conversation with Alfred Snow with her. But I would have to tell her sooner or later before she got the phone bill!

We continued washing and peeling vegetables for the salad. Dad had already prepared the meats for cooking and was outside starting a fire under the grill. I had another question for Mom. All this talk about ghosts and dying had made me think of something.

"What happens to children when they die?"

"Children go to heaven to be with God forever. We'll see them when we get there." She sounded so sure. It was comforting to hear her talk like that.

There was a knock at the door and the Girls filed in. Somehow they had all managed to ride their bikes and carry their backpacks and sleeping bags at the same time!

"Hi, Mrs. Sparrow!" they called to Mom as they dumped their gear in the mud room. That's what we call the little room at the back door where we leave our boots and hang wet drippy things.

"Hi, girls!" she called back. "Will you please help me take these dishes out?"

We carried all the food and plates out onto the patio to the long picnic table covered with a red-checked tablecloth. The patio was between our house and barn. Our rambling antique home had been in my dad's family for over 200 years. Dad's family, the Sparrows, had come over from England and settled first in Boston. When they moved to the Cape, they built our house in another town further up the Cape. Then about 150 years ago, the family moved it to its current location. That's right. They picked it up off its old foundation, transported it through the streets on a horse-drawn barge, to its current location. They plunked it down on a new foundation. And here it has stayed. It was cheaper than building a new house!

My dad grew up in this house. He's a carpenter as I told you and my mom works as a visiting nurse. She goes to people's homes to help out after they've had an operation or serious illness or if people are just too old to take care of themselves. She grew up in our town too.

"It's going to take a while for these coals to heat up," Dad told us. "Why don't you girls run along? I'll call you when the burgers and chicken are done."

That was our cue to go down to the beach. We ran to the edge of the lawn and followed the sandy path through the towering wild rosebushes.

"These roses are going to have plenty of rose hips for jelly this year," I pointed out as we brushed past the pink petals.

"What are rose hips?" asked Abigail.

"They're these seed pods here." I answered, pulling a tiny hip from a bush and showing the girls the hard, shiny, red-orange tomatolike fruit. I opened it so they could see the insides, all full of seeds and surrounded by a sticky layer of pulp. "They're the seed pods of roses. Lots of vitamin C and they make wonderful jelly," I informed them.

"We'll take your word for it, Nature Girl!" teased Mollie, continuing down the path.

"You'll see next month," I promised. "That's when my mom and I harvest the hips and start our jelly making. Maybe you'll come over and help." They agreed that they'd like that.

When we reached the shore, we strolled along. A light fog was blowing in from Womponoy Sound, the body of water between the mainland of the Cape and a group of islands to the south. The breeze was keeping the mosquitoes and nosee'ems away. Do you have nosee'ems where you live? They're tiny bugs, so tiny that you can't "see 'em," but you can feel 'em in your ears, up your nose, and on your skin when they bite! They weren't bothering us tonight, thankfully.

"What did you find out at the library, Muffy?" asked Abigail.

"Well, I could hardly wait to tell you! It seems that Captain Snow was quite a character. First of all, he sailed a ship belonging to my great-great-grandfather George McLaughlin and his partner, Salathiel Lowndes!" she gushed.

Oh no! Mr. McLaughlin, the murdering gambler, was Muffy's relative!

"What else did you find out?" asked Mollie.

"I read that there was some kind of problem between Captain Snow and the ship's owners. For some reason, Mr. McLaughlin and Mr. Lowndes planned to 'relieve Captain Snow of his duties,' as the papers said, as soon as he arrived back from his voyage."

"What was the problem?" asked Abigail.

"I couldn't find out. It's frustrating to research something that happened so far in the past! There was an article about Captain Snow being called before the church elders. One old newspaper made it sound serious."

"I called Mr. Alfred Snow in Cleveland, Ohio, this afternoon," I began. All eyes were upon me as my friends' mouths fell open.

"Say what?" asked Mollie.

"Mr. Alfred Snow. He's the great-grandson of Captain Snow. He told me his version of what happened."

"What do you mean, *his* version?" asked Muffy, sounding surprised and maybe a little defensive.

"Well, Mr. Snow said that Mr. Lowndes and Mr. McLaughlin had the ship insured for so much money that they didn't care whether it sank or not."

"What good is a ship on the bottom of the ocean?" asked Mollie.

"That's what I wondered," I confided. "But Mr. Snow told me that Mr. McLaughlin had insured the ship for so much money that he would make more money by it sinking than he would if the ship came back to port and he sold all the goods."

"That's not true!" yelled Muffy, her face red from anger. "Captain Snow had some kind of problem! All the newspapers and biographies said so. Alfred Snow knows all about it, but he just doesn't want to admit it. Besides, my great-great-grandfather was an upright man."

"Don't get so upset," I said, trying to calm her down. "I only know what Mr. Snow told me. He said that Mr. McLaughlin had huge gambling debts and needed the insurance money as quickly as possible so he could pay them off."

"He did *not* have gambling debts!" Muffy practically screamed at me. Her eyes were filling with tears. "He was a very strict man and he didn't believe in drinking, smoking, dancing, *or* gambling."

"What could Captain Snow's problem have been?" Abigail meekly asked. "Do you think he could have been stealing the cargo and selling it on his own?"

"I don't know," admitted Muffy. "But I'll find out!"

"Maybe they both had secrets," suggested Mollie. Muffy gave her a really annoyed look.

"The town was so small back then," she said, "it would've been difficult to have a problem such as gambling and keep it a secret."

"The townspeople suspected Captain Snow of something," I added. "Whatever it was, he couldn't have been able to keep it a secret either. Let's try to find out what it was."

"It won't be easy," mused Abigail.

We walked on in silence. I stooped to pick up a perfect orange scallop shell lying on the white sand beside a pile of dried eel grass. I put it in my pocket to save for making a "sailor's valentine," one of my favorite crafts. The old-fashioned sailors made their valentines by decorating wooden boxes with shells they collected from around the world. Mine were cardboard hearts glued with shells to be hung on the wall. I wondered if Captain Snow had ever made a valentine for Mrs. Snow.

"How can we solve a mystery when everyone is dead and it's been over a hundred years since the events occurred?" asked Abigail. "My dad is a lawyer and he's never had a case like this! There's no one to question. And I'm sure that the books in the town library aren't going to give us all the details we need. I'm surprised that you found out as much as you did, Muffy—and Laura. I spoke to Slim H. when he came over to mow Grammy's yard this afternoon. He said he heard from his father that the Snows were 'uppity' people who moved away because they thought they were too good for this town."

"Well," began Mollie. "Wait 'til you hear what old Mrs. Wiggins told me! She said that the Snow house had always been haunted, even *before* the Captain and Mrs. Snow died! When her grandmother was a little girl, her mother used to send her over there to buy herbs. She was so frightened of Mrs. Snow that she would pretend to be sick so she wouldn't have to go. Mrs. Wiggins thought her grandmother knew a lot more, but always seemed afraid to tell her anything else."

"That sounds mysterious," Abigail concluded. An accurate summation from Lawyer's Daughter!

Just then we heard our dinner bell ringing. Yes, we have a dinner bell. It's an old ship's bell, which my grandfather got from a shipwreck over on the outer bar. He said it wasn't stealing. After a ship ran aground during a storm or in the fog, the owners of the ship would hire salvagers to save whatever they could from it. Then the townspeople were allowed to take what was left. There's even a little shack near the lighthouse, which was built entirely of wood from ships that crashed on the deadly sandbars surrounding our little seaside town. But that's another story.

Chapter Six

The bell rang again. "Time for dinner!" I announced as I led the Girls back up the hillside to my house. As we crossed the lawn, we ducked under the clothesline and around the corner of the house to the patio.

Dad set a big plate of burgers and chicken down on the table. My mom doesn't believe in hot dogs, if you know what I mean. "Too many mysterious ingredients in them," she says. That was fine with me. I can live without those kinds of mysteries as well!

We found our places around the picnic table laden with salads, drinks, and corn on the cob. It was a feast! My dad had a secret marinade for the meat that made it taste extra special. You would never miss the hot dogs!

"I guess you girls are finished with mysteries now," my father said between bites of potato salad. The Girls and I looked at each other. Mom caught our glances.

"I think they're on a new case already," she told him, smiling.

Now was our chance to say something. We usually kept our mysteries a secret unless we really needed help from an adult. Maybe Dad could help us. We needed all the links to the past that we could get.

"We visited the old Captain Snow house today and had a frightening experience," I told him. "Something invisible caught hold of my hand as I tried to reach for a book on the library shelf."

"Maybe some kind of anti-theft device," he joked.

"It's not funny, Dad," I said. "It really happened."

"Why were you in that old house in the first place?" he asked, suddenly serious.

"Mollie and her friend had gone over there yesterday and heard moaning. The door flew open all by itself and a cold wind blew out so we went over today to investigate," I told him.

"That's private property, Laura," said Dad, frowning. "You girls are not to go into other people's houses without their permission, no matter what condition the house is in! But you're not the first kids to sneak into an old abandoned house," he added, a dreamy look coming over his face as he remembered the past.

"My childhood friends used to sneak into abandoned homes, including Captain Snow's. Funny thing is, they used to say just what you said, that there was an icy wind blowing inside the house. Always scared them away. And the moaning, they heard that too, I remember. I have to admit, I went into the old Atkins house before it burned down, but that doesn't mean you should do it."

Parents are like that. They were kids once and did all sorts of things, but they don't want us to do those same things. Instead, they want us to learn from their mistakes. It makes sense, I guess. They don't want us to get hurt. They want to protect us, but sometimes it seems that they're just trying to keep us from having fun and doing the things that kids do! At least my parents admitted their past mistakes. Maybe now was my chance to tell them about my conversation with Mr. Snow.

"I don't really want to go back to Captain Snow's house, but Mom said we could if we got permission. I called Mr. Alfred Snow, the owner, in Ohio, and he told us we could go in the house and solve the mystery," I blurted out.

"*What?*" asked Mom, shocked by what I'd done. "You did what?"

"I called Mr. Snow," I repeated. "It was your suggestion. I thought it was a good idea," I added, trying to "butter her up," as they say. "The town offices told me that Alfred Snow owns the property and the telephone operator gave me his phone number in Ohio. He's very nice. Captain Snow was his great-grand-father. He told me the death of the captain and his wife broke up the whole family and drove them away from this town. Mr. Snow thinks he knows what killed them. He asked me to publicize the facts so the spirit of his great-grandmother can rest."

"Oh," remarked Mom. She didn't know what to say to all that. The Girls eyed me nervously. They were afraid that we'd all get into trouble now.

"I'll pay for the phone bill with my allowance," I added, hoping to not get scolded.

Dad gave me a look that made me feel very uncomfortable. "Laura, I don't want to reprimand you in front of your friends, but you know that you are not allowed to make long-distance phone calls without our permission."

"Yes, Dad," I admitted. Trying to blame it on Mom hadn't worked. She didn't specifically tell me to call Mr. Snow. It had been sneaky, the way I'd done it. I had wanted to get my own way and hadn't wanted to take a chance of being denied by asking my mom. Now I was going to get punished in front of my friends!

"I'm sorry, Mom and Dad." I thought it was better to not say any more, rather than offer excuses. I hung my head and looked down at my plate, as if that could help.

"If you pay for the call out of your allowance, you may call Mr. Snow again and solve your mystery," Dad said. I was surprised! He was smiling so we all smiled back at him.

"I was a kid once myself," he confided to us, though that was hard to believe. Well, I guess it had to be true. "You did the right thing by calling Mr. Snow to ask for permission, but next time get permission from us first before you make the call. I don't think a cold breeze will hurt you girls. As long as you let us know when you're going over to Captain Snow's and don't walk over any rotten floorboards, I think you'll be all right."

"Hurray!" we cried. Mom was laughing. This was better than I could have imagined—we had my parents' and Mr. Snow's permission to solve our new mystery. We usually didn't like grownups to be involved in our business, but as I said, it seemed we needed them on this case, more than ever.

"Mr. Sparrow," began Muffy. "At the library there were a few books which mentioned Captain Snow and the ship he sailed. One of the owners of the ship was my relative, who my family says was a good man. Alfred Snow says that he, my great-great-grandfather, was a gambler, and he wanted the ship to sink so he could collect the insurance money to pay for his gambling debts. An old newspaper I found at the library told about Captain Snow being in trouble, but didn't tell exactly what..."

"And old Mrs. Wiggins said that Mrs. Snow was scary and the house was haunted even before Captain Snow and his wife died," interrupted Mollie.

"How can we find out the truth about something that happened so long ago?" asked Abigail.

"Well," began Dad, as Mom brought out a plate piled high with homemade chocolate chip cookies. "You have your work cut out for you! You'll have to ferret out the information, but the truth is, it may no longer exist, if it ever did."

"What do you mean?" I asked as I wiped cookie crumbs from my mouth with a red-checked napkin.

"Muffy's relative probably kept business records. There might be old letters tucked away in someone's attic or a bit of gossip passed down from generation to generation. Or maybe not. It's possible no one recorded anything about Captain Snow other than what you've read in the library. If there was more, it could all be gone by now. Lost in a fire or flood or just thrown out. The only way to know for sure is to ask around. It will take some work, but you'll learn about the old days and it should keep you out of trouble for a while!" he laughed. We didn't think it was so funny. Where would we start?

"I'll ask my mom about our relatives," said Muffy. "My aunt has all kinds of stuff. Her desk and cupboard are full of old papers. And my grandmother has a whole house filled with antique trunks and things. There must be some information for us in all that paperwork! Maybe we could spend an afternoon going through it all,"

"It may take weeks," warned Dad.

I shrugged my shoulders. "If that's what it takes...," I said, not finishing my sentence.

"Aren't you girls going to the band concert tonight?" asked Mom.

"We didn't want to miss Dad's cookout and we had to have a sleepover. We'll go next week," I informed her.

After we cleared the table, we helped Mom wash the dishes. Dad cleaned the grill and put it back in the barn after dumping out the coals. We should have made s'mores. You must know "some mores," those yummy snacks made of chocolate bars melted by hot toasted marshmallows when sandwiched between graham crackers. Then we could have put those glowing coals to good use, but we were out of marshmallows. Mom looked out the kitchen window.

"The fog is rolling in, girls," she observed. "Will you all run out and bring the laundry in please? If anything is still damp, hang it up here." She pointed to the clothesline hanging on the wall over the washing machine.

The clothesline was set up so it could be attached to the opposite wall. It was a little embarrassing to have a clothesline in the kitchen. Everyone else in the world has a dryer, but do we? No! My parents have to hang the clothes on a clothesline! Yes, my dad sometimes helps with the wash. I'm surprised we even have a washer! The Girls and I ran out with the old wicker laundry basket and brought the clothes in. Some were still damp, so we stretched the line across the room and began to hang them up to dry.

"Don't you think you ought to sleep inside tonight? It'll be awfully cold and wet out there on the patio," Mom remarked.

"Awww, Mom," I whined. "It'll be O.K. We like cold and wet, don't we Girls?" I tried to sound enthusiastic.

"Sure!" came their doubtful but unified reply.

"Well, if it's too much for you, just come in," she said. It was getting dark early because of the fog, so we went upstairs to "brush and wash" as my mom says and did something you'll think is gross: a "tick check." When you're out all day, roaming the woods and sitting in the grass, you have to check your hair, back, armpits, and other body parts for the little hard, flat, black bugs that embed their pinchers in your flesh and suck your blood out. It wouldn't be so bad if they didn't carry Lyme disease. But let's not talk about that. We did our inspections, put on our jamies, and headed out to the patio to set up our "beds."

Chapter Seven

It was dark now and we could barely see. The outside light above the back door was turned on, but the dark wasn't so much the problem. It was the fog. The light lit up only a hazy patch of the fog around it. I could barely see my friends. We each took a chaise lounge lawn chair, already wet from the fog, and unrolled our sleeping bags on top of them. I put my flashlight on the flagstones beside my "bed."

"Is this what they call 'pea soup'?" asked Abigail, trying to catch the mist with her hands.

"I'll say it is!" exclaimed Mollie. We snuggled down into our sleeping bags and tried to go to sleep. The cool mist of the fog on my face reminded me of the ghost we had encountered earlier! I usually loved the feeling of being surrounded by the fog. It made me think of God's love surrounding me, but now it made me think of that cold "being" who had attacked me at Captain Snow's! With that scary memory in my mind, I began to doze. I must have actually fallen asleep because I awoke with a start. What was that noise? I bolted up as I heard a distant howling! The others popped their heads out of their bags as well.

"W–w–what's that?" asked Abigail in a frightened whisper.

"It's a coyote, I think," I answered. Just then we heard the thundering of hooves as a large animal thrashed through bushes on the slope between my yard and the beach.

"Run for your lives!" screamed Mollie. We leapt out of our sleeping bags and dashed toward the back door. The animal raced over the lawn and off across the road. We could hear it but couldn't see a thing! We huddled together in the doorway, shaking.

"What was it?" asked Abigail.

"It must have been a deer. Chased by a coyote," Muffy speculated.

"Wow!" exclaimed Mollie, exhaling. I guess she had stopped breathing for a while. We were silent. Our hearts were still pounding, echoing the deer's hoofbeats.

"Will a coyote attack a deer?" asked Abigail.

"A pack of them could probably bring one down," Muffy informed her. "I wish they'd never come to the Cape. I hate them."

"I thought you were an animal lover!" Mollie chided Muffy. "Coyotes are natural. They've been driven out of the deep woods by all the new houses being built. It's not their fault!"

30

"Well, my dad says they came over the bridge to the Cape just a few years ago," I countered. "They're taking over because they have no natural enemies and there are plenty of rabbits and cats and little dogs here for them to eat."

"Ewwww," squealed Abigail. "They shouldn't eat dogs and cats! That's awful!"

"One animal is the same as another to them," continued Mollie. "They shouldn't be blamed. It's only natural."

Then we heard it again. That howling! It sent shivers down my spine. This time it was much closer.

"Let's go in," said Abigail, timidly. "It might try to eat us next."

"They're afraid of humans," explained Mollie, though I doubted it.

"My mom says they bit a little girl over in Fairmont," Muffy informed us. Another howl at the edge of the yard sent us into a clinging huddle, but we didn't retreat into the house. I had left my flashlight near the lounge chair, though it probably wouldn't have been much help in such a thick fog. We clung to each other as a shadowy shape moved out of the mist into the hazy light of the bare bulb shining above the back door! My heart was in my mouth as I stared in horror at the form moving closer and closer. We huddled tightly together, too scared to even move inside.

Another howl practically sent us into hysterics, the scared-to-death kind of hysterics, but the sound came from a boy.

"Hi, girls!" It was Louie!

"You creep!" I spat out in my most furious voice. "You just about..." But I stopped myself. I couldn't let him know how much he had frightened us.

"Did I scare you?" he asked, with pride, rather than concern, in his voice.

"You scared that deer," Abigail said, evasively. We granted him that much.

"Mollie told me that you were having a sleepover," he said in his annoying way. We gave Mollie a nasty look. Why did she always have to tell everything to the wrong people? She had done it during our last mystery when she blabbed our secrets to her neighbor Howie Snow. She probably had told Louie everything about our mystery club, the Eel Grass Girls!

"I forgot to tell you all that I ran into Louie on my way over to old Mrs. Wiggins," she began, sounding guilty. "I filled him in on our adventure at Captain Snow's. Let's tell him the rest."

We were silent. Why should we tell him? I didn't even like him. I have to admit that I don't like boys in general, but Louie wasn't just any boy. He was mucho annoying. Consider what he had just done! Yet, he had taken Mollie to Captain Snow's in the first place, so I guess it wouldn't hurt to let him know what had happened to us when we went back with Mollie.

"If it weren't for Louie, we wouldn't even know about Captain Snow's haunted house," Mollie pointed out, which was true.

31

We pulled the lawn chairs into a circle under the outdoor light. I got my flashlight and crept into the house, returning with the leftover cookies, a gallon of milk, and a stack of paper cups stuck under my chin. I passed around the cookies and milk.

"Here's what happened this afternoon," I began and we told Louie about our adventure at the haunted house.

"I can't believe you girls actually got in and went as far as the library!" exclaimed Louie. "You're kind of brave for a bunch of girls."

"Gee thanks, Louie," I said, with a sneer. He was getting to me. I mean, he was making me so angry, I was acting nasty. I didn't want to act that way, but it was as if he were controlling me. I don't like him, but I couldn't understand how he could make me so upset that I didn't even like myself! It's weird! I had to calm down!

Where did you put it?

"What?" I asked.

"What are you talking about?" asked Mollie.

"What are *you* talking about?" I asked Louie.

"What do you mean?" he asked.

"Louie, you said, 'Where did you put it?' and I asked 'What?'" I repeated.

"I didn't say anything," he insisted.

It's at Captain Snow's. This time it was a different voice from the first—two men talking!

I jumped up from the lawn chair and peered into the foggy yard. It sounded as if someone were standing right next to us carrying on a conversation! Though we could hear them, we could see no one. They didn't seem to hear us either!

"Whoa!" exclaimed Mollie, in a whisper. "What's going on?"

"Maybe someone else is here in the yard with us!" whispered Abigail.

"They're on the beach!" cried Louie. "Let's go see!"

"That's the trouble," I said to the others. "We can't see a thing!" But Louie had already disappeared.

Chapter Eight

"Where'd he go?" asked Abigail, looking around into the fuzzy fog.

"He went down to the beach," said Mollie as she got up and moved out of the light toward the dark bluff. "Come on!" We blindly followed her, taking each other's hands, walking single file through the lawn. I picked up my flashlight along the way and switched it on. It wasn't much help, so I turned it off again. The grass was cold and wet under our bare feet. Then we felt the sand of the path leading down to the beach. The fog that had condensed on the overhanging rosebushes fell like rain as we passed among them. When we came out onto the beach, we could see nothing at all. The phrase "lost in a fog" came to mind. We couldn't hear anything either.

"I've never seen fog like this!" exclaimed Abigail in a barely audible voice.

"Well, I have," I replied. "But not for a long time. Where is Louie and where are those people?"

Let's get over to Snow's. The voice was so clear it sounded as if the mystery men were right beside us! The hair on the back of my neck stood straight up. It was, as Mollie would say, surreal!

"Where can they be?" asked Muffy in a hushed voice. "How is it that they sound so close, but we can't tell where they are? And why is it we can hear them, but they can't hear us?"

I couldn't figure it out. There was no wind, just a little breeze blowing the fog in. I say this because you know that the wind can carry your voice.

"It's the fog!" exclaimed Louie. There he was, right beside me! I was so startled I jumped! "I've heard of this before, but I never saw it."

"Saw what?" asked Muffy, puzzled.

"Saw the voices riding on the fog," he replied.

"You mean 'heard,' not 'saw,'" Mollie corrected him.

"Yeah," was his reply.

Just then we heard splashing water, as if the two men whose voices we'd heard had waded into the water. Then it sounded as if they hoisted something into a boat, letting it land with a thump, and then boarded themselves. There was a muffled animal noise! We heard the rumble of an outboard motor. The sound seemed to be right in front of us, but we couldn't be sure. Our senses were playing tricks on us!

"They're going to Captain Snow's!" Louie exclaimed triumphantly as if he had solved the whole mystery.

"They said 'Snow's.' That might not mean 'Captain Snow's,'" I told him.

"The boat's coming toward us. It's going to Captain Snow's and it'll have to go under the bridge!" continued Louie. "Let's go!"

"What are you talking about?" asked Abigail.

"Come on!" yelled Louie, running back up the path. "Where're your bikes?" he called urgently.

"In the barn," I told him, as we stumbled after him back up the hill. "We'll never get there in time."

"Stop complaining," he yelled, bounding through the fog to the barn. When we caught up with him, we helped pull the bikes out of the barn, under the pitiful beam of my flashlight.

"Muffy, you're the smallest," he observed. "You ride on the seat and I'll pedal."

"I will not!" she asserted. "*You* get on the seat and *I'll* pedal."

"Come on! Don't be a 'girl'!"

"I am a girl and if you want to ride on *my* bike with *me*, I'll pedal!" Muffy told him. The rest of us were already on our bikes. Muffy led the way. Louie, balanced on the seat of her bike, held the flashlight so we could see ahead of us. Unfortunately we couldn't see more than a few feet beyond its feeble gleam as we rode single file down Yacht Harbor Road to the bridge.

"They'll be going slow too because of the fog," Louie informed us.

"You mean 'slowly,'" corrected Mollie.

"That's what I said," Louie responded.

"What are we going to do when we get there?" asked Abigail, from the rear of our procession.

"They're up to something," said the brilliant Louie. "Why else would they be going to Captain Snow's in the middle of the night?"

It was slow going with *us*, that was for sure. I was afraid I might ride my bike into Mollie, who was ahead of me—and I was afraid that Abigail would smash me from behind. I was thankful for the streetlights, which helped us stay on the road. We rode past the yacht club and onto the bridge, where we stopped to listen. The faint sound of a motor met our ears. But where was it? It seemed to be coming from Snow Pond. Then silence.

Chapter Nine

"To Captain Snow's," ordered Louie. Great! Now we had two bosses. First Mollie and now Louie. We were used to Mollie ordering us around. She didn't really mean to—it was just her way, but Louie was another story! Yet we obeyed and rode our bikes over the bridge and up the dirt road leading to the haunted house. Were we really going to go there again? At night? In the fog?

"Leave the bikes here," Louie ordered. I had had enough of him!

"I think we ought to put our bikes here," I repeated, acting as if it were my idea. Of course it was what we would have done anyway, but I couldn't stand the fact that he was taking over! I wasn't going to let him make himself our leader. The Eel Grass Girls didn't have a leader—we were all equal. I was glad that Muffy had forced him to sit on the seat of her bike while she pedaled, though I'm sure it wasn't easy for her—and now she seemed out of breath!

We stashed our bikes in bushes that were damp with fog and started up the path through the old overgrown driveway leading to Captain Snow's. Silently we crept along. The fog dripped down like tears, as if the huge old trees were crying. When we neared the house, I felt sad, a feeling I had had here before. I wondered if the others felt it too.

We jumped into the bushes when we heard a woman exclaim, *Look at this fog! Who would believe that we have a full moon tonight?* She sounded so near!

Do we need the moonlight? asked another female. *I'm new at this. Will it work without the moonlight?*

It's better with the light, answered a man, one of the pair we'd heard on the beach, *but it works just fine without it, as long as the moon is there and it's full.*

"Where are they?" whispered Muffy. "I can't see a thing!"

"What are they talking about?" Louie asked, not expecting an answer. None of us had a clue what they meant.

Where's the sacrifice? asked another man. I shivered. Had I heard correctly?

"Sacrifice?" barely escaped from Abigail's lips. What was going on here? These were adults by the sound of their voices. What did they mean by "sacrifice"? What could they be doing?

Here it is, answered another man. His voice sounded familiar, but we couldn't see anything. Without a face to put with the voice, I couldn't recognize him. Then we heard a whimpering and rustling.

"Let's go," pleaded Abigail. "I'm scared!"

"I'm with you," I whispered. "Let's get out of here."

"No!" insisted Mollie. "Let's stay see what they do.

35

"We can't see anything and it sounds terrible!" I said. "I'm going. Are you coming Muffy? Louie?"

"I'm staying with Mollie," Louie said. "We'll come back to your house later."

"I'll go with you," said Muffy, staying near me.

Abigail, Muffy, and I followed the path back to where we had left our bikes, but they were gone!

"We must have left them in some other bushes," remarked Abigail.

"You know we didn't! We left them right here at the end of the drive-way," I declared.

"They must be here somewhere," said Muffy, groping around, but the bikes were gone!

"We'll have to walk home," I complained. Actually I was glad to get away from that place, no matter how I did it.

So we walked down the road and over the bridge. We kept on until the end of Lowndes River Road, where it joined Yacht Harbor Road. All we could see were trees illuminated by the streetlights. They loomed over us like long-haired monsters. Everything else was thick blackness. This new mystery was horrifying. It was one thing to deal with real people, regardless of how mean they are, but it was another thing to deal with ghosts and adults who offer sacrifices at midnight! What kind of people would do a thing like that?

My mind kept going back to another question: Why were those adults meeting at Captain Snow's house? Did the ghost have something to do with their meeting? If ghosts usually come out at night, why weren't the adults afraid to be there at midnight?

When we got to my house, we grabbed our wet sleeping bags from the lawn chairs and brought them inside, along with the cookies and milk we had left out when we had run down to the beach to investigate the voices. What a night!

"My sleeping bag is too wet," Muffy observed when we got into the kitchen.

"Mine too," said Abigail.

"We'll sleep upstairs in my room," I said, leading the way up the stairs. Mom had left the nightlight on in the upstairs hallway as she had every night since I had been given a room of my own. It made me feel safe. I hoped that Mollie and Louie were safe too.

"Should we have left Mollie and Louie there all alone?" I asked, afraid that we had made a mistake. Had we abandoned our friends? I mean, Mollie is my friend. I couldn't say the same about Louie.

"They'll be all right," Muffy assured me. "They'll take care of each other." I knew that they could take care of themselves under ordinary circumstances, but we were dealing with the unknown here! We left it at that, though I was still worried. I hoped they would be back soon.

Muffy helped me pull my bed apart to make two beds out of one. My double bed wasn't big enough for all four of us, so we dragged the mattress off the box spring and onto the floor. Abigail and I stretched a sheet over the box spring and divided up the blankets, but the three of us crawled onto the box spring together. Our pajamas were damp and dirty from our adventure, but we were too tired to care.

"Mollie and Louie can sleep on the other bed," said Abigail.

"He's not staying here!" I exclaimed. Then I thought better of it. "He can stay if he wants to." But that was too weird to even think about.

"What were those people doing at Captain Snow's?" Abigail asked, pleading for an answer.

"Hopefully Mollie and Louie will find out," answered Muffy.

"I don't think we should go back there," said Abigail. "This isn't the kind of mystery I want to solve."

"Well," I said. "The mystery has come to us. If there's something bad going on and we know about it, we have to do something. We can't ignore it." We were silent for a while and my thoughts went back to the sacrifice. But before we knew it, we'd fallen asleep.

Chapter Ten

I don't know how long I was asleep, but I awoke to see Mollie leaning over me.

"Wake up and come downstairs!" she whispered.

I got up. Muffy and Abigail awakened as well. We all crept downstairs. There was Louie sitting at the table, in the shadows of the dark kitchen. The outside light was still burning, illuminating clouds of thick fog still rolling through the backyard, making our kitchen look stark and gloomy by contrast.

"What happened?" I asked in a low voice.

"Those people are scary!" Mollie began. "They stood in a circle, out in the yard, near the house. Then they lit a fire and sang...no—chanted—in some strange language. One woman chanted something and the others chanted in reply. Then they burned something in the fire and a man said weird things. After they chanted some more, they put the fire out and left."

"Yeah," said Louie. "Then we heard those two women, the same ones we heard before, talking about the 'Earth Mother.'"

"What's an Earth Mother?" asked Abigail.

"It's the same as mother nature," explained Mollie. "You know. It's the spirit that makes things grow, changes the seasons, moves the stars in the sky, all that."

"You mean God?" asked Muffy. She wasn't joking. Her attitude was very serious. She believed in God in a traditional way.

"*Some* people think that there's a spirit that holds all of nature together and that we should honor her," continued Mollie.

"How do you know so much about it?" asked Abigail.

"We learned it at school," answered Mollie. "On Earth Day. Our teacher taught us that almost all cultures have a god or goddess of the harvest."

"Let's go back there tomorrow and see if we can find any clues," suggested Louie.

"How about tomorrow afternoon?" I asked. "I want to go sailing in the morning if the fog lifts. How about it, Girls?"

"Sure, let's sail! We can go back to that creepy house after lunch," said Muffy. "But how about you, Louie, do you sail?"

"Nah, I go to camp at the community building every weekday morning."

"Then why don't you meet us at the yacht club after lunch, about one?" Muffy suggested.

"I'm not a member," Louie mumbled.

"It doesn't matter. You can still meet us there," Muffy told him.

"How about the Clam Bar?" Louie asked.

"That's good," agreed Mollie. It was settled. Louie would meet us at one. He slipped out the back door and disappeared into the fog. The Girls and I went upstairs and were asleep before we could even think about discussing our mystery.

Chapter Eleven

The next day we awoke to sunlight streaming through the bumpy little glass panes of my antique windows. A beautiful day for sailing. We could smell wonderful scents rising from the kitchen downstairs. We all awakened at once and wandered down the narrow winding staircase, following the delicious smells.

Our old house is full of cupboards and corners, twists, and turns. We have more rooms than most modern houses, but all our rooms are small. No floors or walls are straight. Sometimes I have the feeling that there are rooms I've never discovered. Or hidden closets hiding ancient secrets. Everything is jumbled up from all the years of Sparrows living in it, adding on, making changes.

"Good morning," Mom called out as we entered the kitchen. Dad had already left for work. Carpenters start their days early, you know.

"Did you all sleep well?" She was well rested and energetic this morning! I guess we hadn't awakened them with all our comings and goings during the night.

We mumbled an unintelligible reply. Our heads were still "full of cobwebs," as my grandmother says, but somehow I didn't like that expression anymore. It made me think of a certain haunted house! Besides, we didn't know what to say. We didn't want to tell her about our escapade in the fog!

"I see that you came in out of that fog. That was smart." We noticed that she had hung our sleeping bags out on the clothesline. And she had taken our family's laundry off the inside line and folded everything up. As they say, "a woman's work is never done!" But knowing my dad, he had helped.

We sat down at the kitchen table and began to gobble up pancakes drenched with real maple syrup. We helped ourselves to scrambled eggs, sausages, and bacon. Luckily my Mom "believes" in sausages and bacon. Breakfast never tasted so good.

"You're a good cook, Mrs. Sparrow," said Abigail. We all agreed. She was a good cook.

"What are you girls doing today?" she asked.

"We're going to take the Catabout for a sail," I told her. The Catabout is my old wooden sailboat, which belonged to my mom when she was a girl. My dad had lovingly restored it. It was the only boat in its class that was still in the water. A few others existed, I had heard, but they were in barns or garages somewhere. Mine was the only one I knew about for sure. It was beautiful, lightweight, and fast.

My sailing skills had really improved ever since I started sailing it. Having your own boat makes all the difference. I have to admit that I used to panic when I was at the helm, but not any more!

"Have fun, but don't forget to wear your life vests. Laura, make sure the dishes are done before you leave!" she called as she swept out the back door to her car and headed off to work. We hardly ever use the front door of our house. It faces the harbor and you have to go through the sitting room and a drafty little parlor to get there. The back door faces the driveway, patio, and barn. We prefer to gather in our kitchen anyway, though we do have the sitting room, parlor, and a library—where we can entertain guests.

"Let's make Fluffernutters for lunch," I suggested as we piled the breakfast dishes in the sink. Mollie washed and Abigail dried while Muffy and I made the Fluffernutters, that is, peanut butter and Fluff sandwiches. Are you wondering what "Fluff" is? It's actually called "Marshmallow Fluff" and it's white, creamy, marshmallow stuff that goes with peanut butter instead of jelly. It's made in Massachusetts, so you might not have heard of it. It's very messy, but we love it. We spent a lot of time licking it off our fingers. We then packed my backpack with the sandwiches, chips, cookies, and some drinks.

We ran upstairs to dress and brush our teeth (that's the kind of girls we were—the type who remember to brush) and then ran down the front staircase and slipped out the "front" door for a change. It looked like a front door, with nice molding around it and an old millstone for a doorstep, but it was like a back door to us since we rarely used it. In the olden days, it was more likely that someone would come up from the harbor beach, I guess. Maybe when my ancestors moved the house to the bluff, they put it down backwards!

Chapter Twelve

"The oars!" I cried as we crossed the yard. "You go on down to the beach and get the dinghy ready and I'll get the oars from the barn," I called, dashing around the corner of the house. We had a huge old barn, which had been built on the property at the time the house had been moved there over a hundred years ago.

I pushed the barn door open. Familiar smells greeted me. There was the smell of hay and oats, though the barn hadn't housed horses or cows for years. There was oil, kerosene, gasoline, paint, mice—too many scents to try to figure out. As I reached for the oars, I noticed an old trunk in the room we used as a potting shed. Why hadn't I ever noticed it before?

I let the oars fall back in their corner and moved into the potting area. Talk about cobwebs! I grabbed a rag from the counter above and dusted off the top of the trunk. Its black leather was cracking on the curved top. The brass latch was unlocked, thank goodness. When I raised the lid, I half expected bats to fly out into my face, though that would have been "highly illogical," as Mollie would say.

Inside were bundles of letters tied with faded silk ribbons or twine. I opened one. The first letter was from my great-great-grandfather Captain Sparrow to his wife, dated 1870. I read it, fascinated. But what was this? Captain Snow's name was mentioned in the letter! I ran out of the barn to show the letter to the Girls, but I stopped and turned back. I didn't want to take the old letter down to the beach. It might get ruined. I carefully put it back into the trunk. Then I ran out of the barn again. Remembering the oars, I ran back to grab them and took off down to the beach, slamming the barn door shut behind me.

"What took you so long?" asked Mollie. She and the other Girls were sitting on the edge of the dinghy.

"We thought you had changed your mind about sailing!" Muffy teased.

"I found an old trunk in the barn!" I exclaimed. "It was full of old letters. The first letter I opened had Captain Snow's name in it!"

"Where is it?" asked Abigail excitedly.

"I put it back. I didn't want to take it sailing. After we meet Louie, we could all come back to my house and look through the trunk. It's our first big find!" This was a real breakthrough—exactly what we needed. Surely there would be information in those letters that could help us solve our mystery! It was too good to be true. And it would be fun to learn more about my family.

"Maybe we shouldn't go sailing," suggested Abigail. "Maybe we ought to work on our mystery instead."

"Look at the sky! Feel the breeze!" exclaimed Muffy, gesturing dramatically. "It would be a crime not to go sailing on a day like today. We're the Eel Grass Girls! We have to get in the water and feel the seaweed around our ankles and the wind in our hair. We'll rifle through those letters when we get back. Come on!"

We sprang up and dragged the dinghy over the heaps of seaweed. Eel grass had been washed up by the high tides brought on by the full moon. We pushed her, I mean the boat, out into the water and jumped in. There was a lot of eel grass floating in the water too. I prefer to be able to see through the water so I know what's in it. I like it clear. I don't like the feel of the grass around my ankles, no matter what Muffy says!

I set up the oarlocks. Muffy took my backpack with the food in it. I placed the oars in the locks and began to row. I didn't tell you, but my Catabout is moored near my house, in the harbor. I always leave the sails on it—they're protected by blue canvas covers. The life jackets are stowed up under the cockpit, a little mildewed, but we don't mind. We're used to mildew, mold, wet, and all those other Cape things.

We rigged the boat without any problem. After tying the dinghy to the mooring, we headed off. I was glad for a change of pace, after the horrors yesterday and last night!

"Where are we going?" asked Abigail.

"How about Womponoy?" I thought it was the perfect day to go out to the island.

"You mean near Deer Island or way out there outside the cut?" Abigail wanted to know.

"Outside the cut," I replied.

"Isn't that dangerous?" questioned Abigail.

"We've been out there before," Mollie reminded Abigail.

"And we almost got killed!" Abigail reminded Mollie, remembering our last mystery.

"But it's low tide!" Muffy explained. "We could almost walk there from Deer Island. See all the boats going in and out of the cut? It's such a beautiful day, everyone is out on the water. If we get in trouble, we can just call for help. See? Laura even has a whistle." She held up the whistle I had attached to a cord on my life vest.

"I'd feel better if we had a cell phone." Abigail wasn't convinced that it would be safe.

"O.K." I gave in with a sigh. "We can stay in the harbor."

"No," said Mollie. "Let's go. Come on Abigail!"

"Oh, you win," Abigail sighed. "But next time tell me in advance, so I can bring my grammy's cell phone."

"And have it get wet?" retorted Mollie. "We're sailors, not techies. We don't need cell phones." Abigail ended the discussion by not saying anything more. I really didn't think it would be dangerous.

Tacking between the moored boats was a challenge, but the harbor was always crowded in summer. One had to get used to it. As we neared a huge fishing dory, Mollie cried out, "Whoa! What's that cage doing down there?"

"Must be a lobster pot," Muffy surmised, looking into the green water.

"No it's not! Stop the boat! I want to see what it is!" Mollie ripped off her life vest, dove overboard, and disappeared into the water! I turned the boat into the wind and luffed the sails. We waited breathlessly for her to resurface. Her head bobbed up. "It's a cage. And there's an animal in it!"

"Is it alive?" asked Abigail.

"Of course not! It has fur on it. The last time I checked, furry animals don't live in the water," Mollie said, with a little sarcasm in her voice. "It's *not* a lobster pot. It's a big cage. Can't you girls see it?"

We peered down into the water. We could see something.

"Should we call the animal warden?" I asked.

"See?" said Abigail. "We *do* need a cell phone."

"Whatever it is, it's been dead a while," observed Mollie, climbing back into the boat. She put her life jacket on over her dripping wet clothes. "We can call the animal warden when we get back from our picnic."

"Who would put an animal in a cage like that?" I asked. "That's really sick!"

No one said anything. It was too icky and creepy—and sick—to even think about. We had wanted a diversion from our mystery and now this! I tried to put it out of my mind. The animal was already dead, I told myself, so we couldn't help it anyway. Yet it made me feel terrible.

We sailed toward the cut. It separated Yacht Harbor from the Sound. The wind was against us, from the southwest, but the tide was still going out, the current in the channel helping us reach the cut before too long. As we tacked through the cut, we could see Wompony Island stretching off into the distance on our left. It was a huge, long sandbar, once the home of a whole village of townsfolk, but that was a long time ago. Now it was a wildlife sanctuary. On the horizon we could see a hazy patch—a fog bank.

"Is that more fog?" asked Muffy, shading her eyes with her hand.

"We have time to picnic before it gets here," Mollie responded with her usual confidence.

We skimmed over the little sandbars to the island and anchored the boat. The island shimmered through heat waves rising from the sand. When we had secured the boat, we walked across the wet flats to the dunes and plopped down on the hot sand. We stretched out and let the warmth penetrate our clothes and hair, into our bodies. It felt so good. We lay there for quite a while, listening to waves gently lapping the shore on our side of the island and pounding on the other side, which bordered the ocean. Gulls called to each other overhead. Tiny shorebirds peeped as they scurried through sea foam along the water's edge. This was heaven.

"Hey," said Mollie, after a while. "Let's go over to the other side and eat."

We roused ourselves and walked along the dunes until we found a path to the other side. It led through the wild rosebushes, lively purple-blue sweet peas, low bayberry bushes, dusty miller with its yellow blossoms and "dusty" gray leaves, and seas of beach grass. From the crest of the dune we could see the old life-saving station in the distance, the only building left standing on the island.

We paused to look. "There used to be a whole village over there," I said, pointing south. "They even had stores and a school."

"I can't imagine it," said Abigail. None of us could. All we could see was miles of beach grass waving in the light breeze, with the fog hovering off the far end of the island.

When we got to the other side, we sat in the sand. Muffy passed around sandwiches and drinks from my backpack. Waves crashed where the sloping beach met the Atlantic Ocean. It was so peaceful. We could see a few motorboats off the shore. Because they were being used for fishing, their engines were turned off. No sound disturbed our peace.

We couldn't help but notice the fog slowly rolling toward us. It seemed far enough away, though. As we ate our chips and cookies, we watched sandpipers running along the edge of the surf looking for food. Abigail made a "potato chip garden" in the sand by arranging chips in a circle. We wanted to stay forever, but we had a rendezvous with Louie. It was time to go.

As we marched back up the dune to the path, we were startled to see a tall man leaning on a piece of driftwood. He was as old and weathered as the driftwood itself. His worn-out Aussie hat and khaki-colored clothes made him appear to have escaped from some outback platoon. The shotgun resting across his knee made us feel very uncomfortable.

"What're you girls doin' out here?" he asked with a sneer.

"We're having a picnic," Muffy replied.

"That your boat over there?" he asked, jerking his head in the direction of my boat.

"Yes," I answered.

"This area is restricted," he informed us. "And you're trespassin'."

"But we're citizens," protested Mollie. "We have a right to go to the beach!"

"Not this beach. Now git!" He pointed the barrel of his shotgun in the direction of the Catabout. It didn't seem wise to argue. We were leaving anyway. The Girls and I hurried along the path. We could see the mist drifting up the island toward us.

Who was that man? I wondered. And why was it suddenly against the law to go to Womponoy? I'd heard from my parents that parts of the island were closed at certain times of the year to protect the nests of birds that lay their eggs in the sand. But I just couldn't believe no one was allowed anywhere on the island ever! And why did he have a gun?

"Who was that nasty old man?" asked Mollie, looking back over her shoulder. "Hey! He's gone." We all paused to look back. He had disappeared!

Chapter Thirteen

"Let's get out of here," Muffy said as she led the way back to the boat. When we got there, we saw that the fog had filled most of the Sound and was quickly heading toward us!

"Come on!" I called. I stowed the anchor and we put our life vests on again. Then Abigail and I raised the sails. Mollie and Muffy pushed the boat out a little, then climbed in. To our dismay, right before our eyes, the fog bank filled in the space between us and the cut!

"Uh oh!" exclaimed Abigail. "I knew something like this would happen!"

"If we sail straight, we'll reach the beach—on one side of the cut or the other," I said, trying to reassure her, and myself, that we could make it home. "Then we can walk the boat through the cut, if we have to, and into the harbor."

"Then what?" asked Muffy.

"Then we can figure out which direction is home and just sail to my mooring. The wind is still blowing from the southwest, so we'll run right into my beach," I added with confidence, though I wished that I had my compass on the boat, rather than on top of my bedroom bureau!

"That would be fine if we were the only boat in the harbor," said Muffy. "No one can see us and we can't see them. Look!"

She pointed to the top of a mast sticking out above the fog bank. A large sailing yacht was in the channel, headed for the cut, but we couldn't see any of it, except the tip of the mast!

"That's strange-looking!" remarked Mollie. "At least we know where *that* boat is—and we can *hear* the motorboats, even though we can't *see* them."

"I'll blow my whistle, then they'll hear us and know where we are," I said and gave a long, shrill blow on my whistle, continuing to sound at short intervals.

We plunged into the fog bank. It was quiet inside the bank and it felt cool upon my skin, reminding me of the ghost again! But I couldn't think about that now. I had to concentrate on my sailing.

We were on a reach headed straight for the cut, I hoped. My plan was to land on the beach just east of the cut. Whether I blew the whistle or not, I knew it wasn't safe to sail in these conditions! I really didn't want to risk our lives. I knew that a lot of serious accidents happen in thick fog!

"We're running aground!" called Muffy as she hopped out of the boat and pulled us to shore. "Where are we?"

"I'll find out where we are," I said as I leapt out of the boat and ran ahead, trying to get beyond the fog.

"Come back or you'll get lost!" Abigail called after me.

"When I call to you, answer me. Then I won't get lost," I yelled back as I searched the area. I discovered we were on the west side of the cut, near the old lighthouse. I ran back, calling out, "Where are you guys?"

"Here, here," I heard, coming from the fog. Then I could see them.

"We're near the lighthouse," I told them. "This way." Mollie held the painter. No, nothing to do with paint! The painter is the line, I mean a rope, on the bow, the front of a boat, used to tie up or pull the boat. I led the way as Mollie walked the boat along the shore, through the cut, and into the harbor. On the inside, the fog was light. I noticed a path through the brush, leading north of the old lighthouse.

"Abigail, let's see where this leads," I called to her as I ran off to follow it.

"Come back!" she yelled. "We've got to get home before the fog catches us."

I had already followed the path to a clearing in the sedge and beach heather, with its sprays of tiny lavender flowers. There, in the middle of the clearing, I came to a halt when I saw the shape of a five-pointed star carefully drawn in the sand! At first I supposed that a child must have drawn it—kids like to draw in the sand, but it was too perfect. Something about it gave me the creeps. The sand was completely smooth all around it. There were no footprints anywhere. Bunches of herbs were placed around the edges of the clearing. They looked as if they had been burned. A child wouldn't have done that!

I ran back to the girls.

"Where did you go?" asked Mollie, annoyed at me for running off.

As we hopped on board and sailed ahead of the rolling fog, I told them what I had seen.

"Probably just some kids playing in the sand," said Muffy.

"Maybe, but it looked really freaky. It was too perfect. And those bunches of burned herbs. What could they be?" I asked. The Girls shrugged their shoulders.

"We've seen a lot of strange things today. We can't forget to call the animal warden when we get back to your house," Mollie reminded us.

"And I want to know this: Why do we have so much fog all of a sudden?" Abigail asked. None of us had an answer for that either.

We sailed back to the mooring without any mishap. Heavy fog blanketed us after we had "put the boat to bed," as they say, and were rowing to shore.

"Wonder what time it is?" asked Muffy, after we had dragged the dinghy up onto the beach and flipped her over. We all had watches, but we rarely wore them.

"It's probably time to meet Louie," said Abigail, while we climbed the hill

48

to my house. The Girls came with me to put the oars back in the barn.

"There's the trunk." I pointed to the huge old trunk pushed under the counter of the potting room.

"Wow! Wait 'til we get into that!" exclaimed Muffy. "But we'll have to go through it after we meet Louie. And remember, we'll have to walk all the way to the snack bar."

"I forgot we left our bikes at Captain Snow's," I said. "Where's yours, Mollie?"

"My bike is gone! Louie and I couldn't find it anywhere! We had to walk back here. Yours were gone too?"

"Yes," answered Muffy. "That means they know about us."

"Who? The ghost or those crazy people?" asked Abigail.

"Whoever," replied Mollie. "The ghost obviously knows about us. But whoever moved our bikes is real flesh and blood. They may know that we were there last night, but they don't know who we are, so we don't have to worry." I wasn't so sure.

I dropped my backpack inside the back door of the house and we filed into the kitchen. I glanced at the clock over the stove. Almost one o'clock—time to begin our journey to the Clam Bar. I grabbed the phone book and looked up the number of the animal control officer. No one was at his office, so I left a message. Then we set off, trudging down the road.

Chapter Fourteen

As we passed by the yacht club, we stopped to peek in. Our friend Billy Jones was in the main room, which had a huge fireplace I don't remember anyone ever using. The clubhouse was basically one big room, with a little kitchen, tool room, two bathrooms, and a loft upstairs. Billy's an instructor—a college kid. He had helped us a lot with our last mystery.

"Hi, girls!" he called out, with a big grin on his face. "What's going on?"

"Oh, we're just going down to the snack bar," Muffy told him.

We waved good-bye and continued on our way. Billy came out and stood in the doorway of the clubhouse.

"Why are you walking?" he asked. "Where're your bikes?"

"Um, they're near the snack bar," I answered, evasively.

Billy gave us a suspicious look. "Why are they there and you're here?"

"It's a long story," said Mollie.

Billy leaned against the doorpost and just shook his head. "Tell me later," he smiled and went back inside.

We walked along. The fog was filling the harbor and blowing down the road like wispy clouds fallen from heaven. We could smell the honeysuckle. I pulled some flowers from the vine spilling over a split-rail fence beside the road and shared them with the Girls.

"What's that?" asked Mollie.

Muffy showed her how to pull the end off the flower and suck the honey out.

"I like to do it this way," I said, pulling the stamen out and licking the honey off with my tongue.

Abigail giggled, "We're little humming birds!" We began to hum, spreading our arms out like wings, running down the road.

We were still laughing when we got to the snack bar. We could see Louie's bike leaning against the side of the little gray-shingled building with its sagging roof. As we rounded the corner, we saw Louie stretched out on the grass. He had his hands behind his head, propping it up so he could watch the boats going in and out of the river under the bridge.

"Where've you been?" he asked in an annoyed tone.

"We've had an adventure!" Mollie filled him in on the animal she found in the submerged cage, the trunk in my barn, and the crazy man with the gun.

"He's the coyote killer," Louie said in a matter-of-fact tone.

"The what?" I asked.

"He's from the federal government. He was sent here to kill the coyotes on Womponoy Island 'cause they're eating those little birds they care so much about," he explained.

"But isn't that against the law?" Muffy asked. "How can it be legal to kill one animal to save another? I hate the coyotes, but I don't like the idea of that man kicking us off the island so he can have it all to himself to shoot them!"

"There's nothing anyone can do about it," Louie continued. "The Feds do whatever they want."

"Let's go find our bikes," said Muffy, changing the subject.

"Let's eat ice cream first," Abigail suggested. We stepped up to the window of the Clam Bar and ordered our favorite flavors. Mrs. Pitts was at the window. She had worked at the Clam Bar ever since I could remember. She wore her long gray hair pulled back in a bun. She had a star hanging from her necklace.

"Is that a Star of David?" Mollie asked.

"Nah. It's a pentagram," she replied, scooping up the ice cream.

"What's a pentagram?" I asked.

"It's a good-luck charm," she explained, handing us our cones.

"Did you see that?" I asked the Girls. "It's the same symbol that I saw drawn in the sand on the beach!"

"It's just a star," remarked Mollie, as we walked toward Captain Snow's, licking our ice cream.

"What are you girls mumbling about?" asked Louie.

I explained about the star I'd seen on the beach. "That sounds very suspicious," he considered. "It wouldn't mean so much if it was just a star, but with that burnt stuff too, it means something."

"I'll research it at the library," said Muffy. "Maybe I can go online and find out what it means. What did that lady call it?"

"A pentagram," I said.

"What did you ask her if it was?" asked Abigail. "A star of what?"

"Star of David. It's a Jewish symbol. It's on the Israeli flag," said Mollie.

"Does it mean good luck to them too? I mean, to the Jewish people?" Abigail asked.

"It represents the star on King David's shield, so it symbolizes protection," replied Muffy. "My uncle's Jewish. He told me about it one time, but the Star of David isn't the same. It's a hexagram with six points, not five."

Louie grabbed his bike and we walked across the bridge, then headed up the dirt road leading to Captain Snow's, making sure that no one noticed us. There were only tourists fishing from the bridge. No one else was paying attention, except for maybe Mrs. Pitts at the snack shop. I saw her leaning out her window, but maybe it was only to wipe a spill of ice cream from the counter.

Chapter Fifteen

"Here's where we left our bikes," I said, looking into a clump of bushes at the end of the old road going up to Captain Snow's.

"And there they are!" exclaimed Mollie as she began pulling them out of the undergrowth, one by one.

"That's really strange!" I muttered, looking the bikes over. "They're just where we left them, only they *weren't* here last night! Someone took them and put them back. That means they're playing games with us."

"But who?" asked Abigail. "I still want to know if it's the ghost or those crazy people?"

"We can just leave them here now while we go up to the house," said Louie.

"Wait a minute!" exclaimed Abigail. "You aren't planning to go back there, are you?"

"Sure," said Mollie. "But let's move the bikes closer to the house this time. I don't want to lose them again." Abigail reluctantly took her bike and looked at me. I wasn't happy about going back to that haunted house either, but we pushed our bikes down the narrow path, which was overgrown with tall weeds and grass. We hid the bikes in the bushes near the house.

Captain Snow's former residence was just as deserted as it had been the day before, with no signs of its late-night guests. We poked around the yard, looking for the remains of the fire.

"Here it is," called Louie. We came over to him and huddled around him, looking down at the ashes and burnt logs.

"What's that?" asked Muffy, pointing to a charred object.

"A bone!" exclaimed Louie, bending down and picking it up. "It's an animal bone. Look!" He stuck it under our noses.

"Euuuuuw! That's disgusting!" squealed Abigail, jumping back. "It might have germs! Don't touch it!"

"Too late now," mumbled Muffy.

Then Mollie asked Louie, "Can you tell what kind of bone it is?"

"It's about the size of a dog's. See? Small and delicate, compared to a human bone. Here's the skull. It's all here. They burned the whole animal. I'd say it was a..." Louie continued, pulling the skeleton out of the ashes.

"I'm going to be sick!" groaned Abigail, turning away. She looked pale, as if she were going to vomit, or cry, or both. "I don't understand what's going on here and I don't want to either. If you want to stay and try to figure this out, fine, but I'm leaving."

"Don't go, Abigail," I pleaded. "You're one of us, the Eel..., I mean, we can't just walk away from this! If they're killing animals, we've got to put a stop to it. We can't let them keep on doing it."

Mollie spoke up, "We don't know if they actually killed the animal. It might have been road kill, a raccoon hit by a car, already dead. Maybe they just roasted it for some reason."

"We heard animal noises," Muffy reminded us. "They said 'sacrifice' and that usually means killing, doesn't it?" No one wanted to answer.

We spun around as we heard the click of the door handle and creak of hinges. Captain Snow's front door slowly opened before our eyes! But no one was there!

"I'm going in there," Mollie said, looking toward the open door. "I'll get one of those books no matter what. That ghost isn't going to stop me! Come on, Louie."

Louie hesitated. He was a boy, so he had to act macho. He couldn't show his fear in front of a bunch of girls. The Eel Grass Girls don't have to play those games. If we're afraid, we say so—and we don't care what anyone thinks.

"I'm out of here!" I turned and raced through the brush toward my bike. "I don't want to be pulled apart by that ghost again! Come on!" I hollered over my shoulder. Abigail and Muffy were right behind me.

"Be careful!" I called back to Mollie and Louie, as I pulled my bike up from the weeds. "Meet us at the Clam Bar!" We quickly rode our bikes down the road and out to the street and pedaled over the bridge to the snack bar.

"I can't believe they dare go into that house again!" I exclaimed, hopping off my bike. We sat down on the grass of the riverbank and looked nervously back in the direction of the old house. "I hope they don't run into any trouble."

"What kind of adults would kill an animal and then burn it?" Abigail asked with a shudder.

"Priests used to sacrifice animals to God," Muffy informed us.

"Why?" asked Abigail.

"It has to do with the death of an animal being the payment for sin." Muffy told us.

"Lots of cultures use sacrifices," I added, remembering statues of gods and goddesses I had seen at the Boston museum. "They want the gods to give them rain, a good harvest, or success in war."

"But who in our town would be sacrificing to whom and for what?" asked Abigail, the Lawyer's Daughter. She wanted the facts, but I couldn't imagine the answers to her questions. Just then I had an eerie sensation on the back of my neck. I spun around to see the snack bar lady peering out her window! That was strange. Why was she so nosey all of a sudden?

Chapter Sixteen

"Here come Mollie and Louie!" shouted Muffy. The two raced toward us on their bikes.

"Look!" exclaimed Mollie, leaping from her bicycle and holding up an old book. I couldn't believe my eyes! She had taken one of the books from Captain Snow's library!

"How did you get it?" I asked, remembering my attempt at taking a book from that haunted shelf!

"We ran into the house, straight to the library. It was cold as ice in there, just like before. A freezing wind was blowing right through the house! We could even hear the windows rattle, but we didn't let that stop us. We ran straight to the back. On the way we passed a closet. Louie opened the door and saw a white robe and some gold plates and goblets stuffed in it, but I went for the library and grabbed this book from the shelf. Louie was with me by then and we dashed out the back door, never stopping 'til we got here!" Mollie concluded, breathlessly. "The ghost didn't get us. We were too fast for her!" she boasted.

"Yeah," Louie attested. "It was kinda scary, but we were outta there before it could catch us!"

"Wow! Good for you!" I congratulated them. I was glad to hear that the ghost could be outwitted. We settled down on the grass. "Let's see what they're hiding from us." We crowded around Mollie to look.

She ran her hand over the worn leather cover. It was plain brown, crumbling with age around the corners, with no title printed on it.

Mollie carefully opened the front cover. The thick yellowed pages had rough edges. She flipped through them, looking for clues, but all the pages were blank!

We were too shocked to say a word! We just stared and waited as Mollie searched page after page.

"What've you got there?" We were startled to see Mrs. Pitts, the snack bar lady, hovering over us! What was she doing? We were silent. I saw that Abigail was about to answer, so I poked my elbow into her ribs to keep her quiet. Something strange was going on with that woman!

Mollie snapped the book shut. "Come on," she said to us as she moved toward her bike. "Let's go." We all obediently followed. I looked back over my shoulder to see the lady give us an evil look!

The five of us headed toward Yacht Harbor Road. I wanted to go to our Eel Grass Palace, but with Louie around, we couldn't. We could never let a boy know about our secret palace!

"Laura, your house is the nearest. We'll go there," suggested Mollie. We followed her to my house. After dumping our bikes in the yard, we filed into the kitchen and crowded around the old wooden table. I got cookies from the counter and poured milk.

"What's with that snack bar lady?" asked Muffy. "Why did she sneak out to spy on our book?"

"Maybe she was just interested," said Abigail.

"No! She was staring at us before Mollie and Louie arrived," I told them. "She even watched us go toward Captain Snow's. I saw her leaning out the window. I bet she's been eavesdropping on our conversations too!"

"She's one of them!" Louie speculated. "She wears that star necklace. It must mean something. We've got to be careful." He was right.

"How can this book be so special if there's nothing in it?" Muffy wondered aloud, searching the blank pages. "It doesn't make any sense! Yesterday the ghost was guarding the book so well."

"And today she let Mollie take it," I pondered.

"If there's nothing in it, it can't be special, unless...unless it's filled with invisible writing!" Abigail exclaimed.

"Yeah!" uttered Louie. "I read about that in one of my comic books!"

Muffy gave him a strange look, which said that she expected as much from him. She didn't waste her time on comic books, but if he could remember how to make the writing visible, then comic books weren't such a waste of time after all.

"Hold it over a candle!" Louie yelled. That was it! I ran to the fireplace and got a candle and matches down from the mantle. Now all we had to do was heat the pages without setting the book on fire!

"Be careful!" warned Abigail. "We don't want to burn your house down." We lit the candle and held the first page over it. Incredibly, brown markings appeared all over the page, but it wasn't writing!

"What's that?" asked Louie. The page was covered with rows of little lines and dots.

"It may be a secret code," Abigail suggested.

"How can we figure it out?" I wondered as we heated up another page. We kept up the tedious process until we had done nearly 20 pages.

"What's the point of all this work if we can't even read what it says?" asked Mollie. We were all feeling tired and discouraged. The lack of sleep from the night before was catching up to me and probably the others too.

"My uncle wrote a book," Muffy began.

"Yes?" asked Mollie, in her impatient way. "He wrote a book and—?"

"About code breaking," she finished.

"Well, why didn't you say so?" asked Mollie, exasperated. "Where is it?"

55

"I left it in New York. He gave it to me when my mom and I visited my grandmother down in Florida. We went over to my uncle's house. He's really my mom's cousin's husband."

"Who cares? Can you get it?" asked Mollie, losing her patience.

"He sells them on the Internet. Maybe he could send me another one, if my mom calls him and asks," Muffy suggested.

"Is this code in the book?" I asked her.

"I don't know," said Muffy. "I never even opened it."

Now we gave her an evil look!

"Sorry!" she whined. "I wasn't interested in secret codes last spring!" We forgave her. I knew how it felt to have a distant relative give you a book as a gift and then never read it. We had all done the same thing, I'm sure, leaving those books on a shelf after writing an insincere thank-you note. Of course we appreciated the thought. A book is better than an ugly sweater that your mom might make you to wear to school. But parents forget about making you read a book.

"Let's not get your mom involved," Mollie said. "Get the phone number of your uncle, or cousin, or whatever he is. Call him and tell him what this code looks like and ask him if it's in his book. If it is, he'll be glad to send you a new copy, I'm sure. O.K.?"

"O.K." replied Muffy.

"Hey! What about the letters in your trunk?" asked Abigail. "We were supposed to look at them this afternoon."

"I'm too tired!" I exclaimed. "I need to take a nap. I can hardly keep my eyes open."

It seemed that we were all too tired. Tomorrow was Sunday, usually a family day for the Eel Grass Girls. We needed a day of rest.

"Shall we meet on Monday morning?" Muffy asked.

"Why not tomorrow?" questioned Louie.

"We take Sundays off," explained Abigail. "We spend time with our families so they'll leave us alone the rest of the week. That way we can work on our mysteries without any interference. But where shall we meet? The snack bar isn't safe anymore. How about the bandstand in the park?"

"Nah. Too public. We need a private place. Your house, Laura," decided Mollie.

"O.K." We agreed the Girls would meet at my house on Monday morning. Louie had camp at the community building every weekday morning, so he would come over at one. Mollie would keep the book. I wrapped it in a plastic bag and stuck it in my backpack, which I lent to her. As soon as they left, I climbed the steep, narrow little stairs up to my room under the eaves and fell asleep before my head touched my pillow.

Chapter Seventeen

What was that? I awakened with a start. Pitch-black darkness surrounded me. What time was it? A wheezy breathing sound came from somewhere in my room! An icy fear swept over me like a huge wave. I groped for my bedside lamp, but it wasn't there! I told myself to calm down. I must have shifted in my bed. I was disoriented. A string hanging from the ceiling would turn on another light, but I was too scared to stand up and reach for it! What should I do?

Just then a light went on in the kitchen downstairs, illuminating the stairway leading up to my room.

"Laura?"" Mom called.

"Mom!" I shrieked. She raced up the stairs, pulling the light string as she entered my room. The bright light revealed the terrible mess that was my bedroom.

"What's wrong?" She rushed over to me. I clung to her, looking around the room to find what had been making that awful noise. Nothing was there! Whatever had made the sound was gone! Had it been a ghost?

All I saw were my sheets, blankets, and mattress heaped all over the floor. Clothes were scattered and draped on my chair and bureau.

"Are you all right?" Mom put her hand on my forehead to see if I had a fever I guess. "What happened to your room?"

"I fell asleep," I mumbled weakly, scanning the room again. I knew I had heard something! But what?

"You're a little warm, Laura. Do you feel sick? Did you have a nightmare?" Mom asked.

"I suppose," I answered, though I was sure I had been awake when I heard the noise. I kept looking into the corners, expecting to see something! Was it just the mystery getting to me? I didn't feel well, but I couldn't get sick now. I felt cold—or was it hot? Mom said I was warm. I know I felt confused.

Mom helped me put the mattress back on the box spring and tuck in the sheets and blankets. My room was messy. The Girls and I hadn't straightened it up after the sleepover. Should I tell Mom about the sound I had heard? Maybe I had just imagined it.

"You all left quite a mess in the kitchen too," she said. "I'm surprised that you knocked the trash over and didn't even pick it up! And what were you all doing with the candle? You know you're not supposed to be playing with matches!"

I followed her down the stairs.

"We were working on our mystery. We were careful."

"Mystery or no mystery, don't play with matches!"

She must have had a hard day at work. She wasn't usually so grumpy, even if I forgot to do my chores or if I did something wrong. I wondered what she meant about the trash. I would never leave trash on the floor! I glanced at the clock over the stove. Wow, it was late!

"Why are you home so late, Mom?" I asked.

"There was a special town meeting. Your dad and I both forgot about it, so we called home and left a message on the answering machine. Didn't you get it?"

"No, I never checked the machine." Mom had already picked up the trash, so I put the milk glasses in the sink and wiped the cookie crumbs from the table. Then I washed the dishes. "Where's Dad?"

"He stayed late at the meeting to talk. There's a new committee of townspeople who don't want our town to grow. They say there're already too many people living here. New houses are wiping out the forests and eliminating the open spaces. We're going to run out of water before long. The coyotes have no place to hunt so they're stalking pet dogs and cats."

"Did you eat dinner?" I asked her, not really wanting to hear her report of the meeting, though I should have been interested the coyote part.

"We stopped by the Nor'easter. Your friend Billy was there. He came out of the kitchen to say 'hi.' Did you eat?"

"No. I was so tired I fell asleep as soon as the Girls and Louie left."

"Louie?" asked Mom. "Isn't he in your class at school?"

"Yes. He's become friends with Mollie, so now he hangs around with us. He's all right, I guess."

"It's late," said Mom, looking at the clock. "How about a snack before you go back to bed?"

I felt a little better now. I wasn't tired anymore. Even if I were tired, I didn't want to go back to my bedroom! I was afraid to sleep in my room ever again, but I was too old to ask Mom if I could sleep with her. Maybe I could read for a while and then fall asleep on the couch in the sitting room. But wouldn't it be creepy to wake up in the middle of the night downstairs all alone? I didn't know what to do.

"Snack?" Mom repeated.

"Uh, no thanks," I stammered.

"Is something the matter?" she asked, showing concern.

"I think I'll do some reading. I found some old letters out in the barn today. I'll go get a bunch of them and read for a while."

"It's awfully late," Mom observed.

"But I've been napping since this afternoon and I'm not sleepy anymore," I told her. She shrugged her shoulders. I got the flashlight and headed for the barn. The moon had risen above the pine trees and was so bright I didn't need the flashlight to cross the yard. My bike was still lying on the grass where I'd left it when I'd come home with the Girls and Louie. I picked it up and pushed it toward the barn.

I opened the door on the side and pulled my bike in, leaning it against the wall where I always kept it. As I moved toward the potting room, I heard something fall deep inside the barn. I stopped and shined my flashlight into the interior of the barn. I saw nothing. It was still, silent. Just a mouse, I told myself. I moved toward the trunk and opened it. I took the top bundle of letters, including the one I had opened earlier.

I closed the trunk and turned to go out. I headed toward the door, but as I neared it, suddenly it slammed shut in my face! I grabbed the handle, but the latch was jammed. It wouldn't move! I couldn't get out! I heard a noise coming from inside the barn. A rustling, something moving. I aimed the light in the direction of the noise. Nothing, no—a shadow! I could hardly breathe! I moved the beam of light to my father's workbench. I grabbed a hammer and whacked the latch so hard it flew up and off the door! I sped toward the house.

Chapter Eighteen

Mom was upstairs getting ready for bed when I got to the kitchen so I was alone downstairs, breathing hard. I heard Dad's truck enter the driveway. I sure was happy to hear him! I waited for him.

"You still up?" he asked, coming through the back door.

I was trembling after being locked in the barn. Dad didn't seem to notice. I was glad of that. Had it just been my imagination? The shadow, I mean. How had the door jammed? Could it have been Louie playing another one of his tricks? Or had it been someone else?

"How was your meeting?" I asked, trying to get my mind off what had just occurred.

"Some people are just never going to be happy," he complained, sitting down at the kitchen table. "They just can't let anything be. They have to meddle in whatever they can stick their noses into."

I didn't know what he meant, but I sat down too, placing my bundle of letters on the table. He continued, "They move to our little town from some big city somewhere. They say they love our town because it's so quaint and natural, but they can't live without their malls and highways! I hate to see the old houses torn down and the forests cleared out, but I don't know what we can do! People want to make money. It doesn't matter to them that they're destroying the natural beauty and polluting our water!"

I felt sorry for my dad. He seemed so upset. He and Mom were always pointing out the places where they played when they were children, but all I could see were big new houses and huge green lawns. They described fields and forests, but they were almost all gone now. New neighborhoods stood in their places. I thought of some of my favorite places to play. The tangle of grapevines we called our Eel Grass Palace. What if someone built a house in the middle of it? I would be really mad—and sad.

"I'm going to read for a while in the sitting room," I told Dad, picking up my letters. "I took a long nap today so I'm not tired."

"O.K. I see you're starting your research." He kissed my forehead and headed up to bed. I turned on the sitting room lamp and turned the kitchen light off. (My parents are strict about not wasting electricity.) I settled down in the deep red velvet of the antique settee to reread the letter I had found that afternoon. I carefully took the yellowed paper from the envelope. Another slip of paper fell into my lap! It was covered with the same markings as in

Captain Snow's book! Why was that code in with my family's letters? I searched for an answer, but found none.

I read through all of the letters and found out more about Captain Sparrow, his wife, and teenage daughter. His son had gone to sea with another captain—Captain Snow! And Captain Sparrow wasn't happy about his son sailing with that particular man. Captain Sparrow's family had lived in our house. It was he who had built our barn—our now creepy barn!

When I finished reading the last letter, I heard something at the window. I looked up to see a dark shadow flitting by! Who was it? I stood up and peered out. Moonlight flooded the yard. The windows faced the harbor so I could see the boats at their moorings, the old lighthouse, and beyond. No one was there. There were old rosebushes growing around the windows, but there was no breeze to blow them across the windowpanes! There was nothing to make a noise, yet I was sure that I had heard and seen something! Maybe it's just an animal, I told myself, but I felt uncomfortable. What kind of animal was big enough to make a shadow across the window?

I dreaded going back to my room, but I didn't want to stay in the sitting room either! I placed the bundle of letters in a cupboard beside the fireplace. I turned off the sitting room lamp and entered the kitchen again, pulling that light on. Something passed by the window! I knew I saw it this time, but what was it? It was no animal. It was human!

We never locked our doors except when we went away for a trip. I wanted to lock the doors now, only the shadow had just moved toward the back door! I didn't want to meet it face to face!

I could see the door. Nothing was there now. Nothing I could see, at any rate. If it attacked me, I could scream, I told myself. My heart pounded in my chest as I rushed toward the door and flipped the lock! I did it! We were safe!

Then it occurred to me that all the windows in the house were wide open. The door facing the harbor was probably unlocked as well. But my parents were home. They would keep me safe. I turned to the stairway. The nightlight was on. I pulled the cord that turned the kitchen light off. I climbed the stairs, wishing that my bedroom were closer to my parents' room, not on the opposite side of the house. A jumble of attics and quirky little rooms separated our bedrooms. I had always enjoyed my privacy, but not any longer.

I turned on my bedside lamp. When I got into bed, I saw it! In the corner of the room! A disgusting blob on the floor! Wet-looking. What was it? Vomit? How did it get in my room? This was too much for me! I switched on all the lights as I ran through the maze of hallways and attics to my parents' bedroom. I didn't care about conserving electricity anymore. Not when my peace of mind was at stake!

Mom and Dad were sound asleep, but I didn't care. They were there. That was all that mattered. I took the extra quilt from the foot of their big four-poster bed, rolled up in it on the rug like a dog, and slept peacefully.

The code looked like this

Chapter Nineteen

"The aroma of my mom's good cooking drifted up the front staircase to my parents' room where I lay on their bed. Dad must have found me on the floor and put me in the bed. What a night! Had I dreamed everything that had happened? Was it just Louie playing tricks on me, locking me in the barn and lurking around the yard? He'd be sorry if it was! Anyway, it was all over now. I'll go downstairs and eat breakfast, just as I always had. It was Sunday. Family day. It would be normal, I hoped.

I hurried down the twisting front staircase and headed for the kitchen, but it was empty! Bacon sizzled in a black cast-iron frying pan on the stove, but no one was there! Where were Mom and Dad? My mom would never go off and leave the stove on!

"Mom! Dad!" I screamed.

My parents ran inside the house through the front door.

"What's the matter?" Mom asked, looking worried. "What's wrong?"

I didn't want to let them know how frightened I was so I said, "You went off and left bacon cooking on the stove! You should never do that! It's dangerous!"

"You're right. I shouldn't have done that," said Mom, going over to the stove. "But I had just put the bacon in the pan when your dad called me out front to see the harbor. I'll turn the stove off now. Let's all go out and have a look."

She did just that. Out on the front lawn we gazed at the water, smooth as glass, calm and peaceful. It was soothing. A graceful heron flew over from Deer Island and landed on the shore near our boathouse. I shouldn't have allowed myself to become terrified, but I really had thought my parents had just disappeared! Our new mystery was spooking me. I was overreacting.

I ate my breakfast in silence while my parents discussed the town meeting. I was beginning to understand why Dad was so upset. I hoped that he and the other townspeople could come up with a plan to prevent our town from becoming "suburban sprawl" as Dad called it. I didn't want to lose the quiet, natural beauty of the town I had always known and loved.

Mom turned to me. "Time to get ready for church."

I bolted up the stairs to my room. Then I remembered the whatever-it-was I had seen on the floor the night before. I didn't want to look, but I did and it was gone! Mom must have cleaned it up. She probably thought that I had thrown up. She hadn't mentioned it though. I would have to ask her about it later.

I went to Sunday school as usual. After church we drove to Muddy River where my grandparents live. We had lunch with them every Sunday after church. They were my mom's parents. My dad's parents had both passed away a long time ago. They had lived with us—or rather, we had lived with them—when I was a baby. I hardly remember them, but I miss them anyway. My parents' memories of them haven been interwoven with my own, so I recall things that I actually couldn't have known.

My mom's parents live in a little cottage that had been my grandfather's grandfather's house, if you can follow that! It stands atop a windswept bluff, overlooking the Sound. It's surrounded by gnarled cedar trees. Grammy makes the same thing almost every Sunday: chicken stew, vegetables, cranberry bread, and apricot sponge pudding (a tangy rubbery dessert no one else has ever heard of.)

As we drove up to the house, I could see my grandparents waiting in the doorway. They know exactly how long it takes us to drive from our church to their home. I dashed out of the car and ran up to Grammy. I kissed her soft wrinkled cheek and Grandpa's scratchy cheek. He smells like peppermint and tobacco.

They always like to eat right away. Over dinner—that's what they called lunch—they asked us about church. They seemed interested, but they never came with us. They had so many excuses. The seats are too hard. The minister speaks too softly. The service is too long and so on. I like church so I can't understand why they don't.

"Maybe we'll go with you next week," said Grandpa.

"Really?" I was surprised to hear him say that.

"Grandma and I are getting a little old. Maybe it's time to get some religion before we go to meet our Maker." I looked at Mom. What was he talking about?

"Grandpa means that he would like to get to know God before he gets to heaven," explained Mom. That was a good opening for me to ask about Captain Snow.

"When you lived in town, did you ever hear of Captain Snow? The man who was lost at sea and whose wife froze?" I asked.

"Oh yes, dear!" said Grammy. "We used to sneak into that old house all the time. It was haunted! So cold. A wind blowing in the house! Even on a summer's day." I was shocked! My own grandmother had sneaked into Captain Snow's house! I couldn't imagine her doing something like that. And she had had the same frightening experience!

"They say the Devil killed them," Grandpa added. That was surprising!

"Why?" I asked.

"My grandmother knew old Mrs. Snow," continued Grammy. "Said she was a very secret person. Did some real bad things, so the Devil took her. But why are you asking about the Snows? You aren't mixed up in any of that bad stuff are you?" She seemed worried about me.

"Oh no, Grammy," I hastily explained. "My friends and I went to the old house and found a book. We felt the cold air and it scared us. I called Mr. Snow in Ohio, who owns the house. He gave us permission to go back to the house, but he said Mr. Lowndes and Mr. McLaughlin, who owned the ship Captain Snow sailed, were responsible for the shipwreck that killed Captain Snow. Mr. McLaughlin had the boat insured and *wanted* it to sink so he could collect the insurance money to pay his gambling debts."

"I never heard that one before!" exclaimed Grandpa. "In fact, I heard that the church was gearing up to run them Snows right out of town. McLaughlin was in on it, as I recall. My granddaddy used to tell me stories about the old sea captains. If you wanted to know for sure, who could tell you? Not a soul left. They're all gone." He shook his head.

"Are there any old newspapers?" I inquired.

"Could be. Could be," muttered Grandpa.

"Do you have anything?" I asked. "Maybe some books or old letters?"

"We've got none of that here," he answered. "Wonder if any of them old church records is still around. Ask the parson, why don't you?"

"Which church was it?" I asked. We had so many churches in town.

"Meeting House Church, it was, I'm sure. That's the one," said Grammy.

That was our church! It would be easy. I would call our minister and ask him if I could see the old records. I'm sure he would allow me to see them. And I was certain I could find some clues about Mr. McLaughlin and Captain Snow!

Our conversation turned to my sailing classes. Then Dad and Grandpa started in about the town meeting. Mom and Grammy and I went out to look at Grammy's garden she had planted close beside the house to shelter it from the Sound.

"This is basil. Smell it," Grammy said, touching a dark green plant, its pungent fragrance rising into the air. It smelled wonderful. "And this is lavender. Take some home and put it under your pillow. It keeps nightmares away."

"Don't tell her those old wives' tales!" Mom scolded her. "An herb can't keep her from having nightmares!"

"What do you know?" asked Grammy. "The smell can calm the nerves and rest the mind. Try it! It's better than a sleeping pill. It's natural—that's what you modern women like, isn't it? All natural? Here, Laura." She handed me a bunch of fragrant, lovely purple flowers with dusty green leaves. I was sure they would keep my nightmares away. Not by magic powers, but from the pleasant smell, as Grammy said.

Soon it was time to leave. We kissed good-bye. In the car Mom told me about one of her patients.

"Laura, I forgot to tell you. Miss Deighton just had an operation. She can't weed her garden for a while and needs help. I told her I would ask you to give her a hand. She'll pay you."

"Sure, Mom. Where does she live?"

"On Pine Street. It's the house behind the one with the columns. Do you know the one I mean?"

"I know the house with the columns. When should I go over?"

"You could stop by tomorrow. She'll be there. She can't go anywhere. Her name is Dorothy Deighton. You'll like her."

I would go by after the Monday morning meeting of the Eel Grass Girls.

Chapter Twenty

I awoke to rain pelting on the little panes of my windows. What a dismal day! At least it was a normal day. No ghost breathing in my ear. Nothing disgusting on the floor in the corner of my room. Only the fragrant smell of Grammy's lavender surrounding my pillow. The herb had worked! I hadn't slept so well in a long time.

I could hear Mom and Dad in the kitchen downstairs. It must have been early, if Dad was still home. I scrambled down the stairs.

"What's up today?" Mom asked me.

"Nothing much. I hope it clears so I can work in Miss Deighton's garden."

"It's supposed to clear up by this afternoon," said Dad. "Got to go!" He kissed us both good-bye and headed out the door, dashing through the rain to his truck. I listened as his truck drove out of the driveway and down the road. I ate my poached eggs and English muffins in silence.

Then I asked, "Mom, did you do any cleaning in my room?" I was thinking of the strange gook on the floor from the night before last.

"No. I've avoided your room ever since the sleepover. Is something missing?"

"Not really. I guess I should straighten up."

"Why don't you do that this morning?" she suggested.

"Good idea. I might find a lot of things under all that mess!" I joked.

Mom cleared the counter. "Wash your dishes," she reminded me. She kissed me on the forehead and whisked out the back door, grabbing a rain slicker from the mud room on her way. I listened to her car drive away. Suddenly I felt lonely. It was the same feeling I had felt at Captain Snow's! I tried to ignore it as I finished my breakfast and washed the dishes. Maybe it was only the rain.

Just then the phone rang, scaring me almost out of my wits!

"Joe Costa here. Animal control," a man announced in a gruff voice and paused. I was startled but then remembered that I had called his office on Friday.

"Oh, yes," I stammered. "My friend saw a cage in Yacht Harbor with an animal in it, on the bottom."

"Sounds like a harbor patrol problem. Why'd you call me?" he asked.

"It was a furry animal like a dog or something. We thought it was strange for an animal like that to be in a cage on the bottom of the harbor," I replied.

"I see your point," he mused. "I'll call harbor patrol and we'll check it out. What's the location?"

"At the mouth of Small Pond River. Near a big fishing dory. I think it might be Howie Snow's dory. If it's not his, it's the kind of boat they use for the fish weirs." I should explain what fish weirs are. They're fish traps made of nets attached to long poles, which are stuck down into the water. The fish swim along the nets and into a trap made of another net.

The animal control officer was telling me that he would call if he found anything. I thanked him and hung up.

My mind went right back to Howie Snow. Hmmmm. Was he a relative of Captain Snow? Why hadn't we thought of that before? Duh! I couldn't wait for the Eel Grass Girls to come over. We had a lot to talk over.

I climbed the stairs and entered my room. It was a mess. I began to pick up my books and dirty clothes. Then I saw it! Dark animal prints on my rug! A monster or some kind of supernatural being had been in my room!

I ran downstairs to call Muffy. I had a phone in my room, but I wasn't going to stay there! Muffy's mom told me she was on her way over. The rain had turned to drizzle, so she probably wouldn't be too wet riding over on her bike. I went to the back door and sat on one of the two benches facing each other in our mud room. I would be safe there. I could run outside if the monster appeared!

Mollie was first to come up the driveway. Should I tell her what I'd found or wait until everyone arrived?

"You look scared! Are you all right?" asked Mollie, sitting down beside me.

"Some kind of creature has been in my room!" I cried. I told her everything: the breathing, the gook on the floor, the tracks on my rug, the shadow in the barn, the locked door, and the figure at the window. "What could it have been?" I practically wailed.

"Do you think it could have been Louie?"

"The paw prints?"

"No, silly! The person locking you in the barn and sneaking around!"

"I don't think so, but we had better ask him. If it was, he's in big trouble!" I was sure that it had been some kind of spooky creature, not Louie.

"The animal officer called. He's going to check out the cage," I told her.

"Good! Will he let you know what he finds?"

"Yes. But let me tell you what else happened!" Once I started talking to her I couldn't stop until I got every scary detail out of my system.

I proceeded to tell her what my grandparents had said about Captain Snow and his wife. "I'm going to contact my minister and look at the old records. What about your friend Howie? He's a Snow. Do you think he's related to Captain Snow? He might be able to give us some information."

"Why didn't I think of that?" Mollie asked herself out loud. "Let's go over there after the Girls get here. Is his boat at the mooring?"

We walked to the sitting room and looked out to the harbor. Through the drizzle we could see that Howie Snow's dory was gone. He was probably setting up his fish weirs.

"That animal in the cage couldn't have been Howie's, could it?" I asked.

"Of course not!" exclaimed Mollie, as Abigail and Muffy rode up. After greeting each other, they took off their rain gear, and we sat down on the mud room benches. I told them everything that had happened to me. Mollie said she had worked some more on Captain Snow's book. She had cleverly used a blow-dryer to reveal the code on about half of the pages. She took the book out of her backpack (and returned my backpack).

"Only half of the book has the code. The rest is blank, for real," she said as she flipped through the pages to show us.

"If only we could read the code!" I complained.

"I called my uncle, uh, cousin, down in Florida," Muffy told us. "He's faxing a copy of the code to my aunt's shop. It should be there by now." We stared at her in disbelief.

"Why didn't you tell us before?" demanded Mollie. Muffy started to offer an excuse, but Mollie cut her off. "Call your aunt now and see if it came in!" We followed Muffy into the sitting room as she dialed the shop. The faxed code was there waiting!

"Muffy, why don't you ride to town and pick up the fax?" I suggested. "Later this morning I have to help one of my mom's patients with her weeding. You all can stay here, if you want, while I'm gone. There are plenty of old letters in that trunk out in the barn. They might have some important information in them we can use. I read a bunch last night. When Muffy gets back with the code, you can decipher the book and a note I found last night in one of the letters."

"You found something with the code on it?" asked Abigail.

"Yes. It's right here." I took the bundle of letters from the cupboard. I opened the envelope and showed the Girls the note. They could see that the markings of lines and dots were the same as in the book.

"You know what this means?" asked Mollie. "Your great-great-grandfather was part of Captain Snow's mystery."

"I've thought of that," I said quietly. I didn't like it though—my relatives being mixed up with Captain Snow! I wasn't sure who were the "good guys" and who were the "bad guys," but it seemed as if the Snows were on the bad side. I wanted my relatives to be on the good side.

We agreed that Muffy should ride into town to get the code. She put on her raincoat, hopped on her bike, and pedaled off down the drive through the drizzle.

"Let's get those old letters," suggested Abigail. We stood up and headed toward the barn.

Chapter Twenty-One

We pushed the barn door open, and I showed them the dangling latch I had knocked open Saturday night.

"Do you really think it was a monster?" asked Abigail.

"A monster or Louie," Mollie told her.

"Or Louie the Monster," I laughed. No one thought my remark was funny. I didn't either, but I wanted to relieve the tension I was feeling.

We entered the ancient structure, glancing nervously into the main part of the barn as we moved toward the potting room. It was dark and quiet. Dim light filtered in through the dusty windows and cracks in the old wooden siding. The trunk stood before us. Why was I always so afraid to open it? But I went ahead and opened it. Nothing flew out into our faces! We each took a bundle of letters and headed back to the house, protecting them under our slickers.

We made ourselves comfortable in the little sitting room facing the harbor. The weather was clearing. We began to read. I gave each of my friends a pad of paper and pencil to take notes. We weren't sure what we would find, but at least we would be prepared.

After a while we decided to take a break from reading, since we weren't finding any clues. The old script written with pen and ink wasn't easy to read. It was tiring us out. We put our work down and headed for the kitchen.

"My letters are from Mrs. Sparrow," said Abigail as we sat around the kitchen table. "They tell about the children, weather, and gossip. It seems that a local girl ran off with a Native American who came to town selling the 'elixir of life.'"

"What's that?" Mollie asked, wrinkling up her nose.

"It's like medicine, I think," I said. "My letters…"

"Wait," said Abigail. "I didn't finish. Parts of my letters seem stiff."

"They were written a long time ago," put in Mollie. "People back then were formal. That was their way."

"But she was writing to her husband. Something's strange about them. Listen to this." Abigail ran back to the sitting room to get the letter. "What happened?" she cried.

We followed her to the sitting room door to find all our letters scattered over the floor! We froze! What had happened? Who could have done this?

"O.K.," said Mollie. "We're the only ones in your house, right?" she asked tensely, looking at me.

"I think so," I whispered. My heart was going a mile a minute. I felt cold and sweaty at the same time!

"Search the house!" commanded Mollie. We crept through the front rooms around to the den and back into the kitchen. Mollie started toward the stairs, and we followed her up. We searched under beds and in closets and cupboards, all through the upstairs and attics. We crept down the front staircase to the sitting room and went around back to the cellar.

Then we heard the kitchen screen door slam shut! We scampered up the cellar stairs to see no one. Nothing. We tumbled out into the yard, but it was empty. I saw a movement in the rosebushes on the bluff sloping down to the beach. We just stood and stared.

"What was that?" asked Abigail, clinging to me. It was safe to say that it was flesh and blood. Whatever it was, it wasn't a ghost. It was still in the bushes—we could feel it watching us. Was it the monster? We backed into the kitchen and locked the door. Then we went into the sitting room and locked the front door.

"They know that we know about them!" exclaimed Mollie. "Now they're after us!"

"Who?" asked Abigail, fear flooding her eyes.

"Those people from Captain Snow's," Muffy answered.

"Are you sure?" I asked. "I don't think it was a person. It was that monster that was in my room!"

"Don't be ridiculous!" Mollie scolded me. "There is no such thing as a monster, but it could have been a ghost! If a ghost can grab you, blow a cold wind, and open and shut doors, it could do this—and all those other things that happened to Laura."

She was right. It could be a ghost! And right in my own house!

"Well, I think it's those creepy adults. And if they're trying to scare us, they're doing a good job of it," added Muffy.

We were really frightened. Ghost, monster, or creepy grownup, one was as scary as the other! Our hands trembled as we picked up the letters from the floor. Fortunately none of them was damaged or missing as far as we could tell.

Even though we were shaken, I decided that it was time to eat. "When in doubt, eat," is one of the Eel Grass Girls' mottoes. We wandered into the kitchen again. I grabbed the peanut butter and Fluff from the shelf and we made our Fluffernutters. It was a little early for lunch, but we needed a snack.

"Where were we?" asked Mollie.

"I had a letter to tell you about," said Abigail, disappearing into the sitting room to find it. She brought it into the kitchen.

"Don't get food on it," I warned.

"I'll be careful," she assured me. "Now let's focus on this. Remember, it's from Mrs. Sparrow to her husband. Here's what she writes: *I went to the well, as you know. Aunt was not there at first, but she spoke later after the others spoke. She is fine, but warned of bad weather to come. She begs us not to follow her path. Mrs. Winter wants more than she did before, but it is worth it.* Now doesn't that sound strange?"

"She went to the well for water. What's so strange about that?" asked Mollie, munching away.

"The well is in the cellar!" I told them. "They lived in this house, Captain and Mrs. Sparrow, his aunt, and the children. Mrs. Sparrow wouldn't have expected to see anyone at the well! Abigail is right! She's speaking in some sort of a secret code. The well must be some other place, maybe some place where they gathered."

"Could Mrs. Winter be a code name for Mrs. Snow?" asked Mollie.

"Could be," I said. "That first letter I found mentioned Captain Snow. It said that Captain Sparrow didn't want his son to go to sea with Captain Snow. There must have been some problem between the two families. But why would Mrs. Sparrow be doing business with Mrs. Snow? And why would she write to her own husband in code?"

"There must have been something secret going on," speculated Mollie, "don't you think?"

"They say that Mrs. Snow was an evil woman," said Abigail. "Maybe it has something to do with that."

"All the old records are at the town hall," I told them. "We could stop by and see if there was a Mrs. Winter living in town at that time, but I think we can assume that the letter has another meaning."

"Who was Captain Sparrow's aunt?" asked Mollie, her mouth full of Fluff. "It sounds as if she had moved out and come back to visit. The letters I read from Captain Sparrow to his wife were dull and boring. He only talks about life on the ship."

"Aunt Sparrow wasn't mentioned in my letters," I said. "They were from their daughter and some relatives in Connecticut. Maybe Aunt Sparrow went on a trip."

"If Mrs. Snow was so wicked, why was your great-great-grandmother her friend?" Mollie asked me. "Especially if Captain Sparrow didn't like Captain Snow?"

"I don't know. It's another mystery." I was a little upset. Somehow my relatives were mixed up with the Snows and it had something to do with whatever trouble the Snows were in! Why else would Mrs. Sparrow write to her own husband in code?

"I've got to go do that weeding," I told the Girls. "I'll be back in an hour or two. Muffy should be here any minute. Tell her she can help herself to the peanut butter and Fluff, if she's hungry."

The Girls walked with me to the barn for more letters. Abigail and Mollie promised to keep on reading. I would be back soon.

Chapter Twenty-Two

Before I left, I grabbed my gardening gloves from the old basket on the potting room shelf and stuffed them in my back pocket. Once on my bike I rode through the light mist down several roads until I came to Pine Street. When I reached the house with the columns on the porch, I peered behind it and could just see Miss Deighton's rambling Cape (that's a style of house) half hidden behind a row of pine trees.

As I slowly pedaled through the deep sand of her driveway, I noticed something about her house that made it different from all the other houses in town. Miss Deighton's door was painted a bright shade of purple! It was pretty but not in keeping with the rest of the local homes. Other Cape homes were trimmed in either black or white or maybe a dark green—never purple! I leaned my bike against one of the pines. The purple door was before me. I knocked and waited for an answer.

"Come in." The voice drifted out from somewhere deep within the old house. I pushed the door open. A spicy smell, like cinnamon and cloves and other scents I couldn't recognize, met my nose. There were hanging plants, piles of fabric, balls of wool, and boxes of clutter heaped on the antique furniture. I wandered from one room to another looking for the occupant.

"I'm in here!" she called. I followed the voice to the kitchen where I found Miss Deighton seated in an antique rocking chair. Beside her a sliding glass door led to a glorious garden bursting with colorful flowers and herbs.

"Excuse me for not getting up," she said. Her face was serious. Maybe she was in pain from her operation. "You must be Laura. Little Laura. You may call me Miss Deighton. Did your mother tell you about my operation?"

"She said you needed help with your garden," I said, not wanting to hear about her operation. I was afraid that she would tell me all the gory details. Grownups love to talk about that stuff! It scares me to even think about a doctor.

"Do you know anything about gardening?" she asked, as if she assumed that I didn't know much. She was a big woman, overweight to be exact. She wore a wrinkled, loose-fitting gray linen top and a long, flowing, purple skirt. Her longish hair was gray-blonde, a little wild. She looked like an aging hippy. I felt uneasy while she stared at me. It was as if she were making some kind of judgment that had nothing to do with whether I could pull weeds or not.

"I pretty much know what a weed is," I said in answer to her question.

"I have always done a good job of weeding," she told me. "So whatever you find growing around my precious plants, all those little green things, are probably weeds. Pull them up. What do you know about herbs?"

"I know the ones my mom and Grammy use in cooking," I told her, feeling that she probably meant something else.

"Herbs can be used for many things," she said mysteriously. "For medicines, tonics, and other purposes." I stood by the glass door. She was beginning to make me feel uncomfortable. "Other purposes?" I supposed she meant love potions or magic spells.

"Love potions and magic spells," she continued. Whoa! Could she read my mind? I just stared at her with my mouth open.

"You'll find some gloves and tools on the table there. Put the weeds in this basket and leave everything on the back step when you've finished. I may lie down and rest for a while. I'll put your money here on the table. If you become thirsty, there's some ice tea in the refrigerator." Her faint smile somehow looked like a smirk. I opened the screen door and escaped into her garden.

I wouldn't wear her gloves, no matter what, but I had taken her basket of tools from the table. She was definitely weird. Why couldn't my mom get me a job with a normal person? I looked the garden over. Everything was wet from the rain, but it was warm and weeds are easier to pull when the soil is damp. I was glad that the sky had cleared.

Flagstone paths led through plots of herbs, colorful flowers, shrubs, and trees. There were birdbaths, wind chimes, birdhouses, and a little pond full of goldfish. It was lovely, even though it was soggy and Miss Deighton was strange.

I put the basket down on the back step then walked down a path, trying to decide where to begin my work. Then I saw something that made my stomach do a flip! Right in front of me I saw a planting of herbs in shape of a star! Was it a just coincidence? Was it a pentagram? I shivered. Could Miss Deighton be one of them? Did she offer sacrifices to the Earth Mother?

I hurried back toward the house. I would begin in the corner. The herbs were big and well established, probably several years old. They were so bushy there was little room for weeds to grow beneath them, but I did find a few here and there. The sun was just peeking out from behind the rain clouds, making the air muggy. Steam began to rise from the flagstones and the wooden steps leading to the house. There was plenty of shade around the edges of the garden, so I hoped I wouldn't become too hot. I was afraid to drink Miss Deighton's ice tea.

It felt as if someone were staring at me. I turned quickly toward the house and saw Miss Deighton slowly rocking in her chair, peering out at me, smiling her evil smile. It made me really uneasy. That woman was not normal!

I continued working but couldn't concentrate. Not that weeding takes a lot of concentration, but I wasn't having much fun with her watching me. When

I looked again, she was gone! The chair was still moving, but she had disappeared! Good!

But just then something zipped through the bushes just in front of me! I jumped back. What was it? The bloodcurdling howl of a cat pierced the air! Don't they usually howl at night? This was really spooky! I wanted to finish up and get out of there!

"Gather me some tansy, dear." Miss Deighton's voice startled me! There she was again, standing in the doorway, leaning on her cane. She pointed to a yellow flower. I took the cutters from the step and cut a bunch. Then I went over to hand it to her, but she wouldn't take it.

"Come in. We'll make tansy tea," she cooed. Did she plan to make me her apprentice? If so, I wasn't interested. I'd tell my mom that this job wasn't going to work out. If Mom wanted to take care of this lady, fine, but Miss Deighton was too wacko for me!

She handed me a teakettle. When I started to fill it from the faucet, she almost turned inside out!

"Don't use *that* water!" she shrieked. "Use this," she cooed, smiling sweetly and in a completely different tone of voice, pointing to a jug on the counter.

"Uh...What's wrong with the tap water?" I managed to ask.

"It...it... isn't pure," she stammered. "I mean, it has chlorine in it. That's not good."

"Isn't chlorine natural?" I asked.

"Not in the amounts they put in our drinking water," she explained, taking a seat in her rocker again.

She instructed me to put the kettle on the stove and take the yellow flowers from the stalks and put them in a teapot.

"You can use the leaves as well," she told me, but I didn't care about her recipe. As I took my gloves off, she said, "Put some of this in," pointing to a bundle of leaves hanging from one of the thick wooden beams spanning the kitchen ceiling. "And a pinch of this," she said, leaning over to push a glass jar of brown powder across the counter toward me.

"There're cookies in here," she said, pointing to a crockery jar. I transferred some to a plate that was waiting on the tiled counter. The flat buttery wafers were flecked with dark something. More herbs, I supposed. They had a pungent smell. That's when I saw them, the bundles of herbs, just like the ones I had seen on the beach!

"What are those?" I asked, motioning to the bundles hanging in a dark corner. Maybe she could give me some information that would help our case.

"Oh, those are for attracting good spirits. When they're burned, the spirits come," she explained, as the teakettle began to whistle. Miss Deighton told me to pour the steaming water over the flowers in the colorful pottery teapot.

"Why do you want good spirits to come?" I asked.

"Well, why not? You wouldn't want bad spirits to come would you?" she snapped. "There are good spirits everywhere. They help our Earth Mother heal the land after all the damage that's been done to it!"

"The 'Earth Mother'?" She had to be one of them!

"Yes, the Earth Mother. You must have heard of her. She created the earth and has given life to everything: people, animals, and plants. But what are men doing? They're ripping up the forests, polluting the rivers and streams, driving animals from their homes! How can she rest with all that going on?"

"But what can you do?" I asked. Yipes! She sounded like my father! I didn't like that thought! Was Miss Deighton the type of person who would attend town meetings and try to change the laws like my dad? Or was she the type to offer sacrifices? Could she be one of the women who was at Captain Snow's house last Friday night? With her recent operation, probably not.

"Our town is too overcrowded," she continued ranting. "You're only a child, but you must have noticed it. Too many people and too many houses. I haven't done any damage to the environment since I moved to town years ago. I bought an older house. I didn't harm a single tree. The developers are the destroyers. They must be stopped—and we'll make sure they are stopped!" She had a strange, faraway look in her eyes. She sounded like my dad, but she gave me the shivers.

"The tea must be done now," she said suddenly, giving me a strange look. "You must try some."

I glanced at my watch. Thankfully I had worn it for once. "Oh, dear!" I exclaimed. "I'm late. I have to go. Thank you anyway. The weeds are in the basket where you told me to leave them. Good-bye!" I said as I backed away from her, bolted out of the kitchen, and headed for the front door. She hadn't left any money on the table for me, but I didn't care. I wasn't going to let her poison me! She took the weirdo prize. I slammed her purple door behind me, hopped on my bike, and rode as fast as I could all the way home—without looking back even once!

Chapter Twenty-Three

Back at my house, the Girls were deciphering Captain Snow's code. I bounded into the house to find them in the sitting room, pouring over Captain Snow's book, the letters, and papers.

"What happened to you?" asked Muffy as I appeared, breathless from my ride.

"That old lady is a lunatic! She tried to make me drink a secret potion! She tried to poison me!"

"Whoa. Wait a minute," Mollie tried to calm me down. "What do you mean she tried to poison you?"

"She tried to get me to drink tansy tea!" I exclaimed.

"So?" inquired Abigail. "I've heard of that."

"So have I and that's why I wouldn't drink it. It can cause you to go into a coma!" I told them.

"Why would she poison you?" asked Muffy. "She could never get away with it. We all know that your mom sent you over there to weed her garden. If you got really sick, the police would find out that you drank tansy tea at her house and she would go to jail. She can't be that dumb."

"Maybe she was trying to drug me to put me under her spell and make me into her zombie," I continued, still shaking. "Her garden is full of herbs and one of the flower beds is planted in the shape of a pentagram!"

"The pentagram supposedly has magical powers," Muffy said. "I found out about it at the library. It's called a lucky shape. Miss Deighton must have planted her flowers in the star shape for good luck. She must believe in it."

"There's nothing wrong with that," said Mollie. "You've got to calm down, Laura. You've been watching too many scary movies. Miss Deighton probably knew what she was doing. The tea is harmless, I'm sure."

"Then you go do her weeding," I suggested, sulkily. "I'm never going back there again!"

"Hey, that's a good idea!" exclaimed Mollie. "Let's all go back there together. Who cares if she pays us or not?"

"You're right!" Muffy agreed. "It's a great idea. We'll work for her and spy on her at the same time!"

"I'm not so sure," said Abigail. "It might not be safe."

"Well," I began reluctantly. "If we all go, I'll go too. She might be involved in our case because she mentioned the Earth Mother. She could know who those people are who were at Captain Snow's the other night. She went on and on about developers, just like my dad did after the town meeting, but she sounded crazy! And she had herb bundles in her kitchen, exactly like the ones I found on the beach. She said when they're burned they attract good spirits."

"Wow! Then we have to go back soon," stated Mollie. "If she's one of them, we could find out who's in the group. Let's go by her house on Wednesday. We'll pretend to be interested in her herbs."

"Whatever," I muttered, still shaken from my near-death experience and not wanting to think about seeing that woman again.

"I forgot to tell you that Louie called last night," Mollie told us. "He has to help his brother do some yard work today and tomorrow after he finishes camp. So I told him to meet us at the ice cream shop tomorrow night at seven."

"If he's not going to be around, we can visit the Eel Grass Palace later," Abigail said.

"That would be fun! What does Captain Snow's book say?" I asked, looking around at all the papers.

"I got the code from my uncle," Muffy held up the fax for me to see. "It matches the code in the book and on your note!" She showed me the code of lines and dots representing the letters of the alphabet. It read "The Pigpen Cipher."*

"Pigpen?" I asked with a laugh.

"Yes, because the alphabet is divided into these squares and diamonds made up of little lines and dots," Muffy said as she pointed out the shapes. "They look like little pigpens."

"If you say so," I teased. "But what do the book and note say?"

"That's the problem," Abigail said. "The entries are just as mysterious as the letters from your great-great-grammy. Look."

She showed me a page from the book and the translation they had made. It read: *Lawrence's lady friend appeared. We could smell the lavender scent she always wore. Lawrence could feel her hand on his cheek. I asked her if she was at rest. She knocked once to reply 'yes.' I asked if she had a message for Lawrence. She answered 'yes' again. She impressed upon me that he would succeed at Lowndes & McLaughlin.*

"Wow! But who is Lawrence?" I asked.

"We don't know. There are lots of names mentioned, but we don't have a clue who any of them are," said Muffy.

"What did the note that was in my letter say?" I was curious to find out.

"Here it is," said Abigail, finding it on the floor. "It says: *What does my aunt say? I wonder if you can indeed speak to her. I must tell you that I have doubts about the Winters. Are they truly our lifeline to the other world? Will we be turned out of the white house, as they may be?* Now that is really strange, isn't it?"

"It is," I replied. "The note must have been written by Captain Sparrow, since it was tucked into his letter. But why would his wife have trouble talking to his aunt? What is the 'white house'?"

"It's all a mystery," answered Muffy. "We don't even know who these people are when their names are mentioned!"

"I'll telephone Mr. Snow again and ask him to give us the names of Captain Snow's children and their relatives," I suggested. "My parents and grandparents can help me with Captain Sparrow's family, though I hate to think of my relatives being mixed up in this."

"Don't worry about it," Abigail consoled me. "Their letters are helping us."

Mollie turned to Muffy, "Do you think those old books in the town library might help us find out who some of these people were?"

"Sure," replied Muffy. "I'll stop by again on my way home and see what I can find. What about the town records, Laura?"

"I'll call the town offices now," I said as I reached for the phone book. I dialed and waited for someone to answer the phone at town hall. The receptionist answered and transferred me to the town clerk, who told me that we were welcome to come in and look through the records as long as we were accompanied by an adult.

"Rats!" I exclaimed as I hung up the phone. "We don't have enough Eel Power to solve this problem. We need an adult!"

"How about Billy?" asked Muffy. "He's technically an adult."

"Billy! Yes!" exclaimed Abigail. "Let's ask him tomorrow at sailing school."

"Then we'll have to involve him in our mystery," warned Mollie. "We already have one of the male species on this case. Do we need another?"

"Unless we can somehow make Louie grow up in a hurry, we need Billy. Or we could ask one of the girl instructors, but we'd still have to involve another person," I pointed out. I was in favor of asking Billy. We knew that we could trust him. The Girls agreed.

"How about a quick sail?" I suggested. It was mid-afternoon and the sun was finally shining. We decided that was a great idea. We tucked all the letters, papers, and the book away in the cupboard beside the chimney of the sitting room fireplace. We grabbed some cookies, chips, and juice and stuffed them in my backpack. We could eat on the boat if we got hungry.

It had turned out to be a beautiful day. No traces of the earlier rain remained, except for a few mud puddles in my driveway, which we jumped over as we headed for the barn to get the oars.

*A copy of the Pigpen Cipher is on Page 123

Chapter Twenty-Four

We heard a strange noise when we opened the door of the barn. It came from deep within the dark cavernous space of the old structure. Something was in there! There was no denying it. We all heard it.

"What was that?" asked Muffy. We stood still to listen, but we didn't hear it again.

"Where's your flashlight, Laura?" asked Mollie, as we quickly stepped back outside and moved away from the barn.

The Girls waited in the bright sunlight while I ran back to the house and got a couple of good flashlights. We reentered the barn. The flashlight beams revealed piles of junk stowed in the depths of the barn over the past century. We crept around two lawn mowers, a small boat, an antique carriage, and an incredible assortment of ancient tools. We heard rustling and glimpsed a movement!

"Wwwwwhat's that?" whispered Abigail, fearfully.

Huddling together and moving as a unit, we edged further toward the far corner, where we had seen the movement. Cowering on an old mattress, looking up at us with sad eyes was—a very thin dog!

"It's hurt!" I exclaimed, noticing a nasty wound on its back.

"Maybe its sick," suggested Mollie. "Go call the animal control officer," she said to me.

I didn't like her bossing me around, but I ran back to the house, looked up the number, and called the officer. He was out, but I left a message and hung up. As I paused, trying to think of whom else I could call, the phone rang.

"Just got your call." It was Mr. Costa. "You got another problem now?"

"Yes. There's a sick dog in my barn. Could you come over, please?"

"I'm no vet! It's your dog?" he asked.

"Of course not! It's a stray, I think. I've never seen it before."

"Better stay away from it, then. I'm on the road. Called in to check my messages. Got time now. I'll be right over. What's your address?"

I gave him directions, then hung up. Why were adults so difficult sometimes? Muffy had come into the kitchen to get some water for the dog. I found a couple of old plastic ice cream containers and filled one with water and one with leftovers. I hoped the dog liked my father's marinade! We went back out to the barn and put the containers down where the dog could reach them. She was very hungry and thirsty. I told the girls what the officer had said about staying away from her, but they didn't budge.

"She won't hurt us," Muffy insisted.

"This must be the animal that was in your room," observed Mollie. "It probably puked because it was sick. She came to you for help."

"Isn't she sweet?" asked Muffy stroking her head. "Wonder how she got hurt?"

"She went back and ate her own vomit," continued Mollie. "Animals do that."

"That's so gross!" screamed Abigail, wrapping her arms tightly around her stomach and bending over as if she were going to vomit.

"I don't know why they do it, but they do," Mollie informed us nonchalantly.

Was this poor animal the monster which had terrified me and my friends? Maybe it had been in my room and rummaged around my house, but it hadn't been the form at the sitting room window! There was still a ghost or some other being that was haunting us!

I heard a truck in the driveway so I dodged between the piles of dusty junk on my way to the door and stepped out. The animal control officer, Joe Costa, parked in the driveway and got out of his truck. He took a long pole from the back, then came over to me. The pole had what looked like a noose on one end.

"In here," I directed him. "Did you find that cage in the harbor?" I asked.

"Nothing there," he replied. When he saw the Girls standing at the back of the barn with their flashlights shining on the dog, he scolded us.

"I thought I told you to stay away from that animal! Get out of here!" he ordered, but the Girls still wouldn't budge. As he made his way nearer, he critically looked the dog over.

"Coyote," he muttered.

"What?" asked Muffy in disbelief. "This is a coyote?"

"Yep."

"What happened to her?" I asked. Even if she were a coyote, I couldn't help but care about her, with her sad eyes and that terrible sore on her back.

"Looks like a gunshot wound. Probably that coyote killer out on Womponoy. He most likely grazed her with a bullet and she got away. Came over here to recover."

"He shouldn't do that! It's not right!" exclaimed Mollie. "That mean old man shouldn't be allowed to hurt animals!"

"There's nothing anyone can do about it," replied Mr. Costa. "The Feds can't be stopped." That was exactly what Louie had said. Could it be true?

"May we keep her?" I asked.

"Are you crazy? This is a wild animal. You can't even keep her while she's recovering, not without a license."

"Then what will you do with her?" asked Abigail.

"Take her to a woman over in Oceanside who's got a license to deal with animals. Then we'll release her into the wild. You girls move back while I restrain her."

The officer moved forward with the pole, but there was so much junk in the barn, he had trouble getting it in position to catch the coyote. The coyote began

81

to growl and show her teeth. She looked very scary all of a sudden!

"Move back!" he shouted at us. In a flash the coyote slipped through a loose board in the siding and was gone! The officer ran through the barn, tripping over debris, trying to catch her. We followed the coyote out to the yard, but she had disappeared.

"Stay clear of that animal and call me if she ever comes back," he told us sternly. "Don't feed her. She's a wild animal and should stay wild. Feeding her will only put you in danger. She may even have rabies. She could attack you." He gave us a serious look before putting the pole back in his truck. He got in and drove away, leaving us standing in the driveway staring after him.

Chapter Twenty-Five

"What do you make of that?" asked Muffy, her hands on her hips.

"That dog, I mean coyote, doesn't want to go to Oceanside. She wants to stay here so we can take care of her," I replied.

"Yeah," agreed Mollie. "She likes you, Laura."

"I wish I had a pet," Abigail complained. "My grammy won't let me have a pet, but if a stray came to her house, I'm sure she'd let me keep it."

None of us had pets, but it was probably for the best since we were so busy all summer long.

"Are we going sailing or not?" I asked.

"Get the oars and we'll meet you on the beach," said Mollie. I went back to the barn for the oars. By the time I got to the beach, the Girls already had the dinghy uprighted and were waiting at the water's edge. We rowed out to my Catabout, bailed her out, and raised the sails.

"Where shall we go?" asked Muffy.

"Let's go over to the old lighthouse and I'll show you the pentagram I saw," I suggested.

"It will be gone because of the rain," surmised Abigail.

"You're right. I'll show you where it was, then. The burned bunches of herbs will still be there." As we set off, I told the Girls that the animal control officer said that he hadn't found the cage. We decided to see for ourselves. He was right. Nothing was there! That was strange. We couldn't imagine what had become of it, so we sailed on. The wind was perfect and we quickly skimmed across the harbor to the beach.

The old lighthouse stood alone on the sandy point, near the cut through. It was no longer a working lighthouse. A family had bought it years ago to use as a summer home. We could see their wash hanging from a clothesline and flapping in the breeze.

"Do you know who lives there?" asked Mollie.

"Don't know. A yacht club family used to live there, but I heard they moved out last year," remarked Muffy.

We reached the shore and pulled the boat up as far as we could. I anchored it well then we looked for the path.

"Here!" I called to the Girls and they followed me. We easily found the clearing, but there were no markings left in the sand; the rain had washed the star away. Strangely, there was nothing left there at all!

"Where're the herb things?" asked Muffy, looking around the edges of the clearing.

"Someone's taken them away!" I was surprised.

"They got rid of the evidence," observed Abigail.

"I don't know why they would," mused Mollie. "Hardly anyone ever comes over here. Why would they feel they had to clear away the herb bundles? Maybe they erased the star too. No one saw you, Laura. It was too foggy. It's weird someone would bother to come back out here and clean up the beach!"

"Why don't we see who lives in the lighthouse?" suggested Muffy, looking in the direction of the old lightkeeper's house.

"Maybe they don't want any visitors," Abigail cautioned. "The kind of person who would buy a house all the way out here isn't the type to want strangers dropping by."

We headed toward the lighthouse anyway, following a narrow path of white sand through the beach grass.

We ambled along, stopping here and there to notice the pretty purple sweet pea flowers and lavender-colored beach heather. We found some long gray and white gull feathers and shiny gold-colored cockleshells.

"My mom told me that she used to call these 'wishing shells' when she was little," Muffy told us.

"Why?" asked Abigail.

"Because she said they're so beautiful that she and her friends thought they must be magical. They believed that if they found one and made a wish, the wish would come true."

"I wish that wishes did come true," said Mollie, "but they don't. We all know that from all those birthday candles we've blown out or twinkling stars we've wished on."

"You should try praying," suggested Muffy. "It's better than wishing."

"It's the same thing," Mollie sighed.

I could see that Muffy was about to argue the point, but we were startled by an old woman walking toward us. She must have come out of the lighthouse. That wouldn't have been so odd, except for the fact that she was carrying a shotgun!

"Whoa!" exclaimed Mollie. "Why is everyone packing a pistol all of a sudden?"

"Get away from here!" said the woman, her cold eyes showing no emotion. We were close to the lighthouse, but we didn't think that we were so close that we were trespassing.

"We're just looking for shells," I told her, holding up a handful of cockles.

"Get away," she repeated, pointing the barrel of her gun at our feet.

"No problem," Mollie said as we spun away from her and quickly headed toward my boat.

"What's wrong with her?" asked Abigail. "I don't think it's legal to point a gun at people like that!"

"What *is* her problem?" Muffy asked. "We weren't doing anything wrong. She doesn't own the whole beach!"

"What is she hiding? That's the question," said Mollie. "Could she be one of those Earth Mother People? I'm all for nature and saving the rain forest, but this is going too far!"

I stopped to look back. The woman was still standing there, watching us. We continued grumbling as we poked our way through the beach grass to my boat. We didn't know if the woman had anything to do with the pentagram in the sand. Maybe she was just a grumpy old woman. I picked up the anchor. We pushed the Catabout off into the water and hopped in.

Chapter Twenty-Six

"Look!" yelled Mollie, as we hoisted up the sails and they filled with the wind. "There's Howie! Sail over and let's ask him about his relatives."

Muffy was skippering, so she steered the boat over to where Howie was mooring his enormous dory.

"Hey, kids!" he greeted us. "What's happenin'?"

We pulled alongside of him and his crew. "Have you seen anyone putting a cage in the water? Over here?" asked Mollie, pointing to the place she had seen the cage before.

"Lobster pot?" he asked.

"No. A metal cage. Like an animal cage. With a furry animal in it," continued Mollie.

"Is this another one of your screwy mysteries?" he asked, giving us a strange look.

"It's just something we saw," said Muffy. "It was here on Saturday, but now it's gone. We just wondered if you saw anything."

"Nope."

"Howie," Mollie went on, "We want to ask you about Captain Snow."

"We're kinda busy right now," he told us.

He was no help. I thought he had learned his lesson after what had happened during our last mystery and that he would be willing to help us this time. But then he had just come in from his weirs and was probably tired.

"Let me know right away if you see or hear anything suspicious," ordered Mollie. Howie nodded as he continued straightening his nets. We sailed on to my mooring.

"Some help he is!" uttered Muffy in disgust. "I thought he was going to help us 'next time.'"

"Well, it wasn't a good time for him to talk to us," Abigail defended him. "Hey, how about going to the Eel Grass Palace? We could go over after sailing school tomorrow."

We wanted to feel like the Eel Grass Girls again. We needed to have some fun and relax. It was a good idea.

"What exactly is our mystery?" asked Abigail while we tied up at the mooring and wrapped the mainsail around the boom. "I know we have a haunted house and we've discovered the Earth Mother People, but what is it that we are really trying to find out? I don't get it."

Mollie rolled her eyes, but I gave her a look that made her stop. "We need to find out who is haunting Captain Snow's house and why," I began. "Then we need to find out why the Earth People are burning animals. Next we have to find out what was in that cage in the harbor and why—and what's up with the lady at the snack bar and that lady at the lighthouse. They're all separate mysteries."

"Oh," said Abigail, still sounding confused.

"Too bad we didn't find out if Howie is even related to Captain Snow," Muffy said as we rowed to shore.

"I'll ask him when he gets home," said Mollie. I can hear him through the trees. He makes an awful lot of noise, always slamming doors and blaring his radio. I'll know when he gets home."

"The library is still open," said Muffy when we pulled the dinghy up on the beach. "I'll swing by on the way home to look in those old books for the names we found in your letters, Laura, and in Captain Snow's book. Maybe we can identify some of them."

"Great! And tomorrow we'll ask Billy to go to the town offices with us," I said. We climbed the bluff to my house. "And I'll ask my parents about our family tree. I'll call Mr. Snow too."

"What shall I do?" asked Abigail.

"How about taking an extra bundle of letters home? Maybe you can find something important," I suggested.

We said good-bye to Muffy as she rode off to the library. Mollie decided it was time for her to go home too. Abigail and I walked toward the barn to get more letters. I had to return the oars anyway. When I opened the door, we heard that sound again! Where were the flashlights? On my dad's workbench. I flicked one on and we crept to the back of the barn. The coyote was back!

"Let's get her some more food and water," I suggested.

"The animal control officer said not to feed her," Abigail reminded me.

"Do you want her to die?" I asked in an annoyed tone. Then I felt bad. "I'm sorry, Abigail, but I don't know what's the right thing to do. If we call the officer, the coyote will run away again. If we leave the food and water near her, we won't technically be feeding her."

"All right," Abigail agreed, but I knew she felt uncomfortable about it.

We went back to the house to refill the water container and get more leftovers from the fridge. Back in the barn, we left them near the coyote, after speaking soothing words to her. We picked up another bundle of letters for Abigail and left.

"Bye, Abigail," I said. She put the letters in her bike basket and got on her bike. "See you at sailing school tomorrow."

She rode off down the driveway and a terrible wave of loneliness swept over me. It seemed so odd. I never had feelings like that before! Yes, I had felt lonely when my best friend at school was sick and I had no one to play with at recess, but this was much worse. It made me feel afraid. As I crossed from the barn to the patio, the quiet and stillness of my yard almost smothered me.

Then I heard it! A door slammed inside my house! The coyote was in the barn—so who was in the house? I shakily crept up to the back door and peered through the screen. Then I heard footsteps! What should I do?

Chapter Twenty-Seven

I sprinted to my bike and aimed for Mollie's house. She lived only a few houses away.

"Mollie! Mollie!" I screamed as I rode up her long shell driveway and neared her house.

She ran out to meet me. "What's wrong?"

"Someone's in my house! Come!" I tugged at her.

"Hold your horses. Wait a minute. You think we're going to search your house, just the two of us? What if it's a burglar? I'm calling the police."

"No! Come on!" I insisted. She reluctantly followed, getting her bike out of the garage. We rode quickly back to my house. When we arrived, all was quiet. We approached the back door, paused, and listened. Nothing. We tiptoed in and made our way from room to room. To our surprise, every closet door, cupboard, and drawer was wide open! Someone had searched my house! But who? And what were they looking for? In the sitting room we saw our old letters and notes still in the opened cupboard, but Captain Snow's book was gone!

"Mrs. Pitts!" I screamed. "She's the only one who knew we had the book! If she hadn't found it here, she probably planned to search your house, then the other Girls' homes, one by one."

"Shouldn't we call the police?" asked Mollie again.

"We don't have any proof that it was Mrs. Pitts," I told her. "Even though we know it was!"

"You're right. I'll help you straighten up and we'll tell the Girls about it tomorrow."

"Why would she want the book anyway?" I asked.

"Curiosity. Or she's afraid that we'll find out something she doesn't want us to know. She's got to be one of those people who were at Captain Snow's!"

"But where's the code sheet? Where're all our translations?" I asked as I rummaged through the cupboard. I found them under the stacks of letters. Mrs. Pitts hadn't known about the code, so she hadn't looked for it. It was safe!

We were upstairs closing all the doors and drawers when we heard a tapping sound. We stopped to listen. It seemed to be coming from the cellar. We looked at each other, then cautiously crept downstairs to the pantry. I opened the cellar door but saw only darkness.

My cellar is a series of small rooms. The first is a round "root cellar" where my great-great-grandparents kept their fruit and vegetables before the days of refrigerators. Then there's the room where the old well still stood, though we've never used it, and there are a few other small musty rooms with walls made of stones.

"What do you keep down there, Laura?"

"Nothing," I replied as we descended the creaky wooden steps into the dark. "Everything's in the barn."

I pulled the string attached to a light bulb. All the rooms lit up. They were empty, yet we could still hear the tapping. It was coming from the room with the well! Suddenly it grew louder! Mollie and I looked at each other in terror! What was making the sound? Just then a horrible scream pierced the air! We lunged back up the stairs, slamming and locking the cellar door behind us.

"What was that?" asked Mollie, leaning against the door, as if she could keep whatever it was from getting us.

We raced out of the house and stood on the patio in the bright sunlight. We were trembling and gasping for breath.

"Did something terrible ever happen in your cellar?" asked Mollie.

"I don't know," I said. "But we have to find out! I'll ask my parents. This is too scary! You don't think it's a ghost, do you?"

We had to solve this mystery! I didn't want a ghost in my own house! Home was a place of safety! Was this the same being who had locked me in the barn and passed by my windows?

"I wouldn't stay here, if I were you!" Mollie spoke solemnly. "Come over to my house." We got on our bikes and rode back to Mollie's. On the way we passed the entrance of Howie Snow's driveway. He lived just next door to Mollie and we could see him unloading his truck.

"Now's our chance," said Mollie, turning down Howie's driveway.

"Please, Mollie!" I begged. "Not now! I'm too shaken up."

"No," Mollie replied. "This might be our only chance to talk to him."

I reluctantly rode behind her.

"Hey, Howie!" she called. I couldn't understand how she could go from encountering a ghost one minute to interviewing her neighbor the next! Howie stopped in his tracks when he heard her voice. He swung around, not seeming very glad to see us. He was peculiar, that was for sure. He had always been nice to Mollie—until we'd asked him to help us with our last mystery. Now he seemed suspicious every time he saw us.

"I wanted to ask you," began Mollie. "Are you related to the famous Captain Snow of Snow Pond?"

"I suppose," was his answer. We waited for him to continue. He didn't seem to want to say any more, but after a long pause he added, "He was an uncle of my great-grandfather. Granddaddy told me that even though the Captain was rich and famous, he and his wife was into the black arts. Our side of the family stayed as far away from 'em as they could, being that they was livin' in the same town."

"Black arts?" asked Mollie, surprised.

"Auntie was famous for communicating with the dead," said Howie, suddenly not seeming to mind the questions. "Granddaddy told me a lot of people were dying in them days. Lots of communicating needed to be done. Old Auntie was raking in the dough. She didn't call up the dead for nothin'. The Captain was gonna be thrown out of the church by the upright and holy townsfolk. They wasn't appreciating the Captain and his family much."

This was amazing! Grandpa was right about the church wanting to throw Captain Snow out. And maybe that was how the house had become haunted, from calling people back from the dead! Hadn't old Mrs. Wiggins told Mollie the house was haunted even before the Captain and his wife had died? I guess it had been worth it to stop by Howie's after all, even though I didn't feel like it. After our encounter with the ghost—or whatever it was—in my cellar, I just wanted to feel safe!

My mind went back to what Howie had said—what exactly had he meant by "communicating with the dead." Did he mean séances? I wondered how they worked, but I kept quiet and let Mollie do the talking.

"Do you know who else was involved?" asked Mollie.

"What's your mystery this time?" Howie wanted to know.

"We want to find out—" My look made Mollie stop. I didn't want him to know about our mystery, but, we wanted his help. We had to tell him something to keep him talking.

"It has to do with Captain Snow's house," said Mollie instead.

"Haunted, ain't it?" asked Howie. Or maybe it was a statement. "I know, I know. You want to find out who's hauntin' the house and why." We were shocked. That was it exactly. Was it so obvious? Yet we wanted to know more than that. We wanted to know about those grownups who were sacrificing animals on Captain Snow's front yard!

"It's Petunia Snow doing the hauntin'," Howie stated. "Couldn't stand them black arts. So one day she just up and disappeared. Didn't approve of her ma's communicating with the dead and stuff. No one knew what happened to her, but Granddaddy said there were rumors. Bad rumors about her own mother getting her out of the way."

We were shocked. What did he mean?

"Who was Petunia?" Mollie asked.

"Captain Snow's youngest daughter. Was engaged to a Sparrow. They wanted to get married, but Sparrow ran off to sea, and she just up and vanished into thin air," Howie said mysteriously.

"How do you know so much?" asked Mollie. "It was so long ago."

"My granddaddy took care of me when I was a tyke. He always told me stories. Smokin' his pipe and talkin'. Miss him real bad, I do."

It was incredible. This story had been passed down from generation to generation. Howie might be the only person alive who had this information. Had the facts changed as the stories were retold? We couldn't be concerned about that now. Why hadn't Mr. Alfred Snow mentioned Petunia? And the Sparrows! Was it Captain Sparrow's son who'd been engaged to Petunia Snow?

"I owe you kids one," said Howie, growing sentimental. "I didn't do right by you on your last mystery." He reached into his parked truck and took a pad and pencil from the dashboard. He began to make a chart of his family tree. He also wrote the names of other men and women alive at that time of Captain Snow who, according to his "granddaddy," were reported to be involved in the Snow's "goings-on."

"Granddaddy said a whole bunch of strange things were happenin' in those days. Said it was real weird. In the years from about, say 1868 to 1871, just before Captain Snow died. If ya have anymore questions, just stop by." He winked at us and headed for his house.

Mollie and I called out a "thank you" to him as we pushed our bikes down the driveway toward her house. We couldn't believe that Howie had suddenly become so helpful and talkative. He was a gold mine of information!

"Now you have to make a family tree just like Howie's," said Mollie.

"I know we have one somewhere. I'll have to ask Dad. The dates Howie gave us were just after the Civil War, weren't they? Now we have the names of all the Snows, but I wonder what could have become of Petunia Snow?"

"Muffy's at the library right now," said Mollie. "Hopefully she'll find some more clues. When we go to the town offices to check the old records, we might discover even more."

We paused to look at the list Howie had given us. "Look!" exclaimed Mollie. "There's a Mrs. Sparrow on this list of old-timers who were into the black arts along with the Snows! You don't suppose that she was your great-great-grandmother, do you? She did write that letter to Captain Sparrow that sounded as strange as Captain Snow's book."

I didn't want to think about that. How could my relatives be involved? "I don't know," I shrugged.

Mollie didn't push me. "Here are some other families we can check out. See, here's Albert Hinkley, Sadie Buck, and Robert Peterson."

"How does a séance work? And why would people want to communicate with the dead anyway?" I asked.

Mollie paused and thought for a minute. "A group of people sit around a table and try to talk to someone who's died. They do it to find out what heaven is like, or to ask them if they're O.K., I suppose"

"That's what I thought, but it's bizarre to think about it, isn't it?"

"Yeah. Do you think that's the reason why the Snows were being thrown out of the church? Because they had séances and Petunia disappeared?"

"That could be it. And maybe Mrs. Snow's ghost didn't want us to know about the meetings, but Petunia's ghost did. That's why I couldn't get the book at first, but you could get it later when you went back with Louie. Petunia's ghost is trying to help us. But whose ghost is in my cellar?"

"We've got to find out. Hey, you'd better call your mom. She must be home by now."

When we got to Mollie's house, I telephoned Mom. She was home, cooking dinner and wondering where I was. I told her I'd be right home, but I remembered that I wanted to call my minister to ask him if I could check the church records. I hesitated. I had never talked to him before, except to say I was fine when he asked me how I was doing, which he did every Sunday after church. Mollie told me to go ahead and call, so I did.

The minister was at the church office and he was friendly. He told me to stop by at five o'clock the next day. It was settled. I said good-bye to Mollie and thanked her for staying with me. She was a true friend, bossy though she was. I rode home. I wouldn't be scared with Mom there, I hoped.

Chapter Twenty-Eight

"Emergency meeting after sailing class," I whispered to the Girls the next morning at the yacht club. We sat with the other kids on the club deck overlooking the harbor.

"What happened?" asked Abigail.

"What *didn't* happen?" I exclaimed, still in a whisper. Billy Jones did the roll call and told us that we would be going out in the 420s today. We cheered in unison. The 420s were usually used only by the older kids.

"We'll have to split up," lamented Mollie. "Muffy, you come with me. Laura, you go with Abigail." I didn't want to argue with Mollie, but she made me angry sometimes. It didn't matter to me who I went with, but I didn't like her telling me as if I were a child or as if it was her job to make all the decisions for us.

"Mollie, I would love to go with you," said Muffy, but let's ask the other Girls." She seemed to know just how I felt.

"I don't care," said Abigail.

"Well then, I'll go with Laura," said Muffy.

"You just said that you'd 'love to go with me'!" complained Mollie.

"It's true, but I like to decide for myself and I think I'll go with Laura, if it's all right with her."

"Suit yourself," muttered Mollie. "Come on, Abigail." Abigail looked back at us and shrugged her shoulders as they trotted down the steep wooden steps to the beach. Mr. Prince, the sailing master, was already on the dock directing pairs of sailors to go with an instructor in each boat. We were assigned to sail with Judy, a blonde teenage instructor.

The boats were already rigged, so we hoped in. The 420s were kept on the dock, so after they were rigged, they were pushed off the dock into the water. An instructor held each boat by its forestay. Muffy and I carefully stepped into Judy's boat. Then she hopped in, pushing off from the dock at the same time.

"What's your name?" she asked me.

"I'm Laura and this is Muffy," I replied.

"Oh, yes. You're famous!" she gushed. "How did you ever solve that mystery? A dead body and those fishermen! Billy Jones told us all about it. And I read about it in the papers, too."

We just smiled but didn't answer. I didn't think she really expected an answer.

"Ever sail a 420 before?" she wanted to know.

"We went out in one once," Muffy answered. "It was really fun. They're so fast!"

As Judy began to explain about the centerboard, rigging, and balance of the boat, I noticed her necklace. A silver star!

"I like your necklace," I complimented her, wondering if it were the same kind of star Mrs. Pitts wore.

"It's a pentagram," she said. "It brings good luck."

I was right! It was a pentagram, but what would Judy have to do with that symbol? We soon found out.

"Do you really believe that?" asked Muffy. She was kind of religious. I don't believe in good luck either, as I told you before, but I wasn't about to say so, or make a big deal about it.

"Yes, because it's true! Ever since I started wearing it, nothing's gone wrong in my life. In fact, good things have been happening. The boy I like called me on the phone. I got a raise at work."

"At the yacht club?" I asked.

"No, at The Tomb. I work there a few nights a week," she told us.

"The Tomb?" questioned Muffy.

"Yeah. It's on Main Street, toward the old village," Judy informed us. "It's awesome in there. We sell all kinds of magic stuff. Books about charms and spells. Herbs. Other stuff. Come by tonight and visit me, why don't you?"

"O.K.," I agreed. It might lead to something. Maybe that's where Mrs. Pitts shopped for jewelry. We said we'd stop by after dinner.

We took turns at the helm, that is, steering the boat. When we weren't skippering, we practiced roll tacks. That's when we tacked by leaning out of the boat, "rolling" it over to what seemed to be the wrong side, until the sail swung over to that side. Then we would leap to the opposite side of the boat to flatten it out. It made the boat go faster, Judy said.

After we felt confident with controlling such a sensitive and tippy boat, all the students lined the boats up to practice racing starts. Billy Jones and a female instructor, Allyson Parks, were in the *Sea Calf*, the yacht club motorboat, and had set up a starting line for us between their boat and a huge bright pink ball held in place by an anchor.

Judy helped us with our starts, roll tacks, and reading the wind and tide. For instance, she taught us to watch the surface of the water for rough patches where the wind was blowing. When you're racing, you want to sail in those patches so you can catch the wind and go faster. It's the same with the tide and the channel. The tide was coming into the harbor, so she told us to stay in the channel going into the harbor but to avoid it when we were headed toward the Sound because the tide would be against us. The current is much stronger in the channel because it's deeper there. There's just so much to know!

We finished up our lesson and sailed the boats back to the yacht club. After dragging the 420s up on the dock and putting the sails away, we ended our lesson with a meeting up on the deck. The minute we were dismissed, we rushed to the picnic table on the lawn beside the flagpole. We huddled together while the other students waited for their parents to pick them up.

"Where shall we go for lunch?" Abigail asked. Food was first on her mind.

"We've got to talk," I told them. "Let's go to the Clam Bar. I have something to say to Mrs. Pitts."

"What?" asked Muffy in surprise. "I thought it wasn't safe to go there."

"We'll keep an eye on Mrs. Pitts," Mollie said. "Let's go."

Chapter Twenty-Nine

The seagulls laughed overhead. The heat rose up in waves from the pavement as we pedaled our bikes past the bustling town pier toward the snack bar.

Mrs. Pitts was wiping down the counter when we arrived. Another woman, also tall and gray-haired, was leaning forward, talking to her in a low voice. I boldly stepped up to the window.

"Have you read any good books lately?" I asked Mrs. Pitts, looking into her piercing eyes.

Her steely gaze met mine. The other woman turned to face me. It was the same woman we'd seen at the lighthouse carrying the shotgun! Were they sisters? Suddenly I was speechless.

Mollie stepped up behind me. The other Girls crowded in behind.

"You do read, don't you?" asked Mollie.

"What do you care if I read?" asked Mrs. Pitts with a sneer.

"Is this your sister?" asked Muffy, noticing the resemblance between the two women.

"None of your business, you snoopy little girls!" hissed Mrs. Pitts.

"What's going on out there?" called a big man, hovering over the grill.

"Just some troublesome little pests," explained Mrs. Pitts.

"We were only asking Mrs. Pitts what she's been reading lately," said Mollie as innocently as possible. "We were just making conversation, not causing trouble."

"What's your order?" the man gruffly called back. We ordered burgers, a grilled cheese sandwich, and sodas. Then we sat down on the grass to wait. The lighthouse lady kept staring at us and Mrs. Pitts leaned out of her window, straining her ears to pick up our conversation. We kept our eyes on her as well and spoke in whispers.

"What was that all about?" asked Muffy. "Why were you asking Mrs. Pitts about books?" Mollie and I explained about someone stealing Captain Snow's book from my house and the scream in the cellar.

"Wow!" exclaimed Muffy. "Do you think it was Mrs. Pitts who stole it?"

"Of course! No one else knew about the book or that we had it," answered Mollie.

"Who screamed?" asked Abigail. "You don't have a ghost in your house too, do you Laura?"

"I hope not!" I declared, though I couldn't think of any other explanation! What would I do if I had to live with a ghost? Would it blow cold wind on me and grab at me with its icy fingers? I turned my thoughts to Mollie's conversation.

"We dropped by to visit Howie Snow. He told us that he's related to Captain Snow and that Mrs. Snow performed black magic and séances."

"What's that?" asked Abigail. "I've never heard of séances."

"Something about talking to the dead," Mollie continued. "The séances helped to haunt the house! And Captain Snow's daughter Petunia suddenly disappeared without a trace! No one ever knew whatever happened to her. Howie's side of the family suspects that something terrible happened to Petunia. Laura has to call Mr. Snow to ask..."

"Last night," Muffy interrupted, "at the library, I read about Petunia in an old newspaper! Her disappearance was reported as a mystery. If Mrs. Snow was into the black arts, it seems very suspicious to me. I made a list of the people I read about. I hope it will help us."

She pulled a crumpled paper from her back pocket, smoothed it out, and read: *Albert Hinkley was accused of poisoning his neighbor's cows. By all reports, it was witchcraft!*

"Hey!" exclaimed Mollie. "He was one of the people Howie Snow told us were involved in the black arts!"

"And a woman named Sadie Buck, who lived on Snow Pond, had a black cat that attacked some children. The kids said that the cat talked to them!" Muffy continued. "Then there was something about a Mr. Peterson whose son turned into what sounds like a zombie!"

"Spooky!" Abigail shuddered. "Do you think all those things really happened?"

"*Something* happened," said Mollie. "And it was serious enough to get into the newspapers."

"Those are the same names that Howie gave us," I said to Muffy. "Except for a Mrs. Sparrow, who unfortunately is probably my great-great-grandmother! You did a great job of researching, Muffy. It sounds as if the 'black artists' were witches!"

"Is it all connected then?" asked Abigail. "I mean the communicating with the dead and the incidents Muffy found reported in the old newspapers?"

"It's the same group," said Mollie.

"How does a séance work?" asked Abigail.

"It's communicating with the dead," explained Mollie. "At a séance people sit around in a circle and ask a dead person to appear."

"Yes," I agreed. "This group was communicating with the dead and they had powers to do supernatural things! They must have *all* been witches!"

"Even your relative?" asked Muffy, giving me a sympathetic look.

"No comment," I replied.

"You don't think those adults at Captain Snow's are witches, do you?" asked Abigail.

"Of course not!" said Mollie emphatically. "They're nature freaks.

Maybe they've gone a little too far with their animal sacrifice, but I'm sure they're harmless."

"Unless you're an animal," said Muffy.

No one said anything more. Abigail took the bundle of old letters from her backpack and gave them back to me. I put them into my backpack. She said they were interesting but didn't contain anything as important or as exciting as the stories Muffy had found at the library. We decided that we would visit Miss Deighton Wednesday morning, work on our notes in the afternoon, and do a little sailing in between.

Our lunch was ready so we paid Mrs. Pitts and took our paper plates to the riverbank, a little way from the snack bar, so we could eat in peace. When I picked up my burger, I noticed a symbol drawn on my plate!

"What's this?" I asked, showing the Girls.

"Looks like trouble," observed Abigail.

"It's some sort of symbol," Mollie remarked.

"I suspect it's a hex sign!" said Muffy, obviously angry.

One by one the Girls picked up their burgers and sandwich to see that we each had the same symbol drawn on our plates! Mollie grabbed her plate and marched back to the snack bar window. We followed her, but the women were gone! And so was the cook! Where were they? I circled the tiny building and found "Cooky" sitting on the back step smoking a cigar. The Girls were right behind me.

"Look what's on my plate!" demanded Mollie, as we surrounded Cooky. He stared at the plate as if he couldn't imagine what Mollie was talking about! He shrugged his shoulders.

"Mrs. Pitts put these drawings on our plates!" Mollie asserted.

"So what?" he asked. "They won't hurt you."

"But they're some sort of a spell! She might be trying to poison us!" Muffy exclaimed. That got his attention.

"She wouldn't do that! If she did, we'd all go to jail! And I'd be out of business!"

"Well then, you'd better stop her from hexing us!" Mollie warned him.

"Why're you bothering Mrs. Pitts and her sister anyway?" he asked. So the other woman *was* her sister.

"We weren't bothering them. They're bothering us. Yesterday we were walking near the old lighthouse, just picking up shells, and that sister of hers came after us with a shotgun!" I said.

"Hmmmm." He twisted his mustache thoughtfully. "What's this about a book?" he asked.

"We had an old book here the other day and Mrs. Pitts seemed very interested in it. She even came out of the snack bar to peer over our shoulders when we were sitting on the grass looking through it," said Abigail, pointing to our favorite dining area, where our lunch was still sitting.

"Mrs. Pitts had a book this morning," Cooky told us. "She was looking at it, then she hid it in her bag under the counter. I really oughtn't do this, but..." He glanced over to the marina next door, where we presumed Mrs. Pitts and her sister had gone. Then he got up and went to the counter. He rummaged around until he pulled out a dirty old canvas bag. Inside was a plastic bag and inside that was Captain Snow's book!

"That's our book!" shouted Mollie.

"Where'd you get it?" asked Cooky, suspiciously.

Mollie paused. She looked at us.

"Tell him," I said.

"We got it from an abandoned house," said Mollie. Cooky looked at us questioningly so Mollie told him that we had permission from the owner to go into the house. The book, Mollie told him, was filled with secret code and someone had stolen the book from my house yesterday afternoon. Cooky opened the book and when he saw that the pages were full of secret code, he knew that we were telling the truth.

Cooky took a package of paper towels, stuck them in the plastic bag, and put the plastic bag back into the canvas bag in place of the book. Then he replaced the bag under the counter. He handed the book to Mollie and sat down on the back step to finish his cigar.

"Mrs. Pitts's been acting real strange lately," he began, "ever since her sister moved into that old lighthouse. All of a sudden she seems...um...different! Jumpy and always looking over her shoulder. Scared of something, but I don't know what. Won't drink the coffee. Brings her own water. Been working for me for years. Hate to see her get this way." He paused and extinguished his cigar. "You kids better get away from here before she comes back."

We thanked him and I gave him my phone number in case he noticed anything else that could help us. Mollie wrapped the book in her windbreaker and put it in the basket of her bike. We sat back down on the grass to finish our lunch.

"I was thinking," I began. "Cooky said that Mrs. Pitts won't drink the coffee. She brings her own water. Well, Miss Deighton almost had a fit when I tried to fill her teakettle from the faucet. Maybe there's something strange going on with the water that only they know about!"

"If that's true, we shouldn't be drinking the water either," said Abigail.

"I don't mind drinking soda," Mollie laughed. "But we should try to find out if they're up to something."

"You're right. But getting back to the plates..." interjected Muffy. "Let's take them along when we visit Judy tonight."

"Say what?" asked Mollie. We told her and Abigail about Judy and her invitation to visit her at The Tomb.

"She said they sell books about spells. Maybe we can find out what this one means," I said, holding up my paper plate. I then wiped off the plates and put them in my backpack. We would meet at the ice cream shop at seven, after dinner. Louie would be there, according to his plan with Mollie. It was settled. We looked up to see that the sisters were back and glaring at us! They sure were bad news, but we smiled back at them, as if nothing had happened...

Chapter Thirty

"It's Eel Grass Palace time!" I exclaimed. Finally we had time to visit our beloved palace and relax.

We pedaled our bikes to the end of Lowndes River Road and turned right onto Yacht Harbor Road. There we followed the old fence surrounding a field of bright-orange daylilies. We arrived at the tangle of grapevines which housed our "palace."

We followed the path through the "Jungle" to our palace, a series of "caves" made by wild grapevines growing for years up and over themselves. We entered our clubhouse and sat down silently to perform our ritual. First Muffy opened the old biscuit tin and took out a bag of marshmallows. Then we reached for the long sticks tucked into the ceiling and pushed a marshmallow on the end of each one. Mollie opened the moneybox and took out the kitchen matches and lit a fire, which we had laid inside a circle of stones. After the marshmallows were roasted, we partook of them in solemn silence.

Abigail reached for the empty vanilla bottle in the biscuit tin, opened it, and passed it around the circle for each of us to take a sniff of the sweet vanilla scent. After the fire had been extinguished, I covered it with sand. We rose and moved to another "house" to view the skeleton of a dead crow. It seemed scary now after finding the sacrificial bones at Captain Snow's, but we had always performed this ritual without really thinking about it. We stared at the skeleton. The bird had died naturally I suppose. And it was "natural" for an animal to have a skeleton, but I didn't want to think about bones right now!

We each had our own "house" in the palace, where we had our own style of decoration. Now we entered our houses to straighten them up. We were comforted by a familiar and safe routine. After a while Muffy wandered into my house to see my interior decorating. I had a new house because of an incident with fox poop. It's a long story.

"I love this place," Muffy said, settling into a corner. I knew she meant the whole palace, not just my house. "I hope that they never bulldoze it and build a giant house here."

"I wish you wouldn't say things like that, Muffy" I said vehemently. I admit I had had the same thought the other day, but I was just beginning to feel safe and secure again after all our frightening experiences. I didn't want to think that our favorite place would ever be destroyed.

"Calm down, Laura. I have a plan. You said yourself that your dad and that crazy Miss Deighton were ranting and raving about all the new houses going up around town. So I was thinking…we should find out who owns this land and try to get our parents to buy it. That way, we'd never have to worry about our palace being ruined by developers."

"Maybe we could get them to buy up every field and tree on the Cape while they're at it," I said facetiously. It would take millions of dollars to do that, but I really wished that they could.

"I'm serious," Muffy persisted.

"What are you girls talking about?" asked Abigail, as she and Mollie squeezed into my house.

"Saving the world," I said dejectedly.

"Saving our town," corrected Muffy. "We need to preserve our palace. I thought we could find out who owns this land so our parents can buy it. Otherwise it won't be long before it's gone."

"What do you mean?" asked Abigail.

"Someone will buy this land sooner or later and build a big house on it," explained Muffy. "You know it's true, Laura. That's why you're so upset just thinking about it. Don't hide your head in the sand as some birds do. Let's ask our parents to help us."

"Why are you talking about this all of a sudden?" asked Abigail.

"My parents went to town meeting the other night and came home really upset," said Muffy. "And Laura told us about Miss Deighton saying that the developers are building out of control. Something has to be done about the whole Cape, but in the meantime we have to save our Eel Grass Palace."

"We don't want anyone to know about it, remember?" Mollie reminded us. "We can't involve our parents. Laura, you found out who owns Captain Snow's house, so why can't you find out who owns this land?"

"I could try," I said. "Then all we have to do is find a buried treasure and buy the land ourselves. That way we can save our palace and no one else will ever know about it!" I was making a bad joke, but I felt discouraged. A problem like this seemed too big for Eel Power!

"Let's go look at the bog," Muffy suggested. It seemed like a good idea. We hadn't looked at the old bog in ages.

We put our houses in order, then walked through our palace to the abandoned cranberry bog that lay beyond it. Cedars and pines had cropped up in the sandy soil, which had once grown millions of bright red cranberries. Now only a few plants survived.

To the east stood a dilapidated barn. It probably had been used to shelter workers from the hot summer sun and to store cranberry boxes and equipment. We wandered over. When we had first chosen the site of our palace, we had peeked into the barn, but we hadn't been very interested at the time. Now we felt compelled to enter. I pulled the old door open with Muffy's help.

The interior was dark and cool. As our eyes grew accustomed to the darkness, we could see stacks upon stacks of wooden cranberry boxes, rusty rakes and shovels, and a little room, which might have been an office. A dusty window admitted the bright sunlight. We found two stools and a desk built into the wall. It was like an old-fashioned school desk with a top that opened up. Inside we found several metal boxes. The paint had mostly peeled off of them. Abigail opened one.

"Look at this!" she exclaimed. "'Snow's Bog' is printed on all these papers! That means that this cranberry bog was owned by some member of the Snow family." We rummaged through the papers: orders for cranberries, amounts owed and paid, records of supplies.

"I wonder which Snow owned this bog?" I asked, as I looked into the other box. It contained more of the same. The third box was locked.

"A treasure box!" Abigail exclaimed. Mollie picked up a rusty screwdriver she found inside the desk drawer and used it to break the lock. But the box contained only letters. We opened one. It was written in secret code!

"More pigpen code!" exclaimed Muffy in surprise. By now we had just about memorized the code. Between the four of us, we were able to decipher the letters, one by one. But they were cryptic messages.

"These letters are just as strange as Captain Snow's book," said Abigail. It was true.

"We'll never get anywhere unless we go to the town offices," I complained. "We have to find out who these people are whose names are in these messages. Plus, we forgot to ask Billy if he would take us!"

"Billy might still be at the club," suggested Abigail.

"Most of the names are only first names and some, like 'Mrs. Winter,' may be code names," Muffy continued. "We have to find out what these messages mean."

We took the box of letters and went back to our bikes. We pedaled down the dusty dirt road past the blaze of orange lilies to Yacht Harbor Road. I hoped we'd catch Billy in time.

Chapter Thirty-One

As we approached the yacht club, we saw Billy just getting into his truck, which was parked in front of the clubhouse.

"Billy, we need your help," called Muffy, afraid that he might get away.

"A new mystery?" he asked, laughing.

"Yes and we need you to go to the town offices with us," said Mollie.

"A paper trail!" he remarked, still smiling. I didn't know what he meant or understand what was so funny about it.

"Could you come with us right now?" I asked. "Please?"

"I'm supposed to go to work at the Nor'easter, but..." He didn't finish his sentence.

"It won't take long," Abigail assured him, but I doubted it. We had years of records to go through. It could take hours—or days!

"So, what's this all about?" he asked, leaning against his truck.

"We'll explain on the way," said Mollie. "Could you take us now?"

Billy nodded "yes" and helped us put our bikes in the back of his truck. Abigail and I hopped in with the bikes while Mollie and Muffy got into the cab with Billy.

Mollie told Billy about Captain Snow and the haunted house. We could hear her through the open window in the back of the cab. She told Billy how we needed to find records for the years just after the Civil War but before the death of Captain Snow.

"What exactly are you trying to find?" asked Billy.

"We found a book at the haunted house and some old letters," continued Mollie. "We're trying to piece it all together."

"I still don't get it," Billy sighed.

"There were some strange things going on in town just before Captain Snow died," I said through the window. "He was going to be thrown out of the church. His wife communicated with the dead. We want to find out about the people involved and what else they were into."

"Communicating with the dead?" he asked. "Good luck!" said Billy as if he thought we would need it. "If you were investigating something that just happened, it would be hard enough, but this was over a hundred years ago! Do you really think you have a chance?"

"We've got to try," said Abigail. We couldn't get discouraged now.

At the town offices, Billy parked his truck and we got out. Mollie told Billy the exact years of the records we needed. He would do the talking. We entered by the side door and followed the signs to the record office in the back of the old building with its white clapboards and dark green shutters. We startled an older woman seated at the records desk.

Billy spoke up. "Good afternoon. We need to see some old records."

"How old are you?" she asked, peering over the top of her glasses. He produced his driver's license, which seemed to satisfy her. She turned away from us to search the shelves and after a short time returned with several huge, ancient books. She carefully placed them on a wide oak table and we sat down to begin our search.

Of course we had no pencils or paper and had to ask for supplies. The woman gave us everything we needed. She also told us how the information was arranged and how to handle the books. It was easy to find what we needed and it didn't take long to copy everything down. We were finally getting somewhere. The town's population back then was so much smaller that it wasn't such a big task.

The first thing I noticed was no family in town had the name "Winter." That meant that the "Mrs. Winter" mentioned in my great-great-grandmother's letter was probably a code name for Mrs. Snow! I didn't like that because it meant that my relatives were involved in whatever strange things the Snows were doing. I whispered the news to the Girls. They felt sorry for me, but if my relative was part of it, it might be easier to find more information to help our case—possibly in the old letters in my barn.

I found the names of the townsfolk that Howie had given us. They seemed to be normal citizens: a farmer, a wife and mother, and a shopkeeper. But according to Howie's granddaddy and Muffy's research at the library, they were linked to Captain Snow's mystery and the strange happenings.

We finished up and thanked the recordkeeper. We had found Petunia mentioned in a census and only one man named Lawrence, whose last name was Bickly. On the way out, I ducked into the tax collector's office to inquire about the owner of the land upon which our Eel Grass Palace stood. It was Mr. Alfred Snow!!! I shared this news with the Girls.

"Wow!" exclaimed Abigail as we walked out of the offices into the fresh air. "If Mr. Snow owns that land, maybe we can make a deal with him about buying it."

"Buy it with what? Clamshells?" Mollie asked.

"What are you girls talking about?" asked Billy.

"Uh, nothing," mumbled Muffy.

"Yeah, sure," said Billy, smiling at us.

"Thanks a lot, Billy," we said, smiling back.

"You won't get in trouble for being late, will you?" asked Muffy.

"I was going in early to help move some supplies downstairs. I still have time to do it now before my regular shift begins." Billy worked in the kitchen of the

Nor'easter. He was saving money for college. The yacht club was only a part-time job for him.

After Billy helped us unload our bikes from the back of his truck, he drove the short distance down Main Street to the Nor'easter.

"Yipes! It's time for me to visit my minister," I exclaimed, looking at the clock on the steeple of the church across the street from the town offices. "Thank goodness for that clock. Otherwise I'd be late a lot more often than I am!" I laughed.

"Why are you going to see your minister?" asked Muffy. I hadn't told her or Abigail about my scheduled meeting.

"I'm going to look through old church records," I told them. "Captain Snow was a member of my church and my grandparents said that he was going to be thrown out for doing something really bad. But he was lost at sea before the church could do anything."

"Can we come too?" asked Abigail.

"It's 'may we come too'?" corrected Mollie. We ignored her.

"I'm sorry, but I think that I should go alone," I said, though I wished they could come with me. "The minister might get spooked if we all show up together. Then we'll never be able to find out what's in the church records. I'll see you all later." Our plan was to meet with Louie at the ice cream shop at seven, then visit Judy at The Tomb.

Chapter Thirty-Two

I left my friends and rode my bike across the street to the church and up the steep driveway to the old white clapboard parsonage in the back. The building also housed the minister's study and church offices, as well as space for rummage sales and ice cream socials. I knocked at the green-painted door, very traditional like most of the other buildings and homes in town, except Miss Deighton's! The minister, Reverend Maxon, greeted me with a weak smile.

"Hello, Laura. Come in." He seemed tired, or bored, as he led the way through the cool, dark building to his study. The old house had a strange smell. It wasn't musty, but I couldn't quite tell what the smell was. A mixture of leather-covered hymnals, newly laundered choir robes, coffee urns, communion grape juice, and new paint.

We entered the study and I sat down in a burgundy leather wing chair. The minister seated himself behind his huge desk and gazed curiously at me. Maybe he thought I had some sort of spiritual problem or wanted to be baptized as well as look at the old records.

"Why do you have an interest in the church records of last century?" he asked in his calm voice. I hadn't thought about it being strange, but I guess it was—for a young girl to suddenly want to read through old records.

"I'll tell you the truth," I began, wondering just how much of the truth I should tell. "My friends and I have discovered a haunted house."

Reverend Maxon's look became quite troubled. He shifted uneasily in his leather chair but said nothing, so I continued.

"In the late 1860s, a certain family lived here in town. The wife was communicating with the dead. They were members of this church. The church was planning to ask them to leave, but the husband was lost at sea. Then the wife died. One of their daughters disappeared under mysterious circumstances. So I thought that the church records might tell me more."

"I see," he replied, apparently focused on something else. Then he said, "Let's go have a look."

He got up from his chair and led me down the hallway to a door. "Our recent records are in the church office up here." He pointed to the little room on the right. "But the older records, going all the way back to our founding, are in the basement 'vault' as we call it."

He flicked on a light. We descended a narrow wooden staircase to the basement where he unlocked a gray metal door and switched on a bare light bulb that hung from the middle of the ceiling. The small room contained metal shelves lined with metal boxes, each labeled with the year of its contents.

"Jerry Mullins, you know, the deacon, is in charge of church records," he explained as he sorted through the boxes, looking for 1867, the year I thought I should start with. "When I first took my job as minister here, I used to come down and look through these old records, trying to understand the town and its people. Then it dawned on me that the old-timers are gone forever. My parishioners are different people. They're modern and this is a 'new age.' It used to be that everyone was a churchgoer and ours was the only church in town. Today, though we have many churches, very few families even think about God in a traditional way. I don't know what to do to change it, or if it even matters."

What was he saying? Of course it mattered. He was discouraged and I knew how he felt. How often I'd asked my friends to come to church with me, but they just weren't interested! Then I remembered Grammy and Grandpa.

"My grandparents are coming to church with us next Sunday," I announced. "We've been asking them for years and they finally said 'yes.'"

"That's nice," he muttered. He wasn't even listening! He was too busy rummaging through the boxes. "Here we are. My, it feels awfully light!" he remarked, setting a box down on a spindly little antique table set against the brick wall. He wiped the dust from the lid with his handkerchief and carefully opened it. It was empty!

"What's this?" he uttered in dismay. He kept looking into the box as if he expected the papers to suddenly materialize. "I'll have to call Mullins right away." He started out of the room, then turned back. He randomly began to open boxes. They were all full of papers and ledgers. Then he looked for the boxes of the years I had asked to see. He found 1869. It was empty as well! Then 1870, then 1868, and 1871. All empty! This had to be more than a coincidence!

"I don't understand it. When I mentioned to Mullins that you had called, he told me that all the records were in order. No one ever looks at these old records. Besides Mullins, I'm most likely the only person who has ever been down here for years. Who could have taken them? No one has broken in," he said, looking at the lock on the door. He paused. "Oh I know!" he exclaimed with relief. "Mullins must have put them aside for you. They must be upstairs in the office. Let's go have a look."

I followed the minister back up the stairs to the office. We looked around for the records but couldn't find them anywhere. Then we searched his study as well. Nothing. Reverend Maxon telephoned Mr. Mullins at the Water Department where he worked, but they told him Mr. Mullins was out taking water samples at one of the town wells.

"I was afraid that this was another theft," the Reverend confided. I looked at him in surprise. He continued, "A lot of little things have been missing here and there. Nothing really valuable so I haven't called the police about it. At first I thought that I was just becoming forgetful, misplacing things, and not remembering where I'd put them. But now I suspect that someone is deliberately taking things, a robe here, a chalice there. We don't lock the church up during the day. Anyone could get in, snoop around, and take things. It's probably some local kids playing a prank."

He sighed. It was upsetting to see him so dejected. I guess that being a minister is a difficult profession. Not everyone sees it as being an important job, or even a real job. But I didn't like him assuming that it was kids who were responsible for the thefts. It could have been anybody. Why do kids always get the blame?

"Now, about your haunted house," he began again. "What do you think is going on?"

I told him what had happened to us at Captain Snow's, leaving out the part about the sacrifice and what my mom had said about it being evil spirits that scared us, rather than the souls of the Snows.

"What do you think it is?" I asked him.

"Of course I don't believe in haunted houses!" he laughed. "Our church has a rite for exorcism, but none of my peers at Bible college took it seriously." I gave him a puzzled look.

"Exorcism is casting an evil spirit out of a house or a person, but we don't believe that demon possession happens today, if it ever did. The demon possessions mentioned in the Bible were probably just cases of mental illness."

"So you mean the Bible isn't true?" I asked, in shock.

"I'm not saying that the Bible isn't true," he said slowly, considering his words. "It's just that what we believe today is different from the old explanations."

"So you don't think there really are demons, or evil spirits, or ghosts?" I asked in disbelief.

"God is good. He's love. We don't have to worry ourselves about evil," Reverend Maxon said complacently.

That was not good. If my minister, a person who should be an authority on such matters, didn't even believe that spirits existed, how could he help us? Of course you're wondering what I'm talking about. You see, I had an idea...

"Reverend Maxon," I began, "even though you don't believe in ghosts, could you come to the haunted house and maybe try out your exorcism? Just in case it does work? The owner of the house lives in Ohio, but he gave us permission to find out what's going on. If you could cast the spirits out, I'm sure he'd appreciate it." The Eel Grass Girls would appreciate it too. Without the ghosts haunting us, we could investigate the house in peace and solve its mysteries.

His whole attitude changed. It was as if I had said the magic words. He perked right up and said with enthusiasm, "Why I'd love to! I don't know why I should be so interested, but I think it would be fun. I'll rustle up some holy water and sanctified oil and my book of prayers and we'll go to it!"

That was strange. A pastor who doesn't believe the Bible or in demons or spirits but gets all excited about casting evil spirits out of a haunted house! Oh well, grownups are a strange kettle of fish, if you hadn't noticed.

"When could you do it?" I asked.

"Well, unfortunately I'm busy tomorrow and Thursday," he said, looking through the calendar on his desk. "How about Friday morning?"

"Friday afternoon would be better," I said, thinking of Louie, who had camp every morning. We couldn't leave him out of this.

"Fantastic! Where is the house?" he asked.

"We'll show you. My friends and I will meet you here at one-thirty. Could we drive over in your car?" I asked. He agreed. I thanked Reverend Maxon and said good-bye. As I walked out of the parsonage to my bike, I was amazed by the transformation in my minister. He had been so glum, but now he was full of excitement. Maybe he could help us after all, even though all the church records I needed were missing.

Chapter Thirty-Three

I rode home and ate dinner with my parents. Dad was happy when I asked him about our family tree. I had never been very interested in family history before. When you have generations of relatives with children and marriages, it could get extremely complicated! After we finished eating our dinner and washing the dishes, Dad went to the old secretary—that's a desk—standing in the library. He searched a drawer and pulled out a long yellowed scroll. As he unrolled it, I could see that it was a family tree, similar to the one Howie Snow had drawn for us. It seemed strange to me that Howie knew his family history by heart.

All our relatives were listed on the branches of the tree. Yes, it was literally a tree with branches and leaves! Dad told me a few stories about some of our relatives, including the old auntie who had died right in our own cellar! Dad recounted the peculiar story.

Aunt Sparrow had been alone in the house when she went down to fetch water from the well, which you remember is in our cellar. Somehow she had fallen over backwards and hit her head on the edge of the stone well. The family thought it was very strange that she had hit the back of her head on the well when she would have been facing it, but there was no other explanation. Was it Aunt Sparrow who had screamed? Was she trying to tell me something? Just remembering that scream sent chills down my spine! But I kept it to myself. I didn't want to tell Dad.

"What about Captain Sparrow's son who went to sea?" I asked.

"How do you know about him?" asked Dad.

"I read about him in some of the old letters I found out in the barn."

"Well, Captain Sparrow wanted his son Edward to go to sea with him, but Edward went off with Captain Snow instead and never came back. He was lost when Captain Snow's boat went down."

"He was?" I was amazed. That meant that Muffy's relative Mr. McLaughlin was responsible for my relative's death too!

"I'm afraid a lot of local men were lost in that disaster. The townsfolk were quite upset, but they blamed Captain Snow. That's what I heard from the old men down at the shore when I was a boy. He had been a famous sea captain but got mixed up in some kind of trouble. It was probably whatever your grandparents were telling you, that bit about Mrs. Snow being really evil."

"Dad, why didn't you tell me any of this before?"

"I thought you were investigating the haunted house."

"But all of this is part of our mystery. The ghost is either Mrs. Snow or

Captain Snow or maybe even their daughter Petunia. It's all connected."

"Who's Petunia?"

"She was the Snows' daughter, who disappeared. Did Edward have a girlfriend?

"I haven't the faintest idea," was his reply. "You might find out from the old letters. As I recall, some of his letters are in the trunk too."

That was great news. But it was time for me to meet the Girls. I thanked Dad for showing me the family tree as he rolled it up and placed it back in the desk drawer. I then ran upstairs to get my backpack. Maybe I should brush my hair. I reached for my hairbrush, but something about it seemed strange. What was it? Then I realized it was clean! Don't think I never clean my hairbrush because I do—once in a while. But it's the kind of thing you would remember doing and I didn't remember having cleaned it for some time. The top of my bureau looked as if someone had straightened it up. Mom must have done it. That was nice of her.

I told my parents I was going to the ice cream shop and they told me to be home before dark. By the time I got to town, it was after seven. I didn't usually wear my watch, as I told you, but I could tell by the looks on the faces of my waiting friends that I was late. Louie was there. Everyone was licking an ice cream cone and sitting at the wooden picnic tables under the trees beside the shop.

"So?" asked Mollie.

"You won't believe it!" I told them. "When the minister and I looked for the old church records, all the records I needed were missing!" I told them that Mr. Mullins must have removed them and how we couldn't find them anywhere. "And Reverend Maxon is coming to the haunted house on Friday to perform an exorcism!" I announced.

"What's that?" asked Abigail, making a face. I explained.

"You asked him to the haunted house without our permission?" asked Mollie. She was really upset.

"I thought you would be glad!" Though disappointed with her anger, I tried to explain myself. "He's going to get rid of the ghosts so we can search the house for clues. Then we won't have to be afraid."

"But how will we ever find out who the ghosts are if your minister scares them away?" Mollie wanted to know. I could tell she was annoyed with me.

"They're evil spirits," said Muffy. "The Snows are long gone. Our job will be easier if they're not around."

"Laura, it would be nice if your minister could help us figure it all out," said Abigail.

"Yes," I muttered. "But the strange thing is that he doesn't believe in ghosts or spirits or anything like that! He's only going to do it because he thinks it will be 'fun'!"

Louie asked, "Are we going to The Tomb or not?"

I ran into the shop and quickly bought a mint chocolate chip cone and met the others at our bikes. We decided to leave them there and stroll toward the old village, where The Tomb was.

I walked beside Louie. "Hey, did you visit my house the other night? Saturday night to be exact?"

"No. Why would I do that?" He was puzzled. "My brothers and I played basketball in the driveway until bedtime. I was really tired after staying up all Friday night. Why?"

"Oh, nothing," I responded. If Louie hadn't walked past my window and locked me in the barn, then who had? The monster had turned out to be a coyote, so who had the window-barn creature been? The ghost? If it hadn't been the ghost, I was afraid to imagine who it could have been!

The Tomb was at the rear of an old rambling house, which had been divided up into many shops. As we walked through the little yard and approached the door leading to the small shop, we saw Mr. Mullins hurrying out of the store! He jumped into a Water Department truck and drove away.

"Hey, that was Mr. Mullins!" I exclaimed. "He's from my church. He's the one who took the records I wanted to see."

"What was he doing here?" asked Louie.

"Let's find out," said Mollie as we moved toward the door of The Tomb.

Chapter Thirty-Four

"Hi, Judy!" we called out to our sailing instructor who sat behind the counter. Wisps of fragrant incense and the scent of pungent herbs met us at the door. Bundles of herbs hung from the low ceiling, the same sort of bundles I had seen at lighthouse beach and at Miss Deighton's!

There were candles, dream-catchers, herbs, bottles of liquids with strange names such as "dragon's blood" and "lizard bile," and new and used books about charms, spells, and potion-making.

"Wow!" we exclaimed all together. It was eerie but impressive.

"How long have you worked here?" I asked Judy, stepping up to the counter.

"Just this summer," she replied. "The shop opened last spring."

"What was Mr. Mullins doing here?" I continued.

"He works for the Water Department," she told us. I knew that.

"Isn't it a little late for him to be working?" asked Mollie.

Judy shrugged her shoulders, "Don't know."

"Look at that!" Louie had just noticed the skeleton of a raccoon, mounted on a block of wood, on the top shelf of a display.

"Where'd that come from?" he asked.

"Jeffrey Silva brings them in. He always has some new animal," said Judy.

"Where does he get them?" asked Muffy suspiciously, possibly thinking of the charred remains we had discovered at Captain Snow's.

"I don't know and I don't want to know," answered Judy with a shudder. "He's a totally freaky guy. The less I have to do with him, the better!"

"I know who he is," I said. "He's in high school."

"His brother goes to camp with me," added Louie. "He's kind of quiet, but he's O.K."

"I can't say the same for Jeffrey," I said. "He probably kills the animals himself." I guess it wasn't very nice to say, but Jeffrey was really weird!

"Really?" Judy didn't like that idea.

"You shouldn't say that unless you know it's true," Abigail reprimanded me. "My father is a lawyer and he says you had better not say anything about anybody unless you know it's true. Otherwise you could get into big trouble."

Mollie rolled her eyes. "Miss Lawyer's Daughter has spoken," she joked. No one thought it was funny.

"Wait 'til you meet Jeffrey," I said. "Then you'll agree."

I took the paper plates from my backpack and showed them to Judy.

"Have you ever seen these symbols before?" asked Muffy. Louie peered over my shoulder.

"Where'd you get those greasy plates?" he asked. Mollie hushed him with the look on her face.

"Tell you later," she mouthed.

Judy took a book of spells from the shelf and leafed through it. "I...uh...can't find one like that."

"I see it! Here it is!" exclaimed Mollie, taking the book from her. "'Evil tidings to the bearer,' it says!"

"*What?*" Muffy practically shrieked.

"That Pitts woman is in for it now!" threatened Mollie.

"What Pitts woman?" asked Judy. "You don't mean Mrs. Pitts from the Clam Bar, do you?"

"You know her?" asked Muffy.

"I've only been eating lunch at the Clam Bar every day for the past 10 summers!" she exclaimed. "Everybody knows Mrs. Pitts. Did she put these spells on your plates at the snack bar?" Judy was concerned.

"Why, yes," I answered. "Do you think she would try to poison us?"

"She wouldn't do that," Judy said, thoughtfully. "She couldn't get away with it."

"Does Mrs. Pitts shop in here?" asked Abigail.

"She may have come in," Judy admitted, but she didn't seem sure.

"Who are your customers?" asked Muffy.

"Mostly kids," Judy replied. "What does Mrs. Pitts have against you?" she asked, gazing at us intently.

We glanced at each other, not knowing if we should tell her anything about our mystery or not. Mollie decided to mention the haunted house and Captain Snow's book.

"You all did such a good job of solving that fishing boat murder," Judy remarked. "I wish I could help you on this new mystery!"

"Maybe you can," said Muffy. "We're suspicious of Mrs. Pitts and her sister. Even Mr. Mullins may be involved."

"Involved in what?" she asked.

"We're not sure," said Abigail. "But we're trying to find out."

"Oh no!" exclaimed Judy, looking toward the door. "Here comes Jeffrey Silva now!"

We busied ourselves by looking at books as Jeffrey sauntered in, carrying an old beaten-up shopping bag. Something big was in it.

"Got some new skeletons for ya," he said as he pulled out the form of a squirrel and plopped it on the counter. A rabbit's skeleton followed.

"Where do you get these?" asked Judy, in an innocent but curious sort of way. I knew she was trying to help us and not arouse Jeffrey's suspicions.

"I find them in the woods or on the side of the road," he answered, not suspecting a thing. "There's no use letting a good animal go to waste after it's been killed by a car or died of natural causes."

"How did you get that coyote?" asked Judy, growing bolder and pointing to the big skeleton up on a shelf beside us.

"Oh, I can't tell you that," remarked Jeffrey, pouting. "You might take my business away from me."

"You know I wouldn't do that," answered Judy, coyly. "I was only curious." She let it go at that and wrote out a receipt for the skeletons. "Lucky will pay you tomorrow if you stop back. He hasn't been around this evening."

"He's never here anymore," complained Jeffrey. "But I'll track him down. Got any more Benny Beans?"

"Sure," replied Judy. "How many do you want?"

"I'll take another hundred." Judy took a small box out from behind the counter and gave it to Jeffrey, then wrote another receipt. His business completed, Jeffrey left.

"What was that all about?" I asked, moving back to the counter. "What are Benny Beans?"

"They're a new candy. The kids love them," she explained, showing us some little brown bean-shaped candies in clear plastic wrappers displayed in a box on the counter.

"What's in them?" asked Muffy, picking up a piece and inspecting it. "There's no writing on the wrapper."

"Don't know," answered Judy. "There's nothing on the box either," she said, showing us the plain unmarked box.

"Where do you get them?" asked Mollie.

"Some old man brings them in. Maybe he's 'Benny,'" she laughed. "Lucky has some of the kids, like Jeffrey, sell them too."

"Who's Lucky?" asked Abigail.

"He's my boss," Judy told us.

"I think this candy is …uh…fishy," said Muffy.

"Yeah," said Louie. "One of the kids at camp is selling them. I'm glad I don't like to eat candy, 'cause the kids are hooked on them. Maybe they've got caffeine in them."

"What do you think, Judy?" I asked.

"I don't know, but I could try to find out for you," Judy offered.

"I'll buy some," announced Abigail. "I'm not going to eat them!" she said in response to our looks of surprise. "Maybe I can find out what's in them."

"Good luck!" Mollie said in that droll way she had of saying things.

"Does a plump lady named Miss Deighton come in here?" I asked.

"Dorothy Deighton?" asked Judy. I nodded. "Oh, all the time. But I haven't seen her lately. She makes these herb bundles. As a matter of fact, we get most of our herbs from her."

"What's all this herb stuff about?" asked Abigail.

"It's...nothing," Judy replied, evading the question.

I thumbed through a book I had picked up from the rack, a slim volume entitled *Green Is Natural*. It seemed to explain the use of herbs, their powers, and the belief in an Earth Mother. I had enough money to buy it, so I did. Judy seemed upset as she rang up the sale. Maybe she was tired from working two jobs.

Some new customers entered the shop and needed help finding some herbs so we thanked Judy and left. We walked back up Main Street to get our bikes at the ice cream shop.

"What do you think about that place?" asked Muffy.

"I think it's peculiar," said Abigail. "Why would anyone want to know how to make spells?"

"They want to be a witch?" asked Louie. I hadn't thought of that, but now it seemed obvious.

"Is that a witchcraft shop?" asked Abigail, horrified.

"It seems like it is," Mollie said. I wondered how a shop like that could exist in our quaint little town.

"And what about that candy?" asked Muffy. "There's something strange about that too. It doesn't seem to be made by a regular candy company."

"We can add that to our list of mysteries!" muttered Mollie.

"What's our plan?" asked Muffy.

Louie had camp in the morning and then had to help his brother again in the afternoon so he would meet us at the bandstand in the park at seven. The Eel Grass Girls would meet at my house at nine in the morning and then visit Miss Deighton to pull weeds. I told them to bring their own gardening gloves so they wouldn't have to use hers. She, and everything belonging to her, was creepy. And I told the Girls we should bring our own water bottles—we didn't want to have to eat or drink anything at her house!

Then we'd telephone Mr. Snow to find out about Petunia. I had to remember to tell Mom and Dad I planned to make another long-distance call so I wouldn't get in trouble again. Next we'd continue to hunt for certain letters from my trunk, especially letters from Edward Sparrow. And I would read the book I had bought at The Tomb.

"It'll take us forever to read all those old letters!" groaned Mollie.

"Don't be such a wimp!" Muffy teased her. "We're first-class Eel Grass Girls and we can do anything."

"Right!" I agreed.

"What's that?" asked Louie.

I looked at Muffy in shock. She'd mentioned our secret name right in front of Louie! How could she!

"Hey, did I tell you about the lawn party at the library?" asked Abigail, quickly changing the subject. We hoped Louie would forget that he had heard our secret name.

"No, you didn't," Mollie shot back, catching on that we wanted to distract Louie.

"It's a tea party they're having on the front lawn of the library to raise money for new books. It's this Saturday," explained Abigail. "Everyone will dress up in old-fashioned clothes. We could come as Captain Snow and his family."

"That's sick," said Mollie in disgust. "I can't believe that you said that, Abigail."

"What's wrong?" Abigail asked in surprise. "It would be a conversation-starter and give us the opportunity to gather more information about the Snows."

"'Conversation-starter'? 'Gather more information'?" mocked Mollie. "You sound like an old lady already!"

"Mollie!" I scolded her. "Be nice. I think it's a great idea. Louie, you could dress up like Captain Snow. What do you say?"

"How much does it cost?" he asked.

"Don't worry," said Abigail. "My grandmother's on the committee and is buying tickets for all of us. It'll be so much fun!"

"Where will we get our costumes?" asked Mollie.

"I have trunks full of old clothes in my attics," I said. "You can borrow whatever you'd like."

"My grandmother has some antique clothes too," Muffy told us. "And I forgot to tell you that my aunt says that we can go over to her house any time to look at the old books and papers she has from Lowndes & McLaughlin. I've already sorted them out. There's a lot of stuff. When do you want to go?"

"More papers?" moaned Mollie.

"Yes. We need all the papers we can get. More papers means more clues, hopefully. How about tomorrow?" I asked.

"My brother needs me to help again," Louie reminded us. "I'll meet you later."

"O.K.," agreed Mollie. "Then we'll meet you at the bandstand at seven."

We called good-night to each other and rode our bikes home through the last rays of the setting summer sun.

Chapter Thirty-Five

Next morning I told Mom my friends were going to help me weed Miss Deighton's garden. I even remembered to ask for permission to call Mr. Snow, but I didn't remember to make sure I wasn't left alone in my house! Before I knew it, Mom was getting ready to leave. Dad had already left for work a while ago and I was in danger of being home alone with the ghost! What could I do? Mom had an appointment and my friends wouldn't be over until nine.

When Mom drove away, I stood in the driveway, wondering what to do. Should I call Mollie and ask her to come over early? No, she would be over soon enough, I hoped. I would feed the coyote. I hurried into the house to get some scraps of food and fresh water, then carried them out to the barn. The ghost wouldn't be able to catch me if I were fast enough, I thought. After I fed the coyote, I would look through the trunk until the Girls arrived.

I propped the barn door open with a shovel so it wouldn't slam shut and lock me in again. I took the flashlight from Dad's workbench and moved to the rear of the barn. I could hear the coyote shift on the old mattress as I came closer. There she was, waiting for me it seemed.

"Good doggy," I said soothingly, wondering if she minded being called a "dog." "How's your owie? Does it still hurt?" The wound seemed to be healing. I put the food down and filled the plastic water container.

"Just relax," I told her. "That animal officer won't be coming back. Just rest and I'll take care of you." She seemed to understand. Her eyes still had a sad look in them.

I went back to the potting shed to look through the trunk. I had time to sort the letters by writer and lay out the piles on an old newspaper. It would take a while to read all these! As I was finishing up, I heard Muffy calling me. Was I glad to hear her voice! I closed the trunk and came out of the barn into the hazy sunshine.

No one was there! I looked for Muffy, but I didn't see her or her bike either. All of a sudden I heard a crash come from the house! Then a scream!

"Laura, Laura, help!"

"Where are you?" I ran into the kitchen and raced from room to room searching for Muffy. The cellar door was ajar. Would Muffy have gone down there? I was afraid, but I had to help my friend.

"Muffy? Please answer me!" I called down into the cellar. There was no reply. I crept down the dim stairs and pulled on the light string. The lights lit up the gloomy rooms, but no one was there. I slowly moved from room to room. All the while my heart pounded in my chest! I retraced my steps and headed back up the stairs. Suddenly the cellar door slammed shut! I heard the bolt slide through the lock! I rushed up the stairs and tried to force the door open, but it wouldn't budge! I screamed!

"Laura, Laura!" I could hear someone running through the house.

"I'm down here! In the cellar!"

I heard the bolt slide back and the door swung open. I fell into Muffy's arms.

"Oh, Muffy! Am I glad to see you!" She led me into the sitting room and we sat down on the red velvet settee.

"Laura, what happened? How did you get locked in your own cellar?"

"I don't know," I told her, still trembling. "I heard you calling me. Then I heard a terrible crash and a scream! I thought you had gone into the house to look for me and something terrible happened to you. When I saw the cellar door open, I thought you must have gone down there. Were you in my house?"

"No. I just got here. I saw the barn door propped open, but no one was there so I came to the house. I was just about to knock when I heard you screaming and pounding on the cellar door. No one was here except you."

"Laura?" It was Mollie and Abigail at the back door.

"Come in," Muffy called. They found us in the sitting room. I was still shaking as I told them what had just happened to me.

"It's the ghost!" Mollie stated.

"Last night my dad told me that old Aunt Sparrow, the one who was mentioned in the letters, died in our cellar while she was fetching water from the well."

"It must have been her!" exclaimed Abigail.

"But the voice was young. It sounded like Muffy!" I insisted. "This doesn't make sense. Even if it were my great aunt's ghost, why would she play tricks on me and lock me in the cellar?"

"Mrs. Snow's ghost doesn't make sense either," Mollie informed us. "It's just the way they are."

"How do you know?" asked Abigail.

"Isn't it time for our weeding job?" asked Mollie, standing up and ignoring Abigail's question.

"Not now!" I protested, looking up. "I can't face Miss Deighton!"

"Well, it's our next assignment," said Mollie, without any sympathy for me.

Muffy asked me, "Do you feel up to going?"

"I'll go, but I don't feel like it," I took a deep breath and exhaled slowly. "My house never had any problems with ghosts until we went to Captain Snow's. What's the connection? Oh! That reminds me. I have to call Mr. Snow."

The Girls sat beside me as I dialed Ohio to talk to Mr. Snow. What if he wasn't home? But he was.

"Hello, Mr. Snow?" I began. "It's me, Laura Sparrow. I have a few questions to ask you." He paused, waiting. "First I want to know about Petunia."

"Petunia?" he questioned. "Never heard of her."

"But she was your grandfather's sister. We heard that she disappeared not long before her parents passed away. She's listed in the town records."

"Well, I've never heard of her!" he insisted.

"Did you ever hear anything about your great-grandmother being involved in the 'black arts'?"

"Never heard of such a thing," said Mr. Snow, becoming upset. "What are you trying to say? That my great-grandmother was a witch?"

"Why, no!" I was shocked to hear him say that. Even though it had occurred to us that she might be something of the sort. "We heard that she communicated with the dead. We wondered if your grandfather had ever told you about it."

"Well, you may be sure no one ever told me such nonsense! You are supposed to be telling the world that Lowndes & McLaughlin killed my great-grandparents, not peddling false rumors! Haven't you done anything useful with your time?"

"My friends and I were able to take one of the books from Captain Snow's library. It was full of secret code, which we deciphered. The entries are all very strange and don't make sense. The deciphered words themselves seem to be some kind of code."

"Well, what else did you find?"

"We found an old cranberry bog and barn. I think you own them too," I ventured.

"Yes. That's right. And I pay plenty of taxes on all that property. My grandfather used to work at the bog when he was a boy. It's all gone now, I suppose."

"No, they're still there. The bog is overgrown, but the barn is still standing. It's in good condition. You should come and see it. The land is so beautiful, it should be preserved forever." Hint, hint.

"If you remember anything about Petunia, would you give me a call?" I asked, giving him my number.

"Keep up the good work! Good-bye." Mr. Snow abruptly hung up on me!

I looked blankly at my friends. "That's rude! He just hung up."

"Maybe he didn't like what you said," suggested Abigail. "Now he knows that his grandfather kept a lot of secrets from him. It probably makes him feel bad."

"I didn't get to ask him about his family tree," I muttered in disappointment. "But I guess we have all that information from our trip to the town offices."

"Let's go pull weeds and get it over with," said Mollie, getting back to business. I wondered why she was so eager to go to Miss Deighton's. I could wait.

On our way out of the house, the Girls said they wanted to see the coyote so we stopped by the barn. As we walked by the potting shed, I told them how I had sorted out most of the letters from the trunk. In the back of the barn, they could see that the coyote was fine. We bade her farewell and rode our bikes to Miss Deighton's. It must have been a little after ten by the time we arrived. We decided to act really dumb to try to get as much information as we could from Miss Deighton.

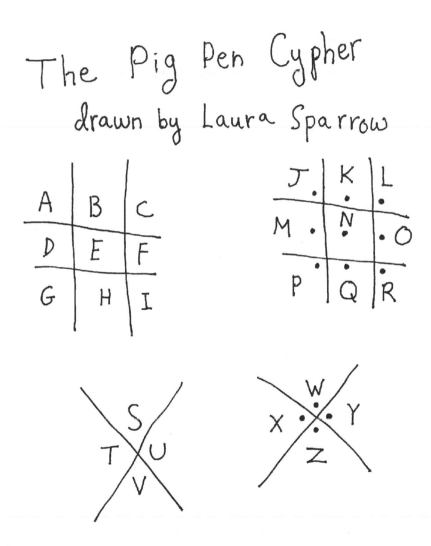

Chapter Thirty-Six

I knocked on the purple door. "Come in" came from the depths of the house. We entered. A horrible, acrid smell filled our nostrils.

"Yuck, what's that?" asked Muffy, wrinkling her nose.

"Herbs!" Mollie speculated.

"It's me, Laura Sparrow!" I called out.

"I'm in the kitchen!" she called back. I led the way through the cluttered rooms to the sunny kitchen. Light poured in through the sliding glass doors, which were thankfully open to let some fresh air blow in.

Miss Deighton was leaning on her cane at the stove. A big black pot was boiling away on one of the burners. Thick green liquid splashed over the sides. The smell was almost unbearable.

"Oh, Laura, how nice to see you. And your little friends," said Miss Deighton with her usual sneer. It was uncanny how she could give a pleasant greeting in such a nasty way. She really wasn't nice. How could Mom have said she was? Mom was a poor judge of character in this case. Miss Deighton couldn't hurt us if we were all together, could she?

"We came to finish the weeding," I explained.

"Oh, of course you did," she said, squinting over at us. Her eyes bored right through us as if she could read our thoughts. Did she suspect our motive for coming back? She paused. "There are the tools." She pointed to a basket beside the sliding door. "I suppose you *all* want to be paid for weeding."

"Oh, no," I mumbled. "Don't worry about paying us. We're just glad to help."

"I hope you won't run off again the way you did last time," she said, looking pointedly at me. I did plan to get out of there as soon as we had finished the weeding and got some information. She made me feel so uncomfortable! Was it the way she glared at me or something else?

I snatched up the basket and we exited into her lush garden. Butterflies floated above colorful flowers still wet with dew and a watering from Miss Deighton I presumed. If it weren't for the pentagram-shaped flowerbed and her strange herbs, the garden would be a lovely place.

"What's wrong with that woman?" asked Mollie. "She's not normal."

"And what is she making in there?" asked Muffy. "It stinks! I bet there are frogs and lizards in it!"

"She looks like a witch to me!" said Abigail with a shudder.

"We could've asked what she's making," said Mollie, reflectively. "We shouldn't be so scared of her."

"I suppose she could be cooking herbs to use for medicine," said Abigail as she sat down to pull weeds.

I asked the Girls if they wanted a tour of the garden. Abigail put down her trowel and followed. The brick and flagstone path led through tall irises and around apple and willow trees. Wind chimes tinkled as we passed. Birds splashed in stone birdbaths.

"How can someone so batty have such a pretty garden?" asked Abigail.

"I don't know how," I said. "But she is and she does."

I pointed out the herbs planted in a pentagram. Then we got to work. There were more weeds than I thought there would be so we worked away steadily. About an hour passed.

"Won't you come in for a cold drink?" Miss Deighton called from the door.

"Remember, we have our own water," I whispered as we moved toward the house. "Think of this as an information break."

"We brought our own water," I said to Miss Deighton, taking bottles from my backpack as we neared the door. "But we don't mind having a break."

"Well, come in," she said impatiently. She seated herself in the rocker. Today she wore a gauzy dress of pale lavender. Her earrings and necklaces were shades of purple as well. Behind her on the stove we saw the black pot still simmering away.

"Do you little girls go to school together?" Why did she have to keep calling us "little"? And why did she act as if she didn't like us?

"Yes," I answered. "I mean, no. We go to sailing school together. I'm the only one who lives in town all year-round."

"Summer children, are you?" she asked viciously. "Your mommies and daddies chop down the trees and dig up the earth to build your big ugly houses just so you can enjoy the good life at the expense of nature, isn't that true? The Earth Mother has been patient, but she has reached her limit. She's getting ready to fight back, you just wait and see! You'll all be sorry!"

Wow! The Earth Mother didn't sound very friendly. This seemed to be a good opening, though. I quickly decided to try to get her to tell us more.

"But Miss Deighton, we agree with you," I immediately responded. "What can we do to stop the destruction of nature?"

"Well, dearie, first you need to find friends who aren't part of the problem," she said, giving the Girls a wicked glare.

Good old Mollie took the cue. "I told my parents not to build a new house, but they wouldn't listen to me!" she announced. I wondered if that were really true.

"My grandmother bought the oldest house she could find!" proclaimed Abigail, catching on.

"My parents live in an old family cottage!" Muffy declared. I was so proud of them. Hopefully Miss Deighton would feel more comfortable with us now and would tell us more.

"Well, bully for you!" exclaimed Miss Deighton sarcastically, not the least bit impressed. "So you've done your part. Isn't that sweet?"

Mollie took a sip of her water. "You said something about the Earth Mother fighting back. What will she do when she becomes really angry?"

"She's already begun," said Miss Deighton, a frightening glint in her eye. "You've heard about the storms, earthquakes, and plagues of the past. More recently we've had the Ebola outbreak in Africa. Scientists have linked it directly to the destruction of the jungles. The hole in the Ozone Layer is caused by industrial pollution and the ruin of the rain forest in Brazil. Think of acid rain. The flu epidemics. It's all part of her wrath!"

She continued ranting, "A few years ago, at the height of the building boom, that terrible storm ripped through the outer bar destroying homes along the shore. The Earth Mother is punishing the world for the misdeeds of the contractors and polluters. They are the enemy. They must be stopped! They must be destroyed!" She was looking off into the distance, probably imagining an army of tree-huggers attacking the contractors with bunches of herbs. It was time to leave.

"Uh, we have to go," I said. She snapped out of her reverie and focused on us. Her eyes burned with anger.

"You want to leave without finishing your work?" she demanded.

"Uh, we have another appointment, but we can come back," I offered weakly, looking to the others for support. I didn't want to come back. I was afraid of her, whether she could give us any information or not, but I had to say something.

"I'll be here," she said, and showing us her cane, added. "I'm not going anywhere."

As soon as we were out of the house, Muffy said, "She's crazy, Laura. I can understand why you wouldn't want to visit her by yourself!"

"Do you think it's true, what she said about the plagues and the storm?" asked Abigail.

"Oh course not!" exclaimed Mollie. "I mean, the plagues are connected with the rain forest, but not with the Earth Mother." I hoped she was right. I had at least two ghosts after me. I didn't need the Earth Mother haunting me too!

We pedaled back to my house for lunch. I made peanut butter and Fluff sandwiches again and we ate out on the patio. Food helps with a lot of problems.

After we had finished eating and had washed the dishes, we got some letters from the trunk in the barn and settled down to read in the sitting room. Mollie organized the notes we had found in the box at the cranberry barn. She began to decipher them. There had to be a reason why the notes were written in strange, stilted language, but what could it be? If only we could figure it out!

I wanted to find some letters from Edward Sparrow. Was he at sea when Petunia disappeared? Did he know that Captain Snow was evil? Maybe Captain Snow wasn't evil, only his wife was. Were the townsfolk upset with him because of his wife?

And what about my relatives? Surely my great-great-grandmother was paying Mrs. Snow for something mysterious and her husband knew about it too. Her letter had said 'Mrs. Winter (Mrs. Snow) wants more than she did before, but it is worth it.' Did that mean that they were evil too? If only we knew exactly what they were doing! It wasn't long before we found out.

We read and read until we were tired. Just as we were about to give up, I found a letter from Edward Sparrow tucked inside a letter from his mother!

"Listen to this, Girls! *Dear Mother, We are leaving San Francisco today. When you receive this letter, I will be on my way to China. I am troubled that Father is unhappy with my decision to sail with Captain Snow. Father is mistaken about him, for he is a good man. I have heard the rumors about the Snow family, but they are untrue. I intend to marry Petunia on my return in the spring. Please send Mrs. Snow and Petunia my regards. Your loving son, Edward.*"

"Wow! So according to Edward, the Snows were fine. No problem," said Muffy.

"But he was in love with Petunia. Maybe he was blinded by love," suggested Abigail.

"I guess Petunia never told Edward about her mother, or he would have known," added Mollie. "Or maybe Petunia didn't know all that was going on either."

"But Edward's own mother was in cahoots with Mrs. Snow," I reminded them. "And his father knew about it. It could have been that Edward was the only one who didn't know."

Still the letter was an exciting discovery. It answered some of my questions. We would add these clues to the bits and pieces we'd already found. They were adding up. The Snow and Sparrow families were definitely linked together in this!

"Who would like to read *Green Is Natural*? I asked. "It explains about the Earth Mother."

Muffy volunteered to read it next. It contained a lot of useful information on herbs. Some of the book sounded superstitious, but some was true, I was sure. I knew that my grammy's lavender helped me sleep. Its "power" was natural and very real. The book was easier to read than the old letters, which were tiring. We needed a change of scenery, as they say. Then I had a bright idea.

Chapter Thirty-Seven

"Let's look for costumes to wear to the lawn party," I suggested. This was the change we needed.

"Hurray!" the Girls yelled as we raced up the front stairway to look in the attics. Room after room contained old trunks filled with quilts, linens, and clothes. We laughed out loud as we pulled out corsets and pantaloons. There were ribbon-trimmed skirts, ruffled petticoats, embroidered blouses, and long dresses. We found boxes of fancy combs, veils, hats, feathers, and gloves, even jewelry. It was amazing what women wore back in the olden days, even in the summer!

"What's this?" asked Abigail, holding what seemed to be a purse rolled up in a piece of silk cloth. She unwound the cloth to find a delicate volume covered in white kid leather. A slip of yellowed paper rested on top of it. It read: "Aunt Sparrow's Diary." There was a silver lock, but fortunately we discovered a key attached by a silk ribbon. Abigail carefully unlocked and opened the diary.

"Is she the old aunt who died in your cellar?" asked Mollie.

"I don't know," I mumbled, looking over Abigail's shoulder. The title page was inscribed "Seraphina Sparrow."

"I'll get the family tree," I said and bounded downstairs to the library. I grabbed my family tree from the desk and ran back up the stairs again. I carefully unrolled the scroll on the floor and searched the branches of the tree.

"Yes!" I showed them. "Seraphina was my great-great-grandfather's aunt. She was the one who died in the house!"

"Let's read her last entry," suggested Mollie. We flipped to the back of the book. A cloud suddenly covered the sun, making the attic grow dark. We looked at each other, wondering what it meant. We paused, but continued searching for the last page. The dimness made us tense.

The final pages were written January 17, 1869. *My dearest diary, I am afraid that this may be the last you will hear from me. I am all alone tonight. My nephew is away at sea, as he most often is, and his wife and daughter have gone to Hyde Park to visit Margaret. My grand-nephew is also away at sea with that wicked Captain Snow, God forgive me. Why dear Edward wants to sail with a man who works for the Devil, I cannot understand. I am so afraid. I cannot forget what I saw tonight.*

Church meeting ended later than usual. Most everyone had hurried home for supper, except the young people. They were staying for choir practice, but first they would go up the steeple to inspect the new brass bell, just delivered from Boston and put in place only yesterday. The sun was setting and Jimminey Crowell and his wife wanted to get home. They were kind enough to offer me a ride. We were the last to leave the church. I don't know why I turned back to look, but I did. That was when I saw Lawrence and Nellie up in the steeple. Nellie was so bright and gay. She turned and leaned over the balcony and Lawrence—I cannot forget the horror of it! Lawrence Bickly picked her up and tossed her over the railing!

I can still see her dark silk skirts billowing out and hear them rustling as she fell—to her death. I screamed for Jimminey to stop the carriage and turn back. Of course he didn't understand. When we returned to the scene, Lawrence had come down from the steeple, and told us all that Nellie had fallen over the balcony. He had tried to stop her, but he said he could not prevent her from falling. He had the audacity to suggest that possibly she had jumped on purpose because she was so distraught over his engagement to Miss Smith, but we all know that it was Nellie who broke off her engagement to Lawrence, and he was bitter about it.

I took Minister Foster aside and told him what I had seen. He told me that I was mistaken. It was growing dark. The steeple was dim against the setting sun. I was old and was at a distance when it happened. But Lawrence knew. He knew that I had seen him because he looked out as he threw Nellie over. He saw me as I leaned out of the carriage. I am afraid. May God rest Nellie's soul and protect me.

"My gosh!" I exclaimed. "Auntie saw Lawrence kill Nellie! Where are our notes from the town records?"

I ran back downstairs again to the sitting room cupboard and grabbed our notes and came back upstairs. We spread the notes out on the rough wooden floor of the attic.

"Here it is!" exclaimed Abigail. "Nellie Nickerson died January 17, 1869, and Seraphina Sparrow died the next day on January 18th! That is too much of a coincidence! Could Lawrence have killed her?"

"Look!" Mollie said excitedly, pointing to one of the pages of our notes. "It says here that Lawrence Bickly married a Melody Smith in May of the same year. Wait a minute! Remember, we read something in Captain Snow's book about Lawrence and his lady friend, remember? Maybe the lady friend was Nellie?"

"I'll go get our papers," I said as I ran back downstairs to the cupboard.

"Here it is," I said breathlessly, as I reappeared with another bundle and spread them out on the floor next to all the others.

Abigail found the entry and read the translation they had made from Captain Snow's book: *Lawrence's lady friend appeared. We could smell the lavender scent she always wore. Lawrence could feel her hand on his cheek. I asked her if she was at rest. She knocked once to reply 'yes.' I asked if she had a message for Lawrence. She answered 'yes' again. She impressed upon me that he would succeed at Lowndes & McLaughlin.*

"I don't get it," said Abigail.

"If she was there with them, why does it say that he 'felt her hand on his cheek'?" asked Mollie.

It reminded me of the ghost who had stroked my face! That was it! "It was a ghost!" I shrieked. "Don't you see? She was invisible! That's why they're talking about the smell of her perfume, the touch of her hand, and the knocking instead of talking!"

We were stunned. We just sat there on the floor while the revelation sank in.

"It sounds as if a group of them were together when the ghost appeared. Hey! Could Captain Snow's book be a record of ghost sightings?" asked Mollie. "The 'well' was probably their gathering place. And what else did that letter say? The one from your great-great-grandmother, Laura, about your aunt?"

"Let me find it," Abigail said as she sifted through the piles. "Here it is. She's supposedly fine and warns of 'bad weather to come.' And she says 'not to follow her path.' If your great-great-great aunt thought that Captain Snow was evil, she may have said some things against the Snows. And she must have said something to Edward. Could it be that?"

"Probably," I mumbled. I was thinking of something else. "Lawrence worked at Lowndes & McLaughlin. And the name Bickly. I've heard that name before, but where? It was a woman. Susanna Bickly...Snow! That's it!"

"What?" asked Abigail, giving me a puzzled look.

"Lawrence Bickly was Mrs. Snow's nephew who worked for Muffy's great-great-grandfather!" I shouted.

"Are you sure?" asked Mollie.

"I think you're right," said Muffy. "Lawrence tried to contact Nellie. That way no one would suspect him of killing her. The ghost didn't tell them that she was murdered, because it wasn't really Nellie who appeared!"

"Then who was it?" asked Abigail.

"Lawrence and Mrs. Snow must have just made it all up! Eureka!" Muffy squealed with delight at her discovery.

"If Lawrence killed your great aunt too, Laura, maybe her soul is haunting your house," suggested Mollie, ignoring Muffy. "I think she's trying to tell you that Lawrence killed her."

Abigail had taken the diary and was looking back at other entries. "Hey! She wrote something about Petunia!"

Crowding around her, we read: *Petunia is gone. Oh where did she go? I fear that her evil mother knows where she is. A place from where she will never return.*

"That's scary!" said Abigail with a shudder.

"So when they supposedly called these people back from the dead, they asked all kinds of questions about the future too," I put in, glancing over some of the translations from Captain Snow's book.

"But it was all fake," said Muffy emphatically. "Mrs. Snow tricked them. And charged them a lot of money for it!"

"Help me!" We heard a girl shriek. "Oh, help me! Help!"

We looked at each other in shock.

"Who's that?" Muffy asked, jumping up. We all rushed downstairs, trying to determine from where the cries were coming.

"Help!" The cry came from outside. We ran out the back door.

"Ahhhhhhh!" She was in the barn! We raced over and threw the door open and ran in.

"Where are you?" I called into the darkness. Silence. Behind us the barn door slammed shut! We heard a padlock click on the hasp! We never locked the barn door, although it did have a hasp in case we ever did. But there was no *lock*. Whoever had locked us in had used their own lock!

"Not again!" I groaned.

"What's going on?" asked Abigail. "This is scaring me!"

"It's scaring us all," I said. "And it's my house and barn that are being haunted! Remember I told you that someone shut me in here the other night?" I reminded them. "Now they've done it again and they've used a lock!"

"But who?" asked Muffy. "And where's the girl?" I took the flashlight from Dad's workbench and we moved through the barn, shining the light around, but no one was there. We looked for the coyote. She was gone too. Then we came to the loose siding where the coyote entered and exited the barn. We stooped down and squeezed out into the bright sunlight.

When we ran around to the front of the barn, we saw a shiny new lock on the door! Dad would have to cut if off when he got home, but now we had a worse problem.

"I don't think a ghost would use a lock like this," I stated. "It was a real person who locked us in the barn for a reason."

"Do you think that person is in your house?" asked Abigail, shaking.

We slowly approached the back door. We stopped to listen but didn't hear a sound, except for a couple of powerboats and someone blowing an air horn out in the harbor.

"Let's go in," Mollie suggested. "Muffy and I will circle around the sitting room and library and then go up the front staircase. Laura, you and Abigail go to the dining room. Check the pantry and the cellar, then go up the back staircase and we'll meet upstairs, O.K.?"

"O.K., but I don't want to get locked in the cellar again." I wasn't kidding.

We crept in, making sure the screen door didn't slam behind us. We circled the downstairs and met in the attics. All our notes, the diary, and my family tree were gone! A door slammed downstairs! We rushed back down, but no one was there. We ran out into the yard but didn't see a soul.

"The sitting room cupboard!" I exclaimed.

We raced back in to check the cupboard. The cupboard door was closed so I hoped that meant that the few letters left inside were safe. My heart sank when

I opened the door and saw they were all gone! The thief had taken everything! Did this mean that it was the same thief who had stolen Captain Snow's book before? I suspected it was.

"Mrs. Pitts!" we exclaimed.

"But where was she hiding?" asked Muffy. "And how could she steal everything so quickly?"

"I've had enough of her!" exclaimed Mollie. "That Pitts woman has gone too far this time. She's going to pay for this!"

"What are you going to do?" asked Abigail, timidly, probably suspecting that Mollie would do something that would get us all into trouble.

"I don't know," pouted Mollie. "She wouldn't be at the snack bar now. She's off somewhere hiding our notes, but she'll go back to work soon...I know! Where are those plates with the hexes on them? We'll put a hex on her! We'll fight her with her own weapons!"

"What are you talking about?" asked Abigail. Mollie appeared as if she would explode with frustration, but she calmed herself down.

"Abigail," she said slowly and softly, as if she were talking to a little child. "Mrs. Pitts drew hexes on our plates, right?" Abigail nodded. "Well, we'll draw the same hexes on our money. Then we'll go to the Clam Bar, order some food, and use the money to pay for the food. She believes in hexes, right? So if we cast a spell on her, it will upset her. And she'll know that we know she's the one who's been stealing our things."

"I'm not so sure that it's the right thing to do," began Muffy. "If we don't like what she does, should we do the same thing to her? It's not right. The Eel Grass Girls are always supposed to do what's right!"

"Muffy!" yelled Mollie. She was on the verge of losing her temper. But she controlled herself once more. "Muffy, this is war. We're going to do it to confront her and see if we can find out more about what she's up to. We're not seriously hexing her."

"Oh," said Muffy. I was sure she had understood that from the beginning, but she believes in always doing what's right. We all did, but Muffy was more strict about it than the rest of us.

"Where are those plates, anyway?" asked Mollie. They were still in my backpack. I located it and got them out and handed one to each of the Girls. We copied the hex sign in ink on our dollar bills, which I don't think is a good thing to do, but we justified it because of our mystery. "We'll give Pitts time to get back to the snack bar. Then we'll saunter over as cool as can be," Mollie explained.

"I still want to know who was calling for help," asked Abigail. "Do you think it's the ghost of your aunt, Laura?"

"It sounded like a girl," I replied. "Not an old lady. I don't know who it was.

Maybe Mrs. Pitts has a little girl working with her, but I doubt it."

"Let's go hex Mrs. Pitts!" Mollie said, heading out the back door.

As we followed her, Abigail asked, "Could we go sailing afterwards?"

"If we have time," I said. I hoped we would. A nice relaxing sail. It was one of my favorite things, but I didn't think I could relax now!

"My aunt said we could go over to her house anytime to look through her old papers," said Muffy. "I know we'd find some clues. When we meet Louie, we can tell him everything that's happened."

"He'll be surprised," I said. I was beginning to feel tired. Too many disturbing things had happened today. The old letters and ghosts were getting to me!

"Where's the coyote?" asked Abigail.

"I guess she's out. Looking for food maybe," I speculated. "Or maybe she's all better now."

"I hope so," remarked Muffy.

We rode our bikes out of my driveway and down toward the yacht club. In the distance we could see Allyson riding away with a small sail, probably a jib, under her arm. She was in charge of sail repair. When we got to the club, Billy and Judy were sitting at the picnic table near the club's flagpole. I was glad that we had two teenagers as our friends. It gave me a feeling of security—something I really needed now.

Chapter Thirty-Eight

"Hey!" called Judy. "I've got news for you."

We stopped and she came over to us. Billy got up to follow. Judy looked at him. She seemed uncomfortable. Mollie noticed her look.

"Billy's cool," she told Judy.

"Yeah," said Billy. "I'm one of them." We all laughed.

"Here's the scoop," began Judy. "Those beanie candies have some herbs in them. They give the kids energy. The kids who sell the beanie candy, like Jeffrey, are supposed to run out every once in a while and tell the other kids they have to go to The Tomb to get more. When they come in, I'm supposed to get them interested in the books, you know, the spells and potions and stuff. They're popular anyway, so it's easy. It took me a while to put it all together, though. I think it's just a marketing idea to make money off the kids."

"So the herbs are like caffeine?" asked Mollie.

"Yeah, I guess so," Judy shrugged her shoulders. "It doesn't really hurt them."

"How do you know for sure?" asked Abigail.

"I don't," replied Judy. "But I am sure that their brains are mush anyway," she laughed. But it wasn't funny. I was surprised that she would say something like that.

"The candy can't be that harmful or your boss wouldn't sell it," I said. "If any of the kids got sick, the police could trace it back to The Tomb without any trouble. Maybe you could give us a list of the adult customers and tell us if anyone says or does anything out of the ordinary. That would really help us."

"Stop by tonight and I'll have a list ready for you," said Judy, with a smile.

"We'll be there," Muffy promised.

"I'm wondering how this business at The Tomb ties in with your haunted house?" asked Billy.

We gave each other a quick glance and nodded that it was all right to tell him some of what we had found out. We told him that we thought there was a connection between the customers of The Tomb, the Earth Mother, Mrs. Pitts, and the foggy gathering at Captain Snow's.

"Hey, you didn't tell me that!" complained Judy.

"Sorry," Abigail apologized.

"Sounds like witchcraft to me," said Billy.

"What?" We were completely shocked.

"It's obvious. They're customers of The Tomb. They're into herb power and the Earth Mother. They sacrifice animals during the full moon. They wear pentagrams and put spells on people. That spells witchcraft," said Billy.

"Wow!" uttered Abigail. "They're really witches?"

"We knew that," claimed Mollie.

"It's green witchcraft," corrected Judy.

"So does that make them good witches?" asked Billy.

"Yes," replied Judy. "They have a lot of good ideas about the environment."

"They sound evil enough to me," observed Billy. "What's your plan, girls?"

"We're trying to find out who is haunting Captain Snow's and my house too," I told him. "We want to find out more about what was going on back then and what's going on now. We're going to look through the old letters and papers that Muffy's aunt has, but our first stop is the Clam Bar to confront Mrs. Pitts."

"I'd like to see that," chuckled Billy. "Good luck!" he called after us as we headed down the road to the snack bar.

It was good to be out on such a beautiful summer day, so clear and bright. The marina store was busy with buyers and the docks were bustling with boats, day sailors, and fishermen. We rode to the Clam Bar. Pitts was stationed at the window.

After leaning our bikes against the little sagging building, we stepped up to the counter to place our orders. Mrs. Pitts acted as if nothing had happened. It almost made me doubt that she was the one who stole the diary and all our notes. Were we making a mistake by suspecting her? I felt really angry and upset though, that someone would come into my house and steal all those things, even my antique family tree! We had to get them back! We had to take a chance.

We ordered the usual. After Mrs. Pitts hollered our order to Cooky, it was time to pay. We each placed our dollar bills on the counter, hex-side-up and plainly showing. Mrs. Pitts reached for the money, but when she noticed the hex sign on one bill and then the others, she dropped the money as if it were on fire! For a moment she was frozen in horror. Then she recovered.

"You little devils!" she shrieked. "You—you—" she stammered, pointing a bony finger in our faces. "I'll get you for this! You'll be sorry! You don't know who you're playing with!"

"What's going on now?" asked Cooky, stepping up to the window.

"It's those little imps, the ones who stole my book!" she cried. We looked up at them blankly, trying to appear completely innocent.

"I'm going on my break," she declared as she took off her apron and slammed it on the counter. She stomped out the back door and disappeared toward the marina.

"What'd you do to her this time?" asked Cooky, with a sigh. "She just came back from a break! A pretty long one, too."

"We just ordered our lunch and tried to pay for it," Mollie explained.

Cooky took the money, without noticing the hex signs we had drawn on the bills and gave us our change.

"I had to tell her that you kids snuck in here and took her book," Cooky told us, meekly.

"Why?" asked Muffy.

"I couldn't let her know that I did it, could I?"

"Thank you *so* much," Mollie said with exaggerated sweetness.

"I helped you get it back, didn't I?" he asked, defensively.

"Yes, but we're here because she stole something else," I told him.

"Again?" he asked in surprise. "She only has a little handbag with her today. If she did take something, I don't know where she put it. She didn't used to take such long breaks," he continued. "But now she disappears for more than an hour at a time. Don't know where she goes or what she does. Was a good worker and did just fine until that sister of hers showed up. Now she's more skittish than a rabbit with a coyote on its trail."

He abruptly turned back to his grill and began to cook our food. If Mrs. Pitts had taken the diary and notes, where had she hidden them? And if she hadn't taken them, who had?

We sat on the riverbank, feeling low. Having our notes stolen wouldn't help us solve our mystery!

"Cheer up," encouraged Muffy. "We'll have fun at my aunt's house. Maybe we can even visit my grandmother later. She said we could look through her old trunks."

"Where do you think Mrs. Pitts is?" asked Mollie, looking around. "I'm going to find that woman." Before we could stop her, Mollie was on her way to the marina. Then she disappeared behind a huge sailboat parked on a trailer in front of the marina store.

"Here's your lunch," called Cooky. We took our plates and drinks and thanked him. We asked what hours Mrs. Pitts worked. He told us her schedule, which was the same as his: everyday from ten to six, except Sundays.

"Should we wait until Mollie gets back before we eat?" asked Abigail, sitting down with her burger.

"I wonder where she went," Muffy said. We noticed Cooky looking out the window in the direction of the marina. Some tourists stepped up to the window to place an order. Cooky was obviously upset about Mrs. Pitts's disappearance. She was nowhere to be seen. Neither was Mollie.

Chapter Thirty-Nine

"I'm going to look for Mollie," I said, getting up and heading toward the marina.

I ducked behind the sailboat and around to the shop. There were some customers looking at outboard motors, but no Mrs. Pitts and no Mollie. I wandered into the next building where boats and motors were being repaired. Only a couple of workmen were there. When I came to the end of the dock, I saw Mollie peering into the window of a small shingled building. I made a "Pssst" sound. Mollie turned and looked toward me, motioning me to keep silent. I crept up beside her. We were on the far side of the building, away from the marina, out of sight of passersby.

"Mrs. Pitts is in there," whispered Mollie, pointing toward the window. "She's talking to a fat man about a 'plan.' I can't make out what it is though."

Suddenly I felt cold and uneasy. What was it? Then I knew, as I glanced up to see Mrs. Pitts looming over us! A big bulky man with a sweaty face and tiny glasses was right behind her. He lunged past her, grabbed us by our shirts, and dragged us into the little building! Inside he threw us up against a stack of wooden crates piled across the back wall! We were so shocked and scared we didn't make a sound! I was angry for not trying to protect myself or making an attempt to fight back! I didn't even try to scream! I just stood there, trembling and waiting to see what they would do to us!

"So who do we have here?" the man asked with a sneer.

"Dirty little troublemakers, I'd say," snarled Mrs. Pitts.

"Do you know what happens to trespassers?" the man demanded. We didn't think he expected an answer. He didn't give us a chance anyway.

"Call the police, Gracie," he instructed Mrs. Pitts.

"Gladly," she responded. She moved toward the door, pretending that she intended to call. There was no phone in the little building. But I wasn't afraid of the police because we were on the marina dock, not their private property. We knew they were bluffing.

"I have a better idea," said Mrs. Pitts, coming back toward us. "Karl, don't you have something in your bag?"

Karl opened up what appeared to be a black leather doctor's bag. He chuckled as he began to take out some sort of shiny object. A cold chill tingled down my spine!

"Maybe a little medicine would make the girls behave," he said. Mrs. Pitts moved toward us, clutching each of us by an arm. A motorboat was revving up its engine in a marina slip just outside, so it was useless to scream now. I stared in terror as Karl edged slowly toward us.

"Maybe this isn't such a good idea, Karl," she said, hesitating.

"Whatever you say, Gracie," he replied, turning and putting back in his bag whatever it was he had been holding in his hand.

"Another time. When you're home alone, Laura. You might just disappear. It would be a while before anyone would notice you missing. And it would be a long time before they ever found you. The same goes for you, Mollie." What did Mrs. Pitts mean? I was afraid to imagine! She laughed hysterically. A shrill cackle, just like a *witch*. She knew our names and where we lived! She was crazy! She released her grip on our arms.

"You may go now. Enjoy your lunch," she snickered as Mollie and I bolted out of the shack, past the marina, and back to our friends at the Clam Bar.

"Let's get out of here!" I cried when we met our friends on the riverbank. "We've got to call the police!"

"And tell them what?" asked Mollie, pulling me back. Muffy and Abigail stared at us in confusion.

"Mrs. Pitts and her friend 'Karl' just tried to kill us!" I told them. "They threatened to come after us sometime when we're home alone. The man had something horrible in his doctor's bag with some kind of medicine in it! We've got to tell the police!"

"You know the police won't do anything," Mollie reasoned. "They'll just ask a lot of questions. Mrs. Pitts will deny everything we say, but she'll tell them that you stole her book from the snack bar. We'll probably be the ones who'll end up in jail!"

"Then what'll we do?" I asked in dismay. "Mrs. Pitts has already broken into my house twice. Not to mention I have a ghost living there too! I'm already afraid to be at home alone! Now I have to worry about that deranged woman sneaking in and doing something terrible to me."

"Well, what about me?" asked Mollie. "She threatened me too! I'm home alone as much as you are. Maybe even more. She knows our names and where we live. And she knows how to creep around without anyone seeing or hearing her either."

"Maybe she's a ghost," Abigail suggested.

After seeing Mrs. Pitts at the snack bar for so many years, I didn't think so, but she sure was evil. "She's a witch," I said. "Maybe Billy's right. They might all be witches!"

"They're no such thing as witches, anymore," said Abigail. "Judy called them green witches, but that's the same thing as environmentalists."

"Great!" I said, throwing my hamburger to the seagulls. I put my soda can in my pocket. We cleaned up our napkins and plates and threw them in the trash. "Somehow

I don't see Mrs. Pitts as an environmentalist. And who is her friend Karl?"

"Whoever he is, he was talking about a plan," said Mollie, taking her bike from the side of the snack bar. "It could have something to do with the environment. Your friend Miss Deighton was all upset about pollution and overdevelopment. If they know each other, they could be working together."

"If only we could have seen those adults on that foggy night," said Muffy. "Then we would know who's in their group. Then it would be easier to find out what they're doing."

"Well," began Abigail, "they may just be trying to protect our town from the wrath and fury of the Earth Mother. That's why they were offering a sacrifice, don't you think?"

"Wrath and fury?" laughed Mollie. "You are too funny! I don't agree with their religion, or in sacrificing poor animals, but this is a free country. If they want to worship the Earth Mother, it's their business."

"Sacrificing poor animals makes it our business!" I said with feeling. "We can't let them do that! We have to stop them."

"To my aunt's," said Muffy, getting on her bike and heading toward the lighthouse. "We need more information before we can stop them and we need to find out more about Lowndes & McLaughlin to solve Captain Snow's mystery, so let's go." We needed a change, that was for sure. No one said a word as we got on our bikes and followed.

Chapter Forty

Past the lighthouse we pedaled and down the road that followed the shoreline. We sped by the fish pier, then turned north into a residential section
of town. We rode down Old Port Road, full of high privet hedges, behind
which we caught glimpses of green lawns dotted with huge bunches of blue
and pink hydrangeas. Muffy's home was in this part of town and her aunt
lived just behind her. We arrived at Muffy's and left our bikes on her front
lawn, then followed a path through the woods to her aunt's house.

Muffy took the house key from its secret hiding place. I can't tell you where that
is—sorry. Muffy unlocked the front door and we entered the rambling Cape house.
She led us to the back of the living room where a huge wooden cabinet stood.

"In here," she said as she opened its doors. The shelves were stacked with old
papers, ledgers, and letters.

"Well, let's get to work," Muffy said as she began handing us piles of
papers and ledgers.

"Here are the piles I made for us the other night. Mollie, you get the business ledgers from Lowndes & McLaughlin. Abigail, you can read these letters
from Mr. McLaughlin and his family. Laura, you take the miscellaneous whatnot." She dumped a box of calling cards, notes, and letters into my waiting arms.
"I'll take these letters to and from I don't know whom," said Muffy. She opened
up the French windows leading to the aunt's beautiful garden. We sat down on the
floor next to the windows where we would have good light for reading the old
pen-and-ink script. Muffy handed us paper and pencils for taking notes.

"Remember, we want names, dates, deaths, and anything that seems unusual,"
she said as she made herself comfortable and began to read her bundle of letters.

"Here's something," said Mollie, as soon as we were settled. "Laura, you told
us that Mrs. Snow's nephew Lawrence Bickly was the Lowndes & McLaughlin
bookkeeper. Look here! He made some big mistakes in his addition."

"I don't believe it!" Muffy exclaimed, defensively, jumping up and peering
over Mollie's shoulder. "My great-great-grandfather would have double-
checked the bookkeeping and would have gone over the ledgers!"

"See for yourself," Mollie said, pushing the ledger under Muffy's nose.
"What do you make of it?"

"Maybe Lawrence was stealing," suggested Abigail.

"If Lawrence wanted to steal money from the company," I said, "he wouldn't
have made obvious mistakes in the ledger. He would have balanced everything
perfectly to cover up his stealing."

"Why would my great-great-grandfather hire a bookkeeper who couldn't even add?" asked Muffy. We looked over the ledger and could clearly see the mistakes, but it didn't make any sense. Even a second-grader could tell his math was wrong.

"I've got it!" shrieked Mollie, scaring us half to death! "It's a secret code! A numeric code. He was trying to say something with the numbers. There's a pattern. See?" She pointed out the variations in the sums. "They're all off by the number five, but it's weird. The sums at the end of the columns are correct! That's why old McLaughlin never noticed."

"What was he trying to say?" I asked. "Why did he have to use a code? He could have easily talked with his co-workers, couldn't he? And he could use the pigpen code to communicate with his witch relatives. Who would see the ledgers other than his co-workers and the bosses?"

"The dead!" answered Mollie, solemnly.

"The dead what?" asked Abigail.

"He was communicating with the dead," Mollie repeated, still skimming the pages. "I'm sure of it."

"That's ridiculous!" exclaimed Muffy. "He was probably just superstitious. He thought Nellie Nickerson would haunt him unless he protected himself with the number five."

"What's so lucky about five?" asked Abigail. "I thought seven was the lucky number."

"There are five points on the pentagram and five is supposed to be the luckiest number of all," Muffy told us.

"I agree with Muffy," I added. "He was superstitious."

"Have it your way," said Mollie. "But I know I'm right." She continued to search the records. "Muffy, may I see if any invisible ink was used in this ledger?"

"All right, but be careful. My aunt won't appreciate it if we burn her house down."

"Picky, picky," muttered Mollie as she lit one of the candles on the dining room table. She held a ledger page over the flickering flame. Sure enough, it revealed a line of pigpen code across the top!

Nellie, forgive me, she read. *It was an accident. You never should have left me.*

"See!" cried Mollie triumphantly. "He's writing to Nellie's ghost and he admits killing her."

"He said it was an accident," corrected Muffy.

"Then why is he asking for forgiveness?" I wondered aloud. "Surely he killed my aunt after she saw him push Nellie out of the church steeple! He must have been using the numbers for communication and protection."

"Wow!" exclaimed Abigail. "That is so horrible! Your poor old aunt!"

She paused thoughtfully, then added, "You don't think Mrs. Pitts would hurt us, do you?"

"This afternoon she and her friend Karl threatened me and Mollie!" I reminded her.

"But they may have just been trying to scare you," Abigail said cautiously.

"They're killing animals, stealing books, and cooking up some evil plot. We have to find out what it is and stop them before someone does get hurt," Mollie stated. "And that someone includes you!" She was right.

Mollie continued searching the ledger for more secret code, but didn't find any, so she blew out the candle. We settled back down on the floor again to search and read. We worked away for a while, finding a few letters from one of Mr. McLaughlin's daughters mentioning the local gossip of blossoming love between some of the young townsfolk.

"Look at this!" exclaimed Mollie again, showing us a ledger that was actually a ship's log from one of Captain Snow's previous voyages. He had sailed Lowndes & McLaughlin ships for years. We read, looking over Mollie's shoulder. The log contained entries by some of the crew members—descriptions of a Pacific Ocean island they had explored on their way to the Orient. It didn't contain any clues for our case, but it sure was interesting!

"Why don't we sit in the garden for a while?" suggested Muffy. "We need a break and some fresh air will clear our minds."

It sounded like a good idea. We put all the papers back in the cupboard and moved out onto the patio. As we admired all the lovely shades of the blue and pink flowers, we heard a tapping noise. We stopped still to listen and looked around. The past few days had been so full of surprises and strange happenings, we were ready for anything!

Chapter Forty-One

The noise was coming from the toolshed which stood at the edge of the yard under the shadow of a giant fir tree. We crept over and peered in through a dusty window.

"It's a bird!" exclaimed Abigail. We saw a big crow flapping its wings against the window. It was trapped in the shed and was trying to get out! Muffy flung the door wide open and the crow whizzed out, cawing loudly as it skimmed over our heads.

"How did he get in there?" asked Mollie, stepping through the doorway into the shed.

"Maybe Muffy's aunt left the door open while she was doing yard work and the crow flew in," I speculated.

"Crows don't do that," Muffy said thoughtfully, entering the shed to look around. That's when we saw it. On the potting table, beside a rusty trowel and green garden clippers, lay a piece of plain paper. Three words, in the pigpen cipher, were scrawled across it. We could read it. It said, "I'M WATCHING YOU."

"I don't believe it!" whispered Mollie. "It's that Pitts woman again! She's following us! First she stole our book, then our notes. Now she knows the code! It's her. I know it is."

"How can you be so sure?" asked Abigail, the skeptic.

"Who else could it be?" Mollie demanded. But if it were Mrs. Pitts, then where was she? We scanned the woods around the yard. Everything was still and quiet. All we could hear was a bulldozer digging the foundation for a new house somewhere in the neighborhood.

"I don't feel safe out here anymore, not with that woman around," said Abigail, obviously afraid.

"Don't be scared," Muffy reassured her. "My house is just next door."

"Then let's go," I suggested. I didn't like the thought of Mrs. Pitts lurking in the woods, waiting to get us! We closed the door of the toolshed.

"You can't scare us!" hollered Mollie, as loudly as she could, while the rest of us moved back toward the house. "We're going to solve this case! We'll find you and expose your evil plot. Everyone will know what kind of witches you truly are. You'll be sorry!"

Only silence answered.

"Let's lock up my aunt's and go to my house," said Muffy.

We went back through the French windows, closing and locking them behind us. At least Muffy's aunt had strong locks on her windows and doors—and she used them. Muffy locked the front door, replacing the key in its secret hiding place. Then we followed the path back to her cottage.

"What's this?" asked Abigail stooping to pick up a little doll lying in the middle of the path. "It looks like you, Laura," she said, holding it up for us to see.

It was a handmade rag doll, only a few inches tall, with real human hair and what looked like nail clippings sewn onto a little shirt with a seagull crudely drawn on it. I stared in amazement as I realized that it did look like me! I always wore a yacht club sweatshirt with a gray and white seagull on the front! The hair was the exact color of brown as my hair!

"It is you, Laura," Mollie whispered. "Why does it have pins stuck in it?"

"Is it a pin cushion?" asked Abigail.

"It's a voodoo doll!" exclaimed Muffy. "Take the pins out, quick!"

"Say what?" asked Mollie. Muffy snatched the doll from Abigail and yanked the pins out, tossing them into the bushes. Then she ripped the hair off it and took the nail clippings out. Dried herbs fell from the doll's torso, as she frantically tore the fabric and cotton stuffing into shreds and flung them into the bushes.

"*What are you doing?*" I shrieked.

"The doll can't hurt you if it's in pieces." answered Muffy, busily dismantling the doll.

"I thought you didn't believe in that sort of stuff," said Mollie, looking at the pieces of my image hanging from the thorns of the blackberry bushes on either side of the path.

"I don't," Muffy explained. "But if Laura does, it might hurt her."

"What do you mean?" Abigail asked.

"If you believe that the doll's magic will make you sick, you'll get sick. Now it can't hurt Laura, whether she believes in it or not," Muffy said, scanning the bits of material and seeming satisfied with the job she had done.

"Well, I don't believe in it, but I feel better that you destroyed the doll," I said. "Thank you. Just last night I noticed that my hairbrush had been cleaned. Do you think that Mrs. Pitts could have taken the hair from my brush and found my nail clippers?"

"It has to be Mrs. Pitts!" Muffy exclaimed. "Or maybe her sister. One of them must have gotten into your house again!"

I guess it could have been either of them, but I suspected that it was Mrs. Pitts. That woman was getting to be really annoying! We continued walking down the hill to Muffy's cottage. Mrs. Pitts was seriously after us. Or was she seriously after only me? And where was she now? Had she been listening to our conversation? She was probably somewhere in the woods watching us!

We barged into Muffy's little cottage and piled into her tiny kitchen, crowding around her antique bamboo table. We decided that it was time to eat. Thankfully Mrs. Cortez was at home to feed—and protect us. Muffy's mom served us homemade beach plum jelly on Ritz crackers. Yummy! A jelly-making mom, like mine!

"Do you girls have outfits for the lawn party on Saturday?" asked Mrs. Cortez. "We have lots of old clothes," I told her.

"Grammy has lots, too," Muffy said, licking the crumbs from her mouth. "She told me everyone is welcome to borrow whatever they need. She has some old letters too. How about stopping by there with me on your way home?"

"I have to get home early," Abigail informed us. "My grandmother wants me to eat dinner with my little cousins, but I'll still be able to meet you at the bandstand at seven. She has an outfit picked out for me. There were lots of things left in her house when she bought it a few years ago."

"Yipes!" exclaimed Mollie. "What time is it?"

We looked at the clock on Muffy's kitchen stove. It was almost four.

"Bye!" called Mollie as she dashed out the front door. "Thank you Mrs. Cortez. I'm late for my tennis lesson. See you in town at seven, Girls." And she was gone.

"I can go with you," I said to Muffy. We cleaned up our dishes, thanked Muffy's mom, and rode with Abigail back toward town.

Chapter Forty-Two

On Main Street, we stopped in front of Muffy's grandmother's house. Abigail left us and continued on her journey to her grandmother's house, leaving Muffy and me alone. We parked our bikes out back. The beautiful old gray and white home stood on top of a hill and overlooked the main street of our town. The backyard sloped down to a huge garden, which extended back to a pond partly hidden by a line of trees. Lilies and blueberry bushes decorated the wide expanse.

We climbed the back steps and Muffy called out at the door as we entered. We found her grandmother at the kitchen sink arranging flowers in a delicate glass vase made in the shape of a basket. I watched her, fascinated.

"Hello, Muffy. Hello, Laura," she said sweetly, putting the flowers aside in the sink as she turned to greet us. "Are you here to look in the trunks? They're upstairs." Drying her hands on her apron, she led the way through the house, past the sitting room where Mr. McLaughlin was asleep in an upholstered wing chair, and up the steep flight of stairs to the bedrooms. The old house had a light and airy feel to it. The ceilings of the pale-colored rooms were high and sunlight poured in through the big windows curtained with wispy white gauze. Carved woodwork bordered the doors and windows, making them so elegant and pretty that Muffy had to pull me along because I wanted to stop and look at every detail. My carpenter father's influence!

"Come on, Laura," Muffy chided me. "We'll have time to look around later, but now we have work to do!" We followed Muffy's grandmother, Mrs. McLaughlin, into a sunny bedroom occupied by a big four-poster bed covered with yellow-flowered quilts and dust ruffles. From beneath the bed she retrieved an old trunk covered with some sort of animal hide, the initials "G.M." in brass studs adorning the top.

"There you are," said Mrs. McLaughlin. "George McLaughlin was Muffy's great-great-grandfather, one of the partners of a big marine shipping company." She opened the trunk and handed us each a bundle of letters. "These are his personal letters to and from his family. Just be careful. They're old and brittle. When you're finished, there are more trunks in the other bedrooms. I hear you need costumes for the tea party. We have lots of old clothes in this house. Have fun! I'll be in the kitchen if you need me." She went back down the stairs, leaving us to search the letters for clues.

We found pleasant letters written by Mr. McLaughlin and his wife to each other on their respective travels from the Cape to Boston, Hartford, and New York by stagecoach, ship, and train. Their trips were for business or to visit relatives. Their sons and daughters were mentioned, but no mysterious happenings. Muffy was digging around in the trunk. Suddenly she let out a squeal that almost knocked me over!

"Look at this!" She held up a wad of notes, which had been stashed in a little cardboard box. In bold pen strokes George McLaughlin had written, "Get rid of L.B." "Mistakes in bookkeeping." "Money missing." "Captain S. cannot be trusted."

"Wow! Could 'L.B.' mean Lawrence Bickly?" I asked.

"I suppose," said Muffy, looking at the old pieces of paper. "My great-great-grandfather must have found Lawrence's mistakes in the ledgers. And he must have discovered that Lawrence was really stealing money from the company, besides using the number five for good luck. 'Captain S.' must be Captain Snow. He didn't trust him either."

"Remember my grandpa said Mr. McLaughlin thought that Captain Snow was going to be thrown out of the church," I told her. "I wonder exactly what he was doing that made Mr. McLaughlin and the church so upset with him. It could have been his wife who was causing the problem, but he worked 'for the Devil,' according to Aunt Sparrow. I guess Mr. McLaughlin wanted to fire both Lawrence and Captain Snow!"

We glanced over most of the other letters, but the chest didn't contain anything else that could help us. These notes were enough, though. They proved that George McLaughlin knew that Lawrence Bickly was stealing from him and that he wanted to get rid of him and Captain Snow. We wondered what had happened to Lawrence in the end.

"Where do we go from here?" Muffy asked.

"We go home, eat dinner, meet at the bandstand, and go to The Tomb. Judy might have something more for us."

"What about the clothes for the lawn party?" Muffy wanted to know.

"I have all those old dresses at my house. You can look through the trunks here and pick something out for yourself. Abigail said her grandmother had a dress for her. Maybe you can find something for Mollie and Louie too."

"I'll ask my grammy to help me."

We placed the letters back in the trunk and pushed it under the bed. After I admired a group of old photos hanging on the wall and a beautiful ship model, we went back downstairs to say good-bye to Muffy's grandmother. Her grandfather was still napping.

"Won't you two stay for dinner?" Mrs. McLaughlin asked as we came into the kitchen. "I made spaghetti, Muffy's favorite."

"I think I'd better go home," I told her, "but thank you anyway."

147

"I'll stay," said Muffy with enthusiasm. "I'll call Mom and ask her if it's O.K.," she said, running toward the phone in the living room.

I thanked Mrs. McLaughlin again and left by the back door. The sweet scent of the lilies wafted over the lawn as I climbed down the stairs to my bike, which was leaning against the side of the garage where I'd left it.

I felt a strange sensation, as if someone were watching me. I looked up. Beyond the garage was a neighbor's house, separated from the McLaughlins' by a tall boxwood hedge. Did I see someone peering down at me from an upstairs window? I couldn't be sure. The sun was reflecting on the glass, making it difficult to see into the room. I pushed my bike into the driveway. Again I felt it! Someone was watching me! I glanced back up to the window next door. The curtain moved! I ran back into Muffy's grandmother's house.

"Excuse me, Mrs. McLaughlin!" I called as I reentered the kitchen. "Could you please tell me who lives in that white house next door?" I pointed to the house across the hedge.

"Oh, you're still here," she said in surprise. Muffy looked up from the salad she was preparing. "An elderly couple, Mr. Wells and his wife, live there; they have for years. But they're health is so poor that their son has moved in with them for the summer. They used to sit out in the sun every day on the other side of their house, but they're too ill now." She paused and looked at me. "Why are you asking?"

"I had the feeling that someone over there was watching me," I told her. "I saw a curtain move in an upstairs window."

"How peculiar," mused Mrs. McLaughlin. "The Wellses can't go up and down the stairs any more, I'm sure. It must have been their son looking out the window. Maybe he was just curious to see a little girl at my house. We usually have only old folks like me coming and going!" she laughed. "I never hear or see anything on this side of their house, except when Slim H. mows their lawn or clips the hedge. I should try to visit them soon if their son will allow me."

Hmmmm. Slim H. He was the caretaker of Abigail's grammy's house too. Abigail could ask him what he knows about the Wellses and their snoopy son. It must have been the son who was peering out at me. But why? Was I really such a "curiosity?"

I thanked Mrs. McLaughlin again and said good-bye to her and Muffy and headed out the back door. No more "feelings" of being watched. I hopped on my bike and rode home.

Chapter Forty-Three

Thankfully Mom was there when I arrived. I had no interest in being home
alone ever again! I felt a new appreciation for her and enjoyed her company,
even while she talked about her job. I also enjoyed feeling safe. I helped her
prepare dinner. Dad came home and we had a nice meal together. I didn't
mention the theft of our notes and family tree or any of the other upsetting
events of the day, but I did tell Mom that we went back to Miss Deighton's.

"That was so sweet of you," she complimented us. "She's a really neat lady!"

"Neat?" I asked, thinking of her cluttered rooms, crowded with herbs,
books, fabric, and who knows what.

"Neat," Mom repeated. "It means 'cool.'"

"Oh," I murmured. An expression from the sixties, I supposed. I wouldn't
call Miss Deighton "neat," no matter what the definition was!

"Who put that lock on the barn?" asked Dad.

"It's a long story," I told him, not exactly knowing what to say. "Someone was
trying to play a trick on us."

"Does that someone have the combination, or do I have to cut it off?"

"I think you'll have to cut it." I quickly changed the subject. "There's going
to be a lawn party at the library on Saturday."

"So you know about it!" Mom exclaimed. "I just bought tickets today!
One of my patients is on the committee, so I bought tickets for the two of us.
I didn't think your dad would be interested in going. Am I right?" She
looked at Dad and he nodded. "Let's look for costumes after dinner."

"But Abigail's grandmother got tickets for all of us Girls," I told her.

"Oh, that's all right. It's a fund-raiser for the library. All the money raised
goes for buying new books."

After we finished our meal and cleaned up, Mom and I climbed into the
attics to find dresses to wear to the tea. I had seen a pretty blue silk dress when
the Girls and I had looked through the trunks earlier. I found the dress again
and showed it to Mom. It was a little too big, but she thought she could alter it
to fit me. She found a green velvet dress with black trim for herself. The fabric
was a little heavy and might be uncomfortable to wear in summer weather, but
she said that it was so lovely she had to wear it anyway. There were hatboxes on a
shelf where we found two good bonnets. To complete our look, we took parasols
from an umbrella stand tucked in a corner.

"We're all set!" Mom announced.

"Thanks, Mom." We carried our costumes downstairs.

"We can air these out tomorrow. The sun might damage the fabric," Mom explained, "so we'll hang them in the shade of our willow tree."

"It's time for me to meet the Girls," I said and kissed my parents good-bye.

I grabbed my bike and rode the short distance to Mollie's house. As I entered her kitchen, her little brother was whining at the dinner table. Mollie's mother was trying to explain that he was too young for whatever it was he wanted. Her family was so different from mine. First of all, she wasn't an only child; she had a brother. Second, her father worked in the city and came down only on weekends. And third, her mom spent most of her time playing tennis and taking her little brother to the beach. Mollie was left pretty much on her own. I was on my own too, but if my mom didn't work, she would spend more time with me, even if I did have a brother or sister.

"Hello, Laura," her mother greeted me. "What do you girls have planned for tonight?"

"We're meeting the other Girls in town," Mollie announced.

"Better brush your hair before you go," her mom said. "It's a little messy."

"Where's my hairbrush anyway?" asked Mollie, eyeing her little brother, Maxwell. "I can't find it. It seems to have disappeared!"

"It must be in your room somewhere," her mom insisted, as she wiped the kitchen counter.

"Some other stuff is missing too," she complained. "Maybe you know where my things are, Maxwell."

Maxwell wasn't paying any attention to her.

"Oh, never mind," said her mom, nervously. "I'll buy you a new hairbrush and whatever else is missing." We said good-bye and left.

"I'll get that little brat!" fumed Mollie, adjusting her red headband.

"Wait a minute!" I exclaimed. "It might be Mrs. Pitts!"

"*What* might be Mrs. Pitts?" asked Mollie, not understanding me at all.

"She may have taken your brush to make a voodoo doll of you!"

"No, she didn't!" insisted Mollie. "It was that brat Maxwell."

"O.K., if you insist. Shall we stop by Abigail's on our way to town?"

We agreed we should and rode past the yacht club toward Abigail's house. I shivered as we passed the marina, recalling the terrifying incident with Mrs. Pitts and Karl earlier that afternoon. Where were those two now? Would they really come after us? I pushed those thoughts from my mind. They were too frightening!

Chapter Forty-Four

We pedaled along Lowndes River Road in silence. The air was cool as we rode through the dark shadows cast by the towering privet hedges that lined the street. Soon we were at the lighthouse where we turned left through a series of narrow lanes bordering Snow Pond. When we reached Abigail's long shell driveway, we saw her playing tag on the lawn with her young cousins.

"Oh, my goodness!" she exclaimed. "What time is it?"

"We don't know, but we think it's near seven," I told her. She dashed inside the house.

"It's past seven! I told Grammy 'good-bye.' She's eating dinner with my aunts and uncles. Let's go." Abigail's parents live in Connecticut. They send her to spend her summers with her grandmother. She hopped on her bike and we said good-bye to her little cousins. "Stay in the yard!" she warned them as we pedaled toward the street.

In town, we found Muffy and Louie at the bandstand already waiting for us. Muffy approached us. "I told Louie about our day. He can't believe that some-one made a voodoo doll of you, Laura," she said.

"Well, what about Karl and Mrs. Pitts threatening us at the marina?" Mollie countered. "That's even worse than a voodoo doll!" As we sat on the wooden steps of the bandstand, we talked about Miss Deighton and the Earth Mother People.

"Wow!" Louie exclaimed. "If those people care so much about nature, how can they go and kill an innocent animal?"

"I don't know, but they did," said Mollie.

"Isn't it time for ice cream?" asked Abigail. We pushed our bikes down the street to the ice cream shop. It was a short distance to the shop and in our town you're not allowed to ride bikes on the sidewalks. We ordered our favorite flavors and sat down at the wooden picnic tables next to the shop to enjoy our cones.

"I found the perfect outfit for you, Louie," chuckled Muffy. "My grammy has the coolest old vest, coat, and captain's hat. I even found a tie and cane. You'll look just like Captain Snow home from his latest voyage!"

"Gee thanks!" said Louie, less than enthusiastic with the news. "Captain Snow never made it home from his 'latest voyage.' It sounds like bad luck to me, dressing up like a doomed man."

"Don't be so superstitious!" Mollie scolded him. "We have to dress up like the Snows in order to be a conversation piece. Once everyone knows who we're supposed to be, we may just meet someone who knows something about the Snows. It's the least you can do." Louie didn't seem convinced, but he would get over it. The lawn party would be fun. We had never been to a dress-up tea party before and the Eel Grass Girls were looking forward to it!

We finished our cones and headed for The Tomb. When we got there, Judy was behind the counter, talking on the phone. A few kids were in a corner looking at what seemed to be a book of spells.

Judy hung up as we entered. "I've got the list," she said, taking a paper from her pocket and placing it on the counter. Just then a man, probably her boss Lucky, came out from the back room. He looked at us, then at the list lying on the counter.

"What's this?" he asked Judy, reaching for the paper.

"It's 'girl stuff,'" said Mollie, snatching it up. "You know, herbal masques, scrubs, and creams, bath beads, scented candles." She stuffed the paper in her pocket and smiled broadly at Judy, "Thanks so much. Can't wait for my next bath." Mollie could be annoying, but her boldness and quick thinking had saved us again!

We thought it would be best to leave, so we headed for the door.

"Not so fast," said Lucky, stepping out from behind the counter and blocking our way! The other kids looked up from their book and stared. When he noticed them gawking at him, he said, "Have a nice day," stepped aside, and let us leave.

Once outside, we grabbed our bikes and rode back to the bandstand.

"Who was that guy?" asked Louie, pushing his bike across the grass.

"Probably Judy's boss, Lucky," I said.

"What a loser!" exclaimed Muffy. "Let's see that paper she gave you."

"Look," said Mollie, after she had leaned her bike against the side of the bandstand. She showed us the paper as we huddled around her, but it was a real disappointment. The "list" consisted of Miss Deighton, Mrs. Pitts, and her sister (no name given), Jeffrey Silva, and Mr. Mullins! Only the people we already knew were customers of The Tomb!

"That's odd," said Abigail. "She must know plenty of other people who shop there. Why would she give us a list like this? It's meaningless."

"Like a lot of other things," I muttered. "And we won't be able to ask her about it until sailing school tomorrow."

"We might as well go to my house and hang out," suggested Mollie. "I have lots of board games we could play."

We rode our bikes through town, past Small Pond, and down Pine Street. We peered up Miss Deighton's driveway as we passed and saw several cars parked along the side.

"Miss Deighton must be having a party," I commented.

"Witches brew and tansy muffins! Yum, yum!" exclaimed Muffy. We all laughed as we rode to the end of Pine Street and turned toward the harbor.

When we arrived at Mollie's house, we could hear her mother reading to Maxwell in the living room. Mollie introduced Louie to her mom. We decided that we would play *Clue*. You know, the game where you find out who the murderer is and where and with what he, or she, did it.

"If only our mystery could be solved this easily!" Muffy lamented. We played a few rounds, but by now it was getting dark. It was time for Abigail, Muffy, and me to get home. The Eel Grass Girls would meet at sailing school tomorrow. Louie would meet us at seven at the bandstand the next night. He stayed to play another round of *Clue* with Mollie. It made me feel strange to leave Mollie and Louie together without the rest of us. Was I a little jealous? I hoped not.

Chapter Forty-Five

The next morning was a perfect summer day. I looked out my window toward the harbor. The old lighthouse stood on the point, no longer an aid to sailors but part of the scenery and part of our mystery. Mom and I had breakfast together. Dad had already left for work. I was thankful Mom was leaving a little later than usual. Her first appointment had been postponed.

After breakfast, I put on my life jacket and slathered some sunblock on my face and arms. Mom and I left the house together. She waited while I took my bike from the barn. Fortunately Dad had cut the lock off. It gave me a bad feeling to remember getting locked in the barn, but I put it out of my mind. At the end of the driveway we parted, going in opposite directions.

At sailing school, I sat with the Girls on one of the crowded benches. Opening meeting was ready to begin. There was Judy. We had to ask her about that dumb list of customers she had given us. After roll call, Mr. Prince explained how we were going to practice making clean tacks. He wanted us to tack around the moored boats in an area of the harbor near my mooring.

Then I saw Judy take Billy aside and begin whispering in his ear, all the while grinning and looking at me and the other Girls! That was a little nerve-racking! What was going on?

The Eel Grass Girls were allowed to sail together without an instructor. We already knew how to make clean tacks, squeaky clean, so crisp and clean you wouldn't believe it. We could use the time to talk. Of course we would take turns at the helm, making a lot of tacks, just in case the instructors were watching us. We wanted to be left alone. After rigging our boat, the *Chubby Quahog*, we sailed out from between the club dock and the town pier and caught a nice breeze, which took us over toward my mooring. Our favorite boat, the *Minnow*, was still in the repair shop after the mishap that occurred during our last mystery.

Abigail skippered first and did a good job. We meandered around the harbor. Some of the other kids crossed our path now and then. We sailed near a big yacht we hadn't seen before. And there at the bow, tied up to the mooring line, was my Catabout!

"Hey!" I yelled. "My boat!" I looked up to the deck of the yacht. An older man with gray hair, a blue blazer, and a captain's cap was wandering around with a mug of coffee in his hand.

"Ahoy there!" I called to him.

"Ahoy there to you, too!" he called back, leaning over the railing and waving. "How are you this morning, young sailors?" he asked in a very pleasant manner, with a smile to match.

"This is my sailboat." I pointed to my Catabout. "How did you get it?"

"It was adrift, so Olga rowed out in our dinghy to fetch it. Brought it back and tied it up. Ho, ho, ho!"

I didn't think there was anything funny about it, but I was thankful that they had rescued my boat. "Come aboard, little maties. Come aboard." He threw down a rope ladder. I took off my life jacket and attached it to the side stay of our Sprite to act as a bumper between the two boats. Otherwise the friction might cause damage. Muffy tied our boat to the ladder and we climbed aboard.

"I'm Doctor Perhonen. Sailed in from the Vineyard a day ago. Too bad, vacation's almost over. Got to get back to my lab at the university. I'm a scientist, you see. Have to work. Hate to leave this place. So lovely here. Olga's still asleep. The others too. So who are you?"

We introduced ourselves, giving our first names only, since the doctor was a stranger. We told him that we were supposed to be practicing our tacks for sailing school.

"Better get along now. I see a motorboat coming over. Must be your sailing teachers." We looked out and saw Billy, Judy, and Allyson in the *Sea Calf*, headed toward us.

I thanked him for rescuing my Catabout. I really was thankful because it could have easily drifted out to sea. The doctor seemed like a nice man. I was glad that Olga, whoever she was, had rescued my boat.

We quickly scrambled down the ladder to the Sprite. We drifted over to my Catabout. Abigail and I got in and pulled the sails up just as the *Sea Calf* arrived.

"Why did you board that yacht?" asked Billy.

"My boat drifted away and the people on the yacht rescued it. I'm going to sail it back to the mooring and then we'll finish our tacking practice."

"Remember, the tacks have to be clean and fast," said Judy. Allyson said nothing. We didn't need any more instruction! We knew how to tack.

"We know, we know," said Mollie. "By the way, I want to ask you about that..."

"Capsize!" yelled someone from across the harbor. We looked and saw that a Sprite had tipped over near the channel. The instructors left us and sped away to help, leaving us alone again.

"So much for our confrontation!" Muffy said, discouraged.

"We'll talk to her later," I reassured her. "If not today, then tonight."

Abigail and I sailed the Catabout to its mooring.

"Lucky for you that doctor found your boat and saved it," said Abigail.

"Don't use that word, please," I told her. It wasn't the "luck" that bothered me, but a person by that same name.

"Hey, what's this?" As we reached my mooring, I saw something floating in the water, something attached to my buoy line.

"What is it?" asked Abigail.

Another voodoo doll! But this time it was floating face down in the harbor! I scooped it out of the murky water and turned it over in my hand. It was made of scraps of fabric, just like the first one, with real hair and nail clippings sewn on the front. And it wore a red headband—just like Mollie! This was bad. Really bad.

Muffy and Mollie had followed us over in the Sprite. They now sailed up beside the Catabout. Muffy held onto my boat as I secured it to the mooring and cut the doll free with my jackknife, which had been my dad's when he was a Boy Scout. I'm a Girl Scout, so I like to be prepared too, especially when there are mysteries to be solved.

"Mollie!" I called to her. "Look at this." I held the soggy little doll for her to see. Abigail and Muffy looked on as well.

"Another one!" Mollie exclaimed. Then a look of shock distorted her face as she realized that the doll was supposed to be her!

"Hey! That's not fair!" she shouted. "Mrs. Pitts is in for it now! This means war!"

"How do you know she did it?" began Abigail.

"Who else could it be?" Mollie asked angrily.

Whoever had set my boat adrift had made the doll and tied it to my mooring. Was it Mrs. Pitts? What was she trying to accomplish by making dolls that looked like us? Was she using her voodoo magic to try to scare us and keep us from solving our mystery? If so, what were they hiding? What was their secret?

Muffy snatched the little doll and proceeded to rip it to shreds and scatter the pieces of fabric and hair in the water.

"There!" she proclaimed. "It can't hurt you now, even if it could."

"That makes a lot of sense," said Mollie, who was now sullen. "But thanks anyway for protecting me."

Abigail and I began to furl and cover my sails. We disengaged the rudder and hopped into the Sprite with the others to finish up the tacking drill. Out in the harbor, we could see the capsized boat, with its drenched sailors, being towed to the club by the *Sea Calf*.

The class was almost over, so we sailed back to the club with the other boats. After every boat had been pulled up onto the beach and the sails stowed away, we clambered up the steep stairs to the deck where we sat on the wooden benches for closing meeting. The hot sun made me feel sleepy. I would close my eyes for just a minute…

Before I knew it, I had dozed off. I found myself in a field. Mrs. Pitts was coming toward me. She was carrying my bicycle over her head! Someone was calling me. "Laura, Laura!"

"Huh?" I awoke with a start. I was still sitting on the bench, but everyone, except the Girls, was gone.

"Wow! I must have fallen asleep. I had the strangest dream. But the strangest thing about it was that it seemed so real."

The Girls didn't seem very interested in my dream. Lunch was on their minds!

"I'm hungry," whined Abigail.

We automatically pushed our bikes out onto the street and headed toward the Clam Bar. When we arrived, we were surprised to see a very robust and jolly-looking woman at the counter.

"Excuse me," I said. "But...uh...where's Mrs. Pitts?"

"She called in sick," the woman told us, with a frown taking the place of her smile. "I'm Cooky's wife." She motioned with her head toward her husband. Her smile returned. "What would you girls like to order?"

We gave each other meaningful glances and gave her our lunch order. As we waited for our food, we sat on the riverbank to discuss this turn of events.

"Mrs. Pitts is sick," I repeated. "I wonder what that means."

"Maybe she's sick?" Abigail suggested.

"That woman's never been sick a day in her life!" Mollie stated emphatically. "She's too mean."

"That makes sense, Miss Logical," said Muffy. I couldn't help laughing out loud. But we did wonder what had happened to Mrs. Pitts.

When our orders were ready, we checked our plates for evil spells. There were none. We didn't really think Cooky's wife would hex us, but we had to make sure. We tried to make eye contact with Cooky, but he was doing a good job of avoiding our glances, which made us suspicious. Before we knew it, Mollie was at the back door of the snack bar. We heard her ask Cooky, "So what's up with Mrs. Pitts?"

"You couldn't leave her alone, could you? No, you and that sister of hers had to keep bugging her until she got so jumpy she can hardly work any more. You made her sick. Now she has a heart problem," he complained, flipping our burgers. "My snack bar's only open in the summer. I have to make my money while the vacationers are here. I can't afford to have my only employee out sick. Now my wife has to take Mrs. Pitts's place. She has another job, you know. Now she has to give that up. I don't know what'll happen to us 'cause Mrs. Pitts is gonna be out for a while."

So that was it, supposedly. "Did she leave anything here? Her bag maybe?" asked Mollie.

"No!" he shouted. We thought we had better leave Cooky alone. When our lunch was ready, we sat on the riverbank and ate in silence. Boats were going in and out of Snow Pond. I felt as if I would fall asleep again, but I didn't. I ate my burger, enjoying the sweet tangy green relish I had heaped upon it.

I loved summer and all the tastes, smells, and feelings that went with it, but this summer had been full of surprises, such as new and scary feelings. A simple trip to a haunted house had plunged us into a tangled web connecting a group of weird adults to strange happenings in the past—and the present. We couldn't fit it all together to make any sense out of it. I was proud to be an Eel Grass Girl, but this mystery was more difficult than I had expected it to be. We had to solve it, though. Even if it meant giving up some of our summer pleasures.

"Now what?" asked Abigail, stretching her arms and arching her back.

"We have work to do," declared Mollie. "A mystery to solve."

"Then what should we do?" asked Abigail, again.

"I have an idea," I said. "How about going by Muffy's grandmother's house?" I was thinking of Mr. and Mrs. Wells. Muffy and I told Mollie and Abigail about them.

"Maybe your grandmother has visited them," I said to Muffy. "If not, I think we should. It seems strange that she hasn't seen them all summer and that their son is peering out of the window at me. That's really suspicious."

We agreed. It was another unsolved mystery, but one we could handle. A quick visit or two were all we needed to solve this one. We hopped on our bikes and pedaled toward Main Street.

Chapter Forty-Six

On the way we were startled by something big moving through the bushes beside the road! A tall figure slowly emerged from the woods. Jeffrey Silva!

"Looking for road kill?" asked Mollie, quickly recovering her composure.

"Yeah. Have you seen any?" he asked, perfectly serious.

"No," we replied. What did we look like—scavengers?

"We have better things to do," remarked Mollie.

"There's no reason to let a good animal go to waste," said Jeffrey in earnest. "It's a shame the way those lousy tourists drive so fast. They kill innocent birds, skunks, possums, anything that tries to get across the street in front of them. They're so busy trying to get their money's worth out of their Cape vacations that they don't stop to consider the wildlife. They just run over them and drive on by."

Suddenly Jeffrey didn't seem so sickening after all. From what he was saying, he really cared about the animals.

"Animals are beautiful. Every part of them," he continued, looking down at the ground and kicking around some old leaves with his worn sneaker. "Their skeletons are wonderful, the way all their little bones fit together." He raised his head. "They look just like human bones only with longer toes like in a cat's leg or longer fingers like in a bird's wing."

"How did you get into it?" asked Abigail.

"We studied wildlife in school. Then when I found a raccoon's skeleton in the woods one day, I took it home, cleaned it up, and mounted it on a piece of wood. I got the idea of putting road kill in a cage in the harbor and letting the crabs clean the bones. They do all the work. Pick the bones clean." I thought I would be sick, but now we knew whose cage was in the harbor and why!

"When The Tomb opened up," Jeffrey went on, "I asked if they wanted to sell the skeletons. Lucky said 'yes.' He sells a lot of them, you know. I make good money. It's a great business."

We didn't know what to say. It wasn't our idea of the perfect job, but he wasn't doing anything wrong as far as we could tell.

"I think dead animals should be buried or at least left in the woods," said Muffy, seeming kind of upset. "They deserve respect. It's not right to display their bones."

"But I do respect them," insisted Jeffrey. "They don't deserve to die that way, not by being run over by a careless driver. If I just pushed them off the road into the bushes, I'm saying it's O.K., we can just forget about them. But if I put them on display so everyone can see how beautiful they are, then their life wasn't wasted."

159

"I don't think we're ever going to agree about this," said Muffy. I could see her point of view as well.

"You kids expecting a hurricane or something?" asked Jeffrey.

"Excuse me?" Abigail was confused by his comment.

"You're wearing life vests," observed Jeffrey.

"Oh," mumbled Abigail. We felt a little silly. "We were at sailing school."

"Hey, didn't I see you kids at The Tomb the other night?"

"Yes," I answered, wondering where this would lead.

"Aren't you Laura Sparrow?" he asked me.

"Yes," I answered. I was surprised he knew my name. Usually the younger kids know all the older ones, but not the other way around.

"You into that witchcraft stuff?" he wanted to know, looking from one of us to the other.

"No," Muffy stated, obviously offended, but she calmed down and added, "We're trying to find out about it, but we're not into it."

Jeffrey looked puzzled, but didn't ask us to explain.

"Why do you sell that candy for The Tomb, those Benny Beans?" asked Mollie. "Don't you think something's strange about them?"

"Yeah," answered Jeffrey. "I do. That's why I told them I'm not selling them any-more. I don't know what they put in that stuff, but it's making the kids act loony."

"Really?" I questioned, hoping he would tell us more.

"Lucky isn't on the level," he replied.

"What do you mean?" asked Abigail.

"He's up to something," explained Jeffrey. "I don't know what, but I do know that it's no good. I'm not into that hexes and love potions stuff, but some of the kids at school are. It all started last spring, when The Tomb opened up. They're too much into it. I mean, it's taken them over. They don't act normal any more."

"Who do you mean?" I asked.

"Like Carrie Coughlin," said Jeffrey. Then looking at me, he asked, "Remember? She used to be all right, for a girl. But then she started creeping around with her 'dark sisters' crowd and she tried to get Josh Kelly to like her. He ended up getting sick and missed school for a whole week. Her love potion didn't work. The principal never knew what was going on, but I knew."

"Wow!" I exclaimed. I remembered Josh getting sick and the change in Carrie and some of the other older girls, but I was shocked. No one in my class suspected it had anything to do with potions!

"Yeah," continued Jeffrey. "Kids say I'm weird because I like skeletons. I do like them, but it's because I like animals and nature. It's different with the kids who're into spells and potions. If they don't like someone, they go and put a hex

160

on him. If I don't like someone, I tell him off, or stay away from him. And if I *do* like someone, I spend time with him, but if he, or she, doesn't like me, I go on about my business and don't worry about it. I wouldn't mix up a potion and try to force someone to like me. Something's wrong with that kind of thinking."

"How about Mrs. Pitts and the other grownups who hang around the Tomb?" I asked. "Do you know what they're up to? Or why Lucky's selling that candy to the kids?"

"Nope," was his answer. He had given us some good information, anyway, but now we didn't know what else to say to him.

"Here's my phone number," I said, handing Jeffrey a scrap of paper on which I had quickly scratched my name and phone number with a stubby pencil. I was the best one to call because I had an answering machine and my parents knew about our mystery. "Call me and leave a message if you see or hear anything strange. We suspect that something 'unnatural' is going on. Something evil. Any information you can give us would really help." Jeffrey looked at us blankly, not understanding what I meant or why we would be interested, but that was O.K. As long as he called us with information, he could think whatever he wanted. We left him searching the roadside as we rode on to our destination.

When we reached Muffy's grandmother's house, no one was home. We decided to visit the Wellses anyway. Muffy told us that she knew them slightly because she had been over there with her grandmother a few times before. She suggested that we pick a bouquet of flowers for them from her grandmother's garden. After we had a nice big bunch of fragrant blossoms, we strode over, going around the tall hedge which separated the two houses.

A little circular driveway led to the house from Windy Hill Road, just off Main Street. The weathered green door looked as if it could use a new coat of paint. It had a glass window, covered by a white lace curtain. I wondered why the Wellses' son wasn't fixing the place up, since he was visiting for the summer. Muffy boldly knocked on the door. No answer. She knocked again and we waited. Still no answer.

"Anybody home?" Mollie hollered and began to pound on the door. I thought she was overdoing it a little. She tried the doorknob. The door was locked. She rattled the door and called out again. There was no car in the driveway, but Muffy told us that Mr. and Mrs. Wells didn't have a car. Surely their son did. And if he had gone out, his parents might not be able to get to the door.

"Maybe their son took them out for a drive," suggested Abigail.

"Open up!" screamed Mollie. "I know you're in there."

She was right. Finally we saw the curtain on the door move and a scary-looking man peer out at us! He had a red face, dark shifty eyes, and black hair. We heard him unlock the door and he opened it up a crack.

"What do you want?" he asked in an angry voice.

"We came to visit Mr. and Mrs. Wells," said Muffy, as sweetly as she could.

"They're not here."

"Where are they?" asked Muffy. The man paused, suddenly confused.

"They're sleeping."

"I thought you said they weren't here," countered Mollie.

"I meant they're sleeping."

"We'd like to visit them," said Muffy. "We could come back when they wake up."

"Well you can't. Go away!"

"Here are some flowers for them," I said, handing him the bouquet. He backed away.

"No! Get out!" He screamed, slamming the door in our faces!

"Hey, wait a minute!" yelled Mollie, but I pulled her away from the door. We felt discouraged. Something strange was going on, but what could we do?

"I've got an idea," I said as we walked back to the McLaughlins' house. "My mom is a visiting nurse. I'll ask her to visit Mr. and Mrs. Wells. She'll be able to find out what's happened to them."

"What kind of a son is he?" asked Abigail. "Why doesn't he want us to visit his parents? I've heard of children trying to take their elderly parents' money or property. My dad had a few cases about that kind of thing. When can your mom visit them and find out what's going on?"

"I'll ask her tonight at dinner. She'll think of something," I assured them. "It won't be the first time that my mom has discovered relatives mistreating their elderly parents or grandparents!"

"Well, my grandparents are out partying!" exclaimed Muffy. "They ought to try to visit the Wellses. I wonder where they are and when they're coming back." She glanced at the church clock across Main Street as we entered her grandparents' yard.

"Oh, no! I'm late!" she cried. "I'm supposed to be at my aunt's shop choosing an outfit to wear in her fashion show at the country club. Got to go! See you at seven. Sorry! I'd better stick these flowers in the birdbath here so they won't wilt. Grammy will find them when she gets home." She plopped the flowers in the birdbath before hopping onto her bike and racing off down Main Street.

"I've got tennis in half an hour," said Mollie. "I'd better go too."

"My grandmother made me promise to spend some time with my cousins this afternoon," added Abigail. "I have to go or I won't be able to get away tonight."

"What about me?" I asked. "My mother won't be home yet and I'm afraid to be there all alone."

"You can come with me," suggested Abigail, "but I think I'm supposed to have 'quality family time' with my cousins. My grandmother says that my friends distract me. I've already tried to get her to let me invite you all over, but she wouldn't let me, not while my cousins are here."

"It's O.K.," I said. "I'll just hang out in town for a while." We pushed our bikes out onto Main Street and said our good-byes. My Eel Grass friends rode away in opposite directions. I felt as if I had been abandoned.

Chapter Forty-Seven

I pedaled toward the little information booth in the center of town. It was a small building, which looked like a tiny house with white painted clapboards, green shutters, and a green-painted door. My plan was to sit on the bench right beside the booth until five, then ride home. I parked my bike and sat down on the wooden bench. It would be interesting to watch the tourists go by in all their strange outfits—Hawaiian shirts with plaid Bermuda shorts and knee-high socks with sandals. I relaxed and was enjoying myself. Until I heard that cry!

"Laura! Laura!" My blood ran cold as I spun around to look. Who was calling me? It was the same voice I had heard in my cellar and barn! It was that girl! The ghost! The tourists marched on by. No one seemed to hear the cry except me. Where was the girl? I searched the parking lot behind me. No one was there!

"Laura! Laura!" it came again. That was enough for me! I was getting out of there and fast! I hurriedly rode my bike to Muffy's aunt's children's clothing store. Unfortunately it was packed with so many tourists and summer people I couldn't find Muffy or her aunt! Maybe they were in the back office, but I couldn't get there. It was beyond the dressing room area filled with mothers and shopping bags. I couldn't find anyone I knew to ask if I could use the phone to call home. I would just use the pay phone down the street.

I left the crowded shop and rode to the end of town where there was a pay phone at Nickerson's Garage. I grabbed the receiver and dug into my pocket for a quarter. Nothing. How could this be? I always had money. At least a handful of change in the bottom of my pocket! I searched all my pockets and found nothing!

It had to be five o'clock by now anyway, I told myself. Mom would be home, so I didn't have to worry. I calmed myself down and rode through the old village, past the lighthouse, down Lowndes River Road, to Yacht Harbor Road. The yacht club was deserted when I passed by. All the lessons and classes were over for the day. I rode along the harbor. It looked so beautiful and peaceful in the sparkling sunlight. Then I heard a car behind me and turned to look. A bike rider has to be careful, you know. It was Mom! Boy, was I glad to see her!

I jumped off my bike and stood beside the road, waving my hands at her. To my horror, the car began to veer toward me! I stared through the windshield and saw that it wasn't my mom behind the wheel! It was Mrs. Pitts! I leapt over a split-rail fence into a field just in time. Mrs. Pitts slammed on the brakes and jumped out. Picking up my bicycle and raising it over her head, she stepped over the fence and stalked toward me. It was just like my dream when I fell asleep at the yacht club!

"Laura, Laura!" Someone was calling me. It was that girl again. I looked around. It had to be a ghost because no one was there. No one but Mrs. Pitts. Then I realized it was Mrs. Pitts calling me! She was a ventriloquist, projecting her voice! It was Mrs. Pitts who had broken into my house and stolen Captain Snow's book, all our papers, and the diary! She must have been the one who locked me in the barn and in the cellar! I should have guessed.

"What's wrong with you, Mrs. Pitts?" I called out to her. I was so angry with her that I suddenly felt brave, for once. "I thought you had a heart problem? I think you do. Your heart is as hard as a stone and as black as the night! You'll never get away with breaking into my house and stealing my things! You'd better give up before you end up in jail!"

Suddenly she stopped and put my bike down. Her face showed no emotion. She didn't seem to see me or hear what I had said, but she turned away from me and stepped back over the fence. She got into her car, just like that, and drove away! I was left standing in the field all by myself.

That was odd, very odd. She hadn't said a word except to call my name. What did it mean? And why was she driving my mother's car? And if Mrs. Pitts had my mother's car, where was my mother? Panic swept over me like a tidal wave. Mom! I had to find her!

It was really hard for me to get my bicycle back over the fence and onto the road, but I did it. I pedaled up the hill through the towering pines to my driveway so fast I was completely out of breath by the time I arrived at my house. My mom's car was parked near the barn! But where was Mrs. Pitts? Where was my mom? Was she all right? I frantically threw down my bike and raced to the house!

"Mom! Mom!" I yelled at the door. No answer. Only a stony silence greeted me. "Mom!" I shrieked. "Where are you?" I couldn't help it—I began to cry. Where was my mother? I was afraid to go into the house. Afraid of what I might find...

I ran around to the harbor side of the house and then noticed a beach towel lying on the grass near the top of the sandy path to the beach. I ran to the edge of the bluff. Looking down I saw my mom leisurely swimming between the moored boats, safe and sound.

I grabbed the beach towel and sped down the path.

"Mom, Mom! Are you all right?" She looked up at me, puzzled. She swam to shore and waded out of the water.

"What's the matter Laura? Why are you crying?" I hugged her tightly even though she was sopping wet.

"What happened?" she asked, holding me away from her and looking intently into my face. "Tell me, what is it?"

"Mrs. Pitts—the lady who works at the Clam Bar—she stole your car and tried to run me over!" I blurted out, pulling myself close to her again, sobbing harder now.

"Stole my car? Are you sure?"

"Yes, I'm sure."

"My car is gone?"

"No, it's in the driveway."

"Then what are you talking about? How did Mrs. Pitts steal it? I don't understand."

"Come and see." I thrust her towel into her hand and dragged her up the path. She tried to dry off as she followed. We hurried up the path and across the yard. When we got to the car, I felt the hood. It was cold, meaning it hadn't been driven for a while.

"When did you get home?" I asked.

"I got through work early today. My last patient was out with relatives so I came home about three-thirty or four."

"Mrs. Pitts must have been driving her own car or someone else's," I told her. "But it looked just like yours."

"Well, that's a relief! I'm glad that no one borrowed my car without my permission," she chuckled. Then she became serious again. "But did she really try to run you down? We'll have to call the police about that."

"Please don't call," I pleaded. "Wait. She's part of our mystery. There are a lot of people involved. If the police pick her up now, it might be harder to catch the others."

"What are you talking about?" asked Mom. "Who's involved in what?"

"We suspect something, but we don't know what and we don't have any proof."

"Well, you have proof that this woman tried to hurt you! I don't like the thought of someone trying to harm my little girl!"

"I didn't get hurt. So *please*—just wait."

"Oh, all right. But you have to tell me more about your mystery. Why is this Mrs. Pitts trying to hurt you? Is she connected to your haunted house?"

"I'll tell you all about it at dinner when Dad gets home."

"Do you think it could have been an accident? That she was distracted and didn't mean to scare you?"

"I suppose," I said, though I didn't believe it for a minute! "I was frightened, but I'll be all right, and I'm so glad you are too!" I hugged her again and we headed toward the house.

I didn't tell Mom about Mrs. Pitts sneaking into our house and stealing our books and papers. Mom would definitely call the police if she knew about that. If the police picked Mrs. Pitts up, it would only complicate things. Then it would take even longer to solve our mystery. First of all, I was sure that the police wouldn't find our books with Mrs. Pitts. Second, she would tell them that *we* were the ones harassing *her*!

Mom and I entered the kitchen.

"I'll start dinner while you take a shower," I offered.

"You look tired, Laura. I don't think you've been getting enough sleep." I shrugged my shoulders in answer. "Well, you'll go to bed early tonight."

"But Mom! I have plans!"

"No. Plans or no plans, you're going to bed early."

I wondered how I would be able to get out of the house by seven to meet my friends in town. I was tired, that was true, but I hated to cancel our meeting. As Mom headed upstairs to shower, I stopped by my room to call Mollie. I sat on my bed and dialed. She was still out. Muffy wasn't home either. I finally reached Abigail.

"I'm glad you're home! My mom won't let me out tonight," I told her. "Do you think we could cancel our meeting? We'll be getting together with Reverend Maxon tomorrow morning anyway."

"That's fine with me! I'm tired too," said Abigail. "These cousins of mine are exhausting. I'll call Muffy and Mollie. Mollie can call Louie."

"Thanks. But listen to what happened to me this afternoon!" I told her about the voice calling to me when I was in town and about Mrs. Pitts coming after me with her car and in the field. "She's a ventriloquist! She's the one who calls to me in a girl's voice! I'm sure of it!"

"Amazing!" was all Abigail could say. After a pause, she went on, "Do you think she could have been hypnotized because of the way she didn't respond to you? You said she just walked away. She could have been in a trance."

"You could be right. But if she was hypnotized, who did it to her? Cooky said that she was normal until her sister came to town. Maybe her sister is controlling her!"

"Yes, it must be her sister. She might be the one stirring up trouble. Let's talk more about it tomorrow."

It was all settled. Abigail suggested that Mollie and I stop by her house in the morning, then meet Muffy at the church. I thought I would just put my head down on my pillow for a minute before I started to make dinner. The next thing I knew, it was morning.

Chapter Forty-Eight

Dad had already left for work by the time I got downstairs to breakfast. I waited for Mom to ask me about our new mystery, but she didn't say a word about it or ask me any more questions so I didn't bring it up. As she got ready to leave for work, I remembered to tell her about Mr. and Mrs. Wells.

"I do know them," she said. "They're a very sweet old couple. I think I'll call the McLaughlin's and ask what they think might be going on with them. It's too early to call them now, but I'll call later this morning. It does seem strange that no one has seen them since their son came to stay with them."

"Thanks Mom. When do you think you could stop by their house?"

"Hmmm. I could do it today. I'll tell the son that they're due for a check-up. He'll have to let me in, or I'll tell him that I'll report him—or something. How's that?"

"That'll be perfect!"

We walked out of the house together and I rode my bike over to Mollie's as Mom drove off to work. Dew glistened on the grass. I thought of the coyote when I passed by the barn. It seemed that she had healed and had gone off. I had looked for her a few times, but there was no sign of her in the barn. It was nice that we'd gotten to know her and become friends. Hopefully she wouldn't venture back onto Womponoy and get shot by the coyote shooter again!

A dew-covered cobweb hung from Mollie's mailbox at the entrance of her shell driveway. The droplets shimmered like pearls. I wanted to capture them and keep them forever, but it's the light and dewdrops and delicate pattern that make a spider's web so beautiful, things that can't be saved. I guess that's part of the beauty of it, knowing that it's something that won't last, that can't be preserved. Like a sunset or moonlight on the harbor.

I rode over the crushed quahog shells that covered Mollie's driveway and parked my bike beside her garage. I entered her kitchen and shouted "Hello!" There was no answer. A chill went down my spine! Where could she and her family be? I didn't want to be alone at Mollie's house either and began to feel afraid. Just as I was about to panic, I heard laughter and voices. I looked out through the back window and saw Mollie, Maxwell, and their mother coming up from the beach. Relieved, I ran out of the house and across the green lawn to meet them.

"Good morning, Mrs. Perkins. Hi, Mollie, Maxwell," I greeted them. I had never been so happy to see them!

"We've been down on the beach catching hermit crabs for Maxwell. We left them in a little tide pool." It seemed that Mrs. Perkins's world revolved around her young son. Mollie was left out most of the time. I guess her mom thought Mollie was old enough to amuse and take care of herself.

"That's nice," I said, as pleasantly as I could. Mrs. Perkins and Maxwell went on into the house, leaving Mollie and me standing in the yard.

"What happened to you last night?" she asked.

"I'll tell you on the way," I replied.

"Well, let's get to Abigail's and head for your church," said Mollie. "Muffy will be waiting for us. Maybe our meeting with your minister will lead to something after all." She had recovered from being angry with me about arranging the exorcism. I too hoped that the meeting would lead to something.

We peeked in the kitchen to say good-bye. Then we hopped on our bikes and pedaled between the pine trees, down the hill, and past the harbor. I stopped and showed Mollie the field where Mrs. Pitts had come after me, carrying my bike over her head.

"Remember when I fell asleep on the deck yesterday after sailing school?"

"Yeah, I remember."

"Well, I had a dream. What happened to me here, yesterday, with Mrs. Pitts, was exactly what happened to me in my dream!"

"No!"

"Yes! I don't believe in dreams coming true, but this one did." I told her about the car, how I thought it was my mom's, but it wasn't. I described in detail how Mrs. Pitts had tried to run me over and had chased me into the field, carrying my bike above her head, just like in my dream. "I yelled at her, the way you would have, but she didn't seem to hear me. She just turned away as if nothing had happened. Then she drove off. It didn't seem real!"

"Maybe it wasn't real. Maybe you were still dreaming."

"Of course I wasn't!" Mollie wasn't taking me seriously. I told her how I thought Mrs. Pitts had stolen my mom's car, but thankfully she hadn't. "Abigail thinks that she was hypnotized. I agree. We think her sister is controlling her. What do you think about that?"

"I think you dreamed the whole thing! No, really, I'm glad that we know now there's no ghost in your house. It has to be Mrs. Pitts calling your name, sneaking around, and locking the doors."

"I think you're right, but the ghost at Captain Snow's is still a problem, the way it grabbed my arm! It's real, whether it's a ghost or a spirit as my mom calls it!"

"They're both a problem," muttered Mollie as we rode on past the yacht club. There were no cars on the road at the moment, so she pedaled up beside me to say, "I called Louie last night. I told him about the Wellses' creepy son. Louie might start feeling left out because he has camp every day and he's had to

169

work for his brother every afternoon. He's going to meet us tonight at the band concert, so let's fill him in on everything that's happened since we haven't seen him for a while. He might be able to come up with some brilliant ideas!"

That would be wonderful if someone could think of something! With all the Eel Grass Girls working together and the added help of Louie, we should be able to figure out what to do about Mrs. Pitts and her friend Karl. And those other animal-sacrificing adults! Yet it was too bad that Louie would miss the exorcism.

As we rode on, I noticed that the weather was changing. Clouds covered the sun. As we rode past the Clam Bar and over the old wooden bridge spanning the river, a light breeze blew over the harbor, chasing wisps of mist toward us.

We continued on toward Abigail's grandmother's house. When we got there, the little cousins were all over the yard, screaming and chasing one another. Abigail was standing near the house, watching. She looked really tired. I wondered how late she had stayed up. Her cousins were wearing her out. This mystery was wearing all of us out, but what could we do? The Eel Grass Girls had to find out what was going on!

Abigail looked relieved to see us coming up her driveway. She was ready to be rescued. She called a quick good-bye to her grandmother and jumped on her bike to follow us out to the street. We could hear her cousins still screaming as we rode toward town. When we neared the church, Muffy was sitting on the grass near the parsonage waiting for us. We parked our bikes and asked her if she had seen the minister.

"He must be inside. I don't know what to expect, but I hope this exorcism helps our mystery."

"It will," I said. "We won't have to worry about the ghosts anymore." I didn't know what to expect when we got to Captain Snow's, but we would find out soon enough. We knocked on the parsonage door. It was thick with countless coats of forest green paint. The Reverend opened it up and gave us a big smile.

"Why, hello girls!" He acted overly cheerful, though it was good to see my minister happy about something. The last time I had talked to him he'd been depressed about his job, yet it seemed inappropriate for him to be too cheerful about an exorcism!

I made the introductions. Then we followed the minister back to his study. Several objects were lined up on his desk. One by one he picked them up and plopped them into his briefcase.

"One bottle of holy water, one vial of sanctified oil, and one prayer book. There we have it. Everything we need to perform a first-class exorcism. This should be fun!"

Muffy looked uncomfortable. I was sure that she didn't think it was right for Reverend Maxon to be so delighted about casting evil spirits out of a haunted house, but she kept quiet. She was learning to keep her opinions to herself, but I could tell it was difficult for her.

Outside, we squeezed into the minister's car. We gave him directions to Captain Snow's, going the long way around by Small Pond, rather than through the center of town. We didn't want to attract any attention. The Reverend drove to Yacht Harbor Road and turned left onto Lowndes River Road, driving past the marina and Clam Bar. We passed over the bridge and mist-covered river, then turned into the dirt road leading to Captain Snow's.

"You should park in here," I said as we neared the overgrown driveway that led to the Captain's house.

"My! This road is impassable!" he exclaimed, pulling his car up to the bushes beside the path. We got out and followed the narrow footpath to the old house. Reverend Maxon was amazed when the dilapidated structure came into view.

"How beautiful this old house must have been! Someone ought to fix it up! Do you really think it's haunted?"

We didn't answer. I led the way across the tangled lawn to the sagging porch and up to the front door. I carefully opened it and we entered. No cold breeze met us. It seemed exceptionally quiet this morning, almost peaceful. It was the calm before the storm, as they say. Just as we got to the center of the room, we heard a noise coming from a closet near the library! It sounded as if someone were in there—and trying to get out!

"Wwwwwhat's that?" Reverend Maxon was terrified.

"You'd better get your things out," I told him, hoping that he would be able to cast the spirits out before they were able to get us.

Mollie slowly edged toward the closet. Reverend Maxon began to tremble and fumble, trying to take the items from his briefcase.

Before we knew what was happening, the closet door flew open, and a choir robe, goblet, and other objects flew through the air straight at the minister! The goblet hit him on the head and an offering plate crashed against his back! It was as if they were attacking him! He raced out of the house, holding his head and screaming, with all the objects flying after him!

I grabbed his briefcase and Muffy helped me take out the oil and water. We opened the bottle and vial and shook the contents over the floor, crying out, "God help us!" Mollie and Abigail joined in. Muffy picked up the prayer book and tried to find the right page. A bookmark helped her find the prayer for exorcism. She read as loudly as she could. Suddenly a feeling of peace flooded the old house. We weren't sure exactly what had happened, or why, but it seemed that the evil spirits had left the house! But where was Reverend Maxon?

"I'd better go find the minister," I said, taking the briefcase and heading out the front door. The Girls followed me. We found the choir robe and other church things strewn all over the yard. We picked them up and went back to the car. There was the minister, sitting on the front seat, crying and wiping his head with a tissue. I just stared at him. What kind of a man was he?

"I've failed!" he whimpered through the car window when he noticed us staring at him. "I ran away. I left you children all alone. I'm so weak!" He shook his head and sniffled.

"We weren't alone," I told him. "We prayed the prayer from your book and I think it worked. The evil spirits left the house. You'd better pull yourself together!" I was feeling embarrassed in front of my friends. My minister was pathetic!

He composed himself.

"Are you all right?" I asked, trying to be a little more sympathetic.

"Yes," he said, unconvincingly. "My pride is hurt more than anything else. It's my job to know how to handle these things. I was totally unprepared for what happened back there. I think we'd better go."

"Look at this choir robe and offering plate. Are they the things that were stolen from our church?" I asked, holding up the robe and other articles.

"Why yes, they could be," he mumbled. "I thought they looked familiar. How did they get here?"

"Do you think it could be Mr. Mullins?" I asked him.

"Mullins! How could that be? He's a deacon! What would he have to do with a haunted house? You're mistaken!"

I didn't say any more about Mr. Mullins because I had the feeling that Reverend Maxon wouldn't listen. Maybe it was just a coincidence that the church records were missing, that we had seen him at The Tomb, and that we had found the stolen church property, but I doubted it.

"If we take these things back to the church, they'll know we've been here," Muffy warned. "Maybe we should leave them here."

"They'll find out sooner or later," I speculated. "They belong to the church. I'm taking them back." That settled, we squeezed into Reverend Maxon's car and drove away from the no longer haunted house.

Chapter Forty-Nine

Reverend Maxon brought us back to the church. We went the long way around again, avoiding Main Street. The silence in the car was very awkward. When we arrived at the church, we got out and stood with the minister on the lawn. I handed him the choir robe and other things from Captain Snow's.

"I'm sorry I let you girls down."

"The evil spirits have left the house. That's what we wanted. The holy water, oil, and prayer worked," I told him, encouragingly.

"They were ghosts!" stated Mollie.

"No, they were spirits," Muffy corrected her.

"Well, I think they're gone for good," said Abigail. "And I hope they stay away from our town from now on!"

"Then the outing was a success?" Reverend Maxon asked weakly, rubbing the bump on his forehead where the goblet had hit him.

"Yes. Thank you. By the way, have you had a chance to talk to Mr. Mullins about the missing records?" I asked, remembering that I still wanted to see them.

"I never seem to be able to get a hold of him. He hasn't returned my calls. I'll ask him on Sunday."

"That will be interesting," said Mollie. I didn't reply. Reverend Maxon wanted to believe that Mr. Mullins was trustworthy. If only he knew!

"I'll see you on Sunday," I said. "Remember my grandparents are coming."

"See you then," he half-smiled and waved good-bye to us. Then he turned and wandered into the parsonage. I felt sorry for him in a way, but why did he trust someone who was obviously dishonest, namely Mr. Mullins. And why didn't he have more faith in God, who could be trusted?

"Your minister's an odd duck," said Mollie.

"Thank you," I replied with a smirk. "He's like a doctor who doesn't believe in medicine!"

"Now that the ghosts are gone, what are we going to do next?" asked Abigail.

"We can search the house without being afraid of them," I replied.

"There's nothing there, remember?" said Muffy.

"All the other books are still there, in the library," Abigail said.

"And we can hide out in the house, without being afraid of those spirits, and...uh... spy on Mr. Mullins and his friends," I suggested.

"Fabulous!" exclaimed Mollie, with mock elation.

Then she looked up at the church clock. "Got to go! My mom's taking me out to lunch—without Maxwell," she proudly announced. "He has a play date. It's time for me to go home to meet her."

"I'm so happy for you!" exclaimed Muffy. "You deserve some of your mother's attention! Grammy and I are going to work on our costumes for the lawn party tomorrow. She's coming too. Louie's meeting me at Grammy's tomorrow morning to get dressed up in his Captain Snow outfit. We'll meet you at the party. Are your costumes ready?"

"I'm ready," said Mollie. "My mom took me to that antique store near The Tomb. They had an all-white outfit just my size!"

"That's great. I have my outfit picked out too," said Abigail. "My grandmother's bringing me. I'm glad she said my cousins are too young to come. How about you, Laura?"

"My mom and I have our dresses. Abigail, since Mollie and Muffy have plans, would you like to come over to my house? We can read some more of the old letters and take a sail, if it's not foggy."

"Did anyone tell Louie that we meet at the band concert on Friday nights?" asked Abigail.

"I told him," said Mollie. "Got to go. See you tonight!"

Abigail said she would like to come over to my house. Mollie rode toward Small Pond and Muffy headed down Main Street to her grandmother's. Abigail and I rode in the opposite direction toward the lighthouse.

"Did you ever get to talk to Slim H. about Mr. and Mrs. Wells?" I asked.

"I never seem to be home when he's around. I'm always off somewhere with my cousins on the days he works. Grammy is taking the little monsters to mini-golf today, so it's safe to stop by the house. Shall we see if he's working now?"

I thought it was worth a try, so we rode to the bluff where her grandmother's house overlooked Snow Pond. Slim H.'s ancient brown truck was parked in the drive. Great!

We dumped our bikes on the lawn and hunted around the yard, but Slim H. wasn't there. We looked for him all over the property but couldn't find him anywhere. He seemed to have disappeared!

"There he is!" exclaimed Abigail, pointing to a weathered-looking man in a ragged straw hat standing in the tall grass. He was gazing at the pond, watching the fog roll in. He seemed lost in thought. We waited. Finally he turned and walked toward us. He greeted us with a quick nod, but walked on by, not suspecting that we wanted to talk to him, I guess. We ran after him.

"Excuse me," began Abigail. "Mr. Slim. Could we ask you a question?"

He stopped and waited for us to speak.

"We're worried about Mr. and Mrs. Wells on Main Street next door to the McLaughlin's. Have you seen them recently?"

He peered down at us from beneath the tattered brim of his hat. His skin was dark from the long hours of working under the hot summer sun. The pale blue cotton shirt and khaki pants he wore were torn and frayed. Slim's heavy work boots were in the same condition.

"Haven't seen them all summer. Son took over. Mean b-------! Sorry. But it's the truth. Don't pay on time, neither. The b   !"

"Do you think the Wellses are all right?" asked Abigail.

"Couldn't be, with that son around." He turned and went to his truck to get out his lawn mower. I guess that was the end of our conversation.

"We didn't learn much," I said as we went to get our bikes. "I don't even know the Wellses, but now I feel worried about them."

We mounted our bikes and rode behind the lighthouse, continuing down the lanes to Lowndes River Road. We were covered in fog as we rode over the bridge. We could see Cooky's wife at the counter of the Clam Bar. The sky was overcast and fog was blowing in off the harbor. It felt cold against our skin. I was again reminded of the ghost, but it was gone from Captain Snow's now. I hoped that it would stay away for good!

I shivered all the more as we passed the marina and I thought about Karl. Who was he? How could we find out?

When we got to my house, we could see that the harbor was enshrouded by a thick fog. Sailing was out of the question.

"Did the coyote come back?" asked Abigail as we leaned our bikes against the barn.

"No, she's gone. I guess she healed and went off to wherever she came from."

"I hope she stays away from that crazy coyote shooter!"

I agreed! I opened the barn door and went to the trunk to get out some more old letters for us to read. All the other letters and everything else we had had in the house had been stolen by Mrs. Pitts!

"Please stay there and hold the door open," I said to Abigail. "I don't want to get locked in here again!" I couldn't forget those two times I had been locked in the barn. It was probably Mrs. Pitts who had done it. She was the ghost who had been haunting my house!

I took a big bundle of letters and we headed for the back door. When we got to the sitting room, I noticed the light blinking on the answering machine and pressed the playback button. The first message was from Mom. She said that she was going to visit the Wellses and would tell me tonight what she had found out. That was good. The next message was from Jeffrey Silva!

"Uh...Hi. I...um...is this your private line? Uh...this is Jeffrey Silva. I was...uh...over to Womponoy 'cause sometimes I can find a dead animal over there. It's probably against the law to take them from there, but I'm not sure. I saw that coyote shooter with a sack full of something struggling, you know, like a animal was in it. He was like putting it in a boat. This fat guy with little glasses was in the boat…He shoots coyotes and he's supposed to get rid of them, but it doesn't seem right for him to catch live ones and then turn around and sell them. I think it was a coyote in the sack. The fat man gave him money. I hid and got out of there quick. Is this what kind of information you want? Bye."

"Wow!" we exclaimed in unison.

"I hope it's not our coyote," I said. "That would be terrible. Now that she's healed I can't bear to think of her getting caught and ending up as a sacrifice for those crazy Earth Mother People!"

"You don't know what kind of animal it was or if that man is one of the group," said Abigail trying to comfort me.

"I'm sure the man was Karl, the one who caught me and Mollie at the marina. They're probably planning another sacrifice. But when? There's no full moon."

"Maybe they don't need a full moon every time. They did it in the fog last time. We could ask Judy. If she doesn't know, some of those books at The Tomb might say when sacrifices have to be made."

"Let's ask her tonight after we meet at the band concert. I'm really angry about that coyote shooter! He's no good! No wonder he didn't want us over on Womponoy!"

There was a third message. It was from Mollie: "Maxwell's play date was cancelled so Mom took us *both* out to lunch. It was a total disaster! They're at the beach now. I refused to go. So here I am. But I have news. Call when you get home."

Just then we heard Mollie at the back door.

"Sorry you didn't get to have lunch with your mom—alone," I said as she came into the kitchen, letting the screen door slam behind her. She didn't look very happy. As she plopped herself down at the table, I asked, "Are you all right?"

"I don't care anymore," she answered, burying her head in her arms.

"Are you hungry?" asked Abigail.

"No," Mollie mumbled. "I just had the most horrible lunch that ever was. I don't care if I ever eat again."

"Well, I do!" proclaimed Abigail, helping herself to the peanut butter and Fluff. She began making sandwiches. Mollie really seemed upset about the situation with her mom and little brother, but what could she do? What could we do to help? We told her about Jeffrey Silva's call. She hardly reacted. I had never seen her like that before!

Abigail and I ate while Mollie hid her head and said nothing. Suddenly she popped up. "Let's take a walk on the beach. I need a change of scenery."

I shivered as I looked out the window and saw the fog billowing across the lawn. It wasn't that I imagined zombies lurching up from the beach and staggering across the lawn, but I felt that it was wise to stay at home. There were dangerous people out there who were after us. I thought it would be asking for trouble if we wandered off into the fog.

"Why don't we just stay here?" I asked. "I don't want to risk finding anything or anyone in that fog. We won't be able to see the 'scenery' anyway." But Mollie wanted to go and Abigail didn't mind.

"Come on, come on," Mollie said. I dragged myself up and put the dishes in the sink. We headed out the door facing the harbor. The two girls marched across the lawn and I followed them down the path to the shore. We descended into even thicker fog as we got to the beach. I didn't feel the least bit comfortable about this. Mrs. Pitts and her spooky sister could creep up without us even knowing it!

We ambled along the shore, sloshing through heaps of soggy eel grass heaped up by the tide. Vibrant blue mussel shells littered the beach. A seagull feather was strewn here and there along with a few oyster and scallop shells.

"We've got to find out who's the leader of that Earth Mother group and if there's something going on other than their sacrificing," Mollie remarked. "I'm thinking the mastermind is Mrs. Pitts's sister."

"What about that man Karl? We've never seen him before. He's probably new in town too, or he could be here just for the summer. Maybe he's the one," Abigail speculated.

"Karl might have a boat moored at the marina, since he was in that shack on the marina dock. My dad knows the Mitchells who own the marina. It's Dad's day off tomorrow. I'll ask him if he can stop by to find out who Karl is. The Mitchells might know."

"I wish Muffy were here," lamented Abigail. "It seems strange for us to be together without her."

"Let's go back to my house and give her a call," I suggested, wanting an excuse to get out of the fog. "She must be finished getting her outfit ready for the party by now."

As we turned around to head back toward my house, two tall, dark shadowy figures blocked our path!

Chapter Fifty

"What are they talking about, Gracie?" laughed a man. It was Karl! "They want to know who our leader is."

We had to think fast. I grabbed Abigail and Mollie.

"Jump into the water and swim for your lives!" I whispered to them. But we didn't. We hesitated. I don't know why.

"Stupid little girls." A female voice—it was Mrs. Pitts! "Get them, Karl!"

That was our cue. We dashed into the water. Unfortunately it was low tide. We had to struggle through shallow water until it was deep enough for us to swim. But it was a good idea. Karl Kenton and Gracie Pitts splashed after us only for a moment, then stopped. They were adults and they didn't want to get wet.

The fog kept them from seeing us, but I was sure that they could hear our movements in the water. We couldn't see where we were going either and the harbor was filled with moored boats. That didn't stop us from forcing ourselves to swim out as far as we could to get away from Karl and Mrs. Pitts. Finally we thought that we must be out of their reach. We stopped swimming and waited, treading water, listening.

"I knew we shouldn't have come out in this fog!" I said softly. "Now what are we going to do? We don't even know which way the shore is!"

"The yacht club is close by," said Mollie. "If we keep swimming in this direction, we should come to the dock."

"If we're lucky," whined Abigail. We assumed that Karl and Mrs. Pitts had given up trying to catch us. What would they have done to us if they had caught us?

We slowly swam in what we hoped was the right direction.

"Hey! I've got my compass!" I exclaimed, pulling it from my waterlogged pocket and reading it. "Can you believe that? We *are* going in the right direction!"

Soon we came to the yacht club dock and clambered up. We hoped that we were safe, but how could we be sure? We still couldn't see a thing. Slowly we moved along the dock toward the beach. When we got there and found the stairs, we raced up to the clubhouse. When we entered, we saw Billy Jones and Judy seated at the big wooden table!

"What's up with you guys?" asked Billy. "You didn't go out sailing and sink your boat, did you?" He and Judy laughed at his joke.

We weren't in a laughing mood.

"Uh...no," I said. "We were just playing around. Could we use the phone?"

"Please?" added Abigail.

"Sure," said Billy. "Don't drip water on anything!" he joked again. It was really a joke because, I'm sorry to say, our yacht club was such a mess no one would have noticed if we'd even thrown buckets of water all over everything! We crowded into the narrow hallway where the phone hung on the wall.

We telephoned Mrs. McLaughlin to ask if Muffy was still there. She was. We asked her to come and meet us.

"Our costumes are all ready!" she gushed. "They look fabulous, even Louie's. Where shall I meet you?"

I was afraid to go to my house, but I was cold and wet. We all were. Mollie's house wasn't safe either because it was near the harbor, too. Karl and Mrs. Pitts could be lurking anywhere in this fog!

After a little discussion, we decided to meet Muffy at Abigail's. It was settled. I hung up the phone. Then we remembered we didn't have our bikes! It would be a long walk to Abigail's—unless we could get a ride from Billy.

I turned to find Billy standing over us with his arms folded.

"Tell me what's going on," he demanded. "I want to know what's happening with this new mystery of yours."

The three of us were shocked. Billy sounded so stern! Then his face broke into a smile, "What's wrong with you girls? You're so jumpy! You've got yourselves all worked up. Don't get so involved. It's not healthy."

Great advice for three girls who had almost been abducted, or even worse, a few minutes ago! Judy appeared from behind Billy.

"It's no big deal," she added. "I think you girls are imagining things. My boss Lucky is a real nice guy and his store and his customers are cool. Mrs. Pitts is a little strange, but so are you!" she laughed. We didn't. Judy seemed to be an expert on saying crazy things all of a sudden. I thought she was trying to help us. Now she seemed to be on the other side.

"Billy, could you give us a lift to the lighthouse?" I asked.

"Sure. All the classes and races are cancelled today because of this fog," he said, motioning toward the window to the thick blanket of gray. He paused and asked, "Where're your bikes?"

"Uh...it's a long story," said Mollie, hoping to discourage him from asking any more questions.

"I've heard that before," he chuckled. "Let's go."

We piled into the back of his truck. Billy and Judy got into the cab. As we drove off, we saw someone coming up the steps from the beach. It was Mrs. Pitts and Karl, who was holding his black doctor's bag! They stopped and stared as we drove away. We stared back and shivered. Not from the wet and cold—from fright!

179

No one was home at Abigail's grammy's house when we got there. That was a relief. I wasn't in the mood for an onslaught of little cousins, but we had to consider the possibility of Karl and his girlfriends knowing Abigail's address as well. It was possible that we weren't safe there either. Maybe not anywhere.

Abigail said we could shower, so we quickly rinsed off in her outdoor shower beside the kitchen door. We changed into some clothes which Abigail offered us. Dry and comfortable, we settled into the old chairs lined up on her porch to eat a snack Abigail had prepared. Muffy arrived just in time to eat. I had rinsed off my compass. It had saved our lives so I wanted to keep it in good condition. We told Muffy everything that had happened.

"Let's make a list of all the people who are part of the witch bunch," suggested Abigail, going back into the house and returning with pencil and notepad.

"It's called a coven," corrected Mollie. "Wasn't that in the green witchcraft book Laura bought? Who has that book now anyway?"

"I gave it to Abigail to read," said Muffy. "It doesn't mention covens. It's about good green witches and all the wonderful things they're supposedly doing to save the planet."

"Yeah, sure, like killing animals, stealing, threatening us, and drugging the local kids. Real good people!" Mollie said sarcastically.

"Let's make a list of all the adults involved: Mrs. Pitts and her sister," I began as Abigail wrote, "Lucky, Miss Deighton, Karl, and Mr. Mullins. I don't think Jeffrey Silva is one of them. The coyote shooter could be one of them, or just helping them."

"What do they all have in common?" asked Lawyer's Daughter. "They all live in town year-round, though we're not sure about Karl or Mrs. Pitts's sister. They're all customers of The Tomb, except for maybe Karl..."

"They're all adults and they're all mean," continued Muffy.

"Is Mr. Mullins mean?" asked Abigail.

"Not that I know of," I replied. "But he took the church records and that's not nice."

"They might have a plan to save the world," began Mollie. "But what I want to know is this: If they're good witches, why are they mean at all? They seem so evil."

"Some people will do anything to accomplish their goals," Abigail said.

"Well, we have a lot of time before the band concert," said Mollie. "Let's make good use of it."

That sounded like something an adult would say. I didn't like the sound of it. Mollie looked at a globe-shaped clear glass vase of flowers on the porch table. She moved her hands over it as if it were a crystal ball.

"Let me see...ah, yes, I see Miss Deighton. She's waiting for a visit from the Eel Grass Girls' Deluxe Weeding Service."

"Oh, please!" I protested. "I can't deal with her. Besides, how are we going to get there?"

"I'll think of something," said Mollie, looking into her "crystal ball."

"I'll get that witchcraft book for you Mollie," said Abigail, getting up from her chair. "You're the only one who hasn't read it yet, besides Louie."

As Abigail disappeared inside the house, we heard a car coming up the driveway. We looked up to see Abigail's uncle's Land Rover, chock full of little cousins, rumbling up to the house. Another car of aunts and uncles pulled in behind it.

"Grammy!" called Abigail, emerging from the house. She handed the book to Mollie. We followed Abigail over to the car. "Welcome home! We need a ride to Laura's house. I left my bike there."

"Well, hello girls," her grandmother said pleasantly. We greeted her and were introduced to the aunts, uncles, and cousins.

"Are you leaving so soon?" she asked us.

"Yes, we have a job to do," Abigail told her. She explained about Miss Deighton. Abigail's grandmother then related our situation to one of the uncles, Uncle Jack, who offered to drive us over to my house to get our bikes. He loaded Muffy's bike in the back of the Land Rover and we took off.

We looked for suspects as we passed the Clam Bar, but we saw no one there. It would appear that the fog was bad for business. The yacht club was also deserted. When we got to my house, we asked Uncle Jack to wait until we had our bikes and were out on the road. We weren't taking any chances. When we were ready to go, we waved good-bye to him and rode off toward Pine Street to Miss Deighton's.

We found Miss Deighton sitting in her kitchen rocking chair, sipping tea. She wore a necklace of small clamshells strung on a piece of purple yarn. Her loose lavender linen shirt was belted with a leather braid and her long purple-patterned skirt looked as if it had once been a tablecloth.

"How nice to see you girls!" she sneered as we entered her kitchen. "I presume you've returned to finish weeding. You ought to take some interest in the world around you. You're not too young to learn about the power of herbs. The Earth Mother has given us herbs to heal and to give us power."

Muffy looked upset. I had a feeling that she wasn't going to keep quiet—and I was right.

"*God* gave us herbs for food and healing," she corrected.

"Yes, that's right," Miss Deighton, smiled. "God, the Earth Mother,

Buddha. We call her by many different names, but she is the same person." I could tell that Muffy didn't agree. Her dark eyes flashed with anger, but she kept silent. We were here to get information, not to have a religious discussion. That usually didn't bother Muffy. She always felt she had to stand up for what she believed was right. I felt that way too. But in this case, arguing with Miss Deighton wouldn't get us anywhere. Besides, we wanted her to think that we agreed with her so we could get more information from her. Muffy finally seemed to realize that.

"All the herbs in my garden are labeled. You must have noticed the markers." We nodded. "Good. After you finish weeding, bring me a bunch of each of these plants," she told us, taking pen and paper from the cluttered table beside her chair and jotting down a list of names. She handed it to me. "Then, when you come in for your break, I'll teach you about them, and you can try them out. You'll see what I mean about their power and healing properties."

"The other night we noticed you were having a party," Mollie said, changing the subject. "We rode our bikes down Pine Street and saw all the cars parked in your driveway."

Miss Deighton seemed surprised and was about to say something but stopped herself. Instead she became defensive and answered, "In my condition, I can't go anywhere, so my friends have to come to me." Then her attitude changed again.

"Why don't we have some tea?" She moved to get up from her rocking chair.

"Uh, we have to go now," Mollie suddenly announced. She headed out of the kitchen. We did the same, trailing her to the front door and out of the house.

"How rude!" exclaimed Abigail, once we were outside. "Why did you do that?"

"Well, Miss Manners, do _you_ want to stay for tea?" asked Mollie.

"No, but you could have been more polite. Now she'll suspect us. It looks bad, not to mention it was rude."

"I don't mind leaving," said Muffy, as she jumped on her bike. "I'm afraid of her tea, whether she's a good witch or a bad one."

"We didn't even do any weeding," I said as we pedaled down the soft sand driveway. "You just whisked us away. She'll wonder what's wrong with us."

"She'll get over it," said Mollie as we rode out onto the street.

Chapter Fifty-Two

"Isn't it time for dinner?" asked Abigail.

"You seem awfully hungry nowadays," observed Mollie.

"She's been thinking of all the goodies they'll have at the lawn party tomorrow," laughed Muffy. "But what I want to know is this: Is it a lawn party or a tea party?"

"It's both," answered Abigail.

"I think it's time to head home," said Muffy. "Why don't we go together, Abigail? If you ride down Lowndes River Road, you'll pass by the marina. We don't know where Karl and Mrs. Pitts may be hiding."

"You're right," agreed Abigail. "I'll go with you. I'll ask Uncle Jack to give us all a ride to the band concert tonight. I don't think any of us will want to ride our bikes at night until this mystery is solved. Am I right?"

We all agreed. Uncle Jack would pick us up at seven-thirty.

"Mollie, could you call Louie?" asked Abigail. "We can pick him up, too. Doesn't he live near you?"

"Yes, I'll call him. He lives two houses down. The yellow mailbox."

"What's our plan for tomorrow?" Abigail asked. "I have to go to the party early because my grammy's on the committee."

"Then everyone else should meet at my grandparents' before one," Muffy suggested. "Grammy said parking will be a problem at the library. Laura, tell your mom she can park beside Grammy's garage. You too, Mollie. Louie already knows, but I think he's riding his bike. See you tonight," said Muffy as she and Abigail pedaled off toward town. They would split up at the stop sign, Muffy going straight to her house in the north part of town, Abigail going down Main Street through the old village to her grandmother's house on Snow Pond.

Mollie and I rode toward the harbor. The fog had lifted and the sky was clearing. It made us feel better—without the fog, but we knew that we were still in danger.

"First, we'll see if anyone's at your house," I told her. Fortunately we saw her mother's car in the driveway. To our surprise, her father's car was there too! He never came down this early on Fridays. He always left the city after work, arriving late at night. Mollie wondered what was going on. She hoped that nothing was wrong.

We entered the kitchen. Her parents and Maxwell were sitting around the kitchen table, playing a board game.

"Mollie!" cried her father, jumping up from the table and grabbing her in a bear hug as if he hadn't seen her in years. "My little Mollie!" Mollie gave me a "What is this all about?" kind of look.

"Why, hello, Laura. Welcome to our home," he said to me, making a grand gesture with his arms. "I drove up early from the city so I could spend some quality time with my wife and kids," he explained. "We've decided to spend more time together as a family. We're all going to play some fun games and have a wonderful time together."

"But Dad," Mollie began to complain, "I go to the band concert with my friends on Friday nights."

"Oh, you can play with your friends any old time," he boomed. "There will be lots of other Friday nights for you and your friends to play, but tonight is family night. We're going to have lots of fun!"

Maxwell gave us a demonic grin. I felt sorry for Mollie. Parents could be so strange. Why do they have to wait until you have something really important planned before they begin to feel guilty about ignoring you and decide to do something about it? I'll never be able figure them out. The band concert wouldn't be the same without Mollie, but I knew it was useless to argue.

"Uh, you *do* remember the lawn party at the library tomorrow, don't you?" she asked her mom, fearing that "family time" might include Saturday as well.

"Of course I do! I bought tickets for all of us!"

Mollie gave me an "I don't believe this" look. But at least she would get to go to the lawn party. That was good.

"Good-bye, Mr. and Mrs. Perkins and Maxwell. See you tomorrow, Mollie," I said and left. But as soon as I went out the door, I remembered that I didn't want to go home alone! I hoped that Mom would be there. The stretch of road between Mollie's house and mine was deserted most of the time. Should I go back and get Mollie? If she went home with me, then she would have to travel back to her home alone. It didn't make any sense. Either way, one of us would be alone on the road. I had no choice but to go on by myself. I slowly picked up my bike and headed down Mollie's long shell driveway.

As I passed the driveway of her neighbor Howard Snow, I heard strange music floating toward me from his barn. It sounded like waterfalls and waves, exotic musical instruments, and tropical birds. Very soothing. I looked down the driveway to see Howie stacking up his lobster pots. He had been a real help to us, I thought, as I rode on and out to the road. He had proved himself to be a friend. Oddly, I didn't feel quite so scared any more as I rode home.

When I got to my driveway, I could see from the street that both my parents were home. Mom's car and Dad's truck were parked near the barn. That was a relief! I pedaled up to the house and waltzed into the kitchen.

My parents were making dinner. I felt safe and secure and happy. Family *is* really important! Then I noticed the radio was playing the same music as Howie Snow's! That struck me as somewhat peculiar. In fact, it was freaky! My parents never listened to music like that! There wasn't even any radio station on the Cape that played that kind of music!

Mom noticed the look on my face. "What's wrong, dear?"

"What are you listening to?"

"It's a new station. It's kind of refreshing, don't you think?" she asked.

"Just started up last week," said Dad. "Sort of New Age. They're always talking about peace, love, and herb power," he laughed, as he took the garbage out to the barn.

I knew it! It had something to do with *them*!

"Who runs the station?" I asked, excitedly.

"Oh I don't know. I haven't been paying attention," said Mom, continuing to chop carrots for the salad.

I began to listen as I helped set the table.

When Dad came back in from the barn, he gave me a strange look.

"Have you been keeping some kind of animal in the barn?"

"Uh...well ...um...," I began, my voice trailing off. I guess I should have mentioned the coyote to my parents, but I didn't want them to call the animal control officer to come and take the coyote away. "A coyote got into the barn. It was hurt, so the Girls and I called the animal control officer right away. When the officer got here, the coyote ran out the back of the barn, so he couldn't catch it. But the coyote came back, so we put food out for it."

"Coyote?" cried Mom. "That's a wild animal!"

"Yes, I know, but it was hurt. We think the coyote shooter on Womponoy grazed her back with a bullet. Then she healed up and disappeared."

"She could have had rabies," Dad said sternly. "You should have told us."

"I'm sorry," I said, hanging my head. I should have told them, but I had been afraid that my parents would panic, call Mr. Costa, and have the coyote taken away. She could have been dangerous, that's true. Probably my dad would have helped me take care of the coyote if I had told him about her. I should have trusted my parents to do the right thing. Maybe I should confide in them more about our mystery.

"Don't you ever do anything like that again!" said Mom emphatically.

"If it ever comes back, tell us," added Dad. "Let us help you decide what's the safe thing to do."

"O.K., I'm really sorry," I said again. My parents forgave me. I was glad that was over. At the least the coyote had healed and gotten away. Hopefully she was safe and not imprisoned, awaiting execution by Karl and his evil friends!

"Dad, speaking of dangerous things, there's a strange man we met down at the marina. Do you think you could find out from the Mitchells who he is?"

"What's his name?"

"Karl. We think he's a doctor."

"Oh, that would be Doctor Karl Kenton."

"You know him?" I asked, incredulously. How could my dad know the maniac who was trying to kill us?

"He's the one who runs the new radio station." I almost fainted!

"Really?" asked Mom. She was perfectly calm. She didn't realize how upset I was. "Do you know him?"

"I met him down at the marina last weekend," said Dad. "He's a friend of the Mitchells. They rent him a room above the marina garage. He's into New Age music and philosophy. He thought it would be good for our town and the Cape to have a New Age radio station."

Good for our town? Yeah, sure.

"What else do you know about him?" I asked. "What kind of doctor is he?"

"He's a psychiatrist or psychologist I think, a doctor who talks to people and helps them with their problems."

Karl was using the radio station to tell the locals, such as Howard Snow and my parents, about the green witch philosophy. This was too much! This was too frightening! What if my own parents turned into witches or zombies! What if I turned into a zombie!

"So, why are you so interested in Doctor Kenton?" asked Dad.

"Oh, I...uh...saw him at the marina and didn't recognize him. He seems kind of quirky to me, so I thought I'd ask." I just couldn't do it. I couldn't tell my parents what had happened. Would I be sorry about this too?

"I don't think he seems so quirky," said Dad. "But then I'm not a little girl," he chuckled. "How's the haunted house going?"

"It's not going anywhere," I said, trying to sound as casual as I could, recalling our morning adventure with the flying offering plate!

At dinner Mom told me that she had visited the Wellses. She explained the situation to Dad and told us, "Their son wouldn't even open the door! He said his parents were napping. I told him I would return on Monday and that I wanted to see them. They're due for a check-up, I said. He'd better let me in on Monday!"

"I'm worried about them," I sighed.

"I am too," Mom answered. She really cared about people. With her work, she went inside people's homes. She saw their private lives. Mom liked to help people, but sometimes their problems, especially those involving relatives, were too big for her to solve. That didn't stop her from trying, though.

The rest of our dinner was quiet as we thought about all the activities of our day. I listened to the radio station intently as we ate. The music made me feel relaxed, but I resisted the feeling, not wanting to be influenced by Karl Kenton! It made me think of herbs—they could be used for good or evil. It was the same with Karl's music. When we finished dinner, I helped wash the dishes and put the leftovers away.

"I aired out our costumes," Mom told me. "Too bad your dad doesn't want to go to the lawn party with us," she teased.

"Not my cup of tea," he joked. We all laughed.

Just then the phone rang. I raced into the sitting room to answer it. It was Jeffrey Silva!

"Is this Laura?" he asked breathlessly.

"Yes. What's wrong?"

"It's Aloma Smits! You know, the cafeteria lady? She's down in the woods near the cedar swamp where the old hunting shack is. And I don't think she's trying out new recipes for school lunch 'cause she's acting really scary and she's got something with her. You've got to check it out!"

"What's she doing?" I asked.

"You've got to see it for yourself," he said and hung up. Great! Now what was I going to do? I couldn't just go, especially with Uncle Jack coming to pick us up!

"Who was that?" asked Dad.

"Oh, just a high school kid."

His eyebrows went up as he waited for an explanation.

"Uh, he had some information about our mystery, but I don't know if it really is."

"Oh," he replied, a smile spreading across his face. I guess I wasn't being clear, but I was glad that he didn't ask me anything else! I ran upstairs to get my backpack, which was one item that I usually put away and kept track of.

My parents knew my schedule of meeting my friends at the band concert every Friday night. I told them that Abigail's Uncle Jack was giving us a ride tonight. I was impatient for him to arrive. When I heard the honking of the Land Rover's horn in our driveway, I kissed Mom and Dad good-bye and bolted out the door. I greeted Uncle Jack, Abigail, and Muffy. I told them what happened with Mollie and why she couldn't come with us, but I would have to wait to tell them about Jeffrey's call. The Girls were disappointed about Mollie. We had a lot to discuss tonight. We would miss her, her comments, and suggestions.

We drove to Louie's. He was waiting beside his yellow mailbox. We introduced him to Uncle Jack as he hopped in the back of the car. We told him about Mollie. It would be awkward without her, especially since Louie was more her friend than ours, but we would have to get over it.

It was still bright outside. It would help with our evening outing. I was glad that the fog was gone! Lots of tourists were on the road, heading back to their hotels after spending a few hours at the beach. I'm sure they were glad to see the fog leave too. Cars were driving toward the local restaurants for dinners of fried clams and lobsters. In town, Main Street was lined with cars and a steady stream of pedestrians laden with lawn chairs and picnic baskets, headed for the bandstand to hear the Friday night concert performed by the town band. But I was anxious to tell the Girls and Louie about Aloma Smits!

Chapter Fifty-Three

We took Abigail's big plaid blanket and headed for our usual spot directly behind the bandstand. Uncle Jack would pick us up at nine. Hopefully that would give us enough time to get to the cedar swamp and visit Judy at The Tomb. Dancing and having fun would have to wait. It just wasn't the same without Mollie being there, but what could we do?

"Jeffrey Silva called," I announced.

"What did he have to say?" asked Muffy.

"He said that Aloma Smits is in the cedar swamp, acting nutty and that she has quote—something—unquote with her!" I made quote signs with my fingers for dramatic effect.

"Something like what?" asked Louie, looking perplexed.

"I don't know and he wouldn't tell."

"What are you waiting for?" asked Louie jumping up. "Let's go!"

"Where's the cedar swamp anyway?" asked Abigail as we hurriedly followed Louie.

"It's down Main Street before you get to the Village," I told her. We left our blanket on the ground, weaving our way through the crowd of seated families until we finally reached Main Street. On the way, we discussed Mollie's situation.

"Well, at least she can't complain about her parents ignoring her anymore," said Abigail.

"They picked a great time to start paying attention!" moaned Muffy. "Thankfully they're not keeping her away from the lawn party. We'll all be together tomorrow."

Then we told Louie about the exorcism as we dodged the tourists crowding the narrow sidewalks of Main Street.

"You mean your preacher got the ghosts to get out of Captain Snow's house?" he asked in disbelief.

"We drove the spirits out with the holy water, oil, and prayer," I told him.

"You mean God did," Muffy corrected me.

I then told Louie about our encounter with Karl and Mrs. Pitts on the beach, Jeffrey Silva's other call about his visit to Womponoy, and the possibility of another sacrifice coming up. Abigail recapped our interview with Slim H. and visit to Miss Deighton. I gave them the information I had received from Dad about Karl and his new radio station.

"Wow!" exclaimed Louie. "You girls sure found out a lot."

"What if the sacrifice is tonight?" asked Muffy as we neared the Village. "If

189

they've got your coyote, Laura, we have to save her."

"We can't go without Mollie!" Louie protested.

"Then we'll have to get her later," I said.

"But how?" asked Abigail.

"Let's ask Judy when the green witches do their sacrifices. We know there's not a full moon. Maybe they only do it on Saturdays or something."

"O.K." said Muffy. "We'll ask her."

"And that's really strange about Karl having a radio station and playing New Age music," muttered Abigail. "Especially because he's so mean."

"It's scary to think of him trying to influence the whole Cape!" exclaimed Muffy. "Besides his green witchcraft preaching, he might even be sending out hypnotic radio waves and secret messages in the music."

"Maybe he's the one who's hypnotizing Mrs. Pitts with his music," suggested Abigail.

"Maybe he is. If he wasn't so evil, his ideas wouldn't be so bad," I said. "The Cape could use some good influence when it comes to preserving nature, but we know that Karl is an evil man! You were right, Abigail, when you said that some people will do anything to accomplish their goals."

"Well, we have a goal of our own," said Muffy. "Tomorrow we'll have to talk to the old-timers and see what they know about the Snows. This might be our only chance to meet some of them. We'll have to make the most of the party."

"I hope none of my friends see me there," Louie said, awkwardly.

"What do you mean?" I asked, suspecting I already knew.

"I'll look like a fool in that old outfit and silly captain's hat!" he complained.

"Oh, pooh!" said Abigail. We burst out laughing, all except for Louie, but he couldn't help smiling. What an expression! He knew he wasn't going to get out of going to the party in costume, no matter what.

Louie was leading the way. It was fairly dark by now. He turned down an alley and then ducked through an opening in a enormous privet hedge, which revealed a path winding through the high grass down to the cedar swamp.

"Jeffrey said she was at an old hunting shack," I told them in a hushed voice. Louie veered left and led us along a narrow log placed over a wet area. We could see a fire flickering in the distance! Next to a little tumbled-down shack was Aloma Smits, bending over a bubbling pot! Beside her stood what seemed to be a person, but we couldn't tell if it was a man or a woman! It was dressed in rags, its eyes were dull and blank!

"She's a witch!" exclaimed Louie under his breath. "And she's got a zombie!"

"A what?" Muffy was startled. Abigail began to tremble as she took in the sight before us.

"A zombie," Louie repeated. "A walking dead person."

"There's no such thing!" Muffy stated, yet the person we saw hardly looked alive! Aloma was chanting as she stirred her pot. Her zombie stood stone still, staring into nothingness.

"What should we do?" asked Abigail. I wondered what we *could* do. Just then Aloma stopped stirring and listened. Did she hear us? She spoke in a low voice to the creature at her side. It turned and began to lurch toward the very place where we were hiding!

"Run!" I cried.

We raced back over the log, but I slipped off and fell knee deep in the mire!

"Help me!" I shrieked. Louie grabbed one arm and Abigail the other, but Abigail slipped and tumbled into the muck alongside of me!

Muffy pulled at me, but I was stuck! Abigail was covered from head to toe in mud! Somehow she was able to grasp hold of the log and pull herself up. I heard the grasses rustling! It was the zombie coming toward us!

"Get me out of here!" I begged Louie and Muffy. They hoisted me up just in time! We sped along the path and back through the hedge. Hopefully the zombie wouldn't follow us out onto the street! We paused, panting and listening. The sounds stopped. The creature must have gone back to Aloma.

"Is that person gone?" asked Abigail, dripping with muck and trembling with fright.

"He—or she—must be hypnotized!" Muffy speculated. "Let's get out of here!"

We jogged up the alley, but stopped when we got to Main Street.

"We can't go down Main Street looking like this!" I told Abigail.

"You've got to get cleaned up!" Muffy concurred. "I know. Let's take the back roads to my aunt's shop. We can give you a bath with her garden hose."

"Great!" said Abigail, absolutely thrilled with the prospect.

"You too, Laura. You stink!" Muffy told me.

"Thank you so much for letting me know," I teased. "But we didn't find out what Aloma was doing."

"Who cares!" said Abigail. "It was something witchy and scary. It's more important to find out who her zombie is."

"Do you have any ideas, Louie?" I asked.

He thought for a moment as he led us through yards and down lanes to the back of the shop.

"Could be Morton Grounds," he told us. "He disappeared last winter. They thought he wandered off the outer bar in the dark and drowned himself in the channel."

"I remember that," I said. "But why do you think it's Morton?"

"They never found his body. But that's to be expected. The reason I think it might be Morton is 'cause my friend Butchy said he saw Morton in the woods last spring. I helped Butchy try to find him, but we couldn't. I think it's him."

"But why would Aloma Smits make him into a zombie?" I asked.

"Why not?" was Louie's reply as we approached the rear of the shop.

A green garden hose was coiled on the side of the white clapboard building. We hosed off in the driveway. It was a warm night, but I felt cold and uncomfortable by the time we finished. I'm sure that Abigail felt even worse! We coiled the hose up and walked back to the park to our blanket. The town band was striking up a lively waltz. We looked out over the sea of families seated on blankets covering the grass. Balloons bobbed above the crowd and children twirled their lightsticks in blurs of colored light.

The area of grass around the bandstand, where the audience was welcome to dance, was brightly lit. The *Rock and Roll Waltz* began to play. Though we were wet and soggy, we joined the crowd around the bandstand and danced our version of rock and roll. I was glad that Louie came down with us and couldn't dance any better than we could!

"Tomb time," announced Muffy as the tune ended. The lights dimmed and the dancers headed back to their blankets. We walked the short distance to The Tomb.

"Let's sneak up on them," Louie suggested. We didn't know who he meant by "them," but we followed him as he crept around the building, up to the open door of The Tomb, and peered into the little shop. There were some teenage customers looking through the books and herbs. Beyond them we could see Lucky and Mr. Mullins in the shop office beyond the counter! Mr. Mullins seemed impatient and ready to leave so we darted into a gift shop on the corner of the old building and waited. Mr. Mullins rushed out of The Tomb, jumped into his truck, and quickly drove away.

"Mr. Mullins!" exclaimed Louie.

"Aha!" I exclaimed. "Deacon and the keeper of the missing church records! He's here again, but what can he be doing? I doubt that he's here on water department business."

"He's got to be one of them!" exclaimed Louie.

"I was thinking," began Abigail. "I don't agree with Earth Mother worship, but what they say about saving the trees and stopping pollution makes sense to me. Can't people believe in that and not be green witches?"

"Of course they can," Muffy replied. "The difference is how you go about solving the problems and how far you'll go to get your way. Laura's and my parents don't believe in the Earth Mother but have the same ideas. They're trying to make changes through the town meetings. Isn't that right, Laura?"

I nodded in agreement.

"What are we going to say to Judy?" asked Abigail as we walked toward The Tomb.

"We'll find out if she has any new information and find out when the

Earth Mother People offer their sacrifices, but we have to watch out for Lucky," I said as we walked into the incense-filled shop.

"Hi, kids!" called Judy as we entered. She was smiling and acted as if nothing had ever happened. Maybe nothing had, as far as she was concerned. Lucky had closed the office door so we were safe from him, at least for the time being. "Did any other interesting stuff happen to you all?" she asked.

"Nothing much," I said, not wanting to say anything important while Lucky was only a closed door away. "Does a fat man with little glasses named Karl Kenton come in here?" I whispered.

"Doesn't sound familiar," she replied, shaking her head.

"How about a 40-something man with a red face and black hair?" asked Abigail.

"Nope. Are they new suspects?"

"Yes," answered Muffy.

"Sorry I can't help you," she replied.

"What about that list..." Just as I was about to confront her with that dumb list of Tomb customers she had given us, the phone rang. Judy picked it up.

"It's for Lucky," she told us, holding her hand over the receiver. "You'd better go. I'll have to get him for the phone call. He knows you kids are up to something and he's angry about it. You'd better leave."

"What do you think of that?" asked Muffy, as we walked back to the bandstand.

"I want to know why she gave us that lousy list!" I exclaimed.

"Maybe she was afraid Lucky would see it," suggested Abigail. "He was right there and almost saw the names on the list."

Abigail was probably right. Judy was trying her best to help us. We shouldn't complain. She'd given us so much information already.

"We didn't get to ask her about the sacrifices," complained Louie. "What will we do about your coyote?"

"We'll just have to hope they aren't planning to do it tonight because I don't know how we can get Mollie out of her house," I sighed. If they were going to do the sacrifice at Captain Snow's, I really didn't want to go back there, even though the ghosts had been driven out. But to save my coyote, I would. If we couldn't go with Mollie tonight, we would have to wait and hope that the sacrifice would be some other night.

As we ambled back to the bandstand, something moved behind a hedge bordering a yard on Main Street! We froze! The blank eyes of the zombie glistened through the leaves!

"It's him!" shrieked Abigail. We raced all the way back to the park.

"He won't follow us here," I said, though I wasn't so sure whether he would or not! We didn't know what to do next. We certainly didn't feel like buying popcorn or cotton candy from the vendors on the sidewalk as we usually did.

Muffy suggested that we go back to our blanket. After stepping over families and blankets, we finally reached our place. Abigail and I tried to make ourselves comfortable by wrapping the woolen blanket around us. We listened to the *Bunny Hop* and *Farmer in the Dell*. These were usually our favorite tunes for dancing, but I didn't feel like dancing now. Neither did my friends, or Louie.

We huddled in the blanket, shivering, but stood up for the *Star-Spangled Banner* at the end of the concert. Then we followed the droves of people out to the street where we waited for Uncle Jack to pick us up. He arrived right on time and drove us home, never noticing that Abigail and I were damp. We took Muffy home first because she lived the furthest away, then Louie. I was last. Our plan was to meet tomorrow just before one o'clock at Mrs. McLaughlin's for the tea party. We hoped that we would have fun and though we wanted to work on our mystery, we wished that there would be no more frightening surprises!

Chapter Fifty-Four

I spent the morning with my mom preparing for the party. But the first thing I did was call Mollie to tell her about Aloma Smits and her zombie. It was too bizarre to be true, she said. It *was* too bizarre. It seemed like a bad dream now that the sun was shining brightly. It was a beautiful day. No fog, so Dad decided to go out fishing in his motorboat.

Mom and I stayed indoors getting ready. We lay out all our clothes on her bed. I got my dressy shoes, picked out a pair of laccy white socks, and found my gloves. Mom curled my hair. I chose blue hair ribbons to match my dress. Mom allowed me to wear a little lipstick and blush. It was so much fun. I couldn't remember ever playing dress-up with my mom before!

As we picked out our jewelry and perfume, my mind kept wandering back to our mystery. We had driven the evil spirits from Captain Snow's house and we had discovered that Lawrence, the Lowndes & McLaughlin bookkeeper, was stealing from his employers. Worst of all, he was a double murderer and was trying to cover up his guilt. And I was certain that Mr. Mullins knew more about Captain Snow than we did. That was why he was hiding the old church records!

I wondered if the events had happened too long ago for us to solve the mystery now. We had only bits and pieces. Something was missing, but I didn't know what. Maybe we could find it in the old letters, but reading them was so tedious! The handwriting was difficult to figure out. And most of them had nothing to do with our case at all!

Then we had the mystery of the animal-sacrificing adults. They were obviously green witches. It could be just a harmless religion, but sacrificing animals was not nice! Karl, Mrs. Pitts, and her sister were so nasty we couldn't help but suspect them of being up to something else, something bad. And someone was drugging kids with strange candy. Karl was trying to influence the Cape with his ideas using his radio program. Though some of his ideas seemed good, he had to have some other motive, considering his character. Maybe we could gather some new information at the party. I hoped so.

At last it was time to put on our dresses and drive to the library. We looked so beautiful. Mom asked Dad to take photographs and put the camera in her antique purse for taking pictures at the library. It was a little difficult to get our huge skirts into the car. Now I understood why the ladies of yesteryear rode in carriages! Lots of room. Not to mention that cars hadn't been invented yet.

We drove to Mrs. McLaughlin's and parked beside her garage, as Muffy had suggested. Mom and I slowly climbed up the back steps to the deck leading to the

McLaughlins' kitchen door, being careful not to trip. It wasn't easy to keep our long skirts up and out of the way. Mrs. McLaughlin, Muffy, and Louie were in the kitchen, making plates of finger sandwiches for the party. Mrs. McLaughlin was on the refreshment committee.

Muffy was dressed in a gauzy yellow cotton gown with a dark brown satin trim. Louie made a perfect Captain Snow in his suit and captain's cap. He looked great! Mrs. McLaughlin wore a lavender silk dress with many ruffles on the skirt. They all wore aprons and looked very authentic in the old-fashioned kitchen as they finished wrapping up the sandwiches.

"Good afternoon," my mom greeted them. "What may we do to help?"

"Welcome!" Mrs. McLaughlin warmly responded. "We're all done. We'll just get our hats, gloves, and parasols." They took off their aprons and hung them on a row of wooden pegs near the door. We each grabbed a plate of sandwiches and followed Mrs. McLaughlin through the house.

"Where's Mollie?" I asked Muffy.

"She called to say that they'll be parking in the town lot because her whole family is with her," answered Muffy. "I think she didn't want to be responsible for Maxwell tearing up my grandparents' house."

We both laughed as we walked toward the front door. Their accessories were lying on a table in the front hall. I helped Muffy with her hat. We looked at ourselves in the gilded mirror hanging on the opposite wall. We looked fantastic! Louie stuck his head between ours.

"I hope my mom takes some good pictures of us!" I laughed. We walked out onto the porch. Mom was standing on the lawn and snapped photos of us as we posed on the steps. Mr. McLaughlin was seated in a big wicker chair on the front porch. The house was on top of a small hill, with a "terraced" lawn rolling down to Main Street. A huge maple shaded most of the yard.

"Have fun!" he called to us as we made our way down the old granite steps leading to the street. We could see other partygoers moving along the sidewalk toward the library: men in white linen suits with straw hats, women and girls in big dresses, bonnets, and parasols, and a few boys in short suits. One boy was rolling a hoop, and we saw a man riding an old-fashioned bicycle! It was so exciting! I had never been to a costume party aside from Halloween and never with adults.

Our excitement grew as we neared the library. The charming red brick structure had been built over a hundred years ago. It was the perfect setting for the party: a wide lawn, a border of tall shady trees, and pretty flower gardens. White linen cloths covered long tables set up under the old elms. There were punch bowls, stacks of sandwiches, heaps of cookies, and elegant cakes! What a feast! We gave the plates of McLaughlin sandwiches to the ladies and gentlemen in charge of the food.

"I'm already hungry!" Louie confided, scanning the tables.

"Let's find Mollie and Abigail before we start pigging out," suggested Muffy.

"There they are," I said as I dragged Muffy and Louie to the tables of antique books for sale and a sea captain's writing desk to be raffled. Mollie and Abigail were watching an older man give calligraphy lessons and a gray-haired woman in an enormous hat tell the guests about old-fashioned bookbinding techniques. On a nearby table was a display of rare children's books and ship logs.

"Hey!" I called out to them. They spun around and curtsied when they saw us, Abigail in layers of pink tulle with a matching hat and Mollie in her all-white gown. We admired each other's dresses and they complimented Louie on his captain's outfit. He even carried a gold pocket watch, his grandfather's. He didn't seem to be the least bit embarrassed!

The scene was magical. It appeared as if we had just stepped out of an old photograph in one of my family's antique albums or a frame hanging on the wall of Mrs. McLaughlin's house. It was fun to see men and women, little children, everyone in antique costumes. But as I took it all in, I suddenly felt as if I were really being transported back to the days of Captain Snow! It scared me because as I looked around. I thought I saw Captain Snow lurking in the crowd! Could Mrs. Snow be adding tansy tea to the punch? Was that Petunia, Lawrence, Nellie Nickerson, and Edward Sparrow over there on the lawn?

"We have to get to work." Mollie's voice snapped me back from my wild imaginings to reality! I shuddered with relief.

"There's an old man over there," she said, pointing to a large man in white linen sampling the tea sandwiches. "Let's begin with him." She led the way.

"Excuse me, sir," she began as we reached him. "Have you ever heard the story of Captain Snow?"

"Why no, I haven't," he replied. He was a big man, as I mentioned, his suit quite crumpled with a line of stains down the front of it. He took a cup of punch from the top-hatted server.

"Wonder if they've spiked the punch?" he asked, taking a sip.

"Excuse me?" Abigail didn't understand. I thought I knew.

"Rum, bourbon," he muttered. "Brought my own." He turned away from the crowd, produced a silver flask from his jacket pocket, and poured a caramel-colored liquid into his punch.

"Ah! Now that's more like it," he exclaimed taking another sip. "Now what was that you children were asking me? Captain who?"

"Captain Snow," Muffy repeated. "He was lost at sea. His wife communicated with the dead and practiced black arts."

The man frowned. "Black arts? You mean they were witches? There's a little witch shop here in town. It's harmless I guess. I've heard they're good witches around here. I make candy for them. They give me all the ingredients I need and I cook it up in my basement. Sell a lot of it. Have you tried it? Benny Beans?"

Oh, my! We were talking to the candy maker himself!

"*You* make that candy?" asked Abigail, in shock.

"Yes. My name is Doctor Benjamin Alexis. Why are you so upset? My candy is quite good. Very good, in fact. You ought to try it."

"The local kids are addicted to it," said Mollie. "It can't be good. What do you put in it?"

"It's very simple. I use sugar, water, and lots of herbs. That's all. No preservatives. Nothing artificial. It's all natural."

"It must be the herbs!" I exclaimed. "What kind do you use?"

"Well, I don't know if I should tell you. But they're harmless, I'm sure. I mean I know they're harmless. Lucky Clark, who owns the shop, gives me all the ingredients, and he wouldn't give me any anything that would be harmful to children!"

"How can the kids be addicted to it if it's harmless?" I asked.

"Children love candy," he said. "You should know that. I would never hurt little children. Never!"

"Did you ever wonder why Lucky wants you to make that candy?" asked Muffy.

"He said he wanted an all-natural treat for the children. Something that today's kids would like. Well, time for more punch." He asked the woman at the punch table for a refill and turned away to add more liquid from his bottle.

"You're hurting yourself, too," Louie said. I was surprised that he would say that to an adult we didn't even know.

"Well, young man," began Mr. Alexis, "I tell you I can stop any time I want. I just don't want to." His excuse sounded very childish.

"My church, across the street there," I said pointing to the old white structure, "has a program to help you if you ever do want to stop."

"I'll keep it in mind. Now if you'll excuse me." He abruptly turned away from us.

"Wait," said Abigail, grabbing his sleeve and almost causing him to spill his drink. "Can't you tell us which herbs you put in the candy, please?"

"It's a secret," he whispered, putting his finger to his lips and walking toward the raffle table.

Chapter Fifty-Five

"Well, now we know the man who makes the Benny Beans," said Mollie. "If only we knew which herbs he was using, we could find out their properties and how they might be affecting the kids who're eating them in large quantities. What'll we do now?"

"Maybe Judy could help us find out," suggested Abigail.

"Here comes my mom," I said as she approached, two elderly, elegant women in tow.

"Girls, I'd like you to meet Agnes and Mabel Weeks. We've been talking about family and guess what? They're not only our distant cousins, but also yours too, Muffy!"

"So nice to meet you girls," said Agnes, with a twinkle in her eye. "Such a lovely party, don't you agree? Mabel and I would like you all to come and visit us this afternoon so we can talk. Come over for tea at four, why don't you? We'd love to have you. Our summer residence is on Seacliff Lane, the white house overlooking Blue Oyster Pond. Do you know which one it is?"

"Yes, I do," said Mom. "We'll be there at four. Thank you."

"Now, don't forget," added Mabel. "We'll see you then. Good-bye." They tottered away, holding on to each other for balance. I wondered if they had known Captain Snow, but no, they weren't *that* old! But they knew something, I was sure of it.

As I watched them move away, I wondered what it would be like to grow old. It must be horrible to become frail and wrinkled, so I wouldn't do it. I wouldn't let it happen to me. Somehow I would stay young forever. I would always be healthy, strong, and wrinkle-free.

"I think they'll be able to help you with your mystery," Mom told us. "They have a lot of old papers and albums, they said."

"Thanks Mom!" She was really great. I was glad she had found Mabel and Agnes.

"You girls and Louie should eat now." Mom led us over to the food tables and we dug in. There were little sandwiches cut out in the shapes of hearts, diamonds, and rounds filled with cucumber slices and greenery. Some were stuffed with pink cream cheese or olives and tuna. We took carrot sticks, pickles, and fruit. Mounds of cookies and brownies stood next to the most beautiful cakes and pies I have ever seen. Mrs. McLaughlin helped us fill our plates with sandwiches. We decided we would have to come back for dessert.

We carried our food and punch to a card table under an elm. Mom wandered off to help Mrs. McLaughlin arrange a new batch of cookies that had just arrived. Louie pulled up an extra chair and we settled down to eat. The sandwiches were delicious! Then I noticed a dark shadow hovering above us and looked up to see Mrs. Pitts! She was wearing an antique gray cotton dress and a darker gray hat.

She leaned over our table and hissed, "Don't get a tummyache!" We just stared at her! What did she mean? And what was she doing here? She didn't seem like the type to enjoy an afternoon tea party. She straightened up and pulled a huge pin out of her straw hat, waved it back and forth in front of our eyes, then slowly pushed it back into her hat. She seemed pleased to see a look of complete horror on our faces. She cackled, then abruptly turned away.

"I'm following her," Mollie said, getting up from the table. "Come on, Louie." Louie obediently followed her. They swiftly took off through the crowd after Mrs. Pitts.

"Why did she do that thing with her hatpin?" asked Abigail, fearfully.

"She wanted us to remember the voodoo dolls she and her sister made of Mollie and me," I told her. "Remember they poked pins in the dolls' stomachs? She's trying to make us sick, but she can't hurt us."

"She wants us to give up, but we won't," added Muffy. "Her voodoo is powerless against us!"

"I hope you're right." Abigail didn't sound so sure. "You don't think she put anything in the food, do you? She wouldn't try to poison us, would she?"

"She can't be that crazy!" exclaimed Muffy, eating a delicate sandwich and washing it down with punch. The appearance of Mrs. Pitts had startled us, but we had work to do.

"Who shall we talk to next?" I asked, glancing over the crowds of townsfolk from another era. "Oh no! There's Karl!"

Dr. Kenton was talking to a small group of adults, looking very much like an old-time politician running for office. He wore an immaculate white linen suit and straw hat, gesturing as he spoke. His listeners seemed spellbound by whatever it was he was saying.

"I'm going to find out what he's talking about." I hopped up from the table and sneaked off to the edge of the group to listen.

"I thought the Cape needed some New Age music and ideas," he was saying. "With all this glorious beauty around us, we should attune ourselves to it, to nature, to the Creator of all, the Earth Mother."

No one in the group was surprised by the mention of the Earth Mother! They seemed to agree with what he was saying. One man spoke up and said, "I love that waterfall music. It's so soothing."

A woman commented, "It's wonderful to have someone on the radio who has some real sense. We can't just sit around while the Cape is being destroyed.

We have to save nature, for the sake of the animals, and for ourselves."

"That's right, Victoria," said Dr. Kenton. "You print it in your newspaper. We have to tell the world to stop polluting, stop building, and put an end to this out-of-control developing."

"That's right." "I agree." "We're so glad you came to our town." The crowd seemed to idolize Karl! And was that Victoria Harden, the local newspaper editor? I slipped away and back to our table.

"Karl must be running for mayor! He's preaching about the Earth Mother and save the Cape stuff. I think that woman with the curly hair is Victoria Harden from the newspaper. Karl doesn't seem to be hiding his opinions."

"But he's not telling about how he threatened us and how his friend Mrs. Pitts put a hex on us," muttered Muffy.

"Where are Mollie and Louie?" asked Abigail, finishing her last sandwich.

"They'll be back," I said, looking around and wishing they would return soon. Mrs. Pitts was dangerous. While we waited, I suggested, "Why don't we look at the old children's books?"

We cleared our plates from the table and wandered over near the book display to inspect the antique children's books with hand-watercolored illustrations. Some were so tiny and cute, their cloth covers embellished with gold. Mollie and Louie reappeared.

"Mrs. Pitts is talking to some of her friends. I'm surprised that she has any, but it seems that she's able to act completely normal, the way she used to be," Mollie told us. "We couldn't find out anything, except that she's a good actress."

As we continued to look at the books, I noticed someone coming up behind us. Karl!

"Beautiful, aren't they?" he remarked to no one in particular. We froze. What did he want? "Who are you dressed up to be?" he asked us. "The 'Little Women'?"

"No," Mollie spoke up. "We're Captain Snow," she explained, motioning toward Louie, "and I'm his wife, the black arts expert, Susanna. This is my daughter Petunia, who mysteriously disappeared because she didn't approve of my profession," she added, pointing to Abigail, who turned as white as a sheet. "And these are my friends who join me when I communicate with the dead at my séances," making a gesture to include the rest of us girls. Karl was actually shocked and just stared at us, not knowing what to say.

"Have you tried the food?" he asked, pleasantly, seeming to have recovered. "It would be a shame to get a stomachache with so many tasty dishes to sample." Wasn't that what Mrs. Pitts had said to us? "What's this?" He bent over to pick something up from the ground. When he straightened up, he was holding another voodoo doll! "Did one of you drop this?" he asked handing it to Abigail.

Abigail stared in sheer terror. She wouldn't take it and backed away. We could see why—the doll was wrapped in pink crepe paper, resembling her dress! The brown hair was the same shade as hers. Quite a few sewing pins pierced the stomach area. We all understood what that meant.

Mollie snatched the doll from Karl. "Too bad it's not a big fat man with a white suit and little glasses," she remarked as she hastily pulled the pins out and began to tear the pink paper away from the body of the little doll, revealing nail clippings sewn to the front of it. Karl gave us a strange look and quickly moved away as we huddled around the doll.

"It's me!" wailed Abigail. "They're trying to cast an evil spell on me! That woman's been in my house! What if I get sick? I don't feel so well. My tummy hurts," she groaned, clutching her stomach.

"Stop it!" yelled Muffy. "These pins have probably been in this doll for hours and you felt fine until you realized that the doll was supposed to be you. Admit it!"

"Well, you're right," said Abigail, embarrassed. We took the doll to the edge of the lawn to rip it apart. Suddenly the raffle lady was at our side.

"Give me that doll!" she demanded. "How dare you destroy an antique like that! Children today are so ignorant! So destructive! Where are your parents?"

"What are you talking about?" I asked in surprise.

"This is an antique rag doll from our display. How did you get it? One of you must have stolen it."

"I'll get my mom," I said looking around for her. There she was. Talking to Karl! I gathered up all my courage, and my skirts, and ran over to her.

"Excuse me, Mom. I need you."

Mom excused herself and came with me. Karl chuckled as we hurried off. What an evil man! How could my mom be fooled by him?

I took her aside and said, "Someone made a voodoo doll of Abigail and stuck it full of pins. Now that lady over there," I said, indicating the woman holding my friends hostage, "says that it's an antique doll from her display. It has Abigail's hair and fingernail clippings sewn on it and it's wrapped in pink paper to look like her dress! I'm sure it's not old. We found two other dolls, one at Muffy's house that looked like me and another one tied to our mooring that looked like Mollie."

"Why haven't I heard about this before?" asked Mom, frowning.

"We didn't know who did it. We didn't know what to say. We want to tear the doll apart so Abigail won't be afraid of it."

"Well, I'll see what I can do," said Mom as we walked up to the irate lady.

"Are you the mother of these hideous children?" the woman demanded, giving us the most hateful glances.

"Hello. I'm Cindy Sparrow and this is my daughter Laura and her friends," said Mom, extending her hand and acting as if the woman hadn't insulted us. "What seems to be the matter?" she asked.

"They've stolen an antique rag doll from my display and I caught them trying to destroy it!"

"May I see it?" Mom asked. The woman handed the doll to her. Mom inspected it. "Why, the doll has human hair, exactly the same color as Abigail's," she remarked, holding the doll's hair up to Abigail's to show the color comparison. "And look how finger nail clippings are sewn to the stomach of the doll. My daughter said that pins were stuck in it. Now what kind of doll could this be? Where are the pins, girls?"

I produced the pins. "These pins are brand new," said Mom, showing the woman the shiny silver pins. "And this crepe paper seems to have been taken from the side of the punch table." She pointed to the pink swag hanging from the table, one section of which was missing. "This paper isn't more than a year old at the most."

The woman was speechless. "I suppose I might be mistaken," she muttered.

"Well," my mom said kindly, "we all make mistakes." The woman turned and went back to her table, without any apology whatsoever!

"How rude!" said Mollie. "Don't grownups know how to say 'sorry'?"

"Some don't," Mom had to admit. "So where did you get this doll?"

"Your friend Karl Kenton handed it to us," I told her.

"Dr. Kenton?" She couldn't believe it.

"Yes and he told Abigail not to get a stomachache," said Louie, finally speaking up.

"That's strange," Mom said thoughtfully. "Even if we don't believe in this sort of thing, it implies that someone does. And that someone is trying to hurt you children. How on earth does it have your hair and nail clippings, Abigail?"

"Mrs. Pitts, from the Clam Bar, has been sneaking into our houses and taking things," I told her.

"Into our house?" asked Mom, her face contorting in confusion.

"Yes," I replied. "But we don't have any proof."

"I suppose that this all has something to do with your mystery and you don't want the police to be called in yet."

"That's right." I still hadn't told her about Mrs. Pitts stealing our family tree and Aunt Sparrow's diary. Hopefully we would get them back, or I would have to tell her sooner or later.

"But I can't believe that that nice Dr. Kenton has anything to do with this doll. He must have found it on the ground and picked it up, not realizing what it was. When he saw your plates piled high with all that food, it's not surprising that he mentioned a stomachache."

We gave her one of our looks so she knew that we didn't agree.

"He preaches peace, nature, and cooperation—all those good things," Mom continued. "I think you're mistaken about him."

"Look!" Louie pointed. There was Karl, hastily walking up the hill toward the rear of the library. Then Mrs. Pitts followed, bustling along in her gray gown, looking nervously back over her shoulder several times. She didn't see us watching. While we were observing her, Victoria Harden also left the group. Another man, large with black hair and moustache, huffed and puffed up the hill behind them.

"That's Mr. Blackwell, the bank president," commented Mom. "Where are they all going?"

Already Mollie had crept to the edge of the crowd and was peering behind the library and suddenly was gone. A moment later she reappeared and told us, "They disappeared!"

Chapter Fifty-Six

"Where did they go?" asked Louie.

"I don't know. They just vanished," Mollie told us.

"Well girls...and Louie," Mom began, glancing at her watch. "It's about time to visit the Weeks sisters. Let's ask your parents and grandmothers if you may come with us."

Muffy found her grandmother selling raffle tickets. Mom bought one, even though we didn't need any more antiques in our house. But the writing table would make a lovely gift, she said. She also bought a few old novels.

"Why don't you join us?" Mom asked Mrs. McLaughlin. "Agnes and Mabel Weeks have invited us for tea. I'm going to take the girls and their friend Louie. The sisters say that they're related to you."

"I did meet them years ago, when my mother was still alive," Mrs. McLaughlin replied. "I'd love to go, but I'm on the committee and have to stay. Tell them I'll call on them soon, would you please? And would you bring Muffy back to my house afterwards, when your visit is over?"

"Of course. Now Mollie, where is your family? And Abigail, we have to find your grandmother too." We found them and after their permission was granted, we walked back to the McLaughlins' to get the car. As we walked across the McLaughlins' lawn, I looked up to the Wellses' house, next door. The curtain moved!

"Look!" I exclaimed. "The Wellses' creepy son is spying on us again!"

"He reminds me of Mr. Greasy," laughed Abigail.

"Who's that?" asked Louie.

"He's an out-of-towner who haunted us in our last mystery. He had black greasy hair just like the Wellses' son," Muffy told him.

"But the Wellses' son has a red face too," I said.

"He'll have more than a red face if he doesn't let me see his parents on Monday!" exclaimed Mom. I was glad that my mom would help us solve the mystery of the Wellses.

We piled into the car and drove up to Seacliff Lane. The white house with tall columns stood overlooking Blue Oyster Pond, but it also had a view of the ocean on the other side. We pulled into the driveway. A brick path meandered through a pretty flower garden to the front door. The Weeks sisters were waiting for us, still in their elegant party dresses. They welcomed us into their home, leading us through the lovely rooms to an enclosed sunroom where a table was set for tea. We were ready for more sandwiches, as we settled ourselves in comfortable chairs.

"Your mother told us that you children are interested in Captain Elkinah Snow and his family," said Mabel as she poured lemon-scented tea into fragile porcelain cups.

"We knew Hannah Snow, Captain Snow's niece," Agnes told us, sunlight glistening on her soft white permed hair, making it resemble a halo. "She was just a child when the Snows were alive, but she knew what went on in that family. When we met her, she was an old woman by that time. She said she was an only child and she never married. Because she had no one to whom she could leave all her family papers and diaries, she left them to us. We never ever even opened her trunk. We had no reason to, but your mother tells us that you are trying to solve a mystery concerning the Snows. I think the time has come to open that trunk!"

"Hannah's name was on Howie's family tree, remember?" Mollie whispered to me. I nodded to her. Mabel continued her story.

"Hannah told us that the Captain was a mild-mannered man, but his wife Susanna was truly sinister. The Captain got in trouble with the church because he couldn't stop his wife from practicing witchcraft," Mabel continued, her eyes sparkling.

"Real witchcraft?" asked Louie.

"Yes!" answered Agnes gleefully. "Honest-to-goodness witchcraft!"

That was a strange expression! Hmmm, real witchcraft! We had read the book about green witchcraft and we had called Miss Deighton a witch, but had we really meant it? We thought Mrs. Pitts was evil enough to be a witch and that Aloma Smits acted like one, but had we really, really thought of either of them being "honest-to-goodness" witches? But they must be! Maybe they were black witches pretending to be green witches!

Mabel continued the story, "The Snows' children were good. One of the daughters, Petunia, disappeared when she was a young woman. Hannah was very close to the girl, though Hannah was much younger. Petunia was opposed to her mother's ways and Hannah always suspected that something terrible had happened to her. Petunia was never heard of again! When her parents died, the other children moved away, somewhere near Boston, and they never came back to the old house."

"Wow!" exclaimed Mollie. "So Mrs. Snow really was a witch!"

"How did she practice her witchcraft?" Mom asked.

"We don't know," answered Mabel. "Hannah never mentioned the details and we thought it would be impolite to ask."

Too bad, I thought.

"How are we related?" asked Muffy, changing the subject while wiping

206

the crumbs from her mouth with a lace-trimmed linen napkin.

"The well-known ship owner George McLaughlin had several sons. One was your great-grandfather. The oldest son was William, who married Polly. They were our parents," Mabel told her, as she sliced slivers of lemon cake. It was too complicated for me to follow. "George's youngest son was Franklin, who married Captain Sparrow's daughter, so we're one big happy family!" She passed us the pieces of cake.

"That makes us cousins, Muffy!" I exclaimed. That much I could understand.

"And we are your cousins, too," said Agnes, glancing at Mabel, whose white bun bobbed up and down as she nodded in agreement. "Isn't it wonderful?"

It was fairly amazing. I liked being related to Muffy and I didn't mind that Mabel and Agnes were my cousins too, but I wouldn't want to be related to Captain Snow—or rather, his wife! Yet I knew that my great-great-grandmother had been involved with Mrs. Snow. There was no denying it! She must have hired Mrs. Snow to communicate with Aunt Sparrow after Aunt Sparrow died in the cellar. That must have been what her strange letter was about!

What had it said? Something about "not following her path" and "bad weather to come." Mrs. Snow knew that Aunt Sparrow disapproved of her! Could the bad weather have been the feelings of the townspeople and the church against the Snows? It was all beginning to make sense now! The "white house" mentioned in Captain Sparrow's letter could have been the church! He too was afraid of being excommunicated!

Mabel poured more tea. We finished our snack and just sat there for a moment, taking in the scene of potted palms and delicate furniture from days gone by.

"I'll need some help with that trunk," said Agnes as she rose from the table. Mollie and Louie excused themselves from the table to follow her up the front staircase, while Mom cleared the table and Abigail, Muffy, and I helped Mabel wash the dishes.

"We live in Milton in the winter," Mabel told us as she sudsed up a glass plate. "We love coming to the Cape for the summer. Our old friends keep passing on, so we have to make new ones. I hope you girls will visit us even after you solve your mystery."

We assured her that we would. Then I noticed a stained-glass sun-catcher hanging in the window, over the sink. It was in the shape of a pentagram!

"What's that star in your window?" I asked Mabel.

"It's our good-luck charm," she replied.

"You don't believe in it, do you?" asked Muffy.

"Why of course we do! When you're our age, you can use all the luck you can get! We call it our lucky star," she told us. "I bought it at a little herb shop in town."

We were surprised! Muffy and Abigail looked uncomfortable. Why would

207

they believe in luck? And why would they use a pentagram? It would have seemed more normal if she had used the symbol of a four-leaf clover or a horseshoe. These two old ladies were customers of The Tomb! They couldn't be involved with the witches, could they? No, no, no!

Mollie and Louie clambered back down the stairs, carrying a small trunk between them and setting it down in the middle of the living room. Agnes slowly followed, holding onto the banister to steady herself. We joined them to open it up and see what clues it might hold for us. Mollie carefully lifted the lid. But at that exact moment, the phone rang.

Chapter Fifty-Seven

"I'll answer it!" called Mabel, as she went back to the kitchen and reached for the wall phone. Mollie's hand was resting on the lid of the trunk, ready to open it and see what secrets it contained.

Mabel soon rejoined us. "That was our handyman, Slim H., on the phone. We had asked him to come over and fix a few things around the house for us and he's on his way over now."

Was this just a coincidence? Or did the sisters change their minds about helping us?

"The children could come back another time," Mom put in.

"Why don't you all come back tomorrow afternoon?" asked Agnes. "We have tea every day at four. We'd love to have you."

They were inviting us back, that was good, but were they trying to get us to come to their house alone, without my mom? I wasn't so sure I liked this.

"That's so sweet of you," Mom replied. "But tomorrow is Sunday and we have plans. The girls have sailing school during the week, but they could call you when they're free. Kids today have such busy schedules! What do you say, girls? And Louie?"

"Thank you for the invitation," said Muffy. "We'll be by soon." I wanted to come back as soon as we could, but these old ladies were beginning to give me the creeps! And it was so disappointing to have to leave now. There was the trunk, full of information and clues regarding our mystery, but we couldn't touch it! Not now anyway. We pushed the trunk from the middle of the floor to the wall. It would have to wait. We thanked the sisters and left.

In the back seat, I could hear Abigail whispering to Mollie and Louie about the pentagram. Mollie gave me a "what's that all about?" sort of look, but I just shrugged my shoulders. Maybe it didn't mean anything. I hoped not.

First we drove back to Main Street to drop Muffy off at her grandmother's. In the car, we Girls made a plan to meet Monday morning. Louie would join us after lunch. The town was still packed with people, but the lawn of the library was almost bare. The party was over and all the goodies had been cleared away, yet a few beautifully gowned guests lingered on. Mr. McLaughlin was asleep in his wicker chair on the front porch. Mrs. McLaughlin was in the kitchen preparing dinner.

We all piled into the old-fashioned kitchen. "Here's you granddaughter," Mom announced. "It was a lovely party. I wanted to ask you though, were you able to visit Mr. and Mrs. Wells?"

"I tried," answered Mrs. McLaughlin. "But no one would come to the door. I'm sure that someone was home. I can't believe that the Wellses are so feeble that they can't even walk anymore."

"Hmmm," said Mom. "I'll find out on Monday. I'm making a house call and their son had better let me in or I'll have the police go over with me."

"Oh, I hope it doesn't come to that!" exclaimed Mrs. McLaughlin.

We said good-bye and exited. Next we drove toward the lighthouse and dropped Abigail off at her grandmother's house, then we drove Mollie and Louie to their homes. I was tired by the time Mom and I finally pulled into our driveway. I couldn't wait to get out of that dress and change into something more comfortable. We could smell something yummy. Dad was at the kitchen stove preparing the fish he had caught for our dinner—a giant bluefish!

"Don't you look lovely!" he exclaimed, as we entered the kitchen. I didn't feel lovely! Only hot, sticky, and tired!

"Thanks," I said anyway.

"By the way, there's a message for you on the answering machine. I can't figure it out. Maybe you can."

I ran into the sitting room and switched on the playback button of the machine. I heard Cooky's voice, "This is Cooky. I got news for you. Mrs. Pitts showed up for work today. I was kinda surprised. My wife was already there to take her place. Then a big guy with glasses came looking for her. They talked a while. I told my wife to listen in, 'cause I've just about had enough of Pitts and her antics.

"Well, my wife, she busied herself, keeping close to them. They talked in low voices, but my wife hears them say the 'usual crowd' is meeting at their 'usual place' Wednesday. Then the man said something about a *sacrifice* being ready. That didn't sound so good. So I thought I ought to call you."

"*Sacrifice*?" asked Mom from the door, not believing her ears. I didn't answer. I was pretty sure that the sacrifice would be the coyote Karl had gotten from the coyote shooter on Womponoy. I still hoped it wasn't my coyote they were planning to use! Whatever animal it was, we had to stop them! I had to tell the Girls and Louie!

The rapid-fire message continued, "So Mrs. Pitts says she's sick and goes off as if I didn't have a business to run. I wish she'd be like her old self 'cause the way she is now, I'd like to fire her!"

"What's going on?" Mom asked. "Is this about the woman who tried to run you off the road and is sneaking into our house?"

"Yes," I told her. "She's acting strange, so we're keeping an eye on her."

"You have to let us know if you think she's really dangerous, but I suspect that you've been annoying her."

I started to object, but decided to let it drop. Mrs. Pitts was dangerous and so were her friends. We would watch out for them. But it was better if Mom wasn't worried about us. I knew that Mom didn't really believe that Mrs. Pitts had been in our house. If she did, she would have called the police, so I just let it go. We didn't need the police involved. Not yet.

Mom and I joined Dad in the kitchen and she told him about the party and our visit to the Weeks sisters.

"I'm sorry I missed all the fun," said Dad with a smile. We knew he wasn't sorry at all! He'd had too much fun catching our dinner!

"I've got to get out of this dress!" I announced, feeling so uncomfortable I couldn't stand it any longer. I trundled up the stairs.

The lawn party had been an experience, but that old style of dressing wasn't for me! Thankfully I live in the days of shorts and T-shirts! I peeled off the dress and headed for the shower. After I was all nice and clean, I put on my jamies. Finally I felt normal again!

Dad was calling me for dinner. Mom had also showered and changed. We arrived in the kitchen at the same time. The bluefish was delicious!

"I'm really tired," I said as we cleaned up the table and I began to wash the dishes. "I think I'll go to bed early."

"Good idea," said Mom. "I think I'll do the same thing. Remember Grammy and Grandpa are coming to church with us tomorrow. We should get there a little early."

I went up to bed and called Mollie to tell her about the sacrifice on Wednesday. She promised to call Abigail, Muffy, and Louie. Soon I heard my parents climbing the front staircase to go to bed also. My dad was in the habit of not staying up late, since he has to go to work so early. It wasn't long before I heard my parents snoring. Yes, my mom sometimes snores too. I smelled Grammy's lavender under my pillow and in no time I was probably snoring myself!

Chapter Fifty-Eight

Sunday was hot. Bright sun streamed into my little bedroom and it was stuffy, though all the windows were wide open. I smelled bacon and coffee. Yum for the bacon. Yuck for the coffee. I clambered down the stairs. Mom and Dad were already seated at the table.

"You remember Grammy and Grampa are meeting us at church today, don't you?" asked Dad.

"Sure! I'm excited."

We took our time eating. Dad mentioned that he'd like me to take him for a sail around the harbor, before summer was over. He wanted to see how well I'd learned to sail since he'd fixed up the Catabout for me. Maybe after lunch, I told him. Mom reminded Dad that she wanted to go over to Oceanside in the afternoon to see a famous herb garden. She said that she had heard it was so beautiful, but I hoped that was all! It was O.K. if she was interested in herbs for cooking or medicine, but not magic potions!

Dad didn't seem very excited about the plan, but it would give them some time to be alone together. I didn't want to go anyway. I could get together with Muffy, even though we didn't usually see each other on Sundays. I knew that Abigail would be busy with her cousins and Mollie's father was still in town. But no way were my parents going to leave me home alone!

We got ready for church and arrived a little before ten-thirty. We waited on the front lawn of the church for Grammy and Grandpa to arrive. At ten-thirty sharp, we saw them pulling into the parking lot. Soon they were coming up the walkway. It was a special day for my family and I felt very proud and happy.

Reverend Maxon stood at the door greeting the parishioners. When he saw my family, he gave me a guilty look, but smiled at my parents and heartily shook my grandparents' hands. We found a pew not too close and not too far back. My grandparents seemed comfortable with the choice. The organ was playing a tune my grandmother knew. She hummed along and swayed a little to the music.

After the choir sang, we all joined in for a few hymns. Then Reverend Maxon made the announcements. All the windows were open and big fans were buzzing away, blowing the air through the church, in hopes of keeping us cool. When it was time for the offering, I looked around for Mr. Mullins, who usually passed one of the plates, but I didn't see him anywhere. I wondered where he could be.

The sermon began. Reverend Maxon preached about the need for more affordable housing for the poor families in town, the evils of war, and the AIDS epidemic in Africa. I usually went to Sunday school with the other kids my age, but today I was allowed to sit in church because my grandparents were there. I really couldn't understand what point the minister was making. He mentioned some very real problems, but he didn't offer any solutions or say anything about God.

After the choir sang again, it was time to leave. My grandparents seemed pleased. I know I was bored and glad it was over! We made our way down the aisle to the back of the church, Mom and Dad introducing my grandparents to their friends along the way. When we reached the door, Reverend Maxon was there shaking hands and asking everyone how they were. He was good at that. When we reached him, he did his usual, but I seemed to make him nervous.

"Where's Mr. Mullins?" I asked.

"He's not feeling well. Left a message on the church answering machine last night. How did you enjoy the sermon?" he asked my grandparents.

"Very contemporary," my grandfather tactfully answered.

"Why don't you come over for dinner at our house?" asked Grammy. "It's all prepared. All I have to do is heat it up. I make a tasty chicken stew."

The reverend couldn't resist a home-cooked meal and readily agreed to come. He would ride over with my grandparents and we would follow in our car. The other deacons said they would close up the church and encouraged the minister to go along with us. We drove to Muddy River to my grandparents' house on the bluff overlooking the Sound.

It was still hot, but a nice breeze was blowing off the water, which made it much cooler than the church. We gave Reverend Maxon a guided tour of the gardens and the old house. He was very interested in everything. He seemed to like my grandparents and they liked him. I thought they would have been more critical of his sermon, but I was glad they weren't. They didn't even mention the hard pews or the stuffy air.

As we sat down to dinner, Grandpa asked the minister to say a blessing. As we began to eat, Grammy asked, "You know our little granddaughter has a mystery, don't you?"

The minister cautiously answered, "Yes."

"Did she ask you if she could look at the old church records? We suggested that they might have some clues for her and her friends."

"One of our deacons, Mr. Mullins, put the records aside for us, but we can't seem to find exactly where he put them," Reverend Maxon explained between mouthfuls of Grammy's stew and cranberry bread. "He works for the water department so he's hard to reach. And now he's out sick. But as soon as he's back to the church, I'm sure we'll be able to locate the records and then Laura can get to work," he added encouragingly. He was still convinced that Mr. Mullins was an honest man. Mom and Dad exchanged glances. It must have sounded suspicious to them, but they didn't say a word.

"What do you know about witches?" asked Grandpa, passing a serving bowl heaped with vegetables. The minister almost dropped the dish. I was surprised too. Why was he asking about witches?

"Why, I don't think about them at all," he answered nervously. "We know there is no such thing as a witch, so I don't bother myself with even thinking about them." He gave a nervous laugh.

"Didn't Laura tell you about that haunted house?" asked Grammy, passing the cranberry bread around again.

"She did..."

"It is haunted, isn't it?" asked Grandpa.

"It's the same evil powers that do the haunting and witching, don't you think?" asked Grammy.

"I suppose..."

"Where is God in all of this?" Grandpa blurted out.

"God is good. We know that. He's not concerned with these types of problems."

"How could that be?" asked Grammy. "God not concerned with evil? What kind of God do you have, young man?"

Reverend Maxon hung his head and sighed. All eyes were upon him. "Maybe that's my problem," he confessed. "Maybe I don't really know God if I think he's not concerned."

"Could be God cares a lot more than you think, but you've been going by what you've been taught at Bible school, not what really is," said Grandpa. Mom and Dad listened as Grandpa continued. "I think you ought to ask God what's what and stop thinking you have all the answers, when you can see plain and clear that you don't."

"You're right," said the minister, shaking his head and heaving another sigh.

"We don't know God so well ourselves, so maybe we could all learn about him together," suggested Grandma.

"You could start by going back to the Bible," I added. "That's what we do in Sunday school."

"Good idea!" said Reverend Maxon, cheering up a little. "I think this is the change I've been needing. I've felt very angry about all problems and injustices in the world, as if I needed to come up with solutions to them all by myself. Of course I've never been able to do that, so I just go on feeling frustrated. I never thought of asking God about any of it! I'll take your advice. Thank you."

It was time to clear the table and for Grammy to serve her famous apricot sponge. Later, we helped Grammy clean up and wash the dishes. After we finished, we walked out to her garden. She picked bunches of flowers and herbs for the minister and us for potpourris, cooking, and to help us sleep better.

I kissed Grammy and Grandpa good-bye and we got into the car. Reverend Maxon and I sat in back.

"What do you know about zombies?" I asked him as quietly as I could.

"Nothing," was all he said. I guess he didn't want to deal with the new twist in our mystery. I let it go. If he tried to help us, it might turn out worse for him than the exorcism had.

We dropped the minister off at the church. He promised to pray about his relationship with God. Hopefully next week's sermon would be more interesting.

One of the deacons came out of the church and greeted us.

"Fabulous offering today, Reverend!" he exclaimed. "By far, the biggest we've had all summer!"

"I didn't notice a bigger crowd than usual," said the minister.

"No. I counted a few less. I've left everything in order. See you at the board meeting."

Reverend Maxon just stood there. My parents said good-bye to him and headed for the car. I hesitated. Something was wrong.

"Jerry Mullins always counts the money," mumbled the minister. His gaze met mine. "Maybe you're right about Mullins. It seems to be too much of a coincidence, that the one Sunday he's not here, we have the biggest offering of the season."

I didn't know what to say, but I was glad that my minister was willing to suspect Mr. Mullins. Maybe he wasn't guilty, but maybe he was. Now that the minister was suspicious, he would be looking for evidence. Not ignoring it, as he had been. I ran to the car but didn't mention it to my parents. Time would tell if Mr. Mullins was one of them or not.

Back at home, I scrambled upstairs to change into my shorts and T-shirt. I could hear Dad calling me. When I got downstairs again he asked if I would like to take him for a sail. It was a perfect day and we had time. Sure I would! Mom wanted to stay home to read one of the novels she had bought at the library yesterday.

"Don't forget the herb garden in Oceanside when you get back," she called out as we exited the back door.

"I won't," Dad responded.

Dad and I stopped by the barn to get the oars and headed for the beach. It was a gorgeous day, hot, but with a breeze. I liked that. We flipped the dinghy over and dragged it into the water's edge. Dad rowed out to the Catabout. We hoisted up the sails and took off. I was at helm and Dad just relaxed, stretched out over the wooden floorboards.

We tacked in and out of all the moored boats. One of our starboard tacks brought us near Dr. Perhonen's yacht. As we sailed into the channel, I looked over my shoulder to see Dr. Perhonen on the deck of the yacht with Karl Kenton! My heart sank. If they were friends, did that mean that Dr. Perhonen had taken my boat on purpose, instead of rescuing it? Was it their plan that I would find my boat during sailing class and then notice the voodoo doll when I returned my Catabout to its mooring?

"Look Dad! There's Dr. Kenton! That other man is Dr. Perhonen. He rescued my boat the other day when it drifted away from its mooring."

"That was very good of him, but you have to be more careful with your boat," Dad said. "You don't want it to drift out to sea!"

I didn't reply. I was now definitely suspicious of Dr. Perhonen. I tacked again, sailing near the old lighthouse. I could see a few cars parked beside the lightkeeper's house. One seemed to be the color of Mrs. Pitts's car, but I couldn't recognize any of the others. I wondered who was there and what they were doing. Was it the Earth Mother group? If it was, then why wasn't Karl there too?

"You wanted to know more about Dr. Kenton," said Dad. "I think I'll have a talk with the Mitchells. They respect him a great deal. I'll try to find out how much they really know about him."

"Thanks, Dad."

"I'll stop by the marina when we get home."

I asked if I could go with him. He said "yes" so I cut our sail short and headed for my mooring.

Chapter Fifty-Nine

Our sail had been brief. We tied my boat up to the mooring, furled the sails, and rowed back to shore. Dad turned the dinghy over near the boathouse and I followed him as he carried the oars up to the barn. I hopped into his truck, while he leaned in the back door and told Mom that we would be stopping by the marina to talk to the Mitchells.

At the marina, we found a teenage boy at the counter of the store. He informed us that the Mitchells had taken the day off. There was nothing we could do about that.

"That's odd!" said Dad. "They're always here on the weekends. I suppose I'll have to talk to them another time. Let's get home. I promised your mom I'd take her over to see that herb garden. Looks like a storm coming up." He pointed to the north where the sky had become dark.

When we got home, Mom was ready and came out of the house to meet us.

"Why don't you invite a friend over?" she suggested.

"I'll give Muffy a call," I said as I ran inside to telephone. But Muffy's mom said she was at her aunt's house. She'd be home soon and would call. What should I do? I didn't want my parents to leave. But I guess I didn't have to worry about Mrs. Pitts and Karl—they were accounted for. And they would have no way of knowing that my parents were planning to drive to Oceanside. I would be O.K. until Muffy came over, wouldn't I?

"Muffy will be over later," I called to my parents from the back door.

"We'll have leftovers tonight," Mom called back, as she hoisted herself into Dad's truck, "so don't worry about dinner. I'll heat them up when we get home."

I hated to see them leave, but what could I do? Mom must have noticed the look on my face.

"We won't be long," she called from the truck window. "We should be home in a couple of hours, before dark."

I watched my dad's truck disappear down the drive. I thought I should do something to keep me outdoors where I would be safe. I didn't want to be in my house all alone. From the patio, I could still hear the phone ring when Muffy called me back. I decided to work on my bicycle, to grease the wheels and chain. It's something I do every spring, but I hadn't done it this past spring. I kept putting it off. Now seemed to be a good time to do it. I took my bike out of the barn.

I reentered the barn to get a can of oil. There was one sitting on top of my dad's workbench. I grabbed a cotton rag as well. You can be sure I propped the barn door open. Out on the patio, I flipped my bike over and removed the chain. My dad recommended soaking it in a can of kerosene to remove all the dirt, but I wasn't going that far. I did oil the chain and all the gears.

I kept waiting for Muffy to call, but the phone didn't ring. Clouds had covered the sun and the breeze had picked up a little. I began to oil the wheels and clean the spokes with the rag. As I wiped down my bike, I noticed that the air had changed. It felt cooler. The temperature had dropped quite a bit.

When I finished up, great drops of rain began to splatter on the patio where I was working! Rain? How could that be? I quickly pushed my bike into the barn, put away the oil, and left the rag on Dad's workbench. I closed the barn door and ran to the house. I locked the back door, then worked my way around the house, closing and locking all the windows and the front door, not forgetting the cellar door, just in case...

Why didn't Muffy call? Of course she couldn't come over now, but I wouldn't mind having someone to talk to in this squall. The wind began to whip and the rain was coming down in sheets! I hoped that my boat would be all right and hold to her mooring. Hopefully my parents were already in Oceanside and not on the road. It was just a summer storm. It would be over soon, I was sure. But it wasn't.

The storm continued. The sky was now black, as dark as night! The wind howled, making our old house shake and shudder! I reached for the phone. I would call Muffy. The line was dead! The wind must have blown the phone lines down. Or had they been cut? I didn't want to think about that being a possibility!

The storm had the force of a hurricane! Rain was falling in buckets. I couldn't believe it! It wasn't even August when the hurricanes usually come, if they do at all. I was afraid. I was all alone and I wasn't able to call anyone for help! What would I do?

I decided to turn on some lights rather than stand in the dark. But the lights were out too! I panicked! Had someone cut the power lines as well? Or had all the lines come down together? Laura, I said to myself, calm down. Get a hold of yourself. Light a candle. You'll be all right. Mom and Dad will be home soon.

I took my own advice and entered the sitting room to get a candle. I glanced out to the harbor and saw only darkness. Suddenly, a bolt of lightning shot across the sky, causing me to jump as it gave an earsplitting crackle and rumble. The lighting gave me a view of the harbor, full of boats bobbing and tugging at their moorings—and of a tall figure lurching up from the beach and across the lawn! The zombie!

No! It couldn't be! I shakily took a brass candleholder from the mantle and lit the candle, then made sure that the front door was locked. Next I entered the kitchen. As I moved toward the back door, another bolt of lightning crackled across the sky, revealing the zombie moving past the kitchen window! My heart pounded as I gasped for breath. It was coming to my back door! I knew it! My courage failed. I should go to the door and double-check to make sure I had locked it. I know I had, but I couldn't move. That was all right. The zombie couldn't get in. I was safe, wasn't I?

The back door began to rattle! He was trying to get in! What would he do to me? Who had sent him? Was it Aloma Smits? Where were my parents? Why didn't they come home? There was no one to help me! I tried to scream. My mouth opened, but no sound came out! I just stood there frozen as the zombie violently rattled the door!

"Help me!" came a voice. Not a man's voice, but a woman's, sounding truly desperate! "Please, Laura Sparrow! Help me! Let me in!"

She knew my name! It was Mrs. Pitts, trying to trick me. I couldn't trust her. She was truly evil. But I didn't have to worry. She couldn't get in, I thought, until I heard the sound of the screen being ripped out of the door frame! And the glass of the back door shattering! I looked in horror as a bony hand reached through the broken window and unlocked the door! The tall gaunt figure of a woman lunged toward me, drenched by the rain, glistening in the flickering candlelight!

Run! I told myself. I can easily hide. It was my house. I can escape her. Hide where she'll never find me. But I stood still, watching in terror as the woman moved toward me, her piercing eyes glittering in fear! Who was she?

Then I recognized her! It was Mrs. Pitts's sister! Her wet, stringy gray hair was plastered to her haggard face. Her wild eyes bore into mine. Leaning forward, she grabbed my arms. Her fingers were like talons gripping my arms, making them hurt! My silence ended as I let out the loudest longest shriek I had ever made, but no one heard me. The raging storm was louder. I dropped the candle. It sputtered and went out at my feet. Total darkness surrounded us.

I closed my eyes and continued to scream. I could feel her looming over me. I stopped screaming and could hear the water dripping from her dress onto the linoleum floor. I opened my eyes. I couldn't see her and in the dark my heart pounded so loudly that I thought it would burst. I had to focus. Was she going to try to hurt me? Was she dangerous?

"Help me! Laura Sparrow, help me!" she pleaded. I wanted to cry, but the tears wouldn't come. My heart continued to pound. Where were my parents? I felt so frightened. What should I do? What *could* I do?

"Please!" she pleaded again.

"I'll light the candle." My voice was feeble. I waited for her to release my arms. She slowly unclenched her hands and I bent down to pick up the candle. I set it on the table. I was still holding the matches in my other hand, but I was so unsteady that it took several tries before I could light the wick.

"Let's sit down," I said, shakily. She obeyed. Feeling a little more confident when she took a seat, I asked, "Are you Mrs. Pitts's sister?" I knew that she was, but I had to say something. I wondered why she, the lady who had come after us with a shotgun, the mastermind of the Earth Mother group, was at my house in the middle of a storm asking me for help.

"I would like to help you," I told her. "What do you want me to do?"

"I'm Sally. My sister Gracie is bad. Her friends are bad. They want to hurt you. They want to hurt your friends. You must help."

"How can I help you? What do you want me to do?" I asked again.

Suddenly her eyes became distant, glassy. She abruptly stood, bumping the table and almost upsetting the candle. Knocking the chair over, she turned and lurched toward the back door!

"Wait! Tell me what you want. How can I help you?" I grabbed the candle from the table and followed her, but she charged out the back door and disappeared into the storm! She hadn't told me anything! I closed the door and locked it, but the cold wind blew in through the broken window. I put the candle down on the counter, got the dustpan and brush from the broom closet, and swept up the glass the best I could.

I took my sweatshirt from a hook on the mud room wall and sat back down at the table. I shivered as I thought about what had just happened. That glassy look in her eyes reminded me of something...I know! It was the way Mrs. Pitts had looked when she came after me in the field, with my bicycle over her head! She had acted so strange, as if she couldn't hear me. She had suddenly turned and left, just as her sister had done. Was she hypnotized? If Sally were also hypnotized, then who was controlling her? Could it be Karl?

I hoped my parents would get home soon! Just then I saw headlights coming up the driveway! Dad parked the truck and he and Mom raced through the rain toward the house. The storm had let up a little. I met them at the back door.

"Laura!" Dad exclaimed. "What happened to the door? Is the power out?"

"It got broken in the storm," I said, not wanting to tell them about Sally. "The power is out. The phone lines must be down too because the phone is dead."

I wished that the phone were working so I could call the Girls and tell them what had just happened, but I would have to wait until tomorrow.

"I'll fix this window and screen tomorrow," said Dad. "For now I'll staple a plastic bag over it." Which he did.

"You're right," said Mom to me, after trying a light switch. "There's no power. We saw a few trees down on our way back home. The power lines must be down somewhere. We didn't get very far on our trip. As soon as we realized there was going to be a storm, we turned back. It was so sudden!"

I hugged Mom. "I'm glad you got home safely! Next time, don't go out in a storm like this! I was so frightened!"

"We had no idea it would be so bad," said Mom. "It's letting up now. I'll light a nice fire and some more candles. We can cook pioneer style in the fireplace."

That would have sounded like fun, if I hadn't been recently frightened almost out of my wits! But I helped take the food out of the fridge and tried to calm down. Dad lit a bunch of candles too and helped built the fire. We heated up leftover bluefish in the frying pan and ate potatoes and a green salad. We ended our meal with fresh fruit for dessert.

The wind howled a little more and rain beat against the windowpanes as we washed the dishes by candlelight, but I was sure that the storm was dying. Mom suggested that we go to bed early again. I didn't mind.

"Would you like to sleep in our room tonight?" Dad asked.

"I'll be O.K. Maybe I could keep a light burning in my room?"

"I'll get you a storm lantern," he said, taking a candle into the dining room. He came back with an old-fashioned lantern. "This will burn all night long and won't cause a fire," he told me as he lit the wick. We all climbed the back stairs together and Dad set the lantern down on my bedside table after removing a pile of junk to the floor. Mom tucked me in and they both gave me a good-night kiss. I felt safe and secure now that they were home. The storm was subsiding. I would be able to sleep.

As I lay in bed, I couldn't help but shiver as thoughts of Sally swept through my mind. She had really frightened me. I wondered how she had found me. How could I help her? She hadn't told me anything. What she said was what we had already suspected. It was obvious that her sister and Karl were "bad" and tying to hurt us. Though I could see that she was desperate, I couldn't help but wonder if Karl had sent her to trick me, to confuse me even more. I couldn't decide what was true. While I pondered this, I was swept away by the sweet smell of Grammy's fresh lavender to the land of Nod.

Chapter Sixty

Monday morning was overcast. I looked out my window to see that the harbor was choppy. My Catabout bounced on the waves. I was glad to see she was safe. The yard was scattered with leaves and branches. What a storm! And what a scary encounter with Sally!

When I came down for breakfast, I found that my dad had already repaired the screen and the glass on the back door and had left for work. He was incredible! I ran out and picked up the twigs littering the yard. Then it seemed as if the storm had never occurred, except for the memory of Sally

I remembered that Mom planned to visit the Wellses today. I reminded her to call me as soon as she saw them. She promised she would.

"We might help Miss Deighton with her weeding again," I told her. She was impressed that we were helping her patient, not realizing that we hadn't done much work and that we mainly wanted information from her!

I was sure glad to see Mollie riding up the driveway as Mom was leaving the house. That was a relief! I didn't think I could bear being home alone even for a minute after last night! They greeted each other as Mom hopped in her car and drove away.

"Wait 'til you hear what happened to me!" I exclaimed as Mollie sat down at the kitchen table. I told her the story of Sally's visit in the storm.

"Wow! That's the scariest thing I've ever heard! How does she want you to help her? I thought she was the leader of the whole group."

"I was thinking that maybe she was sent by Karl to confuse us."

"That could be. The way she wandered away was the way Mrs. Pitts acted in your story about your bicycle in the field, like a...a...zombie?"

"It wasn't 'a story'!" I told her. "It really happened. But maybe someone is making her into a zombie! Maybe Aloma Smits! She could be their leader! And she has them all under her control!"

"I suspect Karl," Mollie stated.

We were about to discuss it further when Muffy and Abigail arrived. We told them what had happened.

"Yipes!" exclaimed Abigail. "That's too creepy!"

"But what are you going to do about Sally?" asked Muffy. "What if she really does need our help? Maybe her sister forced her into the group and now she wants out."

"That's not what Cooky said," Mollie reminded us. "Remember he said Mrs. Pitts was fine until Sally showed up. I think she's trying to trick you, Laura."

"I don't know," I sighed. "I don't know what to believe anymore."

"What are we going to do about the sacrifice?" asked Muffy.

"We'll go to Captain Snow's on Wednesday night," said Mollie. "We can tell the animal control officer to meet us there and he can catch those crazy people with the coyote. That would be a good start."

"Well, they can't get away with this!" threatened Abigail, suddenly becoming bold. "They think we're just little girls! They'll find out who they're dealing with—the Eel Grass Girls!"

"Yeah," Mollie chimed in. "The Eel Grass Girls and Louie to the rescue!" We laughed and it made me feel good to be surrounded by my friends, laughing. But the reality of the situation soon overtook my mind again. We had a plan to save the coyote, but we still didn't know who was controlling Mrs. Pitts and her sister. We thought it could be Aloma Smits. Then I told the Girls about the sail I took with my dad.

"We saw Karl with Dr. Perhonen on his boat."

"Then he must be one of them," remarked Muffy.

"It would seem so," I agreed. "He probably took my boat so that we would find the voodoo doll when we sailed back to my mooring. We saw a bunch of cars out at the old lighthouse. I think I saw Mrs. Pitts's car. But Karl wasn't with them. He was on the yacht, so it seems strange that they would have a meeting without him. Then Dad and I went to the marina to find out about Karl, but Dad's friends, the Mitchells, weren't there."

"Why are they trying to hurt us with their spells?" asked Abigail.

"They want us to stay away from Captain Snow's," I said. "But we won't! We'll be there on Wednesday, but what shall we do in the meantime?"

"We might as well go weed," Muffy suggested.

"Do you think we can get any more information from Miss Deighton? I hope it's not a waste of time," said Abigail.

"What do you suggest we should do instead?" asked Mollie, rather piqued.

"Let's go," I sighed. I couldn't think of anything else. Then I had an idea. "What about going over to the lighthouse? Maybe Sally would talk to us."

"The water's too rough," observed Abigail, looking past us through the sitting room window to the harbor. "Maybe we should wait. It's still windy and it might rain again."

"To Miss Deighton's now. Then sail later, if the wind dies down," said Muffy.

"I'm not afraid of the wind," I boasted, feeling brave again.

"If we sail, it should be after we meet Louie," advised Mollie.

It was settled. We rode over to Miss Deighton's. Her house seemed awfully quiet for some reason. No one responded to our knock on the purple door and our "Anybody home?" We tried the door. It was unlocked, so we entered.

The house was quiet, too quiet. We crept toward the kitchen where we always found her, but when we got there we saw her rocking chair overturned on the floor! Miss Deighton's cane lay beside it! Papers and pencils from her little table were scattered all over the floor! She must have fallen, but where was she now?

"What happened?" Abigail asked, worriedly glancing around. "Where's Miss Deighton? Where did she go?"

We searched the house. No one was there! Could someone have kidnapped her? But who? We were terrified! Who could have done this and why? Then I heard something.

"Did you hear that?" I asked. Muffy looked at me blankly and shook her head. I was sure I had heard something, but I didn't know what the sound was or where it had come from. I looked around, then opened the screen door leading to the garden. Beyond the flowers and winding pathway lay a toolshed.

"Come on!" I called to the Girls, as I dashed out the door and hurried down the path to the shed. The Girls followed. All the scents of herbs and flowers filled the air, stirred up by the wind blowing in from the harbor.

When we got to the shed, I noticed that it was locked with a padlock, the same kind that had been used to lock us into my barn! I took a garden shovel that was leaning against the shed and gave the lock such a hard whack that the hasp broke off the door. I was getting good at this! I pulled the door open and gasped. Miss Deighton, bound and gagged, was lying on the dirty wooden floor! She lay very still!

"Miss Deighton!" cried Abigail, rushing into the shed, her eyes brimming with tears. "Oh no! She isn't...is she?" Abigail didn't want to say the word. Muffy followed us into the shed and felt Miss Deighton face and hands. They were ice cold. She took the gag off her mouth and untied her hands and feet.

"How did you hear her?" asked Mollie. "She's not even moving! She couldn't have made a sound."

"I don't know," I muttered. "I can't explain it. Maybe I just felt that she was here."

I was about to ask Mollie to go back to the house to call 911 when Miss Deighton moaned and began to stir. Her eyelids fluttered, then flew open with a look of terror contorting her face. She wildly struggled to sit up, but in a moment she recognized us and lay still again.

"Oh, it's you!" she sighed, closing her eyes for a moment. When she opened them again, she noticed that Abigail was crying.

"Stop crying!" she barked. "Nothing's broken." She struggled to sit up again, so we helped her into a sitting position.

"Should we call an ambulance?" asked Abigail, in between sobs. "And the police?"

"No, no! Don't do that!" She seemed annoyed or afraid. I couldn't tell which. "I don't want to involve them!" she said, arching her back and moving her limbs, one by one. "I need my cane. Go get it for me, one of you." She was sure being awfully mean and bossy for someone who had just been rescued!

I ran to the house and quickly returned with the cane. We helped support Miss Deighton as she stood up. With the aid of her cane, she was able to step down from the shed and hobble through the garden to her house. Abigail ran ahead and uprighted the rocker. We helped Miss Deighton settle into it.

"I ought to lose some weight," she muttered as she arched her back again. "As soon as I recover, I'm going on a diet, possibly."

We stood waiting for her to give us an explanation of what had happened to her. She quickly rocked back and forth, looking straight ahead. Finally she looked up at our waiting faces and spoke.

"Someone is trying to get rid of me, it seems. Don't know who it is. Can you imagine, they wore ski masks?" she asked, forcing a laugh. "Ski masks, on the Cape in the summer! And black sweatsuits! They must have been sweating like pigs, whoever they were. They didn't speak. One of them was quite large and wore glasses under his mask. I don't know who he was, but the other man could have been someone I know." She paused, rubbing her elbows and feeling her ribs. The big man sounded to me like Karl, but who was the other man? And why were they after Miss Deighton? She was one of them, wasn't she?

"Do you know a doctor named Karl Kenton?" I asked her, wondering how to get information from her, but without letting her know too much of what we knew. We couldn't trust her, not yet.

"From the radio station?" she asked.

"Yes, he has a New Age station that just started up."

"Well, what about him?"

"Your description of the man with the glasses sounds like him."

"But why would he do this to me? I've never even met him. I heard he moved to town about the same time I had my operation." She seemed to be considering something. Then she blurted out, "That's ridiculous! I've listened to his radio station. He's on our side. He loves the Earth Mother! You children have your heads full of nonsense!"

"Who do you think the other man was?" asked Mollie.

"I'm not sure...I mean I don't know! But why are you here? You just happened to drop by?"

"We didn't get to do any weeding the last time we were here," explained Muffy. "We just wanted to finish our work."

"Who would want to hurt you?" I asked, suspecting that Miss Deighton might know who the other man was. "There must be someone you suspect."

"I don't know anyone who would want to hurt me," she snapped. "I have my own group of friends, the ones whose cars you saw parked here the other night. We meet on a regular basis to celebrate the Earth Mother." She paused, considering something, then went on.

"Those men who threw me in the toolshed are dangerous! I don't know why they came after me, but with them lurking around, we must all be careful. Get me that book from the counter," she said to Mollie, pointing to a big book covered with shedding leather.

"What's this?" asked Mollie, picking up the book and handing it to her.

"It's an 'herbal,' a book about herbs and their uses," explained Miss Deighton as she opened it up. It was ancient and looked like a witch's handbook to me! We crowded around Miss Deighton. As she flipped through the pages, I could see that it was full of spells and recipes for magic potions!

"We need a basic recipe for warding off evil. It will keep you girls safe." She thumbed through the pages. "Here it is." Firmly implanted in her rocker, she directed us to the kitchen counter where we found measuring spoons and a pottery bowl. She told us which jars of herbs to get, taking a spoonful of this and a pinch of that until we had concocted a pile of seasonings filling the bowl. We mixed them well with an old wooden spoon. Then she told us to each take a handful of the mixture and put it in our pockets, which we dutifully did. Then she asked us to bring her the leftovers, which she stuck into both pockets of her voluminous purple skirt.

"Thank you Miss Deighton, but we have to go now," I said, noticing the clock on her wall. We had to eat lunch and meet Louie. "But what about you? Will you be safe here?"

"I'll call my neighbor Betty. Hand me the phone." Abigail gave the phone to Miss Deighton, who telephoned her friend. She would be right over, she promised. We waited until she arrived. Betty lived on Pine Street, so she was there within minutes. She barged right in and introduced herself. She was the same type as Miss Deighton, an aging Hippie Flower Child, and we were sure Miss Deighton would be safe with her. Betty began preparing lunch, not at all aware of what had happened to Miss Deighton that morning!

"I'll be fine. They'll think I'm still in the shed," Miss Deighton said to us in a low voice while Betty put the tea kettle on the stove. "Come back soon. The weeds are taking over my garden!"

As we said good-bye, she thanked us. I almost thought she wouldn't. I couldn't understand why my mom liked her so much. She was so weird and she was a witch! Probably Betty was, too. We left by the purple door. Once outside, we talked as we pushed our bikes through the deep sand in her driveway.

"Why is Karl after Miss Deighton?" asked Abigail.

"She must not be part of his group," said Mollie. "There must be two Earth Mother groups."

"I wonder if it's because of us," said Muffy, stopping in her tracks as she realized that that must be the reason. "One of them must have seen us coming over here! It's our fault!"

"You really think so?" asked Abigail.

"What else could it be?" asked Mollie. "If Miss Deighton is one of them, Karl should know. He must think that she's told us something, but what?"

"She said she doesn't know Karl," I protested. "It was the other man she recognized."

"If Karl came to town when Miss Deighton had her operation, maybe he took over the group and that's why they don't know each other," speculated Muffy.'

"But she said that her group was here the other night," said Abigail. "Mollie must be right, there are two groups. Maybe they have one member in common and he's the one she recognized!"

"Yes!" exclaimed Muffy. "And he's the one who told Karl about us and Karl wanted to be sure that Miss Deighton wouldn't give us any more information!"

"Then we'd better be more careful," I warned my friends. "If they could do this to Miss Deighton, what would they do to us?"

Muffy took the herbs out of her pocket and began to drop them in the driveway.

"Not 'til we're on the street!" I said, looking back over my shoulder. Then realized that Miss Deighton would still be sitting in her rocking chair and wouldn't be able to see us anyway.

We rode our bikes to the end of the driveway and onto Pine Street, where we dumped the herbs in a clump of bird berry bushes beside the road. We didn't believe in their power to keep us safe. Yet we knew that we were in danger.

Chapter Sixty-One

We rode to my house and parked our bikes against the barn. First I checked the answering machine. There was a message from Mom. She had visited the Wellses and said they were fine. The son was odd, but his old parents seemed to be in good health. She would go back and check on them again in a few days, she said. We were glad to hear some good news.

In the kitchen we prepared peanut butter and Fluff sandwiches. Abigail got the milk from the fridge. Muffy helped make the sandwiches and Mollie served us fruit salad. We took everything out onto the patio to eat. The top of the picnic table was cracked from where it had blown over during last night's storm. It was still a little windy and overcast, but the patio was sheltered from the breeze by the house and it was warm enough to enjoy the outdoors.

"We aren't really going to go over to the lighthouse, are we?" asked Abigail, looking nervously out to the harbor.

"Do you have a better idea?" asked Mollie. "We have to find out what's going on with Sally. Does she need our help, or is she just trying to trick us? If any of the others are there, we can spy on them too. I have a tape recorder we can use. We'll sneak up on them and tape their conversation. Then we'll have the proof we need."

I said. "We could sail over tonight."

"In the dark?" asked Abigail, aghast. "What if it's still windy? Wouldn't that be dangerous?"

"Don't be a scaredy-cat!" Mollie ignored Abigail's concern. "You all can sleep over at my house. My dad's gone back to the city. Louie can meet us later on—for the sail. It'll be fun."

Abigail didn't seem convinced, but she gave in. There was no use arguing with Mollie. We finished eating just before one. It was time to meet Louie. We rode our bikes out onto the street and past the harbor. As we passed the yacht club, we saw a group of instructors just leaving. Judy and Billy were among them.

"Hey, kids," Judy called out as we approached. "What're you up to?"

"Just heading over to the Clam Bar," answered Muffy.

"What're your plans?" she asked.

"Nothing much," I answered, as Billy joined us.

"We're having a sleepover at Mollie's after we sail over to the old lighthouse," Abigail told her. We couldn't believe Abigail said that! Usually she didn't say that much, but now she was blabbing our plans to everyone! When she saw the looks on our faces, she knew she had done something seriously wrong.

"Just kidding," she said to Billy and Judy, with a silly laugh.

"I hope so," said Billy. "Maybe you girls ought to stay closer to home until your mystery is solved."

"We've got to go," I said, pedaling down the hill. The others followed and we rode past the marina to the snack bar. Louie was lying on the grass, waiting for us. From the empty paper plate and soda can, it appeared that he had already eaten his lunch.

"What took you so long?" he asked. "Order your lunch because I've got news."

"We already ate," Mollie told him. Then she took the green witchcraft book out of her backpack. "Before I forget, here's the witchcraft book. You're the only one who hasn't read it. It explains a lot. Now tell us what happened."

"When Mollie called me last night she said something about Laura's mom going by to see old Mr. and Mrs. Wells. I must have said their name 'cause when I got off the phone, my Aunt Lydia, who was over for dinner, told me something really freaky. Listen to this! She used to date Jared Wells, the son of those old people, and she says that Jared disappeared years ago. He got into some trouble and didn't get along with his parents so he went out West somewhere. She thinks he lives in Salt Lake City, Utah. The strange thing is that she said he was really handsome and the thing she liked best about him was his wavy blond hair!"

We were speechless. Wavy blond hair? No way was the man we had seen at the Wellses' their blond-haired son! Who could he be?

"Can your aunt get in touch with the real Jared?" asked Abigail.

"She already called information to get his phone number. I hope you don't mind that I told her what Mollie said. Aunt Lydia's real concerned about the old man and woman now. She couldn't reach Jared so she left a message on his answering machine and she's waiting for him to call her back. She'll let me know as soon as she hears from him, but we don't have an answering machine and Aunt Lydia works late."

"Wow!" exclaimed Muffy. "If Jared has wavy blond hair, who is the dark-haired man at the Wellses' house? You have to call your aunt tonight to see if she got in touch with Jared."

"Maybe they have another son," said Muffy.

"Aunt Lydia said Jared was an only child," answered Louie. "So I told her and my mom about the man. They said he must be someone else! Aunt Lydia has to find Jared and he's got to come back and help his parents!"

"The dark-haired man is an impostor! Why is he living with the Wellses, pretending to be their son? I've got to tell Mom!" I exclaimed.

We sat on the grass watching the boats go under the bridge. The tourists leaned over the edge of the bridge, throwing bait to the crabs—I mean fishing.

"It makes me angry," Mollie said, "to think of that man holding the old couple hostage! If only your mom knew, Laura."

"I wish she had known before she went over there this morning!" I exclaimed. "But why do you say he's holding them hostage, Mollie?"

"Because he's controlling them, by keeping them indoors and not letting them out," she replied. "Making them pretend that he's their son. No wonder he doesn't want any visitors."

We told Louie about Miss Deighton. He was shocked. Now we all had to be extra careful.

"Hopefully we'll get some information of our own tonight," said Muffy.

"What do you mean?" asked Louie.

"We're having a sleepover at Mollie's and we're going to sail over to the old lighthouse later, once Mollie's family is asleep," I told him.

"What?" asked Louie in surprise. "You girls are going to sail at night?"

"You're not afraid, are you?" I asked.

"I'm not afraid, I just didn't know that girls could sail at night."

"You think we're too stupid?" asked Muffy, miffed.

"No," mumbled Louie, obviously at a loss for words and feeling more than a little awkward. "I just never thought about it before. I...uh...I'm sure you can do it," he said, still sounding skeptical. Boys are so weird sometimes. They think girls are stupid, but I have to admit that sometimes I think the same thing about them!

"I'm glad you're not scared," said Mollie. "Because you're going with us and you have to help. You have an extra life jacket in your boat, don't you, Laura?"

"Sure. Who's at the Clam Bar today?" I asked, craning my neck to see who was at the counter.

"Cooky and his wife," answered Louie. "They're awfully quiet and look kind of glum."

"Hopefully they can find someone to take Mrs. Pitts's place," said Muffy.

"How about a swim?" suggested Abigail. "My cousins are gone, so it's safe to come to my house. Snow Pond is crowded and muddy, but the water is...O.K."

"There're too many boats," complained Muffy.

"Then we could look for crabs, or catch minnows. Come on," she persisted.

"All right, if your grandmother will give us ice cream," I said.

"You know she will," Abigail replied.

After Louie threw his trash away, we waved to Cooky's wife and rode off to Abigail's house. It wasn't such a great day for the beach, but we would make the best of it. When we arrived, Abigail's grandmother welcomed us with ice cream and cake! Abigail was fortunate to have such a loving grandmother. And she was around, at least most of the time, so Abigail didn't have to be afraid the way Mollie and I did.

Chapter Sixty-Two

We sat on the porch while we ate, watching the wind blow the silver leaves on the "silver leaf" trees. The leaves are green on the top, but when the wind blows, the silver undersides show, giving the trees a shimmering effect. Then we gathered up buckets, nets, and shovels and headed down the hill to Snow Pond. We spent the afternoon catching crabs (hermit and blue), and minnows. It was very muddy. Eel grass floated out with the tide. But it was relaxing and we had fun. It felt good to accomplish something, even if it was only catching and releasing crabs and fish.

Later as we walked back up the hill to Abigail's house, we noticed something lying in the road. At first I thought it was a toy, accidentally dropped by a child on her way home from the beach. A pang of panic began to rise in my body as I saw that it was another voodoo doll! This time it was clearly Louie! We stood and stared.

"Hey! It's me!"

"Rip it apart!" ordered Muffy.

Louie bent down to pick it up. He studied the details of his image: brown hair, T-shirt, jeans. It was amazing, but at the same time scary, that someone had spent so much time on a doll for the sake of harming someone. Louie carefully took the pins out of the stomach area, one by one, and then tore the doll apart, pulling off the clothes then the limbs. Tearing out the stuffing, he tossed the pieces into the bushes.

"I guess I was expecting this," he muttered. "On the same day that you gave me the witch book, I get a voodoo doll. I don't like this."

"None of us do," said Muffy. "But we're all in it together. I hate to think of what they'll do next!"

Mrs. Pitts, or whoever, had been into all of our houses, except for Muffy's. We were silent as we continued up the hill toward Abigail's. Her grandmother brought tall glasses of lemonade to us as we sat sulking on the porch.

"Are you girls all right?" she asked. She couldn't help but notice our mood.

"Oh yes," replied Abigail. "We're just trying to make plans."

"I'd better call home and let my mom know about the sleepover," Mollie said with a sigh. Usually a sleepover was a happy occasion, but with our new mystery, it was part of our job! Mollie went inside to use the phone. A few minutes later she was back. "It's all settled. You're all invited for dinner too. Louie's included. Oh, and Muffy, if you don't want to go home to get your pajamas and toothbrush, I have extras you can use."

"Thanks. I didn't really want to ride all the way home just to get mine."

"Muffy, why don't you call your mom about the sleepover? I'll ask Grammy for permission and then pack," said Abigail, going into the house.

"On the way to Mollie's, we have to stop by my house so I can pick up my things," I said.

When Abigail reappeared, we decided we might as well head on over to Mollie's. We thanked Abigail's grandmother for the snacks. As we rode over the bridge, we noticed that the water was still choppy. Cooky and his wife had plenty of customers: tourists, fishermen, and marina visitors.

Past the yacht club we rode to our first stop—my house. My friends waited in the kitchen while I quickly packed my bag, grabbed my life jacket, and didn't forget my compass. I checked the answering machine. No new messages. I wrote a note for Mom, telling her about the sleepover and about Jared Wells. I hoped that she would call Louie's mom and Aunt Lydia. Perhaps they could make a plan to see if they could find out who that strange man was and why he was pretending to be the Wellses' son. Then we continued on to Mollie's.

When we got to her house, a note on the kitchen table greeted us. It was stuck on the top of a big box of pizza. It read, "I've taken Maxwell to the movies. Here's a nice pizza for you and your friends. There are cookies in the cupboard and sodas in the fridge. Help yourself and don't forget to brush your teeth and floss."

"Can you believe that?" muttered Mollie in disgust as she plopped down in a chair at the table.

"What's wrong?" Abigail asked.

"What's wrong? My mother should be here. I thought she and Dad were 'turning over a new leaf.' Family was going to be a priority. I said 'family' not 'Maxwell'! What did I expect?" She put her head down on the table.

I felt sorry for her. Mollie's house was quite a contrast from Abigail's, with her grandmother serving us treats or Muffy's, with her mom giving us snacks when we were at their cottage. My parents were attentive when they were home. I could understand how Mollie felt that her mom had abandoned her, leaving her home all alone, even when she knew Mollie was having guests over for the night.

"We're here," Abigail said trying to comfort her. "We'll have fun."

"But what if you weren't here? She does this all the time. She doesn't know about the danger we're in, but even if she did, she's so afraid of making a mistake with Maxwell that she ends up making an even bigger mistake with me! And besides that, she's turning Maxwell into a monster. It's wrong to give that little brat all her attention and ignore me!"

"Your father seems to want to spend more time with you," I said. "Isn't it getting better now that he's coming down earlier on the weekends?"

"I suppose," she sighed. "Let's eat."

The pizza was cold, so we heated it up in the microwave. We all felt better after we ate.

"Now we'll have to wait for them to get back before we can go over to the lighthouse," complained Mollie, kicking her shoes off under the table.

"We could stuff pillows under the blankets of your bed to fool your mom," suggested Muffy. "Or is she the kind of mom who would come in and make sure we were asleep and give you a kiss good-night?"

"I think we could fool her," said Mollie, cheering up. "She wouldn't come in the room, because she 'respects my privacy,' so she says. Maybe it's a good thing after all that she's gone. We'll mess up the bathroom, leave our clothes lying around, put pillows under the blankets, turn out the lights, and shut the door. She might peek in, but that's all. Great thinking, Muffy!"

"That way Louie won't have to leave and come back," I added, looking at him munching away on a cookie.

"I'm going to call home," I said. "I want to be sure my mom got the message about Jared Wells." Mom answered the phone. She and Dad had just finished dinner. Mom had found my note and the news about Jared really shook her up! She had already telephoned Louie's mother, who told her that Lydia was still at work. Louie's mom would call my mom as soon as Lydia reached Jared. She told me to have fun and she'd see me tomorrow.

"Well, there's nothing left for us to do except sail," said Muffy, jumping up from the table. We left our glasses there rather than wash them. That way Mollie's mother would notice them as soon as she entered the kitchen and would assume that we were home and in bed asleep. We girls dashed upstairs to brush our teeth and floss, as we had been instructed in the note from Mollie's mother.

Then we changed our clothes in Mollie's bedroom while Louie waited downstairs. We borrowed some of Mollie's clothes and left ours lying in the hallway and bathroom, so it would appear that we had changed into our pajamas. We grabbed pillows from the chairs and beds and stuffed them under the covers of Mollie's twin beds to make it look as if we were sound asleep. Abigail grabbed her backpack and we turned off the light and closed the door, then clambered downstairs to Louie.

We took our life jackets, marched out the back door and across the lawn to the stairway leading down to the beach. It was dark, too dark. Remembering our last walk on the beach, I began to panic and drew back. Could Karl and Mrs. Pitts be waiting for us in the dark? Maybe the zombie was there! I hesitated, but the others went on ahead, Louie in the lead. Cautiously I followed.

The sky had been overcast all day. Now the cloud covering hid the stars and moon from view. We could see distant lights coming from the old lightkeeper's house. There were lights on the bluff coming from other houses and on the harbor from a number of yachts. We could hear music and laughter from Dr. Perhonen's large sailboat, which was moored in its usual spot.

"Let's check out Dr. Perhonen on our way over to the lighthouse," suggested Muffy. "He's having a party. Maybe Karl and Mrs. Pitts are there."

"But we'll have to be careful," Abigail said. We would be.

We followed the shoreline to my boathouse, where my dinghy lay waiting, but then remembered the oars!

"Oh no!" I groaned. "The oars!"

"Go get them," commanded Mollie in her familiar military style.

"My parents will hear me going into the barn! They'll catch me. I know they will. They're that kind of parents. They have radar that catches me when I'm doing something that's wrong."

"What are we doing wrong?" asked Mollie. "Sailing at night isn't a crime."

"But it's dangerous," Abigail informed us.

"Maybe it's not such a good idea," said Louie. But his comment made Mollie even more determined to make our plan work.

"Then I'll go get them," she announced, turning toward the path leading up to my house.

"Oh, I'll go," I sighed, moving ahead of her. "But someone has to come with me."

Of course they all did. And I was glad. I didn't want to have to wander across my yard, or anywhere, alone. Especially on a dark night like this.

We filed up the sandy path through the tall rosebushes to my yard. I could see my parents through the sitting room window, my father reading the newspaper and my mom reading her antique novel. They looked so quiet and peaceful. Would Karl and his friends ever try to hurt them? I hoped not.

It made me feel guilty sneaking around my own yard, with my parents thinking I was safe and secure at Mollie's house. And I was the one taking my friends on a potentially dangerous adventure! I hoped that our adventure would be a safe one. We crept around the edge of the yard to the barn. I quietly opened the door and entered.

"Please hold the door open," I whispered to Abigail. "I'll never trust that barn door again!" I thought about the coyote. Where was she now? With Karl? Waiting to be barbecued by those Earth Mother worshippers? We had to find a way to rescue that animal, whether it was "my" coyote or not!

It was dark inside the barn, but I knew just where the oars were. They were leaning in the corner opposite my father's work bench. I reached out my hand, half expecting someone to grab my wrist, but no one did. I drew the oars to me and came out. Abigail closed the door and we all continued back to the beach. My parents were still sitting under the lamp, never suspecting what we were doing. But it was better that way.

At the beach we righted my dinghy and pulled it to the water's edge. I rowed the Girls and Louie out to my Catabout and we began rigging the sails. Louie didn't know what to do, so he just sat in a corner of the stern and stayed out of the way. It was so dark that it took longer than usual to get the sails up, but that was all right. We weren't in a rush.

I made sure everything was shipshape before we left the mooring. We headed straight toward the lights of the old lightkeeper's house, next to the defunct lighthouse.

"Muffy, could you hand me the flashlight?" I asked. "It's in the toolbox, in the bow." She rummaged around in the pitch black until she found the box, then handed the flashlight to me. I looked at my compass. I wanted to get a bearing so we would be able to sail back in the opposite direction when it was time to come home. The bluff where my house was would be dark by then. Only a compass reading would get us to my mooring without any problems.

Doctor Perhonen's yacht was on our course, so we sailed silently toward it. There was quite a party going on and by the lights onboard, we tried to recognize the guests, but Dr. Perhonen was the only person we knew. No one on the boat seemed to notice us. We wondered if the guests were part of the Earth Mother group anyway.

I headed into the wind and we came to a standstill, grabbing onto the mooring of a nearby motorboat. We listened. It sounded like a regular cocktail party with ice clinking into glasses, loud voices, laughter. There was a woman with an accent. Maybe that was "Olga," who Dr. Perhonen had mentioned to us. We couldn't hear anything important, only phrases here and there. At least the yacht gave us enough light to see our way past a number of smaller boats moored nearby as we sailed on toward our destination.

There was a good breeze. We quickly skimmed over the water to the old lighthouse. It was a little scary as we moved away from the yacht because of the darkness. We could hardly see, but the lights from old lighthouse guided us to a safe landing on the beach.

"I bet Mrs. Pitts and her sister are partying, too!" suggested Louie.

"I suppose her guests would be Lucky, Karl, Mr. Mullins, and Mr. Alexis," smirked Mollie.

"I hope they aren't there," I said. "We won't be able to talk to Sally if they're there."

"But we'll find out a lot if they are," said Muffy.

We pulled my boat up on the beach and secured the anchor. The tide was still rising and would be turning soon, but I didn't think I had to worry about my boat becoming beached. We weren't planning to stay long. The white sand of the path through the beach grass almost glowed, leading us to the old house. I set out first. The Girls and Louie followed.

"Do you girls have a mystery club or something?" asked Louie. I wondered why he had waited until now to ask about our club. I thought I knew what he meant, but I asked him, "What do you mean?"

"Well, you solved a mystery, so I was thinking you might have a mystery club. With a name and dues and code names for each other?"

"We don't have dues or code names, but we do have a secret name for our club," said Abigail. "No boys allowed."

"That's the name?"

"No!" Muffy almost laughed. "She means it's a girls-only club."

"I don't want to join it! The guys would laugh at me if I joined a girls' club," he was quick to add. "I was just wondering."

"We appreciate your help," said Muffy, feeling a little guilty, I suppose. "You're the one who told us about Captain Snow's house in the first place. And you're with us now."

"Hush!" whispered Mollie. "We're getting close."

We moved toward the lightkeeper's house, beside the old lighthouse. Of course it hadn't been used as a lighthouse in years. The keeper's house and a few out buildings stood together near the point. They were surrounded by sand dunes and scattered bayberry bushes. Through the windows we could see people inside. There was Mrs. Pitts and a man. We crept nearer to a window to get a better look at the man and the others, but when we got close enough, you won't believe what we saw!

Chapter Sixty-Three

There in the center of the room, sitting around a large oak table, were Mrs. Pitts, Mr. Mullins, Lucky Clark, Karl, Mr. Blackwell, Victoria Harden, and Aloma Smits!

"Hey!" whispered Louie. "It's the cafeteria lady!"

"Wonder if she brought over her stew from the cedar swamp for refreshments?" I joked. "I hope her zombie isn't around!"

"All the rest of them are here," observed Mollie.

"Except Sally," I remarked. "I wonder where she is? This is her house."

"What are they doing?" asked Abigail. They were holding hands and had their eyes closed.

"Séance!" Muffy whispered.

"What?" asked Louie.

"It's when they call someone back from the dead," Muffy explained.

"That's what Captain Snow's book is about. And those notes we found. This is what Mrs. Snow used to do."

"Who are they calling back from the dead?" asked Mollie. We watched, waited, and listened. Mrs. Pitts seemed to be the leader. We could hear every word through the window.

"Oh, no!" exclaimed Mollie. "I forgot my tape recorder. Now we'll never have any proof!"

"Hush!" hissed Muffy.

"Mrs. Snow, Mrs. Snow, please come to us," Mrs. Pitts commanded. "We have questions for you regarding your dealings with Lawrence Bickly."

"Lawrence Bickly!" repeated Mollie in a hushed echo.

"We want to know where he buried his fortune. We need that money to carry out your plan to take over this town, for the good of the Earth Mother."

We couldn't believe our ears! Take over the town? What did they mean? And how were they planning to do it?

"Your plan is our plan as well," continued Mrs. Pitts. "We know that you worshipped the Earth Mother and you are with her now. We worship her too. You instructed Lawrence to get all the money he could from the evil Mr. McLaughlin and Mr. Lowndes. He was able to amass a fortune, but he wasn't a true believer. He didn't continue on with you and the work after your passing, but kept the money for himself. We haven't been able to reach him. Please come to us and tell us where the money is."

"Wow," exclaimed Muffy, in a whisper. "I wonder how they know so much about Mrs. Snow and Lawrence? We weren't able to find out anything about a treasure!"

"They must have other sources," I put in, but I was afraid to imagine who those other sources could be. We waited for Mrs. Snow to respond. Suddenly there was a loud knock on the table. Everyone around the table gave a start. We did too.

"Mrs. Snow!" Mrs. Pitts called out. "Where is the treasure?"

A series of tappings followed. It sounded like Morse code.

"It's buried under the barn at the cranberry bog!" Karl blurted out. "Under the office floor! But what cranberry bog? There must be hundreds of bogs in this town! Ask her which one!"

"Which cranberry bog, Mrs. Snow? Please tell us," pleaded Mrs. Pitts.

But Mrs. Snow was silent. She didn't respond.

"I think we'd better leave," mouthed Muffy. When we turned to go, we noticed a shadowy figure moving along the path! We froze. Who could it be? Aloma Smits's zombie? Suddenly it disappeared!

"Let's get out of here!" said Abigail, sounding scared. We quickly followed the path back to where I had anchored my boat. When we got there, it was gone!

"That person we saw must have set it adrift!" I exclaimed. "My poor boat!" I hoped that the outgoing tide wouldn't take her out to sea! I was worried about her, but I was also worried about us. Was the zombie lurking nearby? And how were we going to get home!

"We'll have to walk to Herring Beach," said Louie. "Come on." He led the way, cutting through the beach grass to avoid going near the lighthouse. The sharp blades of the stiff grass lashed our legs as we hurried through. We headed for the dirt road, which led from the lighthouse to the beach parking lot about a half a mile away. We kept looking back over our shoulders as we trotted along, but we didn't see the dark figure, or anyone else, following us.

"Was that really Mrs. Snow's ghost in there?" asked Abigail, fearfully.

"Oh course not!" exclaimed Muffy. "It's got a be a hoax."

"Then who was it?" Louie wanted to know. No one had an answer.

"What do you think about the treasure?" asked Mollie.

"And under which cranberry barn is it buried?" asked Abigail.

"It could be Mr. Snow's barn," suggested Muffy.

"What barn?" Louie wanted to know.

"Just a barn we know about," I answered evasively. The barn was too near our Eel Grass Palace for me to tell him outright.

"There's an old barn off Yacht Harbor Road," he said. "An old dirt road, beside a field of daylilies, leads way back to an old bog and barn. I haven't been in there in a while, but it might be the one."

My heart sank. He already knew about our bog! But if he hadn't been there in a while, maybe he didn't know about our Palace. He could never know!

"Do you think it might really be the same barn where Lawrence hid his treasure?" Abigail asked Muffy.

"There aren't many cranberry barns left," Louie cut in. "I've seen plenty of old bogs, but not barns. And that one has an office too. Mrs. Snow said the treasure is under the office floor. We ought to go over there tomorrow and check it out."

Great! Now Louie would have to come within a few yards of our Eel Grass Palace! I never dreamed that this kind of situation would ever come up! I guess there was no getting around it.

"What time?" I asked. We were now on the dirt road running from the lighthouse to the beach parking lot. I was puffing as we trudged through the deep sand and I glanced over my shoulder again. "Don't you have to work for your brother after camp?"

"Not tomorrow. I just have to be home by five, 'cause my mom likes me to be home for dinner."

"We have sailing in the morning anyway," I said. "Meet us at the Clam Bar at one."

"We should hurry before the others get there," said Abigail.

"They'll never be able to find it!" exclaimed Mollie.

"Don't be so sure," warned Muffy.

We agreed to meet at my house at seven. We didn't tell Louie that we already knew about the barn. We'd tell him later. For now we had to concentrate on getting back to civilization!

We slogged on through the deep sand of the road used by Sally and her friends to drive to and from the old lighthouse. Finally we reached the firm hardtop of the beach parking lot! A few vehicles were parked there, facing the Sound. We could see the dark shadows of the lifeguard benches lined up along the shore. Then we saw it! Billy Jones's truck! We ran toward it but stopped short when we saw that Billy was inside with a girl and they were *kissing*!

"Ewwwww! Gross!" squealed Mollie in disgust.

"Who is it? Who's he kissing?" asked Abigail, leaning forward.

"Oh no! I never imagined he would ever do a thing like that!" I groaned. It had never occurred to me that Billy would ever have a girlfriend, but it was one of those things that happen, I guess.

"What's wrong?" asked Louie. I couldn't explain it to him, so I didn't try. We were at the truck now and Mollie boldly knocked on Billy's window. Boy, was he surprised to see us! He didn't seem very happy though.

"Hi Billy," said Mollie, as he rolled down the window. "What are you doing here?"

"What are *you* doing here?" he asked in return, sounding annoyed. I guess

239

he didn't appreciate us interrupting him in the middle of his romantic evening. But we were stranded and we needed help. We peered past him to see who the girl was. Allyson Parks! She was another instructor at the yacht club. She didn't seem very happy to see us either.

"You've got to help us," began Muffy, stepping up to the truck. "We need to get back to town."

Just then we heard something in the distance. The sound of a vehicle! Muffy stopped talking to listen. We turned toward the noise. It was coming from the lighthouse. We could see headlights bouncing along over the dirt road, coming toward us. We instinctively leapt into the back of Billy's truck and laid low until the vehicle passed through the parking lot. It was a town water department truck! It had to be Mr. Mullins!

Chapter Sixty-Four

"Follow that truck!" Mollie called to Billy.

"Here we go again," he muttered as he revved up his engine and turned his truck around to speed out of the parking lot. His comment referred to our last mystery, when he helped us to get somewhere in a hurry, in the middle of the night. "This is getting to be a habit with you guys," he called through the open window in back of the cab.

"What's this all about?" asked Allyson.

"I'll tell you later," said Billy as he wove his way around the curves of the narrow road, leading to the main street.

We could see the water truck at the stop sign at the end of the road. The truck was turning right, toward town, but after a short distance, it veered left onto a little road leading through the woods. We didn't follow too closely, but we were afraid of losing him. He was probably just going home, but we wanted to follow him just to make sure. Suddenly he turned off the road and headed toward the town water tower!

"What's that guy up to?" asked Billy. "See that sign? It says this is a dead-end road. We'd better park here and follow on foot." He pulled over into a clump of bushes and we tumbled out of back of the truck.

"Oh no!" I exclaimed in horror as it hit me. "He's going to poison the town water supply!" It seemed so obvious. Why hadn't we put it all together before? Mr. Mullins worked for the town water department. The Earth Mother People were plotting to load the town water supply with some sort of drug that would cause the entire town to come under their influence! No wonder Mrs. Pitts wouldn't drink the water! Or Miss Deighton either! But if she knew, why hadn't she told us? We would have to ask her about that later.

"They'll use the same drugs that Mr. Alexis puts in his candy!" I exclaimed. "With all those doctors in their group, they don't have any problem getting drugs. They'll poison us all!"

"Dr. Alexis uses herbs," corrected Abigail.

"Herbs, drugs, it's all the same," said Mollie.

"What are you girls talking about?" asked Billy.

"Mr. Mullins is one of them!" I urgently explained. "He's one of the 'good' green witches gone bad. They want to save the world by taking over the town. They're going to do it by poisoning the water!"

"Then we've got to stop him!" Billy exclaimed.

We could see that Mr. Mullins had parked his truck at the top of the hill near the tower. We crept up the road and hid behind his truck. It was difficult to see, but we could hear Mr. Mullins making a clunking sound. He was carrying something. It sounded like a metal box. We listened as he hurriedly began to climb the tower!

"I'll get him," announced Billy, running forward. I started to cry out to tell him to stop, but Mollie clamped her hand over my mouth.

"Be quiet! Let him go," she said.

"Why?" I asked in dismay once she had released her grip. "He might get hurt!"

"Billy can handle himself," she said. I wasn't so sure. He was confronting a desperate man. Mr. Mullins seemed determined to carry out his plan. He started up the metal ladder, which curved up the side of the huge structure. He was obviously familiar with the tower and moved quickly, but Billy slipped and stumbled behind him on the narrow rungs. Mr. Mullins must have heard Billy following him because he began to move faster. Billy moved faster too, convinced that Mr. Mullins had to be stopped from doing whatever evil he intended to do. Allyson gripped my arm so tightly it hurt. I guess she liked Billy a lot.

It was dark, but we could now see the shapes of the two men against the side of the pale-colored tower. We could still hear Mr. Mullins stomping up the rungs. Then Billy must have reached him because we could hear them begin to struggle. We clung together as we looked up helplessly. Then we heard a cry from above and saw a body toppling over the rail!

"Billy!" shrieked Allyson, pulling away from us and rushing forward. We watched in horror as the body fell at our feet. Then the metal box hit the ground beside it and broke open. Little glass vials flew out all over the soft pine needles. We stared in terror at the body. It was Mr. Mullins! We looked up and saw Billy's form racing down the metal ladder. We stood frozen. When Billy reached the ground, he sprinted over to us and felt the pulse in Mr. Mullins's neck.

"He's alive. We've got to get help." He looked at me. "Laura, run to the nearest house and call the police—and an ambulance."

Abigail and Louie came with me as I ran to the first house on the road. We banged on the front door with all our might, screaming for someone to open up. Finally an old man in his pajamas and slippers shuffled to the door and slowly opened it, looking sleepily out at us.

"Call the police and get an ambulance! Someone's been hurt up at the water tower," I blurted out. The old man just stared at us so I asked, "Where's your phone?" The man stood aside and pointed to a small table just inside the door. It was so dark I could hardly see, but I pushed past him and snatched up the receiver. It was the old-fashioned kind of phone with a rotary dial! Without being able to see properly, how could I dial 911?

"Where's your light?" I screamed. He flicked a switch near the front door.

Though I could see, I still fumbled with the phone, trying to dial. By the time I finally got through, I was almost in tears!

"This is Laura Sparrow!" I hollered into the phone the instant I was connected. "Send an ambulance to the water tower. Someone fell off. Send the police. He has chemicals." Of course I had to repeat this several times, until I was nearly hysterical! "If you don't get here right away he'll die!" I shrieked. "I'm hanging up now so you'd better send the police or you'll be the one in trouble!"

I held back my tears as I hung up. How could adults be so difficult? Why was it so hard to understand what I had said? 911 was supposed to help people, not drive them crazy and waste precious time by asking the same questions over and over again!

The old man was still standing at the front door blinking at us, wondering what was going on. As we thanked him for the use of his phone, we could hear the familiar sirens of the town's police cruisers in the distance. I began to feel safe again. Abigail, Louie, and I raced back up the hill and got there just as the cruisers pulled in.

"What seems to be the problem here?" asked a young policeman as he emerged from the cruiser. His partner had noticed Billy, Mollie, and Allyson standing over Mr. Mullins, and he had rushed to their side, feeling for Mr. Mullins's pulse as he lay unconscious.

Billy explained how we had followed Mr. Mullins to the water tower and how he and Mr. Mullins had fought up at the top before Mr. Mullins had lost his balance and fallen. Another cruiser arrived and the ambulance. Mr. Mullins was carefully placed on a stretcher and transferred to the ambulance, then rushed off to the hospital 20 miles away. One cruiser accompanied the ambulance to the hospital.

The police picked up the box of chemicals and asked us to follow them back to the police station. As we walked toward Billy's truck, Abigail said, "He was going to poison the water!"

"How did he think he could he get away with it?" asked Billy. "He works for the water department! He'd be the first person the police would suspect."

"Then what was he doing?" asked Allyson as we climbed into the back of the truck. Now Allyson knew about part of our mystery. I hoped she wouldn't talk about it and tell the other instructors. We followed the cruiser to the police station, where we pulled up and parked.

"Maybe Mr. Mullins was just going to take water samples or do some sort of testing," said Billy, forlornly, as we climbed out of his truck. "Which would mean I'm going to be in really big trouble!"

We were shocked. It had never occurred to us that Mr. Mullins wasn't part of an evil plot. When Billy saw the look on our faces he asked, "Didn't you kids think that maybe this guy wasn't up to anything? I don't know why I let myself get sucked into your crazy mystery games again! Why are you so suspicious of him anyway?"

"First of all, it's not a 'crazy mystery game,'" said Mollie. "And second, he stole all of the church records that we need for our case."

"But we don't know that for sure," cautioned Abigail. "Maybe your minister has found the records by now Laura, somewhere in the church."

"Well, he stole the choir robe and goblet and other things from church," I continued.

"But someone else could have stolen them," Abigail said, reflectively.

"He's been hanging around The Tomb and acting strange," I said.

"Yes," Mollie agreed. "But that's no crime. Being at the old lighthouse isn't a crime either. For all we know, Billy may be right. Mr. Mullins was just doing his job at the water tower. We interfered with it and now we may be responsible for him breaking his neck!"

A cold shiver went up my spine. What if that were true? What if we had risked the life of an innocent man, just because we had let our imaginations run wild? What if we were wrong about Mr. Mullins? Not only that, but now we had involved Billy. And because he had been the one to struggle with Mr. Mullins, he would be the one to get into trouble.

"This is the last time I'm going to help you goofy girls," said Billy in disgust as we entered the police station. We didn't bother correcting Billy, reminding him that Louie was a boy. We felt just terrible! No one said a word, as we waited for the officers to finish filling out their report. If they called our parents, we would have a lot of explaining to do!

"I wish we'd never followed Mr. Mullins," Abigail whined.

"I'm scared," said Muffy. "What if he's really hurt? What if Billy goes to jail? What are we going to do?" We had no answers and we were very afraid.

Chapter Sixty-Five

A young officer with a buzz cut was on duty at the desk under the glaring fluorescent ceiling lights. A captain came out of the back office and he motioned for us to enter. The Girls and I squeezed onto two chairs, while Louie took the other chair. Billy and Allyson stood.

"He'll live," said the officer, sitting down behind his metal desk. "Just had the wind knocked out of him. That thick bed of pine needles broke his fall. Said he tried to stop you from going up the tower," he told Billy, giving him a stern look.

"What?" asked Billy in disbelief. "*He* tried to stop *me*?" We couldn't believe our ears! Why had Mr. Mullins told the police that?

"What were you all doing up there anyway?" the officer asked us, looking from one to the other.

"*We* were following *him*!" protested Billy.

"You were following him?" he asked. "That's not what he said."

Billy glanced at us. Mollie took up the story. "We were at the beach when we saw Mr. Mullins's truck coming from the old lighthouse. We couldn't understand why a town water department employee would be out so late at night so we trailed him. When we saw him head to the tower and start to climb up with that box, we were afraid he was going to poison the town water."

"And why would he do a thing like that?" asked the policeman, leaning back in his chair. "Why didn't you assume that he was going to do some water testing?"

"In the middle of the night?" I asked.

"Why not? You don't know when it ought to be done, do you?"

That was true. We suddenly felt very foolish and very scared. Maybe we had made a terrible mistake!

"You're lucky he's not pressing charges," continued the officer.

"*What*?" asked Billy again, not really comprehending what was going on.

"He's going to be fine, so he won't be filing charges against you kids, but you'd better stay away from the town water tower from now on. It's not a safe place to play."

We were shocked and relieved! We were free to go, he said. We scurried out of the police station, afraid the officer might change his mind. We hopped into Billy's truck and he drove us to the yacht club, where we could talk—and think. We tumbled out of the truck and over to the benches on the deck overlooking the harbor.

It was still dark and overcast and the sea breeze blew against us. We could see lights on Dr. Perhonen's boat and lights still shone from the old lighthouse. Who was still there? And where was my little Catabout? Hopefully not drifting out to Nantucket!

"What just happened back there at the police station?" asked Billy. "Did that Mullins jerk really tell the police that *he* tried to stop *me* from climbing the tower?"

"Yes," answered Muffy. "That proves that he was doing something wrong. He put the blame on you, so the police wouldn't suspect him."

"But thankfully he didn't get hurt and he didn't get us into trouble," added Abigail.

"That's the 'up side,'" said Mollie. "The 'down side' is that the police will never test the chemicals in those vials and we'll never know what's in them and what Mr. Mullins was going to do. He must have been trying to poison the water! What else could he have been doing? He'll try it again sometime when he's going about his routine business. Then no one will be able to stop him!"

"But he could never get away with it," insisted Allyson.

"Maybe the police didn't pick up all the vials!" I exclaimed, ignoring Allyson's logic. "When Mr. Mullins's box hit the ground, the vials flew out all over the place, remember? Some of them might still be there. Let's go back to the tower and look. If there's a vial or two still there, we can send them to a lab and have the chemicals tested. That way we'll have proof that he was trying to poison the water supply!"

"Didn't you hear the police officer tell us to stay away from the water tower?" asked Billy, sounding exasperated.

"Come on!" I pleaded.

"No! You can go back on your own tomorrow or I don't care when, but you're not getting me into any more trouble. If Mullins had pressed charges, I'd be in jail now! It's all just a game to you kids!"

"It's not a game to us," corrected Mollie. "We're the ones who are being haunted! We're the ones in danger. They know we're on to them."

"And what about me?" asked Billy. "I'm involved now, too." He paused as we waited. "Oh, all right," he sighed.

"We really appreciate all your help," said Muffy sincerely.

"You poor things," sympathized Allyson. I wasn't sure about her, but she was there and there was nothing we could do about that. She was already involved, whether she or we wanted her to be or not.

"Hop in and let's go look for those vials," said Billy, in resignation.

We obediently jumped into the back of the truck.

"Have you got a flashlight?" asked Mollie through the cab's open window.

Billy said he did. Just then I had a frightening thought! On our way to the snack bar earlier that day, we'd stopped by the yacht club. Abigail had told Billy that we were going to sail over to the lighthouse later that night. Billy and

Allyson just happened to be in the parking lot, right where we would see him. Could they be part of the group? Had one of them been the dark figure who pushed my boat adrift? I tried to push the thought out of my mind.

But now we were nearing the water tower. If my suspicion were true, then the struggle between Billy and Mr. Mullins had been a hoax! Maybe Billy and Mr. Mullins were friends and that's why Mr. Mullins wasn't pressing charges! But it couldn't be!

Billy parked in the same spot as before. He took his flashlight from the pocket of the truck. The huge dark water tower loomed above us. Mollie took the flashlight from Billy. Once we arrived at the place where Mr. Mullins had fallen, she panned the area. "Look!" she exclaimed as the beam fell on a sparkling glass vial filled with a blue liquid.

Muffy scouted an area beneath the tower. Abigail bent over, looking through the pine needles. Even in the dark, she was able to spot a vial containing a pink liquid. Mollie handed the vial she had found to Abigail who then put them both into her backpack.

"Don't you girls have a curfew?" Billy suddenly asked, still not including Louie.

"My mom thinks we're in bed asleep," answered Mollie. "We're having a sleepover," she told Billy and Allyson.

"And you?" Billy asked Louie. "I don't think we've been introduced."

"This is Louie," said Muffy. "He lives near Mollie."

"Hi, Louie," said Billy. "O.K., we've found two vials. I think that's it. Let's go. Next stop, Mollie's house."

Billy dropped us all off at the end of Mollie's driveway. We thanked Billy and said good-bye. We walked toward the house, following the white shells of her driveway through the dark pine trees.

"Don't you think it's odd that Billy just happened to be at the beach parking lot?" I asked. It was crazy to think that Billy was involved, but I had to share my fears with the others.

"I think it was odd that he was kissing Allyson Parks," giggled Abigail.

I told them my theory about Billy. "He's the only person who knew we were going to the lighthouse and he just happened to be there. Maybe he was the dark figure lurking on the path—the one who had set my boat adrift!"

"How could you think that?" asked Mollie, in disbelief.

"That's ridiculous!" echoed Muffy. "I don't believe you. And I never would!"

No one could believe it. Maybe they were right. I hoped so, but it seemed to be too much of a coincidence.

"What are you going to do about your boat?" asked Abigail.

"I don't know. It could be anywhere by now," I lamented. "It might be in the middle of the ocean!"

"I'll help you look for it," offered Louie. I didn't like the thought of wandering down on the beach in the dark, but my boat was more important than my fears. We crossed Mollie's lawn past her dark house to the wooden stairs going down to the beach. The Girls sat and waited on the steps while Louie and I continued on down to the shore. The tide was still going out so it was useless to look for my Catabout on this side of the harbor, but I had to look for her anyway. Though we wandered up and down, peering into the darkness, my boat was nowhere to be seen. We dragged ourselves back up the steps, exhausted.

"I'm going home," announced Louie. "First thing in the morning, I'll ask my mom if Aunt Lydia got hold of Jared Wells. See you at the Clam Bar at one."

"Then it's to the bog to find that treasure," I said. "See you then." And he was gone.

"I've never been so tired in my life!" complained Mollie as we crept into her house and up the stairs. We pulled out the pillows, took their places, and were immediately asleep.

Chapter Sixty-Six

I awoke to complete silence. Bright sunlight streamed in through the big clear panes of Mollie's shiny new windows. Her house is so modern, neat, and clean compared to mine. My house is clean, don't misunderstand me. But at Mollie's, all the corners meet each other evenly, the floorboards are straight and flat, and there aren't any cracks in the moldings or spiders or cobwebs like at my house.

It seemed late, so I jumped up to look for a clock. There wasn't one in Mollie's room. I went downstairs to look for Mollie's mom. No one was home! A note on the kitchen table read, "Took Maxwell to the beach. See you later! Mom." I found a clock on the kitchen wall. Nine-fifteen! Yikes! We had only 15 minutes to get to sailing school!

I raced back upstairs, calling to the others. They were sleeping so peacefully, but it was time to go!

"Wake up! We're going to be late!"

"Who cares?" moaned Mollie, rolling over and hiding her head under the covers. "I can't move. Go on without me."

"You don't want to be left here all alone," I reminded her, seriously. "Get up, get up!"

With a lot of groaning and complaining, they dragged themselves up, one by one. Good thing we were already dressed. It would save some time.

We left the room a mess and tumbled downstairs to the kitchen, only to discover that Mollie's mother hadn't prepared any breakfast for us. In fact, we couldn't find anything at all to eat, except a box of granola bars and a quart of orange juice.

"That makes a complete breakfast," Mollie claimed. It wasn't my idea of breakfast at all, but it was better than nothing. As I mentioned before, Mollie's family was different from mine. Mollie didn't look as though she were suffering from malnutrition. I guess her diet wasn't hurting her. We gobbled up our granola bars and washed them down with the juice. We quickly brushed our teeth and headed out the door. We took our bikes from the garage and pedaled toward sailing school as fast as we could go.

I saw Billy Jones taking attendance. My stomach did a flip when I remembered the night before. Was he our friend or our enemy? As we sat on the wooden benches in the bright morning sunlight, I thought about our plan for the day. After sailing school, we would meet Louie. Then we would visit the old cranberry barn to see if we could find the buried treasure. If we could find it before the Earth People did, that would mess up their plan, whatever it was, because they had mentioned at the séance that they needed the money to carry out their plot.

I would remind the Girls not to mention our Eel Grass Palace to Louie. We would have to pass right by it to get to the barn. Louie would never notice. He would never know about it. He could never know! It was one of our biggest secrets!

Hopefully Louie would have news about his aunt locating Jared Wells. I wondered why Mr. and Mrs. Wells didn't say anything to my mom when she visited them. If he wasn't their son, they should have said so. It was a mystery.

Roll call had ended and Mr. Prince was telling us that we would practice racing today. We would rig our boats and meet at the starting line the instructors would set up. I didn't see Judy on the dock. It seemed as though she was absent today. I guess even sailing instructors get sick once in a while.

The Girls and I grabbed some life jackets from the bin inside the clubhouse. Ours were on my lost boat. We chose the *Chubby Quahog* again. It was fast and in good condition. All the boats were supposed to be in good condition, but some of them had centerboard problems, which could cause all kinds of other problems while racing or just plain sailing.

Mr. Prince came up to us and said, "You girls will have to split up. You're too big to all squeeze into one boat."

"Aw, come on!" exclaimed Mollie.

"Laura, you and Abigail take the *Classy Clam*."

There was no use arguing with Mr. Prince. We rigged the boats and set out, sailing side by side.

On the water, we were quiet. Tired was probably what we really were! I know I was exhausted. The starting line was just east of the channel. The first leg of the course would take us right by Dr. Perhonen's yacht. Who was he? Why was he moored in our harbor? He wasn't at the séance, but he was a friend of Karl's. Was he a New Age fan? An Earth Mother worshipper? A warlock?

Abigail was at the tiller. She would skipper the first race. We got a late start, but we weren't the last boat over the line. She kept a steady course and passed by the bow of Dr. Perhonen's yacht.

"Isn't that my Catabout?" I asked as I saw my boat tied to the yacht's anchor line—again!

"What are you going to do?" asked Abigail.

"I'm going to get it back! That old doctor isn't going to get away with stealing my boat. Especially since this is the second time he's done it!"

"Maybe he rescued it again. That's what he did last time."

"That's what he said, but I don't believe him. It's too much of a coincidence."

"But he's moored here, halfway between your mooring and the light-house," observed Abigail. "It does make sense that he's always around and sees your boat when it's adrift."

I didn't want her to be right. I wanted the doctor to be guilty. I wanted some-one to blame. Abigail hesitated, so I took the helm and came to a landing beside the yacht. The rope ladder was down.

"Hold on to the ladder, Abigail. I'm going on deck."

As I climbed up, I saw that the boat was deserted. I called out, but there was no answer, so I climbed back down again. It was too spooky.

"Let's tow my boat back to the mooring," I said. I untied the Catabout and cleated it to the stern of the *Classy Clam*. We began to sail over to my mooring, but it was slow going.

"We'll come in last," complained Abigail, looking at all the other boats rounding the mark and heading out toward the channel again.

"This is more important," I told her. Finally we arrived. I moored my boat and hopped in it to furl the sails and make sure everything was shipshape. As I removed the rudder, I noticed something written in dark pencil on the tiller! More pigpen code!

"Abigail! Come here! Look at this!"

Abigail tied the *Classy Clam* to my mooring and climbed aboard the Catabout.

"What is it, Laura?"

"Someone has written a message on my tiller! It says, 'We're watching you'!"

"That's what they said in the note we found in the toolshed at Muffy's aunt's house!"

"They're spying on us, watching everything we do! But they can't watch us every minute, can they?" I looked up to the bluff where my house stood and scanned the harbor. That's when I noticed someone on the deck of Dr. Perhonen's yacht with a spyglass, looking in our direction!

"Uh oh! They're spying on us, right now! Let's go!"

My boat was secured to her mooring. I retrieved the Girls' life jackets and we sailed off in the *Classy Clam*. I was at the helm again. We headed toward the yacht again and I came up along side of her.

"What are you doing?" asked Abigail, afraid of what I might be planning.

"I'm sick and tired of that man stealing my boat! And spying on us! Ahoy!"

"Ahoy!" called the doctor, peering down over the edge of his yacht. The rope ladder was still dangling down.

"What were you doing with my boat?" I asked in a slightly rude tone of voice while I climbed up. Abigail secured the *Classy Clam* and followed. "And why are you spying on us?"

"Oh, it's the midnight sailors! Oh, ho, ho!" he laughed. "We watched you sail over to the lighthouse last night. Wondered what you were up to. Have a spyglass here," he said, holding up the instrument in his hand. "We were curious, but you disappeared. Next thing we knew, your boat was drifting in our direction. You can't seem to hold onto your little boat, can you?" he chuckled. I wasn't laughing. In fact, I was boiling mad!

"Olga went out to fetch it again. Good old Olga. Loves to row."

"It seems like quite a coincidence that my boat keeps drifting away and Olga is always there to rescue it."

"Yes. Convenient for you that Olga saves your boat every time! Now tell me," he asked, lowering his voice, "what were you doing over at the lighthouse last night?"

Abigail and I looked at each other, wondering how to answer. It was none of Dr. Perhonen's business. Plus, he was a friend of Karl Kenton. I decided to address that issue first.

"On Sunday, my dad and I were out sailing and we noticed Dr. Karl Kenton on your boat. Is he your friend?"

"Karl? Oh I met him at the marina. He's into that New Age stuff. A lot of rubbish, if you ask me. Tried to talk me into his little scheme. Needs a lot of money. Green witches and whatnot. I'm a college professor and researcher. It wouldn't do for me to get mixed up in all that nonsense!"

Did that mean that Dr. Perhonen wasn't one of them? How could we be sure? He might be trying to trick us.

"When I was just over at my mooring, I saw you looking at us through your spyglass. What were you doing?"

"I just got back from town. Took the motor launch over to the marina. Called a taxi from there. Had to do a little shopping. Olga's still asleep, you know. Not a morning person. When I got back, your boat was gone, so I looked around. Saw you over at your mooring. Just wanted to make sure that it was you who had taken the boat and not someone else, you know."

Was he telling the truth? If so, then who had written the warning on my tiller? Was it Olga? Or someone else?

"What kind of research do you do?" I asked the doctor. I'd decided to try and find out more about him. He had mentioned that he was a scientist the first time we had met him.

"Water pollution. It's all around us, everywhere. Have a big grant. Find all the bad things in our drinking water, dangerous levels, how they get in, how to get them out. All those good things. Very interesting work. Love it. Just love it."

Hmmm. Dr. Perhonen was a research scientist working with water pollution. Another coincidence? Or part of the plot?

"Does Dr. Kenton know about your work?" Abigail asked.

"Never asked. That bag of hot air just goes on and on about his little group and what they're up to. Peace, love, and herbs. All that. Never got a word in edgewise. Just after my money, that's what I think."

I had an idea. "When are you going back to your lab?" I asked.

"Leaving on Thursday or maybe Friday. Got to get back to work. Don't want to leave, but the university won't let me stay on vacation forever. Don't teach in the summer, but lab work goes on. C'est la vie. Want to stay here. Put a mini-lab on the boat. Have a few things here. Like to test the water. Can't help it."

"Abigail. Where are those vials?"

"Uh, right here," she said, descending the ladder and grabbing her backpack from the bow of the *Classy Clam*. Back on deck, she rummaged around for a while before she was able to produce the glass vials.

"Oh, ho, ho! And where did you get these?" asked the doctor, holding them up to the light.

"It's a long story," I told him. "Do you think you could tell us what's in them? If it's some sort of chemical or poison?"

"Poison, you say? Why would you little girls have two vials of poison, I wonder?"

"It's a long story," I answered for a second time. "Can you find out what they are in your mini-lab?"

"Quite possibly. Quite. You never told me about your sail last night. Does this have something to do with it?"

"Maybe. We're not sure." I was afraid to tell him. But it was fairly amazing that we had just happened to meet a real scientist who could tell us what those chemicals might be. I sure hoped that they weren't' chemicals used to test the levels of acidity or bacteria in the water system. In that case, we would really look foolish. Then I had another idea.

"Have you still got those candies from The Tomb?" I asked Abigail.

"Yes, I just saw them in my bag." She dove back into her backpack and began searching again.

"We have something else we want you to check out, if you could, please," I added. "It's a homemade candy that's being sold in town. We think there's something bad in it."

"You don't mean Benny Beans, do you?"

We were stunned. How could this old man, who had just sailed into town, know about Benny Beans? Unless, he was one of them?

"Ha, ha, ha! My old friend and former university classmate Dr. Benjamin Alexis makes that candy. He didn't major in candy making at college. No. Ha, ha, ha! But the man's fallen on hard times. Likes the bottle if you know what I mean." We just stared at him. The bottle? Then Doctor

253

Perhonen made a motion of someone drinking from a bottle. Then we understood. Yes, we had guessed that Mr. Alexis had a drinking problem.

"Couldn't keep a job. Moved down here to the Cape to escape the world. Wouldn't hurt a flea. Wouldn't do it. No, no, no. You can believe me. His candy is just fine."

"Would you please test it anyway?" I begged. "And tell us what's in it and if it would hurt a child who might eat a lot of it? Please?"

"All right, dearies, but you can trust Alexis. Wouldn't hurt a fly. I told him, 'you'll never make a fortune cooking up candy in your basement!' But the poor fellow doesn't know what to do with himself. Quel dommage!"

Abigail finally found the candies and handed them to the doctor.

"You little girls certainly involve yourselves in a lot of schemes. What are you all up to? Sailing at night, playing with vials of poison, worrying about candy?"

"We're just trying to be good citizens," offered Abigail.

"Did you or Olga notice anything strange about my boat?" I asked the doctor. "Like something bizarre written on the tiller?"

The doctor gave me a blank stare. No, I guess they hadn't noticed. If they had, it wouldn't have made any sense to them anyway, except if they had written it themselves! I guess whoever had set my boat adrift must have done the writing.

"Please don't mention any of this to anyone. Not anyone at all," I begged him. "Please promise. Don't tell Dr. Alexis or any of your friends, or even Olga. And especially not Dr. Kenton. Promise?"

"I promise! You can count on me. And, after we eat our breakfast, I'll get right to work on these vials and Benjamin's candy. Then shall I call you with the results?"

"Yes, please! Let me give you my phone number," I said.

From his coat pocket Dr. Perhonen took his cell phone and entered my phone number into its memory.

"Do you have a fax?" he asked. "I could fax you the results."

I gave him Muffy's aunt's fax number at her shop. "Just write 'Attention Muffy' on it, please."

"Well I'm so glad we met again," he beamed. "Now I have a little mystery of my own to solve. I just love mysteries. Scientific research is a mystery, you know. How about you youngsters? Do you like mysteries?"

"Uh, sure." Sailing class would be over soon. We had to get back to the fleet. I was surprised that no one had come to get us, but I guess everyone was too involved with the races. We thanked the doctor, climbed back into the *Classy Clam*, and sailed over to join the others at the finish line.

Chapter Sixty-Seven

"What happened to you?" called Mollie as we sailed up beside her. We turned our boats into the wind and I held onto the *Chubby Quahog*. "We've already finished the race and now we're going to sail the same course again, only in reverse, just for fun."

"I saw you on that yacht," said Muffy. "What happened?"

"They had my Catabout again! They even watched us sail over to the lighthouse last night. Olga supposedly found my boat drifting and rescued it again. And there was a message written in pigpen code on my tiller!"

"No!" exclaimed Mollie. "What did it say?"

"It said, 'We're watching you.'"

"Wow. Could it be true? It does seem as if they know wherever we are," said Muffy, "and where we'll be."

"And Dr. Perhonen is *not* a friend of Karl. He's a research scientist. Remember he told us that before? His specialty is water pollution!"

"You're kidding!" Mollie exclaimed.

"We gave him the vials and Abigail's Benny Beans. He has a lab right on his yacht! But he knows Mr. Alexis and insists that the candy is harmless."

"Of course he would," muttered Mollie. "You shouldn't have trusted him with the vials! If he tests them, fine. We'll have our proof. But if he's one of them, we've lost our only chance to ever find out what was in them! And to find out what Mr. Mullins was going to do!"

We heard the air horn blow, telling us that we had three minutes until the start of the next race. We pushed away from the *Chubby Quahog* and headed toward the starting line. Mollie and Muffy followed. We got a good start and came in fourth. Muffy and Mollie made third place. We were happy for them. As we sailed back to the club, we noticed a tall, blonde woman on board the yacht talking to Dr. Perhonen. It must have been Olga. They were looking our way and pointing at us. It made me feel uncomfortable—and suspicious. Maybe I had made a mistake in trusting him.

We beached the Sprites and pulled them up to the tide line. After we unrigged the boats and put the sails and rudders away, we galloped up the stairs to the clubhouse and found seats on the gray benches. For the closing meeting we discussed something called "buoy room." It was the reason for a few problems during the last race, when some of the boats collided with each other while rounding one of the buoys. It was quite complicated, but I listened even though we hadn't been involved.

"Let's go eat," said Abigail, as soon as we were dismissed.

"I hope Louie isn't late," Muffy said. "We have digging to do. When we go over to the old barn, don't anyone mention our Palace, O.K.? We don't want Louie to know about it. Agreed?"

Of course we agreed. We had never thought about the possibility of anyone ever finding our secret place, but now we would be taking a boy to the barn just beside our Eel Grass Palace! We would have to be really careful.

We hopped on our bikes and rode down past the marina to the snack bar. Cooky's wife was at the window. She didn't seem very happy to see us. As we stepped up to the window, we peered past her to say "hello" to Cooky, but he wasn't there!

"Where's Cooky?" asked Mollie.

"Ain't here." Cooky's wife kept her eyes down. She wouldn't even look at us!

"He's not sick, is he?" I asked.

"He had business to attend to. What's you order?"

We gave her our lunch orders and sat on the grass while we waited for her to fry our burgers. Wonder what business Cooky had. It certainly was strange.

When our lunch was ready, we paid and took our plates and sodas back to the bank of Lowndes River.

Mollie lingered at the counter.

"Have you heard from Mrs. Pitts?" she asked.

"Nope."

Mollie gave up and joined us.

"I wonder what's going on. Cooky and his wife aren't very friendly any more. In fact, they act as if they don't like us. They must be hiding something."

"What would they be hiding?" asked Abigail.

As I ate my burger, I took up my pastime of looking for four-leaf clovers in the grass. It wasn't hopeless, but I was just beginning to think I may never find one again, when suddenly I did!

"Hey, Girls! Look at this!" I held it up for them to see.

"Good work, Nature Girl!" complimented Mollie.

"Is it real?" asked Muffy. "You're not kidding us, are you?"

"No. Look," I showed them that it wasn't just a regular clover with an extra leaf cleverly added to trick them. After they each had a look, I safely tucked it into the pocket of my shirt. I would add it to my collection.

"We need some luck about now," muttered Mollie. Muffy was about to say something, but didn't.

"Well, I don't know about you, but I need some ice cream," announced Abigail. It sounded good to me, so we all walked back to the counter to order and were surprised to see Cooky coming in the back door! Mollie ran around to the back of the snack shop. We followed her.

"Where have you been?" she asked him.

"I've got nothing to say to you," he answered, turning away from us.

"Was it them? Does it have something to do with Mrs. Pitts?"

"No comment." He shut the back door in our faces!

"It does have something to do with them!" exclaimed Muffy. "They must have threatened him. Now he's afraid."

"Then let's leave him alone," Abigail suggested. "They may have come after him because he's been talking to us."

I agreed. Cooky had helped us as much as he could, yet still I wondered who had threatened him and what had they said.

We went back to the counter and ordered our ice cream and then sat on the bank to eat. It was a beautiful sunny day. So peaceful. We were taking our time because we were waiting for Louie. As we licked our cones, we saw him riding toward us.

He leapt off his bike and threw it to the ground, almost crashing into us!

"Whoa, Louie!" exclaimed Mollie. "Slow down!"

"Jared's on his way!" he erupted, breathlessly. "He's flying into Boston tonight and taking the bus down to Smithport. Aunt Lydia's gonna pick him up. No one's supposed to know. You didn't tell, did you?"

The Girls shook their heads "no."

"I told my mother," I said. "And she told my dad, but they won't tell anyone else."

"Good, 'cause Jared's going to surprise that crook. He's going straight to the police when he gets here. Then they'll all go to his parents' house. They'll catch that guy and find out what he's been doing to those old folks!"

"Well, that's good news!" said Muffy.

"Cooky and his wife are acting very antisocial," I told him. "They won't talk to us. We think someone has threatened them."

"That figures," he said, thoughtfully. "I'm going to put in my order. I'm real hungry."

Louie ordered his lunch and we sat with him on the grass as he ate. I showed him my clover and he seemed filled with admiration. He had never found a four-leaf clover in his life.

"It's a good sign," he said.

"I don't believe in luck," I told him. "But I'm glad I found it because they're so rare. We do need help. We've got to find that treasure before the others do."

"When is Jared getting in?" asked Muffy.

"He'll be here about eight."

"And he's going to the police right away?" asked Abigail.

"Yeah."

257

"Come on, Louie," prodded Mollie. "Hurry up and eat. We've got work to do."

"What are we going to do for shovels?" asked Louie, finishing his hot dog and chips.

"There are plenty of them in the barn," I said.

"How do you know?" he asked, his eyes wide open and staring at me. "You've been there before?"

"Sure," said Abigail, matter-of-factly, happy to see that Louie was impressed. "We've all been there. Just the other day we were in the barn, in the office. We found..."

We gave her a look, so she stopped. Louie was almost "one of us" but not quite. We didn't want him to know everything!

"What did you find?" he asked.

"Let's go," said Mollie. "We'll tell you later."

I shivered as we rode past the marina. Even the thought of Karl gave me goose bumps! He was probably at his radio station, wherever that was, preaching about nature and herb power. That was fine, as long as he wasn't following us!

We stopped at the end of Lowndes River Road and turned right. The field of lilies was ahead of us. We turned down the dirt road and made our way to the end, then rode along the old path around the overgrown bog to get to the barn. Though we weren't expecting anyone to find us, we hid our bikes behind the barn where I had noticed a broken door the last time we were there. We entered, closing the door behind us.

"Wow!" exclaimed Louie. "This place is awesome! Look at all this stuff!"

He ran his hand over the old tools hanging in place and scanned the piles of boxes. Mollie was the first to grab a shovel. We each took one from the rack and moved toward the office.

"Let's get the chairs out," said Muffy, taking one and placing it outside the door. We helped take the other chair and a few boxes out. It was then that we saw that the entire floor was built in pieces that could easily be removed. It was a small room, making it awkward for us all to be digging at the same time.

"Let's get to work," I said, beginning to dig in the middle of the floor. Each of us took a corner. Louie ran out and got a couple of buckets for us to put the dirt into. It was crowded and we kept bumping into each other, but the earth was soft and easy to dig.

"I found it!" exclaimed Abigail almost right away. We saw the top of an old rusted metal box peeking out from under the dirt. We dug around the edges of it and helped her get it loose. Finally she was able to pull it out.

"Here it is! The buried treasure!" It was the same sort of metal box as we had found in the desk drawer last time, only this one was more rusty from being buried in the ground. It wasn't locked. As Abigail carefully opened the box, its rusty hinges broke. Inside were stacks of paper money, hundred dollar bills, and small bags of gold coins! We were so excited that we almost didn't hear the voices outside. But we did hear them and we froze in horror!

"Oh no!" I groaned, Muffy and I snatched the shovels and buckets, hiding them behind a pile of cranberry boxes outside the office, as Louie and Mollie frantically replaced the floorboards. Abigail clutched the box as I almost threw the chairs back into the room as we raced for the back door. The five of us slipped out as someone pulled open the big sliding door at the front of the barn. I tore my sweatshirt off and threw it to Abigail to wrap the box in. She tossed it into the basket of her bike. We quickly pushed our bikes around the edge of the barn and made a frenzied dash for the road.

When we reached the Yacht Harbor Road, we stopped.

"We have to find out who it was," said Louie. "I'm going back."

"No!" cried Muffy. "It's too dangerous! If they see you, they'll know we're the ones who have the treasure."

"Maybe they don't know that he's one of us," said Abigail.

"Meet us at the yacht club," Mollie called out as Louie crept back up the road toward the path leading to the old barn. Louie looked back and nodded "O.K." That was the last we saw of him.

Chapter Sixty-Eight

At the yacht club Billy was recording race scores on the bulletin board. He looked up as we entered the clubhouse.

"You look as though you've seen a ghost!"

"Something like that," said Muffy, panting from our desperate bike ride.

Abigail had carefully lifted the treasure box, still wrapped in my sweatshirt, from her bicycle basket and carried it into the clubhouse.

"What've you got there?" asked Billy.

"Uh...something," stammered Abigail. Billy shrugged.

"Have any of you been by The Tomb lately?"

"We were there on Friday night," I answered. "Why?"

"Judy didn't show up today. She never even called. I'm worried about her."

"Maybe she's sick," Mollie suggested.

"Maybe. But when Mr. Prince called her cottage, no one answered. She's renting a cottage with a bunch of girls. One of them is Sandy something, who works at the ice cream shop. Let's swing by and see if Sandy knows what's wrong with Judy."

"Laura, you and Muffy go with Billy. Abigail and I'll stay here to wait for Louie," said Mollie.

"Where's Louie?" asked Billy.

"Uh...um...we'll tell you later," Mollie replied.

"Be careful!" Muffy admonished Abigail. "Guard that box with your life."

"Don't worry," Abigail reassured her. "I will."

The three of us left the clubhouse and drove to town in Billy's truck. It was a short ride. We parked on the street in front of the ice cream shop. Inside, a couple of teenage girls were behind the counter.

"Hi, Sandy," Billy greeted the one with a honey-blonde ponytail. "We're looking for Judy."

A strange look came over Sandy's face. She stared at us with her mouth open, then closed it. Finally she said, "Oh, she's not feeling well."

"What's wrong?" asked Billy, concerned.

"Uh...She has a stomach virus."

"Why didn't she call the club and let us know?"

"Um...She did, but she couldn't get through," the girl said, nervously. "The...uh...line was busy."

Billy hesitated. "The sailing master called your cottage, but no one answered."

"She's...uh...really sick. But she'll be better soon. You don't have to worry."

Billy turned and walked out. We followed.

"She should've called," muttered Billy.

"She tried," Muffy said. She must be really sick. Billy was anxious about her. He was a good person. Maybe I had been wrong to suspect him.

Back at the yacht club, we were surprised to find that Louie still hadn't arrived.

"We're worried about Louie," Abigail told us.

"O.K., Billy. Here's what we'll do," Mollie began. "We'll drive over to the...uh...place where we left Louie and search for him."

"And where did you leave Louie?"

"We'll show you. It's not far," I explained. We all hopped in his truck and drove to the intersection where Lowndes River Road meets Yacht Harbor. "Pull into that driveway over there at the Singers'."

Billy pulled into the long shell driveway opposite the dirt road that led to the barn. The Singers didn't seem to be home. They were members of the yacht club and we knew them, so we thought it would be all right to leave the truck there for a few minutes while we looked for Louie. Parking it on the street would be too obvious.

"Muffy, stay here with me," pleaded Abigail.

"Good idea," said Mollie. "Stay with Abigail and watch the road, but keep hidden."

The rest of us hiked up the dirt road bordered by the field of bright orange lilies and followed the path back to the barn. Louie's bike was hidden in the bushes at the end of the path, just before the bog. That meant he was still there.

"What is this place?" asked Billy. "I hope we're not trespassing on someone's private property! I don't need any more visits to the police station!"

"Shhhh! You don't have to worry. It's an old bog that was owned by Captain Snow, the one who built the haunted house," I explained in a whisper. Billy started walking toward the barn. "Someone might be in there," I said to him. I motioned for him to follow us as we sneaked around to the back door and peered in. All was quiet. We silently entered and moved toward the little office. What met our eyes really shook us up!

It looked as if wild animals had ripped the office apart. Dirt was everywhere! The chairs had been thrown out, one on either side of the doorway. The floorboards were in pieces. But where was Louie?

"What's this all about?" asked Billy as he surveyed the scene.

"We were looking for something," I told him. "After we found it, we heard voices and escaped before whoever it was got in."

"What did you find?" Billy was looking at all the holes dug in the office floor.

"What Abigail has in the truck," I explained evasively. Billy didn't pry.

"How did you lose Louie?"

"He wanted to find out who it was who came in after us," Mollie told him. "So he came back. They must have caught him!"

261

"Well, let's look around," said Billy in a serious tone. "If they did catch him, they may have tied him up and left him here somewhere."

We searched the barn, including a couple of closets and the loft, but Louie was nowhere to be found! They had kidnapped him!

"Billy! We have to call the police! They've taken Louie!" I cried.

"Maybe he just wandered off." Billy didn't seem that upset! What was wrong with him? Maybe he knew more about boys than we did.

"Why would he do that?" Mollie sounded annoyed. "He knew we were waiting for him at the club. His bike is still here. They've got him for sure!"

"Who's got him?" asked Billy

"Those Earth Mother People, of course," she replied.

"O.K., but I think we should give him a little more time," said Billy. "Maybe he's in the woods here."

We went out and looked around outside the barn and in the bushes, but found nothing. I felt almost sick. They had Louie and there was no telling what they would do to him! Mrs. Pitts and Karl had threatened us. They had tied up Miss Deighton and left her for dead. What would they do to Louie?

As we headed toward the path, we heard a rustling in the bird berry bushes. We stopped and clung to each other. Was it Karl? Or Mrs. Pitts? The zombie? Flushed and bubbling with excitement, Louie emerged.

"I found someone's secret hideout!" he joyfully exclaimed.

"Why were you snooping around in the bushes while we were waiting for you back at the yacht club?" I scolded him.

"But I found something real cool! It's like little houses and there's a..."

"*Shut up!*" screamed Mollie. We never used that expression. I was shocked that Mollie had lost her temper, but our worst fear had come upon us! Louie had discovered our Eel Grass Palace!

"What's wrong?" Louie was completely confused.

"First of all, we thought you'd been kidnapped," I began. "Second, you haven't told us who was in the barn." I had to change the subject. Louie had to forget that he'd seen our palace!

"I don't know who they were."

We stared at him, puzzled.

He continued, "I went around back of the barn to look in, but when I got there they were already in the office. I crept up to the window, but that's when they were getting the shovels. When I went back to the door, they were in the office digging. I went back to the window, but by that time, they'd left 'cause they couldn't find the treasure. I ran 'round to the front of the barn, but they were gone. I never saw their faces."

"That's ridiculous!" stated Mollie. "How could you have not seen them?"

"I don't know," Louie shrugged.

"Didn't you hear their voices?" I asked.

"Yeah. They were swearing, but I couldn't tell who it was."

"You found a treasure?" asked Billy.

"Something like that," I said. He didn't ask any more about it.

"How did they ever find this place?" Billy questioned.

"They must have called the town offices. They probably suspected that the Snows owned it. The tax collector would have told them," I said. If I'd been able to find out who owned the land, certainly anyone could.

"You kids ought to be careful," Billy told us. "Let's get out of here."

Louie pulled his bike out of the bushes as we followed Billy back to his truck. Abigail and Muffy were glad to see him, but just wait until they heard that he had found our Eel Grass Palace! Louie threw his bike into the back of the truck and we drove to the yacht club.

"Thanks, Billy," we said.

"Anytime. I'm glad to help you find your lost sheep," he joked. I was glad he had forgiven us for the catastrophe of the night before.

Out on the lawn of the club, Muffy suggested, "Let's go to my aunt's shop. We can leave our treasure in her office safe."

"Good idea," I agreed.

We took Yacht Harbor Road to Sylvia's Way and on to the shop. When we arrived, Muffy said, "They'll never think that my aunt has it if they should come looking for it."

"Do you think they'll try to get it back from us, whoever they are?" asked Abigail, timidly clutching the treasure box.

"I don't know," I replied, not wanting to scare her, but it seemed logical that they would. They knew we had been to the lighthouse and had overheard their séance. So they would suspect that we were the ones who had taken the treasure. They wanted it. They would try to get it back.

"What'll we do with all that money?" she asked.

"It was stolen from my great-great-grandfather's company," said Muffy. "Grammy once told me that his partner Mr. Lowndes had only one daughter, but she never had children, so he had no heirs. I guess the money belongs to my family."

"But we need it!" I exclaimed.

"I know!" beamed Muffy. "It's the treasure we needed to buy the…" She stopped short before she gave away our secret. But what kind of a secret was it now? Louie had already discovered our Eel Grass Palace! This was the worst day of our lives, in one sense! How could we make him forget? But now we had enough money to buy the land from Alfred Snow, so in a way, it was the happiest day of our lives!

263

"To buy what?" asked Louie.

"Nothing," I said. "It's just a dream." Louie let it go.

Muffy took the box from Abigail and disappeared into the shop. She reappeared a little while later to tell us that her aunt had securely locked our mystery money box in her office safe.

Louie looked at the clock on the church steeple. "I've got to go now. My mom wants me home early for dinner tonight, 'cause she's going to the bus station with Aunt Lydia."

"You're going too?" asked Muffy.

"Yeah. Aunt Lydia said I should go. It's 'cause of me she knew that something was wrong at the Wellses."

"I wish we could all be there when the police confront that creep," I muttered.

"Me too," the others chimed in.

"Call me tonight and let me know what happens," Mollie told him.

"Then call us," I said to her. "We all want to know."

Louie nodded his head in agreement. Then he hopped on his bike and rode off. As soon as he left, I wondered if he would be safe riding home alone. Maybe he wasn't scared. If he were, he wouldn't admit it, but I sure would be!

"Want to come over?" I asked. "We could go for a swim."

"I've got tennis," said Mollie.

"My grandparents invited me over for dinner," said Muffy, looking up at the church clock. "They eat kind of early, so I'd better be leaving soon."

"How about you Abigail?"

"Is it safe to go to your house?" she asked.

"It's early, but my mom might be home." It was settled. We would ride with Muffy as far as her grandmother's, go down Pine Street, drop Mollie off at her house, and continue on to mine. Abigail and I would have a nice swim. I would ask Dad to give her and her bike a ride home in his truck. It wasn't safe for her to be out riding alone either. Later, we would call each other as soon as we got news from Louie. As for our Captain Snow mystery, we would have to think of a plan to stop the sacrifice the next night.

When we arrived at Mrs. McLaughlin's, we decided to make our plan for Wednesday. I told the Girls, "I'll call the animal control officer when I get home. We can meet him after dark tomorrow night near Captain Snow's. Then when those Earth People try to sacrifice the coyote, they'll get caught. That will be the end of them and their cruelty."

"We hope," said Mollie. "Why don't you all come over to my house in the morning?"

"Let's meet here at grammy's house instead," said Muffy. "I don't feel safe riding alone all the way to your house anymore. Abigail and I both have to pass some lonely places to get to your house, Mollie. What do you say?"

We agreed. "And don't forget we have an appointment with Agnes and Mabel to view the contents of their trunk," Abigail reminded us.

"'Have an appointment'! 'View the contents'!" I laughed. We snickered at her choice of words. Sometimes she could be funny without knowing it.

"If we have time, we could sail over to the old lighthouse again," I added. No one seemed very interested in that, so the three of us said good-bye to Muffy and rode off.

We swung by Mollie's and stayed only long enough to make sure that her mom was home. After we said good-bye to Mollie, Abigail and I continued riding on to my house. I was glad to see Mom's car in the driveway. She wasn't in the house, but when we looked down the slope to the beach, we saw that she was swimming.

"Let's leave our backpacks in the house," I said. We turned back and entered the sitting room through the front door. As we passed through the little room, I noticed the message light blinking on the answering machine.

"Hi. This is Louie. Bad news. Jared Wells ran into a lightning storm so his plane had to land out West somewhere. He won't get out of there until late tonight, which means he won't get here 'til tomorrow morning. He has to take a bus from Boston. Mom said I could miss camp to drive with her and Aunt Lydia to the bus station. They both have to skip work, but this is important, and they got time off. I'll call you tomorrow. Bye."

"Wow," said Abigail. "That complicates things."

I called Louie and told him our plans. Then I called Muffy and Mollie to let them know the news. I asked Abigail to stay for dinner, so she called her grandmother to tell her. Then we ran upstairs, left our clothes in a heap on the floor (we were already wearing our swimsuits), and headed for the beach.

"Mom," I called out. "Jared Wells ran into a lightning storm. He won't be in until tomorrow morning. Louie, his mom, and aunt are going to pick him up at the bus station."

"That's great! Not about the storm, but that he's arriving soon. I'm glad that one mystery will be solved. We'll find out who that man is and why he's posing as the Wellses' son. Come on in! The water's beautiful!"

After a nice cool swim and relaxing dinner, Dad and I drove Abigail and her bike home to her grandmother's house. Before I went to bed, I found the shirt I had been wearing and took the four-leaf clover out of the pocket. I stuck it between the pages of one of my books. I would find it in the winter and remember this day.

It wasn't that late, but the sleepover, or rather "lack-of-sleep"-over, had left me pretty tired. Grammy's lavender sent me right to sleep.

Chapter Sixty-Nine

The next morning was overcast and a little breezy. I was very anxious to get Louie's call, but it might not come for a while. I got dressed and ate breakfast with Mom. She gave me the phone number of her morning patient so I could call her as soon as I heard from Louie. She waited as I rode my bike to Mollie's driveway before she turned and drove in the opposite direction to her first appointment.

I could hear Maxwell whining and complaining as I neared the kitchen door. Mollie was ready to leave and bolted out.

"My little brother is such a pain!" she complained.

I didn't know what to say. I didn't have a brother or sister and sometimes wished I did. I thought that it would be fun to have a little kid to play with, but Mollie couldn't stand Maxwell. I guess he wasn't much fun. Mrs. Perkins just couldn't say "no" to him. He was really too spoiled.

We rode to Mrs. McLaughlin's. Muffy was already there. We met her in the kitchen.

"Did you hear what happened?" asked Muffy breathlessly.

"No, what?" we asked in suspense.

"My aunt's shop was broken into! Someone smashed a window and tried to blow her safe open! Can you believe that?"

"Were they able to get it open?" I asked, fearing the worst.

"No! But they sure made a big mess of things and practically set her shop on fire!"

"No one was hurt," added Mrs. McLaughlin, entering the room. "It was the first time anyone has ever tried to break in. The police came immediately, but the culprits got away."

"Wow!"

We didn't mention the treasure box to Muffy's grandmother. It was secure and still in the safe. It must have been "them," whoever it was who'd come to the old barn after we found the treasure. Probably Karl and Mrs. Pitts, but how had they known that we had put the treasure in the shop safe? Could they really be watching us all the time? That was a chilling thought! Or was it Billy?

I felt terrible knowing that it was our fault—the break-in and all the damage to the shop. We would have to pay for it with some of our treasure money. It made me feel really guilty, especially since we couldn't tell anyone about it.

"Why don't you girls have some lemonade and sit out on the front porch while you wait for Abigail?" suggested Mrs. McLaughlin.

"Were you able to visit Mr. and Mrs. Wells?" I asked her.

"Oh, I've been so busy. I telephoned, but there was no answer. I must get over there again. It was easier when they sat out on their lawn chairs every day. Now that they stay inside all the time, it's more difficult."

"Did Muffy tell you about their son?" Mollie asked, forgetting that it was supposed to be a secret.

"Yes. It's so strange," she replied. "I guess their real son will be arriving this morning."

"Yes," I told her. "The police will be with him when he gets here. They'll catch that fake son and set the Wellses free."

"It's terrible that an impostor could just move in and take over without anyone realizing what had happened!" she exclaimed. "I'd never met their son. I wish I could have done something to help!"

"You'll be able to visit them from now on," said Muffy. "Jared and the police will confront that man and make everything right again."

"I hope so," muttered Mrs. McLaughlin. "Muffy told me that you wanted to visit Agnes and Mabel. I telephoned them earlier and they're expecting you."

"We should go over there first," I said to the Girls. We sat on the front porch, sipping our lemonade and waiting for Abigail. Because the weather was overcast, the town was more crowded than usual. Cars lined the street and traffic was moving slowly.

We saw Abigail in the distance. When she arrived, Mrs. McLaughlin had a glass of lemonade all ready for her. We sat on the porch until she had finished drinking. Then the four of us rode over to Seacliff Lane to visit the Weeks sisters.

The two elderly women greeted us at the front door.

"Won't you have some ice tea?" asked Mabel.

"No thank you," Muffy replied. "Grammy just gave us lemonade."

"Won't you try just a little of our tea?" Agnes asked. "It's made with herbs from our garden. It's good and good for you too."

Muffy gave me a look. Why were these old ladies, our distant relatives, trying to force us to drink their herbal tea? I couldn't decide if we should trust them or not.

"Which herbs did you use?" asked Mollie.

"Oh, a little of this and a little of that," Mabel replied, vaguely.

"How do you know it's safe?" asked Abigail, grimacing at the glass Agnes was holding out to her.

"I suppose we don't really know," speculated Agnes. "But it's never hurt us."

"Could we look at the trunk, please?" asked Mollie, getting back to the reason why we were there. Mabel and Agnes were suddenly making me feel very uncomfortable!

"Why, of course."

The aged sisters led us into their living room where we had left the trunk against the wall. Mollie and Abigail pulled it into the center of the room and unlatched it. A musty odor rose up from the trunk as Mollie opened the lid. Inside we found clothes, lace gloves, a dried daisy chain wrapped in tissue paper, a Bible, and a journal!

Abigail opened the journal and began to read: *This morning, as I finished my mending, I heard voices in the garden. Looking down I saw Mother and Mrs. Hutchings. They discussed which herbs Mrs. Hutchings would need to use in making a potion to ensure that Wendall Smith would fall in love with Mrs. Hutchings's homely and shrewish daughter, Sarah.*

Why, oh why, does Mother dabble in witchcraft? She can make good money selling her herbs for cooking and medicine. Surely my own mother is a witch!

"Can you believe that?" exclaimed Mollie. "This must be Petunia's journal! How did Hannah get it?"

"After Petunia disappeared, maybe the Snows gave it to Hannah, or possibly after the elder Snows passed away and their other children closed up the house, she obtained it."

"It's just terrible, isn't it, to have to live with a witch for a mother!" said Agnes with feeling. Maybe they were sincere after all.

Abigail continued reading: *If only Father would put a stop to it, but he says nothing. He seems afraid. He may be frightened of Mother. He does not answer me when I question him. The whole town believes that he must be as evil as Mother. They want to excommunicate us all from the church! Even so, Father will not speak a word against Mother.*

Edward will be going to sea with Father soon. His family does not approve of it because of Mother, yet Edward's mother regularly attends her meetings. Edward doesn't know. His aunt speaks out against us. I understand her feelings. Everyone is against Father and against our family, but it is all Mother's fault!

Many of those who speak against us are the same ones who come to Mother's séances. The meetings are secret, so only those involved know who is in the group. But those who come speak against us so as not to arouse suspicion. They speak against Mother and Father in public, yet they come to Mother in private, asking her to bring back their dead, to tell the future, or to prepare potions and spells.

It is all so terrible and horrifying. I have pleaded with her to stop, but she tells me to keep silent. I have grown to fear her as well. She has no natural affection for us, yet my sisters are too busy with their beaux to notice the change in Mother. Brother is active with his friends and tells me I have imagined it all. No matter what they say, I know she is not the mother we once knew.

It made me feel sorry for Petunia. She knew how evil her mother was, but no one would listen to her. I wonder if she had ever told Edward.

"So Mrs. Snow was a real witch!" declared Muffy.

"She helped the locals mix up magic potions and she held séances!" continued Mollie. "Those Earth Mother People are holding séances too. And they said that Mrs. Snow worshipped the Earth Mother. She had a plan and they are carrying it out!"

"The Earth Mother?" asked Agnes, brightening up. "Isn't she the one that nice Dr. Kenton talks about on his radio station?"

Oh no! They were already Karl's converts! I couldn't believe it.

"You don't really believe that stuff about the Earth Mother, do you?" asked Muffy.

"Of course not!" exclaimed Mabel. "But we do agree with the doctor about the need to preserve our town. We've seen so many changes over the years and I'm sad to say that not many of them have been for the better."

That made me feel a lot better! But I wondered about Mrs. Snow's plan that the Earth Mother People were carrying out. When we had overheard their séance at the old lighthouse, we had heard that her plan was the same one that the group had now. We hadn't given it much thought, but we should have. Was it about poisoning the water system? Was it turning the citizens into zombies? It had something to do with controlling everyone in town, I was sure.

"What else does the journal say?" asked Muffy.

The other diary entries were similar. Except for one. Abigail read: *My heart's desire is to marry Edward. His family does not approve of me, yet I believe that he will go against the wishes of his parents. Nevertheless, if he decided not to marry me, my desire would be to travel to India to serve as a nurse in Doctor Douglas's mission hospital in Madras. I could use my knowledge of herbs and medicines to heal the less fortunate. Sometimes in the evening, I imagine myself beneath the palms, dressed in colorful silks, eating saffron rice. I would spend my life telling the 'Good News' of the Bible to the lost souls of India.*

"Do you think that's where she went when she disappeared?" I asked.

"No one will ever know," said Mabel, shaking her head.

"Do you think that hospital still exists?" Muffy wondered. "I bet I could find out on the Internet! I'll go to the library and research it."

Just then the telephone rang. It was Mrs. McLaughlin. She asked to speak with Muffy, whose face turned white as she listened to her grandmother. We held our breath as she hung up the phone.

"That was Grammy. She wants us to come home right away. Jared Wells is there. He went to his house with the police to rescue his parents, but when they arrived, no one was home! Mr. and Mrs. Wells and that creepy man are gone! They searched the whole house. They don't know what to do next, but the police are going to keep watch on the Wellses' house in case they come back. Louie, his mom, his aunt, Jared Wells, and the police are all there at my grandparents'."

Where could Mr. and Mrs. Wells be? What had that man done to them? Agnes and Mabel stared blankly at us.

"It's another mystery," Abigail weakly explained.

"Well, dears, why don't you take this day journal with you and read it through when you have time?" offered Mabel. "You may find some more important information in there. I hope you can discover what happened to Petunia. I hate to think of her encountering her demise."

"Excuse me?" asked Muffy.

"Oh, never mind," said Mabel. "You all run along now."

We thanked her and Agnes. I guess we could trust them, even though they believed in luck from a pentagram! Muffy tucked the journal into her backpack. We said good-bye as the sisters closed the door. When we walked through their garden to our bikes, Mollie stooped down to pick up what I thought was a flower lying on the path. She stiffened as she turned around. Her face was as white as chalk! Oh no! What was it?

Chapter Seventy

Mollie extended her hand to show us another voodoo doll! This time in Muffy's image!

"Not again!" exclaimed Muffy, snatching the doll from Mollie's hand and ripping it apart. "They're not going to hurt me with their snips of fabric and cotton stuffing!"

Bits of hair, cloth, and cotton batting—that is, the stuffing—fell onto the path of Agnes and Mabel's garden. Abigail scooped them up and threw them into the bushes. We were stunned, but I guess we should have been expecting it. Now they had made a voodoo doll of each of us! Then I realized something.

"But Muffy," I said. "Don't you see what this means? They're following us! They know where we are! Every moment! They knew we were coming here! They're watching us, just as that message on the tiller of my boat read and the one in the toolshed. They see us, but we don't see them." It sent a shiver down my spine. Then a worse thought hit me—maybe Agnes and Mabel were part of the group! Maybe the witches network included most of the town already and that was why their messages and voodoo dolls were everywhere! I kept this thought to myself. What good would it do to make the others suspicious of my new relatives, and everyone else?

"We have to get to Grammy's house," said Muffy, urgently. "The doll has been destroyed, but that means that they've been in my house!"

Now she knew how the rest of us felt. It was really terrifying to think of strangers, evil strangers, snooping around your own home! We quickly pedaled back to Mrs. McLaughlin's. Everyone was still there except the police. We were surprised to meet Jared Wells. His wavy blond hair was the first thing we noticed. Then we saw how upset he and Aunt Lydia were. Louie, his mom, and the McLaughlin's showed concern as well. We could see a police cruiser was parked across the street from the Wellses' house, in the parking lot of a bed and breakfast inn.

Mrs. McLaughlin invited everyone for lunch. As we ate in the dining room, we couldn't help glancing over to the house next door, hoping to see the old couple, even though the high hedge blocked our view of the yard and first floor. Jared told us his story.

"I was in college. My grades were bad because I was staying out late with my friends, making the rounds of all the bars, playing my guitar, and living it up." He glanced at us nervously, so I assumed that he meant taking drugs. He cleared his throat and went on.

"Once when I came home on vacation, my dad tried to talk to me about where my life was going. Mom told me that they had cut back a lot on their lifestyle so I could go to a good college, but it annoyed me that they were trying to tell me how to live my life. I was really angry with them. I didn't want to hear it, so I just stood up, walked out of the house, and never came back. That was more than 20 years ago. Can you believe that? I never once called my parents or wrote them a letter that whole time." He hung his head and slowly shook it back and forth. His eyes filled with tears. He cleared his throat again and went on.

"Lydia was able to find me by tracing a letter I had written to a mutual friend of ours. He had told Lydia, at the time, that I was out in Salt Lake City. That was years ago, but I've been there ever since. I can't imagine who that man is, the one pretending to be me!"

"He's about your age and height," I said. "He's like you, except he's ugly with black greasy hair and a red face."

"Hmmm. Sounds like...no. It couldn't be."

"Who?" Mollie asked. "He must be someone you know. Otherwise how else would he even know about you and your parents?"

"Anyone could've heard about me."

"But who were you thinking of?" persisted Mollie.

"Well, a long time ago, I visited a friend of mine in Denver and I met an acquaintance of his, a real estate man, actually a sleazy developer, named...uh...I can't remember. Jim? Joe? He had black greasy hair and a red face just as you described. Anyway, we were talking about our roots. He said he was from New Jersey.

"When he found out I was from the Cape, he seemed overly interested. He wanted to know all about the Cape and my family as well. At the time, I didn't think much about it, so I answered all his questions, though I didn't like him at all.

"It makes me feel worried and angry. If he's the one who's staying with my parents, what could his motive be? Why would he do it? And why would they go along with it? That's the bigger question."

We were silent, considering. It sounded as if this real estate man could be the one, but why? What could he possibly gain by pretending to be Jared Wells? And why would Jared's parents allow him to move in with them? None of us had any answers. And now the three of them had disappeared!

After we finished eating, Lydia suggested that she drive Jared around town to see all the changes that had occurred since Jared left so many years before. She borrowed Mrs. McLaughlin's cell phone in case the police found Jared's parents. Louie's mom went back to work. Louie, the Girls, and I helped Mrs. McLaughlin clean up, while Mr. McLaughlin took up his watch on the front porch. Then we went out to the backyard to talk.

"I have to help my brother," Louie announced, looking up at the church clock. "He's mowing lawns down on Skunk's Neck."

"How about a sail?" I asked the Girls. "If you all want to go, then we could ride with Louie as far as Skunk's Neck."

Mollie said, "O.K. Then let's plan to meet at seven at the bandstand. We can have another sleepover at my house. Just before dark, we can go to Captain Snow's and wait for the Earth People."

"How are we going to do that?" I asked. "Your mom won't let us stay out after dark."

"O.K.," said Mollie. "Then I'll tell my mom that I'm sleeping at your house, Laura. She won't notice when we get in late and she probably won't think twice about it if she finds us all sleeping in my room in the morning."

"That would be a lie," declared Muffy.

"So what? I don't care," stated Mollie. "I'll be the only one who's telling a lie anyway. It's for the good of the coyote and to catch the witches."

We didn't like it, but at least three of us could tell our parents the truth. We would be sleeping at Mollie's. The rest of our plan we would keep to ourselves.

Chapter Seventy-One

We hopped on our bikes and pedaled with Louie down Main Street, past Small Pond, and along Pine Street. Miss Deighton's house looked quiet. Betty's car was parked in front. At Skunk's Neck we split up. As Louie continued on his way, we saw Billy's truck approaching from Gull Lane. He pulled over and stopped next to us.

"I'm glad I found you," he said. "I have to get to my job at the Nor'easter now, but I'm worried about Judy."

"Did you talk to her?" asked Abigail.

"No. I tried calling her again and there's still no answer. She's been acting a little strange lately too."

"How?" I asked.

"I don't know" was his answer.

"Shall we go over to her cottage and see if she's all right?" asked Abigail.

"Yeah. Why don't you hop in? I've got a little time, I guess," he said, looking at his watch. He jumped out of his truck to help us put our bikes in the back. Mollie and Muffy got into the cab while Abigail and I scrambled in next to the bikes.

"Where's her cottage?" I asked Billy through the open window in the cab.

"Off Main Street, on Aster Place, behind your aunt's shop, Muffy. Near the windmill."

"Which cottage?" Muffy asked.

"There's a yellow house on the left with three cottages behind it. Hers is the first one I've been told."

"You'd better park behind my aunt's shop," suggested Muffy. "We don't want to attract attention."

"Why not?" asked Abigail. "We're just visiting a friend. We're not doing anything wrong."

"Even so, we'd better park at the shop," said Mollie. I agreed. Billy pulled his truck up on the grass in the shade of a pine tree, behind the shop. We hopped out and wove our way on foot through yards and driveways, cutting over to Aster Place. It was easy to find the yellow house with its three cottages. No one seemed to be around. Billy stepped up on the cottage porch, opened the screen, and knocked on the door. No one answered.

We peered into the nearest window. A black shade covered it. We circled the cottage. All the windows were shut and covered!

Billy called out, "Judy! Are you in there? Are you all right?"

Still no answer. Billy tried the door. It was unlocked. He looked in. We crowded around him and peeked in as well. We scanned the room, looking for

Judy. We could see four beds lining the bare wooden walls, two on each side of the small room. But they were all empty! No one was there! Billy entered. One by one we followed.

The first thing we noticed in the dark and stuffy interior, besides Judy not being there, was an altar that took up the entire back wall of the tiny room! Candles, flowers, and fruit were heaped upon a narrow wooden table. Several large cloth dolls laden with gold jewelry, stood on the table. One of the dolls, a woman dressed in colorful skirts, held a fake candle, with a light bulb that had been left burning.

Without a word, we each began to search the place. I began by looking under one of the beds. I found a Ouija board! Under the pillow was a pack of Tarot cards! As our eyes became accustomed to the dark, we could see shapes and symbols, similar to the hex sign Mrs. Pitts had drawn on our plates, marked on the floor and walls!

Muffy and Mollie found books of spells and potions. There were jars of herbs and bottles of strange liquids. Abigail pointed out piles of Benny Beans on a shelf! I wanted to find a diary or journal, but we couldn't find anything like that.

"I can't believe this!" exclaimed Billy. "Judy's taking this green witch stuff too seriously!"

"She is," agreed Abigail. "By the way, we shouldn't be here. It's not legal."

"Legal, schmegal!" Mollie laughed.

"I'm getting scared," said Abigail, glancing around at the altar and all the symbols. "Can we go now?"

"It's 'may we go now?'" corrected Mollie. "We might as well. We have enough evidence that Judy and her roommates are into witchcraft."

As we left the cottage, Abigail asked, "Do you think they're green witches or black witches?"

"I couldn't tell you for sure," said Billy, as we walked back toward the shop. "But it doesn't look very *good* to me, all those weird dolls and symbols!"

As we walked, Abigail asked, "It isn't against the law to be a witch, is it?"

"You're the legal expert," said Mollie with a smirk. "You should know."

"Just ignore her, Abigail," answered Muffy. "It depends on which law you're talking about." We knew that she was thinking about the Bible.

"No," said Mollie, with an air of authority. "There are no laws."

"There might be some old laws against witchcraft," Billy put in.

"Well nowadays, a witch would only get in trouble if she broke some other law as well," continued Mollie. "The U.S. of A. guarantees freedom of religion."

"Some religion!" scoffed Billy.

"But where's Judy?" asked Abigail. "If she's sick, she shouldn't have gone out. She should have been in bed."

"This doesn't add up," said Billy. "Something's not right."

We had reached Muffy's aunt's shop and sat ourselves down on the back step to talk. Suddenly Muffy's aunt appeared at the door.

"I thought I heard voices!" she remarked, smiling at us.

"We're really sorry about the break-in," I said to her.

"Those kinds of things happen," her aunt replied. "Just another mess to clean up. This fax came in for you last night, Muffy. With all the confusion, we didn't even notice it until now. It's a wonder it survived the explosion!" She held out a sheet of soot-smudged paper.

Muffy jumped up to take it. She thanked her aunt, who went back to work. We peered over Muffy's shoulder. It was the fax we were expecting from Dr. Perhonen! It read, "Vials contain water-testing solutions. Candies contain sugar, water, and thyme, horehound, rosemary, and lemon oil—nothing that would hurt children, even in large amounts. Don't worry your little heads. Regards, Dr. Perhonen."

"What's that about?" asked Billy.

"You remember the big yacht that was moored in the harbor?" I asked him. "We boarded it the other day because we found my Catabout tied up to it." Billy nodded.

"Well, the skipper of that yacht, Dr. Perhonen, is a research scientist, and we gave him the vials we found at the water tower. We also gave him some of the candy they sell at The Tomb. It's all harmless, I guess."

"Do you really expect me to believe that?" exclaimed Mollie. "It can't be true! The candy must to be bad if all the kids are addicted to it! And Mr. Mullins had to have poison in those vials. I know! It was the vials that the police took that had the poison in them. And they'll never test them! Now we won't ever have any proof! I think Dr. Perhonen is one of them, anyway."

"He could be," I speculated. "We were so close to having some evidence against those Earth People! Now we have nothing. And what are we going to do about Judy?"

"We'll go back to the ice cream shop and confront Sandy," said Billy. "She'll have to give me some answers." We were all disappointed about the fax, but what could we do? Right now we had Judy's disappearance to deal with. It was another, but unrelated, mystery. We got into the truck and drove the short distance to the ice cream shop.

Sandy and her friend, peering through the large front window, saw us coming and began to whisper frantically.

Billy walked in through the screen door and we followed close behind. He announced, "We just stopped by your cottage to check in on Judy, to see if she needed anything. But she's not there."

"Oh," said Sandy, her eyes darting from her friend to Billy. "She called us around lunchtime and said her mother's sick. She's...uh...in the hospital and wanted Judy to come home to Connecticut right away. Judy'll probably be back in a few days."

"That's too bad about her mom," said Billy. "But how could she drive home if she's so sick?"

"She was feeling much better."

"O.K. Thanks."

Outside we talked as we got into the truck.

"I'm calling Mr. Prince. He has the home phone numbers of all the instructors. He'll make sure that Judy arrives home safely and he'll find out how her mom is doing."

"Do you really believe that story?" asked Mollie in amazement.

"Why not?" he asked. "If it's not true, we'll find out soon enough. You girls are too suspicious of everyone and everything!"

Billy had to get to work. He agreed to give me a call as soon as he got word from Mr. Prince that Judy was safely at home in Connecticut, if indeed that was where she had gone! If not, we couldn't imagine what had happened to her, but we were sure that Sandy and her friend knew! Billy helped us get our bikes out of his truck and headed for the Nor'easter.

Chapter Seventy-Two

"I think we ought to go for a sail," said Mollie. "We can't do anything else." Then in an undertone she added, "Until later tonight. Hey, did you call the animal control man, Laura?"

"I forgot."

"How could you? The sacrifice is tonight! And it's your coyote!"

"I'll call," I assured her. So much had been going on, but Mollie was right— how could I forget? I would call as soon as we got to my house. The coyote was important and we were the only ones who knew about the sacrifice, other than the witches. It was up to us to save her.

Then I thought about Miss Deighton. How was she doing? I felt as if we should call her, but if she had really been attacked because of her association with us, we ought to stay away from her. She might be afraid to answer the phone anyway. Fortunately she had Betty to watch after her.

And what about Mabel and Agnes Weeks? Should we be concerned about them, or were they part of the coven? I couldn't tell for sure about those two. Were our parents safe? Mrs. Pitts, or whoever it was, was sneaking into our houses to gather hair and nail clippings! Would she sneak into our houses again and harm our families and friends? Then there was the zombie lurching around! These were scary thoughts! But there was no turning back. We had to be brave.

"Laura, what exactly is our plan tonight?" Abigail asked.

"We'll meet Joe Costa, the animal control officer, at Captain Snow's where we'll wait for the witches to show up," I told her. "And I do believe that they are witches, not just 'Earth People' or 'Earth Mother Worshippers' or whatever we've been calling them before. When they begin to make their sacrifice, Mr. Costa will arrest them all and save the coyote."

"Sounds very simple," said Mollie, in her mocking tone. "Anyway, I think we'll need a cell phone. 'Cause we'll be at Captain Snow's and Mr. Costa will hide near the bridge or at the marina. When we see that they're ready to roast the coyote, we'll call Costa on the phone. He'll come in and make his arrest."

"Don't use the word 'roast,'" pleaded Abigail.

"Mr. Costa won't be able to find us if he's never been to Captain Snow's before," I pointed out, not making an issue of Mollie's insensitive comment. "It'll be dark."

"O.K. We'll have to take him with us," said Muffy. "We can meet him in town. Then we can all go to Captain Snow's before dark and wait there together.

"We could meet him at Abigail's house," suggested Mollie. "Then we could walk around Snow Pond to the path Louie and I used, which goes up to Captain Snow's. That way the marina people won't see anything. We don't know if they're in on it too."

"That's a good plan," I said. "Now let's stop by Abigail's to borrow her grandmother's cell phone. We might need it anyway to call for help."

"I'm glad that you're willing to try some technology," quipped Abigail. Then she sounded like her old self when she added, "Maybe Grammy will have a snack for us."

We took our bikes and pedaled down Main Street past The Tomb and the lighthouse to Abigail's. As she predicted, her grandmother had a snack already prepared, lemon meringue pie, which she served to us as we sat on the porch. It was heavenly! She readily lent Abigail her cell phone. Abigail immediately made sure that 911 was in the speed-dial memory.

After our snack, we rode down Lowndes River Road, past the marina over Yacht Harbor Road, alongside the yacht club, and up to my house. I had to call the animal control officer. I went straight to the phone. I saw there were two messages on the answering machine. The first was from Billy.

"Hey, Laura. Billy here. Mr. Prince called Judy's home in Connecticut. Her mom answered. She's perfectly well and not in the hospital, plus she hasn't heard from Judy in over two weeks. No one ever answers the phone at the cottage, she says. I think Judy's in some kind of trouble and her roommates know what's going on. Talk to you later."

"Wow!" Muffy exclaimed. "Now Judy's missing, too!"

"What do you mean?" asked Abigail.

"Mr. and Mrs. Wells are missing," Mollie explained, with mock patience. "And now Judy's gone!"

"But it's not related," reasoned Abigail.

I didn't respond to their comments but listened to the next message. It was from Muffy's grandmother.

"Jared and Lydia are taking a break at the Nor'easter. We called them on the cell phone to let them know that we haven't heard any news. We'll call again when we hear something."

"Well, that's that," I said. "I'm going to call the animal control officer."

Saving the coyote was the most important issue for now. Of course I only got Mr. Costa's recording, but I left an urgent message.

Then I had an idea. "Shouldn't we call the police too?" I asked the Girls. "We might need them as a backup."

"I guess it wouldn't hurt to have them ready," surmised Muffy. "Joe Costa won't be able to handle all those witches if they get nasty."

I wondered how much to tell the police chief. We had worked with the police before, hadn't we? But still, it seemed awkward. The Girls stood by and watched me dial again.

"Hello, this is Laura Sparrow," I began. "I'm one of the girls who helped with the *California Girl* mystery."

"Oh yes. How are you?" said the police chief.

"I'm fine, but we have a problem. Uh, I want to tell you about some trouble we discovered."

"Is this another one of your mysteries?" he asked in a tone that made me not want to tell him.

"Our last mystery turned out to be quite important," I reminded him.

"You're right," he sighed. "Tell me what you've found."

Why did he have to be so difficult? We were helping him do his job, protect our town from evil, root out the bad people. He made it sound as if he were doing me a big favor by even listening to me! It made me feel really annoyed. I was tempted to just hang up, but Karl and Mrs. Pitts were dangerous. We would need the police to help us, sooner or later. I was thinking that maybe I should wait 'til later to tell him...

"We just want you to be ready to send someone in if we need you later tonight," I said, suddenly feeling that that sounded kind of dumb.

"Oh," the chief replied. I guess he wasn't very interested. "Just give us a call," he said and hung up! I guess that was the end of that!

"What did he say?" asked Muffy.

"He's not interested. But he will be," I assured them.

I found the phone book under the telephone stand. Joseph Costa. I looked up his home phone number and underlined it. If he didn't call us back soon, I would call him at home.

"I wish he'd hurry up and call back," I said.

"Maybe he went home for lunch," suggested Abigail. "You should try him at home now."

"It's too late for lunch," snapped Mollie.

"I'll try anyway," I said and dialed.

"Tell him that the coyote shooter sold an animal to Karl," said Muffy. "That should interest him. Tell him about the bones we found at Captain Snow's. He ought to meet us there. The problem is, we don't know what time."

"I'll get my grandmother's cell phone," offered Abigail, our technology expert. "I'll put Mr. Costa's number on the speed dial, so we can just press 'two' and it will automatically dial him. 'One' is for the police."

"Hello."

"Is this Mr. Costa?"

"Yep."

"This is Laura Sparrow. You came to my house the other day to see about a sick coyote, remember?"

"Still in your barn?"

"No. She ran away. But we have another problem. Is it legal to sacrifice an animal?"

"I never heard that one before! I guess that would be considered animal cruelty. Who's doing the sacrificing?"

"There's a group of adults who meet at night. They're really creepy. We think they're going to sacrifice a coyote tonight and we wonder if you could stop them."

"Well, I suppose."

"Good. We want to take you to the place before it gets dark so we can hide and wait for them to show up. The place is Captain Snow's house, overlooking Snow Pond near the bridge. Do you know where it is?"

"I know the bridge."

"Then let's meet in town at the bandstand at eight. The sacrifice will be after dark, maybe as late as midnight. We think the coyote came from Womponoy. Is it illegal for the coyote shooter over on Womponoy to sell coyotes?"

"He's not supposed to be selling anything. That bum was hired to shoot the coyotes, but I think they ought to ship that nut back to wherever he came from and let nature take care of itself. If he's selling animals for sacrifices, he's going to be in big trouble with me. How did you kids find out about this?"

"We have our sources."

"What's that?"

"We'll tell you later."

It was settled. I thought we should meet Mr. Costa in town because we would be there anyway, meeting Louie. I was glad we could work with Costa. Maybe this would be the way we could stop the witches. If they were arrested for animal cruelty, and it was all over the local paper, that would be the end of them, hopefully. But Victoria Harden was the newspaper editor. Maybe she wouldn't print the story—or worse, she might change it, so the witches would be portrayed as heroes, or victims. That wouldn't be good.

"Do we have time for a sail?" asked Abigail.

"Sure. Let's go," I said as we marched out to the barn to get the oars. Why not go for a sail? We had planned it, but somehow it didn't seem like a good time to go off. I didn't really know why. Could it be that our mystery was becoming more complicated by the moment?

Chapter Seventy-Three

I carried the oars to the beach and the Girls helped me pull the dinghy to the water's edge. Heaps of eel grass had been washed up by Sunday's storm. It was a good thing that the Eel Grass Girls weren't "washed up" as well. We were united in our determination to follow through with our mystery!

I began to think about the ghosts. The ghost at Captain Snow's had been either Captain Snow himself, his wife, or his daughter Petunia. It could also have been Nellie Nickerson, though she had died at the church. The ghost at my house seemed to be only the voice of Mrs. Pitts. My old auntie had spoken to us through her diary, as had Petunia through her journal. They had given us more information through their writings than the ghosts had through their hauntings. In fact, if the ghosts had wanted to contact us, to help us find the murderers or guilty parties, they certainly hadn't helped us much at all.

"Now that we have a cell phone, I don't feel so scared about sailing anymore," said Abigail.

"Let's go back to the lighthouse," I suggested. "Maybe we'll be able to talk to Sally."

"I don't think that's such a good idea," said Abigail. "It's so isolated out there and we know that bunch is dangerous. Any of them could be there. It's not safe. Even with a cell phone."

"Oh don't be such a scaredy-cat!" Mollie exclaimed. "It's daylight. They can't do anything to us with all these boats around," she said, motioning to the scores of boats which filled the harbor. "There are plenty of tourists out on the beaches too."

So we rowed to my Catabout and pulled up the sails. It was a perfect afternoon for boating. Soon we were on our way, headed toward the old lighthouse. The sky had cleared and sunlight bounced off the glittering water.

"Where's Dr. Perhonen's yacht?" asked Muffy. It was gone!

"Maybe he's sailed off for a day trip," I suggested. "Or he could be at the marina."

"Or he could have left town!" said Mollie. "After he gave us that phony information about the vials of poison, he decided to skip town on us!"

I hoped that wasn't the case! My heart sank as I realized that the doctor may have been Karl's friend after all and had lied to us about knowing him. But what could we do about it now? We sailed on. I didn't feel so happy about our afternoon anymore. As we glided out into the harbor, my attention was drawn to the water and sky, which were the most beautiful shades of blue, and my mood lightened again. The breeze blew at my yacht club baseball cap and strands of my brown hair flew across my face. How could I feel bad with so much beauty, and the Eel Grass Girls, all around me?

When we reached the beach near the old lighthouse, I anchored my boat. No one would push her off in the daylight, I hoped. I was tired of losing her. We furled the sails and set out along the sandy path leading to the lightkeeper's house. When we arrived, the place seemed deserted. Not a stitch of clothing flapped on the clothesline. The only sound we heard was a gull overhead, laughing.

"It's awfully quiet around here," said Abigail, looking over her shoulder. "I am not a 'happy camper.'"

Mollie walked across the porch and looked in through the windows. No one seemed to be there. We didn't see any cars. We snooped around the out buildings. I don't know what we expected to find. When we passed by a small barn, I heard a slight noise.

"What's that?" asked Muffy, stopping.

"What?" questioned Mollie. "I didn't hear anything."

"I heard it too," I said. "It sounded like a kitten. The noise came from this barn."

Muffy helped me slide the weathered door open enough for us to enter. The old barn was filled with rusting metal bed frames and junk of all descriptions, but in the center of the barn, the floor had been cleared. As we crept in, we noticed a large trapdoor in the middle of the floor! The Girls and I pulled it open.

"A kitten must be trapped down there," I told them as we peered into the inky blackness below. As our eyes became accustomed to the dark, we realized that there were two big burlap bags in the shallow crawl space beneath us! Strange sounds met our ears as the bags wiggled on the sandy floor!

"What's that?" asked Abigail in dismay.

"Help!" came a muffled cry.

Mollie and I jumped down. With my jackknife I cut the ropes which tied the bags. Inside the bags were an old man and woman! Could they be Mr. and Mrs. Wells? If so, how did they get here?

"Call the police!" I shouted up to Abigail. Mollie and I helped the old couple out of the musty-smelling bags. Their eyes were blindfolded. Muffy handed us a sturdy crate to stand on, so we could get them out of the crawl space. We helped Mr. Wells and his wife up into the barn. Muffy took a water bottle from her backpack and held it for them while they took a drink. They seemed dazed and weak. I was afraid they might not make it!

"Are you the Wellses?" asked Muffy. They could barely nod "Yes."

"The police are on the way," said Abigail. "Muffy, I called Grammy and asked her to call your grandmother so she can tell Jared."

"Jared?" asked Mrs. Wells, her eyes full of confusion and hope.

"Yes, your son Jared is in town," Muffy told her gently. "He's been trying to find you. What's been going on?"

"Jared is here?" asked Mr. Wells, not yet believing his ears. "Jared is really here after all these years?"

"Yes," I told them. "It's true. You'll be all right now. The police are on their way. Will you tell us what happened to you?"

Mr. and Mrs. Wells gave each other nervous glances, but remained silent. They were obviously afraid. Very afraid of someone. Probably their impostor "son." In the distance we could hear police sirens. I looked out through the dusty barn window to see a cruiser and two ambulances, one from town and one from Muddy River, speeding as fast as they could over the sandy road leading from the beach parking lot to the old lighthouse. Muffy and I stepped out of the barn to meet them.

The EMS workers from the ambulances rushed into the barn where Mr. and Mrs. Wells sat on old wooden fish crates. They were put on stretchers and all their vital signs were checked as the EMS workers asked them lots of questions about their condition. When they were sure that the couple was stable, the police began to question them about their disappearance.

Mr. and Mrs. Wells told the police what had happened. Late the night before, they had awakened to find themselves being blindfolded. Someone prodded them with what felt like a gun and had driven them away in a strange car. Their kidnappers, at least two people, hadn't spoken a word. They felt themselves put into rough burlap sacks and lowered into the crawl space. They had been underneath the barn until we found them.

Another car drove up just then and screeched to a halt. It was Lydia and Jared. Jared leapt from the car and raced to the barn. "Mom! Dad!"

"Jared!" They hugged each other and started to cry. I felt like crying, too. It had been a horrendous shock to find two old people tied up in sacks! And now to see them having a happy reunion with their long-lost son was almost too much to bear.

"I'm so sorry I stayed away so long and didn't even contact you in all these years. And now this! Who did it?"

"We don't know, son," answered Mr. Wells, calmly.

"Was it that man who's been pretending to be me?" Jared asked, trying not to show his anger.

"We don't know. That man just appeared one day last spring. He threatened us. He told us that we would never see you again if we didn't do just as he said."

"That dirty rat! What else did he tell you? Why did he pretend to be me?"

The old couple eyed each other apprehensively. Timidly Mrs. Wells said, "He told us to pretend that he was our son. We don't know why he did it. He talked on the telephone quite a bit, but he used his own cellular telephone in the other room, with the door closed, so we could never hear his conversations. He often went out but told us not to leave the house or use the telephone. We were so afraid. We wanted to see you again, so we didn't dare disobey him."

"Why didn't you call us?" asked one of the policemen.

"We were afraid for Jared. That man told us that he was the only person who knew where Jared was. If he found out that we had told anyone anything, especially the police, he said he would hurt Jared. No one would ever be able to find Jared and we would never see him again. It would be our fault, he told us. We couldn't live with that thought, so we did just as he said."

"What's his name?" asked Jared, clenching and unclenching his fists.

"We don't know," Mr. Wells informed us. "He never told us."

The police then asked us how we had located the elderly couple. Why were we out here in the first place? We told them that we were out for a sail and had wandered over to the old lighthouse, when we heard noises coming from the barn. Everyone listened to our story. Then the police peered into the windows of the old lightkeeper's house and knocked at the door. No one answered.

"We can't search the house without a warrant," one of the police told us. "I'll radio the chief and see what he can do."

It was then that we noticed that Aunt Lydia was holding Jared's hand. Hmmm...The EMS man told the police that the Wellses should go to the hospital, so the police suggested that Jared and Lydia follow the ambulance over to the hospital in Smithport.

Jared asked his parents to give the police permission to search their house for clues, but the police said they doubted they would find anything important. But, if Jared insisted they would do a thorough search, they promised. It seemed strange to us all that the man posing as their son had suddenly taken them away and then disappeared himself.

"We don't know if he was the one who brought us here or not," said Mrs. Wells in a frail voice. "It may have been someone else. They may have taken him away as well."

No one had thought of that! There were so many questions that needed to be answered. The ambulance was ready to leave. Jared and the police thanked us. We were heroes, they said. Mr. and Mrs. Wells were loaded into one of the ambulances and Jared followed them to the hospital with Lydia at his side.

Chapter Seventy-Four

"I'm glad old Mr. and Mrs. Wells are safe," said Muffy as we watched the vehicles roll down the sandy road toward the parking lot. "And Jared is here to take care of them. They'll be much healthier now that they can get out of their house, without their fake 'son' keeping them prisoner and terrorizing them!"

"I don't get it," complained Abigail as we turned to walk back to our boat. "Who kidnapped them? Wasn't it the 'pretend' son of Mr. and Mrs. Wells?"

"No one knows," said Mollie. "I wonder why the kidnapper left them out here. The fake son could be tied up somewhere out here too, maybe in the old lighthouse or one of those other buildings. Or he could be the kidnapper."

"You might be right, Mollie!" I exclaimed. "Excuse me," I called to the police as I jogged back to the cruiser. "Shouldn't we search a little more? Maybe the man who pretended to be Jared is still here. He could be tied up somewhere."

"We need a warrant," explained the officer.

"Shouldn't we at least call out and listen to see if someone else is here?" I asked.

"All right," the policeman reluctantly agreed. We shouted and looked around the outside of the buildings, but heard and found nothing. I reentered the barn, scanning it for clues. As I moved to the trapdoor to close it, I had an idea. Jumping down into the crawl space, I looked into the dark corners. That's when I saw it. Another burlap bag!

"Hey! Officer!" I shouted. Everyone came running.

"There's another sack down there," I told them, pointing to the corner.

The officer and his partner sprang down and grabbed the sack, pulling it out. The EMS workers from Muddy River peered over to see who was in it. They cut the rope and pulled the sack open. It wasn't the fake son, but Sally!

"Oh my goodness!" exclaimed Muffy. Abigail began to cry. "Is she..."

"I've got a pulse," said the EMS person. "No observable injuries," he concluded after looking her over, "but she's unconscious. We've got to get her over to Smithport right away."

"Who is she?" asked the officer. "You know her?"

"She's the sister of Mrs. Pitts, who works at the Clam Bar, on Lowndes River. Sally owns the old lighthouse here."

"Know who would have done this to her?" he asked, looking down at us.

"No, we don't," answered Mollie. It was true; we didn't know for sure. "But it was probably whoever tied up Mr. and Mrs. Wells, don't you think?"

But why? What was the connection? Our minds were racing. Why was

Sally stashed under the barn along with Mr. and Mrs. Wells?

The ambulance men put Sally on a stretcher and whisked her away.

"Well, girls," said the officer. "You had a good hunch. I think I'll go back to the station and get a search warrant to go over this place. Thanks. If we hadn't found her, I don't know..."

We knew what he meant. The officers left us and drove back to the station.

"Sally will be safe now, I hope," said Muffy. "She knew she was in trouble. And you were able to help her, Laura."

"Do you think it was the witches who put Sally and Mr. and Mrs. Wells under the barn?" asked Abigail, wiping away her tears.

"That's what I think," said Mollie. We all agreed.

"Are you O.K., Abigail?" I asked.

"Yes," Abigail replied, sniffling. "I feel good about helping to save the Wellses and Sally, even though it was scary. But I want to go home now."

It did feel wonderful to know that we had helped them. We had "been in the right place at the right time" and rescued three people from disaster! But now we had even more unanswered questions! The Girls and I ambled toward my boat, feeling good but perplexed. Thankfully my Catabout was still waiting for us at the beach. We had a smooth sail back to the mooring.

I could see Mom standing on the beach. She was in her swimsuit and dove in, swimming over to meet us at the mooring. She hung onto the side of the boat as we furled the sails.

"Wait 'til you hear what happened to us!" I called to her. She climbed into the boat as we told her about finding the Wellses and Sally.

"That's incredible!" she exclaimed. "I do hope they'll all recover! And I'm so proud of you all. It's good that Jared is here to take care of his parents now. I'm glad you had Abigail's grandmother's cell phone to call for help. But what happened to that man who was pretending to be their son?"

"We don't know," said Mollie. "No one's sure if he was the one who did the kidnapping or not."

"You girls were brave to investigate the sounds and call the police for help," Mom continued as she slipped back into the water and we transferred ourselves from the Catabout to the dinghy. "Why don't you heroes stay for dinner?"

"Thanks, Mom," I beamed.

We rowed in as Mom swam to shore. She dried off and we all climbed the path to our house.

"Uh...Mollie invited us for a sleepover tonight. Is that O.K.?" I asked Mom, feeling slightly guilty about our plans for the evening.

"Sure," she replied, not suspecting a thing.

Mollie telephoned her mom to ask if she could stay over at my house, as was her plan, and the other Girls called their parents as well to ask permission to stay for dinner at my house and to sleep over at Mollie's. We were all wearing our swimsuits under our clothes (as we usually did), so we left our clothes at the house and ran back down to the beach for a quick swim. It was late afternoon, but still hot enough to make the cool water feel refreshing and calming after a wild afternoon. When we came up from the beach, we helped Mom with dinner. Dad came home before too long and we told him about our adventure.

"Sounds like a rough bunch to me, whoever's doing these things! I hope you girls are being careful. Anyway, it ought to make the front page of the paper!"

"I can't imagine who in our town would be tying people up and leaving them to…" Mom began.

Just then the phone rang. It was Louie's mom. She had already heard from Aunt Lydia about how we found Mr. and Mrs. Wells. She was so proud of us, she said, but she wanted to know where Louie was!

Chapter Seventy-Five

"Louie went down to Skunk's Neck, after lunch, to help his brother mow lawns," I told her.

"Danny said he never showed up. I was hoping that he was with you girls. Now I'm worried! Louie's a good boy. He wouldn't just go off somewhere! Where could he be?" she asked, sounding tense. "I'm going to call the police. With all these strange things going on, I'm sure they'll look for him. Usually they won't, not even for a child, until they've been missing for at least 24 hours!"

That seemed like a dumb rule to me. "We'll call you if we see him. He's supposed to meet us at seven at the bandstand."

I told the Girls that Louie was missing. Mollie said she hoped that he was just wandering around somewhere, but we doubted it. He had meandered off when we left him at the old barn, but that was different. Louie was a serious boy when it came to work. He wouldn't promise to help his brother and then go off and do something else! Maybe the zombie had gotten him!

Since it was already dinnertime, we decided to eat first, then go out to look for Louie. As soon as we had finished eating and the dishes were washed, I grabbed my backpack. Out the door we dashed and rode our bikes to Pine Street. It was the last place we had seen Louie. If he hadn't reached his brother, he must have disappeared somewhere between that point and the house where his brother was working. On Skunk's Neck we split up to search through the bushes, two of us on either side of the road.

"Look!" Mollie yelled after a few moments. "Here's his bike!" Louie's bike had been thrown in the bushes about 15 feet from the road! The rear fender was badly bent! The wheel was crooked, as if it had been hit by a car!

"Oh no!" Abigail wailed. "They ran him over! And now they've taken him away!"

"Hopefully he's not badly hurt! What will they do to him?" Muffy asked. "Their voodoo dolls didn't work, so they've turned to kidnapping! I hope Louie will be all right and not end up in a burlap sack in some isolated place!"

"This is really serious!" wailed Abigail. "We never should have let him ride down this lonely stretch of road all by himself! We should have ridden with him as far as the house where his brother was working. It's all our fault!"

"How could they have known he would be here all alone?" asked Muffy. "I didn't notice any cars going by. All we saw was Billy's truck. How do they always know where we are, where we're going, and what we're going to do? And we never see them."

"Call the police, Abigail," commanded Mollie. Abigail took out her grandmother's cell phone and dialed. Then Mollie gave her Louie's number and she called his mother.

"Aren't you glad I have Grammy's cell phone?"

Mollie just grumbled rather than admitting that technology was helping us.

In no time, the police arrived. It was the same two officers who had met us at the old lighthouse.

"What's going on now?" one asked. We showed him the crumpled bicycle. Though he told us that he had been at the station when Louie's mother had called about Louie being missing, he still wasn't convinced.

"Kids ditch their bikes all the time. Their friends do it as a prank, or the kid gets a ride home in a car, or goes off into the woods expecting to come back to pick up his bike later. Doesn't mean a thing. That's why we give these things 24 hours."

"That's ridiculous!" cried Mollie. "Can't you see that the bike has been hit by a car! This is a 'hit and run' accident! After all you've seen today, do you really believe that this is nothing?" she almost shrieked. "Louie was going to help his brother mow lawns right down the street there." She pointed toward Skunk's Neck. "He always keeps his word. That was six hours ago. No matter what you think he may have decided to do, he would have shown up at home or somewhere by now! Obviously he's been hurt!"

"Guess you're right," mumbled the officer, scratching his head. At this point, Louie's mom and older brother, Danny, arrived in Danny's truck. When she saw the police and Louie's bike, she became hysterical.

"What happened to my boy?" she wailed. The police officers had no answer. Danny explained how he had expected Louie to help him after lunch, but the boy had never arrived. One officer took notes while the other attempted to lift fingerprints from the bike. When they were finished, Danny put the bike in the back of his truck. Louie's mom was frantic, but there was nothing she could do.

The police drove off. We didn't have much faith that they would find Louie. This was a bad situation.

"Do you children have any idea who could have done this?" his mother asked us. Danny gave us an angry look, as if we were somehow responsible. I guess he knew that Louie had been hanging around with us and we were up to something.

"We had a plan to meet Louie at the bandstand at seven," I told them, avoiding a direct answer. "I'm sure he's all right. The bike is only a little bent. He'll show up, you just wait and see. We'll call you when we find him."

I tried to sound confident, and I really was hopeful, but this didn't look good. They made us promise to call them immediately if we heard or saw anything concerning Louie and then they drove away. We rode to Main Street to the bandstand. Somehow I hoped that Louie would be there, but he wasn't. Something else was there waiting for us. A note lying on the steps of the bandstand!

It was written in the pigpen cipher! It read, "You are next. That money is ours. We will get it and we will get you."

"Whoa!" we exclaimed together.

"Can you believe that?" asked Abigail. "That means they have Louie and they're coming to get us! And they definitely know we have the money!"

"But how did they know we'd be here?" asked Muffy, looking around.

"Maybe Louie told them," Mollie speculated. "But this is getting to be perfectly dreadful! They knew we were at your grandmother's, Abigail, to leave another doll there. Then they knew when we were at the Weeks sisters' because they left a voodoo doll there. And now this!"

"Are you saying that Louie is one of them?" asked Muffy, in shock.

"Of course not!" she protested. "I'm just saying that I don't know how they know where we are and that they could have tortured Louie to find out that we were coming here tonight."

That was a horrible thought. As we talked about it more, we realized that it seemed that they knew our plans even before we did. I refused to consider that Louie could be on their side! They knew what we were doing, even when Louie didn't. No way could he be involved! Especially now that he was missing too!

Besides, he usually never knew what we would be doing long enough in advance to tell anyone else. The only way they could know our plans was for them to be watching us every minute. They had to be hiding in the bushes, behind the trees, always listening to our conversations. There had to be a bunch of them letting the others know where we would be. That was very unnerving!

"We promised to call Louie's mom," Abigail reminded us. She used the cell phone to call and told her that we were at the bandstand, but Louie wasn't there. We promised to let her know if we found him.

"Shouldn't we meet Mr. Costa somewhere else since they know we're here?" asked Muffy, scanning the park and the hedges bordering it.

"But where could we meet?" I asked.

"We were supposed to meet at my house." Abigail reminded us." We'll be going to Captain Snow's by way of the pond anyway. It makes more sense."

She called Mr. Costa. He was just getting ready to leave so Abigail gave him directions to her grandmother's house. We hopped on our bikes and rode there to meet him.

"What will you tell your grandmother?" I asked.

"Don't worry," said Abigail.

When we arrived, the house was deserted.

"Where is everybody?" asked Muffy.

"Grammy probably went out to dinner with Uncle Jack."

"I thought he left with all the cousins," I remarked.

"No. He doesn't have any children, so he's staying 'til the end of the week."

We hid our bikes near the road, in order to get them later without arousing the attention of Abigail's grandmother. Then we sat on the split-rail fence and waited. Time ticked by very slowly. It was getting dark, but Mr. Costa didn't arrive.

"You'd better call him again," Mollie told Abigail.

This time the animal control officer didn't answer. Abigail left a message telling him that we were waiting. She gave the address again and her cell phone number.

"What if he calls you in the middle of the sacrifice?" asked Mollie, annoyed as usual.

"I've put the phone on mute," she calmly told Mollie. "It vibrates and this little light blinks red."

"Someone has to go to Captain Snow's and someone will have to wait here for Mr. Costa," I said.

"I'll wait," offered Muffy. "Mollie, why don't you stay with me? Laura and Abigail can go on. But where will we find you?"

"We'll hide near the top of the path," I said. "That way we'll be able to see everything and it'll be easier for you to find us."

"But you don't even know where the path is!" exclaimed Mollie. "Maybe I should go and you stay here, Laura."

"Just tell us where it is," I said.

"Oh, all right! There's a red dinghy on the beach. The path right behind it goes up the bluff. I hope you can find it."

"I don't like this," began Muffy. "It's not good to split up. It makes more sense to stick together. Splitting up means more of a chance of something going wrong."

"Then what do you suggest?" asked Mollie. "It's getting darker. Someone has to get there first, before the witches."

"O.K.," consented Muffy. "But we have to remind Mr. Costa to put his phone on mute too before we meet you or we'll be asking for trouble."

So it was decided that Abigail and I would go on ahead. She and I followed the shoreline of Snow Pond to the dinghy. We could see the path behind it leading up to the haunted house. I felt very uncomfortable. Terrified to be exact. It had seemed like a logical plan to separate, but now that only Abigail and I were going up the path alone in the dark, it didn't seem like a very good idea to me. But we had to try to save the coyote and catch the witches!

Chapter Seventy-Six

As we trudged up the path, I thought of Louie. I hoped the police would be able to find him. They had to, wherever he was, and get him back. If the witches had him, where would they be keeping him? How would anyone ever find him? They could have hidden him anywhere! If the police couldn't find him, somehow we would have to do it!

We climbed the steep, narrow path leading up the hill to the bluff. From there it was only a short distance through the brush and pines to the old house. We could see it looming before us. We crept into the brush, hid ourselves, and waited.

Abigail had the cell phone in her hand, waiting for it to vibrate and blink, but it was still. We then realized that we had no way of contacting Muffy and Mollie unless they went into the house. We figured they wouldn't do that unless Abigail's grandmother came home, which would be awkward. They wouldn't be able to explain why they were there and Abigail wasn't. And where was Mr. Costa?

The minutes crept by. It became darker and darker and spookier and spookier. An owl's hoot almost made my heart stop beating! Far off in the distance we heard a coyote howl. My thoughts went to "my" coyote. Was she the one the witches were planning to sacrifice tonight? I hoped that we would be able to save her, or whatever animal they had.

"Maybe they're not meeting here," Abigail whispered. "Or they've changed their plans, or their 'usual place' is somewhere else."

If that were so, then where would it be? The old lighthouse? It could be anywhere! How would we ever find them?

"No one's coming," sighed Abigail. "I'm going to call Mr. Costa one more time, then I'll call Grammy. She can tell the Girls we're giving up."

"Go ahead and call, but let's not give up," I whispered. "They may not begin their ceremony until midnight."

"I'll never be able to stay awake," she complained, dialing the phone. Still Mr. Costa didn't answer. She tried her grandmother. No answer there either.

"What are we going to do?" she asked.

"Wait."

Suddenly I heard a noise in the bushes behind us! The zombie! Abigail and I clung to each other! What would we do? Just then a light appeared inside Captain Snow's house! It was an eerie glow, a flickering flame. Maybe it was a kerosene lamp. The sounds of rustling had stopped. It was just an animal—a small animal I hoped. We watched the house. More lights appeared.

"It's them!" I whispered to Abigail. "Their meeting must be inside this time. Let's go."

"Are you sure we ought to go near?" she asked, her voice quavering.

"We can't see or hear a thing from out here."

All of a sudden I felt a huge hand yank me up by the back of my sweatshirt!
"Hey!!!"

Abigail too was lifted into in midair, her legs kicking! I struggled, twisting every way, trying to see my captor. And though I craned my neck, I couldn't see his face! I couldn't see who had Abigail either. Roughly we were carried to the house! Inside Captain Snow's was the last place I wanted to be! My fear grew as we approached the old wooden door!

"Let me down!" cried Abigail.

At the porch, the person holding me kicked the door open and dropped me to the floor. I landed heavily, in a heap. Abigail landed beside me. I looked up and couldn't believe what I saw! There, standing around us, in a circle lit by several old storm lamps, were Mrs. Pitts, Victoria Harden, Mr. Blackwell, Aloma Smits, and Lucky Clark! And it was Karl Kenton and Mr. Mullins who had snatched us up out of the bushes and dragged us in! The entire coven of witches was here! The blood left my body! I had never been so scared in all my life! And this was going to be the end of my life, I just knew it!

We heard something move in the corner. In the dark shadows, lying on the floor, was the form of a person! A boy! It was Louie tied and gagged! At least we had found him, but what could we do to help now that we were prisoners ourselves? What were they planning to do with him? What would they do to us? A big burlap bag lay next to Louie. Something squirmed inside!

"What do we have here?" asked Mrs. Pitts, with her evil sneer. "Too nosey for your own good, aren't you? You'll be sorry now!" She laughed the most wicked laugh I had ever heard. A cold shiver shot down my spine!

At that, Louie turned his head and his eyes met ours. They were filled with sheer terror! That made us even more frightened! This was definitely the end!

"Abigail!" I mouthed, turning from our captors. "Call the police!"

I hoped that she would hit the speed dial and connect with the police. When they answered, they would send a cruiser to rescue us. But with a cell phone, could they trace the call the same way they can from a home phone, and find out your address? We never knew if they could or not because as soon as Abigail slipped her hand into her pocket, Mr. Mullins ripped the phone away from her and threw it down on the floor so hard that it broke into a thousand pieces! Now our only hope was that Joe Costa would arrive and Mollie and Muffy would lead him to us! Where were they anyway?

"Think you're going to call for help?" Karl laughed hysterically. "No one's going to help you! Not now and not ever! No one will ever find you! We got rid of Sally and that meddling old couple. You kids are next in line to disappear!"

Just then the old front door creaked open. A dark figure dressed in black and wearing a long cape swept into the room. It was the form of a young woman! Oh no! It was Judy! We should have known. But no! It wasn't Judy, it was Allyson Parks! What was she doing there?

"Who do we have here?" she asked, noticing me and Abigail lying on the dusty floor. With her black lipstick and heavily made-up eyes, she hardly looked like the sailing instructor we knew or rather thought we knew!

"Just those annoying little snoops!" hissed Mrs. Pitts. "But we have plans for them and their boyfriend over there," she said, nodding in the direction of Louie.

When Allyson saw the look of shock on our faces, she laughed a wicked laugh. "What did you expect? Did you think I was some sort of fairy godmother?"

One of our sailing instructors! Someone we had never suspected! Billy Jones's girlfriend! If we had to choose a teenager to suspect, it would have been Judy, not Allyson!

Allyson threw back her head and let out a ghoulish howl! She was even scarier than Mrs. Pitts! Her face was contorted. "I bet you're wondering how we always knew where you were and where you were going. Well, I put a little 'bug' in your backpack, Laura. Look and see!"

I ripped open my backpack. After dumping out the contents and sorting through, I looked inside again and felt a small disc stuck beneath a tiny tear in the lining! A microphone! No wonder they always knew our plans! And it was Allyson who had betrayed us!

"Tie them up," Allyson ordered. Why was she giving the orders? Was she their leader? It couldn't be! She was only a teenager! How could she be telling the adults what to do! But Karl and Mr. Mullins obeyed, taking ropes from a box next to Louie and clumsily tying our hands behind us. The rough rope chafed my wrists!

"We're all here!" announced Allyson, looking around the circle. She stood in the center as the others joined hands.

"Where's Jim?" asked Lucky.

"You know he's not coming," Allyson responded in a nasty tone. "Why do you keep asking? You know he has to stay in the background."

"Yeah, but I don't like it," Lucky responded angrily. "He never shows up. If he's one of us, he should be here."

"You know his reasons," quipped Allyson. "So drop it." Lucky still seemed upset, yet didn't say any more. Allyson continued, "We're ready for phase two. Karl, you run the announcements on the radio. Victoria, you do a feature on the 'land trust' in your paper, then in a week or two, run an editorial. Mr. Blackwell, talk up the 'trust' at all your board and civic club meetings. All of you, talk it up. The donations of land and money will go directly to our fund.

Mr. Blackwell has the paperwork ready at the bank for donors.

"Of course once we get the treasure out of that safe on Main Street, we'll be well on our way," she added, giving us a look of utter hatred! "Then we go to phase three when we introduce the land trust at town meeting, run ads in all the Cape newspapers, and get more donations. Before you know it, every inch of open space will be ours. Wild and free—forever—for the Earth Mother!"

"Hail! Hail!" chanted the group. They swayed back and forth, their eyes closed. Then Mrs. Pitts called out in a loud voice, "Oh spirit of Mrs. Snow! Come to us! Come to your house and guide us! Your treasure has been stolen, but we will get it back. We will use it all to buy land. We are trying to return all the land to our Earth Mother and we will. By any means possible. Oh come to us!"

They continued to chant and sway. Their dark shadows, cast by the flickering storm lamps, danced over the crumbling plaster of the old walls. Abigail and I inched ourselves toward each other until our backs were touching, hoping to untie the ropes that were cutting into our wrists.

The chanting suddenly stopped and we froze. Allyson announced, "Something's wrong! Mrs. Snow isn't responding! Maybe it's because of those kids. Get rid of them! Throw them down the old well."

"Wait a minute!" She paused. "First put them in those sacks over there and add one of those spiders to each sack before you tie them up. Give me that jar."

Lucky took an old Mason jar from the box on the floor and handed it to Allyson. It was filled with big brown spiders!

"These are Brown Recluse spiders. They will kill you or maybe they won't. Let's find out."

"No!" Abigail shrieked. "No, don't do this to me! Please!"

I could hardly breathe! How could this be happening to us? Louie tried to squirm away, but it was no use!

Karl and Mr. Mullins lunged toward us and dragged us to the opposite wall, where Louie lay. Lucky tossed a couple of sacks to them from the box beside Louie. They began to pull the musty old sacks over our heads, but they stopped abruptly when the door of the house was flung open again! We expected the worst!

Chapter Seventy-Seven

Were we ever shocked to see Reverend Maxon!

"Halt!!!" he cried as he entered the room, looking very tall and powerful. He quickly took in the startling scene before his eyes: Abigail, Louie, and I being stuffed into sacks in one corner; a circle of adults, holding hands as the storm lamps exaggerated their ghoulish expressions; and a scary-looking teenage ringleader at the center of it all. Karl made a quick move toward Reverend Maxon, but Mr. Mullins grabbed Karl, holding him back.

"He's a reverend! Leave him be!"

"Going soft on us, Mullins?" asked Karl with disdain.

"I didn't want to do it, Reverend, but they made me!" Mr. Mullins cried out.

"Shut up, Mullins!" hollered Lucky. "Don't say another word!"

"Lucky found out that I was stealing from the church! He blackmailed me!"

Lucky leapt onto Mr. Mullins and wrestled him to the ground. A terrible struggle broke out. Just then the police chief with several officers flew through the door, their guns drawn!

"Everybody freeze!" shouted the chief. "Hands up!"

The old parlor suddenly flew into chaos! At the sight of the police, Mrs. Pitts fell to the ground in a swoon! Lucky tried to escape, but Mr. Mullins latched onto him so he couldn't move. A policeman snapped a set of handcuffs onto Lucky. But Mr. Blackwell, Karl, and all the others took advantage of the commotion and scattered, racing toward the French windows and crashing out into the dark. The police followed, but the witches, knowing their way around the old house and grounds, quickly disappeared. The officers didn't dare shoot. One by one the police returned empty-handed!

Thankfully none of the lamps were overturned during the confusion. If they had been, the old house would have surely burned to the ground! We handed the jar of spiders to the chief. He didn't seem real interested in them. He was busy radioing for an ambulance to get Mrs. Pitts.

"Take these two back to the station," he told the officers, referring to Lucky and Mr. Mullins, who had also been handcuffed. He asked the reverend to follow them, but Reverend Maxon had bent down to untie us and asked if he could stay. The others left as the chief looked at Mrs. Pitts to assess her condition. "Looks as if she fainted," he concluded. "Who's in this other sack?" he asked, noticing the wiggling burlap bag beside us.

"We think it's a coyote," said Abigail. "The witches were going to use it for a sacrifice."

"Witches?" asked the chief. "Is that what's going on here?"

"Yes," we replied.

"Well, I'll be," he uttered, but he didn't say "what" he'd be. "Nick, can you believe that?" he asked the remaining officer. He then radioed Joe Costa. "The animal control officer spent most of the evening breaking up a real bad dog-fight. Both dog owners and several bystanders got sent over to the hospital! Busy evening for us all."

That explained why Mr. Costa had never come to help us. He had been fur-ther delayed by writing up citations and reports. It was the worst dogfight in the history of the town. No wonder he had never shown up!

"I'm not opening that sack!" the chief told us. "Costa will take care of that when he gets here. In the meantime, I need you to give me a list of who got away. We'll get the cruisers out to round them up."

We told him everyone who had been there. "Nick," said the chief, "you bet-ter wait out at the street for the ambulance. Otherwise, they'll never find us!"

As Nick left, I asked Reverend Maxon, "How did you know we were here?"

"I couldn't help thinking about Jerry Mullins. I knew he was guilty and realized that letting him get away with stealing wasn't going to help him. I called the police and told the chief that I would come down to the station to make a statement. The chief told me to wait until tomorrow, but I felt compelled to do it tonight.

"It wasn't very late, so I telephoned your home, Laura, to ask you about your suspicions of Jerry. When your mother said you were at Mollie's, I telephoned her house and when Mrs. Perkins told me that Mollie was at your house, I knew you girls were up to something. I wasn't sure, but when no one was home at Jerry Mullins's either, I had a hunch that you would all be here. I told the police and I was right! The chief had had a call from Laura earlier, so he suspected trouble."

"You sure were right!" I said. "And we're really glad! If you hadn't come in just when you did, I hate to think of what would have happened to us! Thank you!"

In the distance we heard the ambulance siren. The same EMS workers who had responded to the call at the old lighthouse came up the path with a stretcher, following Nick and his waving flashlight. They quickly loaded Mrs. Pitts onto the stretcher.

Louie was badly bruised, so the chief had the EMS workers look him over before they whisked Mrs. Pitts away to the Smithport hospital. Louie was fine, except for his bruises and scratches. He was cleaned up and got a few bandages. The ambulance left with the unconscious Mrs. Pitts. Nick went back out to the street to wait for Joe Costa. The chief then asked Louie to tell his story. We couldn't wait to hear how the witches had kidnapped him!

"I...uh...was riding my bike down Skunk's Neck to help my brother mow lawns when a car drove up behind me and ran right into my bike, sending me flying! At first I was just really annoyed, thinking it was some dumb tourists too busy looking at the sights to watch where they were going. When I turned around and saw it was Karl, I was really scared, so I tried to run. But he hauled me into that big car of his before I could get away."

So that was what had happened! Just as we suspected.

Joe Costa finally arrived accompanied by Nick, Mollie, and Muffy! Were we ever glad to see them! Mr. Costa had just reached Abigail's when the call from the chief came in.

When Mr. Costa saw the wiggling sack, he asked Officer Nick to help him take it outside. We all went out to watch. Nick held his flashlight so we could see. Joe Costa carefully untied the sack. "My" coyote was inside! We could see the scar from the bullet wound on her back. She was so thin and dehydrated that we gasped, but she seemed to recognize us!

"Let's look in that box in the parlor," I suggested. "Maybe there's something we could put water in." Mollie and I ran into the house, grabbed one of the lamps, and rummaged through the box. We found an empty can. I took the water bottle from my backpack. Back outside, I filled the can. The coyote lapped up every drop of water.

"Keep back!" ordered Joe, but it was too late. The coyote was in such a pitiful condition, she couldn't possibly have been dangerous even if that had been her nature, which it wasn't.

"This is the same coyote that was in my barn," I told him, pointing to the scar on her back. "The coyote shooter over on Womponoy caught her and sold her to Dr. Karl Kenton, one of those men who got away."

"You have any proof?" asked the chief.

"Yes, a kid named Jeffrey Silva saw it happen," Muffy told him.

"O.K., O.K.," he muttered. "I want someone to start from the beginning. I understand that Mullins was stealing from the church, but what's the connection to all the other folk who were here tonight?"

I told the story, "Lucky Clark owns The Tomb, that new store at the end of town that sells books on witches and spells. You know Victoria Harden from the newspaper and Mr. Blackwell from the bank. They were going to influence the townspeople to give money and land to some 'land trust,' we heard them say. Allyson Parks is an instructor at Yacht Harbor Sailing School. She seems to be their leader and Dr. Karl Kenton has the new radio station in town. He has a doctor's bag and he threatened to give us a shot of some medicine, trying to scare us into leaving them alone. Aloma Smits works in the school cafeteria and Mrs. Pitts works at the Clam Bar. Mr. Mullins, you know, is a church deacon and works for the water department."

"The night Mr. Mullins fell from the water tower," said Abigail, "he was trying to poison the water system! We followed him there to try to stop him."

"Poison the water system," muttered the chief. "That's what you said before."

"Yes!" I exclaimed. Then it hit me! "Aloma Smits works in the school cafeteria! Part of the plan must have been for her to add the herbs or drugs to the school lunches too! They probably had teachers involved in their plot too, to teach the kids about the Earth Mother! It wouldn't be so bad if they only offered their personal opinions. I could accept that, but why do they have to use evil to get their way?" That was it! Or at least part of it. The witches were trying to control the entire town, using every means available!

"And I eat school lunches!" lamented Louie.

"Me too!" I said. "Maybe she wants to turn us all into zombies, once our minds are gone because of the drugs!" I trembled at the thought.

"They were the ones who broke into Muffy's aunt's shop," Mollie told the chief. "We found some money and asked her to keep it for us. We wanted to tell you all about our mystery, but we had no proof to give you. We thought you would just laugh."

The chief looked at us. He knew we were right. He wouldn't have listened to us!

"You should have brought the money you found down to the station. Then the shop office wouldn't have been blown up! Next time let us handle these things. But never mind about that now. My men will pick up the whole gang. We're still looking for that guy posing as Jared Wells, but we can't find him. He seems to have disappeared into thin air. And Sally, Mrs. Pitts's sister, is so confused she's not any help. She can't remember a thing! Seems as if she was hypnotized, or she's doing a pretty good job of faking it! What's this animal got to do with it?"

"We told you," Mollie cried. "They're witches! They sacrifice animals to the Earth Mother!"

"Who?"

"Their goddess, the Earth Mother. Dorothy Deighton, down on Pine Street can fill you in about it. She's a 'good' witch, a green witch. These others are supposedly green witches too, but they've gone bad. They're black witches now. They want their 'land trust' so badly that they'll do anything to get it. They want to control everyone in town to think exactly the same way they do. The land trust sounds good, but we don't understand why they have to be so mean about it. They locked Miss Deighton in her toolshed the other day. If we hadn't stopped by to weed her garden, I don't know what would have happened to her!"

During all this conversation, Reverend Maxon had remained silent. Louie didn't say anything either. The chief radioed the station again and then told us that he was taking us in to file statements about what had happened and all the information we had. We took the lanterns out of the house and used them to light our way back to the police cruiser. Joe Costa carried the coyote back to his truck. The police chief had handed the jar of spiders to Louie, who gingerly gave it to Mr. Costa.

"I'll take this coyote over to the lady in Oceanside," Mr. Costa told us. "This animal will recover in no time and then I'll release her near the harbor. She'll be all right, if we can get rid of that coyote shooter! We'd all be a lot better off without his meddling!"

We thought we understood what he meant: the coyote shooter was not a good person. Our town and wildlife would be much better off without him roaming around with his shotgun! Yet the answer to the coyote problem wasn't clear to me. We had nothing against the little birds the man was sent to protect, or against the government in general, but this individual was illegally overstepping the boundries of his job just to make some extra money. And that wasn't right.

The chief and Nick got into the front seat of the cruiser. The Girls jumped into the back. Louie and I drove with the Reverend. We drove through the dark night to the station where we told the whole story all over again. We were relieved that it was over now. Our mystery had been solved. We could relax again and enjoy our summer vacation! Little did we know what Thursday would bring!

Chapter Seventy-Eight

It had been a late night. After we had been questioned at the police station, Officer Nick had called our parents to come pick us up. When they saw Reverend Maxon with us at the police station, they didn't yell at us as much as they would have. But we had a lot of explaining to do and somehow we did it. Louie's parents and brother were overjoyed to see him. They hugged him so much he was getting embarrassed. They were so glad that he was all right, though he needed a lot of cleaning up! We formed a quick huddle and agreed to meet at the Clam Bar for lunch and a celebration! All our mysteries had been solved in one day!

Then we all went home. Before I was trundled off to bed, Mom told me that I had a message on the answering machine. It was from Mr. Alfred Snow!

"I will be arriving tomorrow afternoon at the Smithport Airport," the message said. "A limousine is meeting me and will take me to the Inn on the Bay where I will be staying for an undetermined amount of time. I am expecting you, your little friends, and their families to join me for dinner at the inn at seven tomorrow evening."

That was a surprise! Mr. Snow was finally coming to visit after staying away his entire life! Our mystery was solved, so it was the perfect time for him to come. It would help settle things. We could ask him about buying the Eel Grass Palace and old bog property!

"Mr. Snow is arriving tomorrow!" I told my parents "We're all supposed to meet him for dinner tomorrow night at seven at the Inn on the Bay!"

"That would be lovely," said Mom. "He picked a good time to come, now that your mystery is solved."

Dad shrugged his shoulders. "Does that mean I have to wear a jacket and tie?" he asked, not sounding very happy.

"I'm afraid so," said Mom. "But it's off to bed for now!"

I gave them a quick kiss good-night and climbed the stairs to fall into bed without even taking my clothes off. I was asleep before I knew it.

It was amazing that any of us Eel Grass Girls made it to sailing class on time the next morning! We sat on the wooden benches in the bright morning sun. I whispered to the Girls about Mr. Alfred Snow. We were all excited that we would be meeting him in person and having a dinner party at the Inn on the Bay, the most elegant restaurant in town. We had so many questions to ask Mr. Snow, but we had no time to talk now. Class was starting.

Billy Jones took attendance and then announced that we would be playing a sailing game that morning. It was called "Pirate." He explained that we would start out with a pirate boat filled with neon-yellow tennis balls. The pirate boat would trail the other boats and attempt to throw the balls into the boats. If they succeeded, those boats would then become pirates as well and help chase the rest of the fleet until all the boats had become pirates. The last boat to become a pirate would be the winner. It sounded like fun, but my mind was still on the night before! Had the police caught everyone? What had happened to Allyson? She had seemed to be a friend! It was so hard to believe that she was the leader of the coven. She was now probably behind bars in our town's little jail!

"I know we're eating at the Clam Bar after sailing school," said Abigail, "but how will Louie get there?"

"I don't know," said Mollie. "His bike is all messed up."

Just then, the instructors came out of the clubhouse. I was in a state of shock when I saw that Allyson was with them! I shivered all over to see her! Hadn't the police been able to catch her? If not, why wasn't she afraid the police would find her at the yacht club? The four of us just stared and didn't hear another word that Billy said.

Before we knew what had happened, everyone else was down on the beach and we were left alone on the deck with Allyson.

"What's wrong, girls?" she asked sarcastically. "You look as though you've seen a ghost."

"We thought the police..." began Muffy, not knowing quite how to say it.

"Arrested me?" Allyson's tone was mocking. She threw her head back and laughed recklessly. "Why on earth would they do that? They found me at my cottage and questioned me, but I didn't do anything wrong. There's no law against getting together with my friends. And that old coyote, I told them I didn't know a thing about it. Who's to say that I did? I've got nothing to fear, but I'm sorry to tell you that I can't say the same thing about you and your little boyfriend. You're the ones who ought to be afraid. You can't stop us. Last night you were lucky, but you'd better stay out of our way from now on. There are lots of places in this town where five dumb kids could disappear—and never be found!"

I bounded for the beach steps to get away from Allyson, but Mollie grabbed my arm.

"You don't scare us," she told Allyson, looking directly into her eyes. "You think we're dumb and that's fine. You'll see how 'dumb' we are!"

Mollie turned and dragged us down to the shore to rig our boats. I was visibly shaking. I just couldn't believe it! The police had let Allyson go free! That meant that the whole gang was probably free and carrying out their plan!

"She can't scare us!" declared Mollie. Unfortunately, the rest of us were scared, really scared! I had hoped that all the witches would be behind bars and we would be safe, but nothing had changed, except that the witches were even more angry with us than ever! We chose the *Classy Clam* and *Chubby Quahog* again, but we were even more upset when we noticed that hex signs had been drawn inside our boats! Abigail and I looked in all the other boats around us, but the hexes were only in ours. Allyson must have drawn them to scare us! Suddenly I didn't feel like sailing.

"Look at those hexes!" Mollie remarked angrily. "I feel like going back up there and telling her off!"

"It wouldn't do any good," Muffy sighed. "She wants to make us upset. It gives her a feeling of power."

"Then what are we going to do?" asked Abigail in dismay.

"We'll finish our sailing class," I said, "and after we eat our lunch at the Clam Bar, we're going to the police station. They have a lot of explaining to do! From there we should visit Jared and his parents and maybe Miss Deighton. We're all still in danger!"

I wanted to talk to Billy, but we wouldn't have the chance until after class. We had to tell him about Allyson! We rigged our boat and sailed out into the harbor. The game was fun, even though we weren't in the mood for games. Playing Pirate improved our skills at the helm and strategies for speed. If only we could escape the witches as easily!

After class, Allyson made sure that she had Billy's attention. It was obvious that she didn't want us to be alone with him! Before we knew it, he was in his truck and driving away! We would have to catch up with him later.

Then we saw Judy! She sauntered over to us.

"Are you O.K.?" I asked.

"Sure," she replied. "I got into trouble, but there was a concert over in Smithport that I really wanted to hear. I couldn't get stuck at this place when Death's Door was playing at the wildest beach party of the summer!"

Boy, was she strange! Mollie rolled her eyes as we hopped on our bikes.

"What a loser!" she remarked.

"She probably won't be asked back as an instructor next summer," I added as we rode along. "She's lucky she didn't get fired! But she'll probably think that it was her pentagram that helped her to not lose her job at the yacht club."

We rode our bikes to the Clam Bar. Cooky and his wife were there. We went around back so we could tell Cooky what had happened to Mrs. Pitts, but it seemed that he already knew all about it.

"So now you've put her in the hospital!" he yelled. This was not the response we had expected.

"She was at Captain Snow's house!" Mollie hollered back, which wasn't very nice to do. Cooky was raising his voice, but I didn't think Mollie should do the same. "She fainted when she saw the police. We didn't do anything to her. Why are you yelling at us?"

"I'm sorry," he said, calming down a little. His wife was now standing beside him, looking angrily at us. "I just wish she'd come back to work so my wife can go back to her old job again. You kids've got Mrs. Pitts all riled up!"

"She was up to something, whether we ever found out about it or not," I said. "You said yourself that she changed ever since her sister showed up. We're trying to solve the mystery so everything can go back to normal."

"Yeah, normal," said Cooky in disgust. "I can't wait!"

We placed our lunch order and sat on the riverbank to wait. As we watched the boat traffic go under the bridge and out into the harbor, I happened to glance over to the marina. Guess who I saw? Karl Kenton!!!

"Oh, no!" I wailed. The others looked up and couldn't believe their eyes either!

"What is he doing here?" asked Muffy. "He's supposed to be in jail! I have a bad feeling that the police didn't do their job very well!"

"You can say that again," said Mollie emphatically. Karl looked over at us and quickly turned away. He jumped into his car and sped down the road toward town.

"He's sure in a hurry," commented Abigail.

Suddenly a police cruiser barreled over the bridge and screeched to a halt in front of the marina. Two officers jumped out. Moments later they hopped back into the cruiser and raced away, following Karl.

"They'll catch him now," Mollie predicted. "The cops are doing their job after all." It was comforting to know that at least one "bad guy" was going to be caught!

Our lunch was ready. As we ate, Louie arrived. He was riding a big bike, probably his brother's. He nodded "hello" to us and stepped up to the counter to order. Then he sat down on the grass with us.

"Jared called this morning. He found something important, a paper under the desk. His parents got out of the hospital and he's staying with them. That guy rearranged some of the furniture so they wanted Jared to move it back the way it was. That's when he found the paper. It must've fallen under the desk. He didn't tell the police yet because he thinks that you girls know something that you haven't told anyone yet. I promised him I'd take you over after lunch." Louie got his lunch and sat down again.

"What could the paper be?" asked Mollie. We couldn't imagine.

"Don't know," answered Louie between mouthfuls of hamburger. "I told him about what happened at Captain Snow's last night. Boy was he surprised!"

"He'll be even more surprised when he hears that Allyson isn't in jail!" Mollie uttered. "But the police may have picked up Karl by now."

"What?" exclaimed Louie, putting his hamburger down. "How can that be?"

"We don't know," Muffy told him. We were confounded by it.

"Mr. Snow is arriving tonight," I told Louie, changing the subject. "We're supposed to meet him at the Inn on the Bay at seven. Your parents are invited too."

"Huh?"

"You heard her," said Mollie. "You'll have to get dressed up again."

"I'm not going!" Louie stated. He sounded as if he really meant it. I didn't think he would enjoy the dinner anyway. He hated getting dressed up it seemed.

"All right, but you'll have to meet us here tomorrow so we can take Mr. Snow over to the haunted house," continued Mollie. Louie agreed to that. We were excited about Mr. Snow's arrival.

"But the house isn't haunted any more, remember?" I said.

As soon as Louie was finished with his lunch, we rode our bikes by the lighthouse to Main Street and on to the Wellses' house. Mr. and Mrs. Wells were seated in lawn chairs beside their little circular driveway. Mrs. McLaughlin was seated next to them, chattering away. The older couple seemed tired, but happy and relieved. It must have been a trial for them to be cooped up in their own house all summer. Now it was wonderful for them to be free and to have their son home again after so many years of being away. At least one part of our mystery had been solved and brought to a happy ending!

Chapter Seventy-Nine

"It's the children who rescued us!" they cried as soon as they saw us. "Oh, children! We didn't thank you for all you've done! If it wasn't for you, I don't know what would have become of us! And because of you, our son has come home as well!"

They embarrassed us, but we were pleased because we knew it was true. If we hadn't been concerned, Lydia would never have found out that an impostor was living with the Wellses. And because we just happened to be investigating the old lighthouse, we had discovered them in the barn. It was more than "luck," and I don't believe in luck anyway as I mentioned before.

Jared came out of the house. We told him about Allyson not being arrested and Karl being chased by the police. He frowned but said nothing.

We asked if we could use the phone. The Girls wanted to tell their parents about the dinner party with Mr. Snow at the Inn on the Bay. We went into the sitting room to use the phone on the desk. One after the other they called. Fortunately everyone would be able to attend. As we turned to go back outdoors, Jared entered the room with a piece of paper in his hand.

"Look at this!" He placed the paper on the desk so we could all gather around it to see. It was some sort of legal paper about a "land trust." It didn't make any sense to me.

"I was thinking yesterday, that whoever put my parents in that barn must have had something to do with that creep who was here pretending to be me. I finally remembered his name: Jim Loggins. I called my friend out in Denver to double-check. None of it made any sense to me—until I found this paper under the desk when I moved my parents furniture back to where it used to be."

"What exactly is it?" asked Louie, looking puzzled.

"See?" asked Jared excitedly, pointing to the fine print that covered the page. "It's about a 'land trust.' Loggins set up the trust and was working with that group that kidnapped Louie. Their plan was for the townspeople to donate land and money to the trust. Loggins wanted everyone to believe that the land would be preserved, but there's nothing in here about preservation! And the trust is in his name! All he had to do was dissolve the trust and start developing! There would be nothing anyone could do to stop him! I'm a lawyer so I understand what this paper means. Jim Loggins was going to take over the whole town! He's a very clever man! Most people would never read every word of this, especially if they believed in the trust. His scheme was almost foolproof."

"Wow!" exclaimed Louie. "So he tricked the whole bunch?"

"It would seem that way," answered Jared.

"I still don't get it," said Abigail.

"It's so clear," said Mollie. "Loggins is a developer. He wanted to make money by developing land and building houses. Those crazies thought that the land trust would save all the land for the Earth Mother, but Loggins wanted it all to himself and in his name so he could get rich! Am I right?"

"You are right," agreed Jared. "The whole group was deceived."

"It serves them right!" exclaimed Muffy. "They used evil for what they thought was a good idea, but now they've been made fools of!"

"Let's go to the police," said Jared. "But first I need some wheels."

We followed Jared outside to the shed. He entered and came out with an old bicycle. We watched as he dusted it off with a rag, squirted some oil on the chain, reentered the shed to find a bicycle pump, and inflated the tires. We said good-bye to his parents and Mrs. McLaughlin and pedaled off to the police station.

When we arrived, we were given a cold reception. The police chief invited us into his office, but didn't offer us a seat. Of course there weren't enough chairs and hardly enough room for all of us to even stand in the small space. The chief leaned back in his chair and looked from one of us to the other. Finally he spoke.

"After Jerry Mullins made his confession, Reverend Maxon decided not to press charges."

"Why not?" Mollie blurted out.

"Because Mullins was being blackmailed, he says, by Lucky Clark. Somehow Clark suspected Mullins of stealing money from the church. Mullins was part of the "Save the Earth Club," but he wanted out. The problem was he knew too much. Clark kept Mullins from leaving the group by threatening to tell the reverend about his stealing."

"But what about the night when Mr. Mullins went to the water tower?" asked Muffy.

"He noticed that someone was following him so he drove to the tower, figuring he could get away from you. He thought that whoever it was tailing him wouldn't follow him up the tower, but that kid Billy Jones took off after him. He was just trying to get away from you. We had those vials in his box analyzed off Cape and the report came back that they were only testing chemicals."

"So he wasn't part of the plot?" I asked, incredulously.

"*There is no plot!*" the chief said with conviction. "You girls have way too much imagination for your own good!"

"But you saw them there at Captain Snow's with your own eyes!" I confirmed. "They were trespassing! They had Louie tied and gagged! They were going to sacrifice that coyote! They were going to do something evil!"

"Lots of people sneak into that old house," the chief replied blandly. "The owners don't even care about it. If you want me to arrest them for trespassing, I would have to arrest you. You were there too, you know. Anyway, they all promised not to go back there again."

"We have permission from Alfred Snow of Cincinatti, Ohio, to go into that house," Mollie told him. All the while Jared kept silent. He was listening intently.

"Maybe the whole lot of them had permission for all I know. I don't care."

"Is Lucky Clark still in custody?" asked Muffy.

"We had to let him go," the chief replied. "Mullins forgave him for his blackmailing scheme."

"Then what about Louie?" I asked.

"Don't know who tied him up. We can't risk arresting the wrong person."

"Ridiculous!" muttered Mollie under her breath.

"What about the coyote?" asked Abigail, meekly.

"It's doing fine."

"But they shouldn't have had it in the first place!" exclaimed Muffy. "They got it from the coyote shooter! Mr. Costa said that was illegal!"

"Then he can take care of that! It's not my department."

"Did you test the candy? The Benny Beans that they're selling at The Tomb?" I asked.

"Lucky Clark said he was trying out a 'natural' candy on the kids. There's nothing in them but harmless herbs."

"Couldn't you catch any of those witches?" asked Mollie. Jared suddenly gave her a strange look. I realized that no one had explained the whole situation to him. Louie had told him some of what had happened last night, but Louie hadn't told Jared all the details I was sure.

"Who says they're witches?" the chief asked. "You gave me names of the most respectable citizens in this town! Yes, I spoke to them. Stayed up all night questioning them. And they weren't very happy about it I can tell you! Said they have a citizen's action committee to buy up the vacant land and put it in a trust. It's a good idea that'll help our town. If they have a thing for Mother Nature, that's their business. They aren't hurting anyone."

"But what about my parents?" asked Jared, finally speaking up. "Someone left them for dead in that isolated barn! Are you telling me there's nothing wrong with that? And Louie here is all black and blue. I'm sure he told you what those people did to him."

"But we don't know for sure who did it," the chief blustered. "There's no connection between your parents and this group. That impostor fellow has disappeared without a trace. We called the Denver police after you gave us the tip, but I have a hunch he won't be going back there any too soon. We don't know who hit the boy's bike and left him at that house. He said it was Dr. Kenton, but I don't buy it and the kid can't prove it."

Louie just stood there with his mouth open. How was he supposed to prove that Karl ran him down? Why wouldn't the police believe him? This was too much!

"How are Mrs. Pitts and her sister?" Abigail asked.

"Somehow Mrs. Pitts faints every time she sees a police officer! The doctor over at the hospital seems to think the two of them have been hypnotized or someone is doing some kind of mind control on them. The sister is scared real bad, but Pitts seems angry. We're trying to get them to talk.

"If it makes you feel any better, we did send a cruiser after Dr. Kenton. We wanted to follow up your story about the doctor's bag, Miss Sparrow. We didn't get around to it last night, but Dr. Kenton left town just before the officers got to the marina."

"Thank you, officer," said Jared. He turned to us. "Let's go."

"But what about the..." I began, but Jared put his finger to his lips to make me hush. He didn't trust the police chief either!

Outside Jared continued, "Let's go to my house and discuss this further. You need to fill me in on the witches, chemicals, candy, the water tower—everything!"

Chapter Eighty

Back at the Wellses' house, Mrs. Wells served us cookies and milk in her crowded parlor. We settled back in the plump upholstered chairs covered with white lace doilies. Mrs. Wells seemed very pleased to have her house back and to have it the way it had been before—without the presence of a stranger and with the company of her long-lost son. Between bites of cookies and sips of milk, we told Jared our story from beginning to end. He listened without saying a single word.

"Hmmm," he said when we finished. "Well, I have to tell you that I've had some experience with witches. When I moved out west, I had a girlfriend who got into witchcraft. At first I thought it was harmless, but she kept getting deeper and deeper into it. She was attracted to the feeling of power it gave her. Then she focused more on the supernatural aspect. She liked being able to control things and people. She took me to one of her meetings. I admit I was curious, but I saw more than enough to convince me that I didn't want anything to do with it! When I heard their chants and realized they were bowing down to the Devil himself, I left! I never even spoke to her again.

"Some of these witches seem to be the peaceful kind," he continued, "such as Miss Deighton and her friends. She believes in the power of herbs for medicine, yet she also believes in superstition, like when she said some of the herbs would keep you safe from danger. She wants to save the town, but she hasn't resorted to evil the way the others have. What I've noticed about witchcraft is this: people start out innocently enough, but the more they get involved in it, one thing leads to another until they're putting spells on their neighbors and trying to poison barking dogs. They preach love, but rather than helping people, their intentions become warped in the end! Thank goodness Miss Deighton hasn't come to that point yet! I'd like to help you kids to stop the evil ones. I have a plan."

I finally had hope again that just maybe this case would turn out O.K.!

"First, we'll go by the library and make copies of this paper. I'll leave one here at the house for safekeeping, and we'll take the rest with us."

We walked over to the library, which was only a few buildings down Main Street. While Jared was getting help with the copy machine, Muffy went on line in the computer nook. Believe it or not, she was able to find Douglas Missionary Hospital in Madras, India! She e-mailed them, asking if a Petunia Snow had ever been a nurse there a very long time ago. Hopefully, they would e-mail back. We looked up to see Jared standing in the doorway with the copies in his hand.

"Where are we going?" asked Louie.

"You'll see," Jared told us. "Let's get our bikes."

We walked back to the Wellses' and Jared went inside to leave a copy of the paper in his father's desk. He handed us each a copy. Then we rode to the bank and parked our bikes in the rack out front. It struck me as strange that the bank would have a bike rack. How many adults ride their bikes to the bank? A lot, I guess. Or maybe more children have bank accounts than I thought. Anyway, we entered the air-conditioned lobby and Jared walked straight toward the open door of the president's office. We could see him sitting behind a huge wooden desk. A look of horror came over his face when he looked up and saw us. He ordered his secretary, who was standing at his side, to shut the door, which she did, just as we were about to enter! Jared knocked on the door and the secretary put her head out.

"Mr. Blackwell is very busy...with a client. He can't be disturbed."

"There's no one in there," asserted Jared. "Tell Mr. Blackwell that Jared Wells and his friends are here to see him. We have an important document we think he would like to see."

The door shut, only to reopen a moment later.

"Mr. Blackwell will see you now," chirped the secretary, leading us into the spacious office. Leather chairs were pulled up for each of us. Mr. Blackwell was sweating and mopping his forehead with a white handkerchief. He stood and reached over his desk to shake hands with Jared.

"Mr. Wells! How nice to see you! What may I do for you?"

"You could read this document," answered Jared, taking the paper out of his pocket and handing it to Mr. Blackwell.

The banker skimmed over the sheet, his face turning white, then red, then almost purple with rage! An exclamation was about to burst out of his mouth, but he controlled himself, thinking better of it.

"Where did you get this?"

"It was at my parents' house. You know that Jim Loggins, the real estate developer, was holding my parents hostage."

Mr. Blackwell turned white again. We could see that thoughts were racing through his mind. Of course he should have made a comment about Jared's parents. If he hadn't been part of the group, he wouldn't have known anything about them, but he gave himself away, as Jared had hoped he would.

"That scalawag duped us! An environmentalist who had worked for the government, he told us! Ha! We trusted him! He worked with us to develop a plan to save this town! We had our papers drawn up. But according to this document, the land trust was just a hoax to acquire land for him to develop at a later date! How did he think he could get away with it?"

Mr. Blackwell fell heavily into his chair and buried his face in his hands. He looked up at Jared and asked in a low tone, "Who else knows about this?"

"No one."

"Except all these children." Mr. Blackwell made a rude gesture toward us. Suddenly he snatched the paper up from the desk and ripped it to shreds! "I'm a very busy man. You'll have to leave now!"

Jared was one step ahead of Mr. Blackwell. He took another paper from his pocket. "The original," he said, holding it out of Mr. Blackwell's reach. We each took out our papers and held them up. Mr. Blackwell's face turned red as Jared led us out of the office. Mr. Blackwell stood speechless, glaring as we filed out.

"What a nasty old man!" exclaimed Muffy. "Did your plan work or not?"

"We'll see," said Jared. "We have several more stops."

We rode past the gas station to the local newspaper office. Victoria Harden was at her desk, talking on the phone. At first she looked scared, then suspicious, then annoyed. By the time she got off the phone, she had a very unfriendly attitude. She looked like the type of person who worked out in a gym, her sleeveless blouse showing off the defined muscles of her tanned arms and shoulders. She tossed her long curls and looked Jared in the eye. He handed her a copy of the document. Victoria read it carefully, her face showing all the emotions of Mr. Blackwell's.

"Who are you and where did you get this?" she asked angrily.

"I'm Jared Wells. Jim Loggins, the real estate developer who held my parents hostage, left it at their house. I thought you might want to use it in your story."

"What story?"

"The story about my parents being held prisoner in their own home."

"I don't know anything about it," she replied, defensively.

"Don't you have contact with the police?"

"Of course I do."

"Then they should have given you the story about my parents' kidnapping and how they were tied up and left for dead at the old lighthouse!"

"Getting back to this...this...Loggins," said Victoria, changing the subject. "You said he's a real estate developer. He told...I mean I heard...Well how do you know what he is?"

"Are you going to print the story or not?" asked Jared taking control. "If you're not interested in what happened to my parents, there's the news about a number of respectable townspeople being tricked by the same out-of-town developer. The group almost had a run-in with the police just last night. That would be quite interesting to read. You wouldn't know anything about that either, would you?"

"No, I haven't heard anything about that," Victoria responded, but not very convincingly, as she squirmed in her office chair. "If I could get that story, I would definitely print it."

"The police can give you all the information you need," Jared assured her, though in my opinion the police didn't seem to be cooperating at all.

"Who else knows about this?" asked Victoria, nodding toward the paper.

"Only you. And Mr. Blackwell."

"What did he say?"

"He ripped up his copy and threw us out."

We turned to exit, leaving Victoria holding her copy of the paper and nervously reading it over.

Chapter Eighty-One

Aloma Smiles had a summer job selling swimsuits on Main Street. I was surprised that Jared knew exactly where to find her. He must have "done his homework," as they say. We stopped by the shop and handed her a copy of the paper. She couldn't make any sense of it at first, but even without a legal background, she realized that Loggins had deceived her and her little group. She trembled as she read through the paragraphs, but said nothing. At last she looked up at Jared and then at us. After we waited a while in dead silence, we left.

Following Jared's lead, we pedaled down Main Street to The Tomb. You can imagine our surprise to see it all closed up!

"I should have expected this," muttered Jared. "Let's continue." He hopped back on his bike and headed past the lighthouse. Soon we were at the marina. I told Jared to talk to the Mitchells. They were both in the store. I introduced Jared and my friends to them.

"Is Karl Kenton here?" asked Jared, though he knew that Karl had gotten away.

"He's left town!" said Mrs. Mitchell. "Can you believe it? After all the work he put into that radio station of his, he said that the Cape wasn't ready for his ideas, so he's moving up to Maine."

"It seemed to me that people liked his ideas," added Mr. Mitchell. "I thought everything was going swell for him. He could have run for selectman! I'm sure he would've won the election! We were sure surprised when he packed up and left—and in such a hurry! As if he were being chased by something!"

Hmmm. Being chased? They were right! Had we chased him out of town? I would like to think so, but I would have felt better if Karl were behind bars. Out of town was the next best thing.

"We were surprised when the police came by just after Dr. Kenton had left," said Mrs. Mitchell. "I'll let you know when we hear from him. I'm sure he'll write, once he's settled down in Maine."

Jared thanked them for the information and we walked out to our bikes.

"Do we have another stop?" asked Louie as we pedaled back toward the bridge.

"One more," Jared told us.

"Could we have ice cream first?" asked Abigail. Of course the answer was "yes!" We rode next door to the Clam Bar. Cooky's wife served us but acted as if she didn't know us. That was O.K. Once we had our cones, we sat on the grass beside the river. Jared was almost like one of us.

"I haven't been here in years," he exclaimed. "You know, this Clam Bar was around when I was a kid. I used to fish for flounder from the bridge.

Believe it or not, I once sneaked into Captain Snow's house myself!"

"No!" exclaimed Mollie.

"What happened?" asked Louie.

"It was freezing cold inside, though it was a warm early fall day. My friends and I ran out and never went back!" he laughed. "Well, kids, we've visited everyone on my list, except for one. Now they know that we know that they were deceived by Jim Loggins. He's gotten away, but not with his trickery. This plot is over! He'll probably go off to another community and start all over again with another scam. At least the Cape will be safe, for now. Karl will be preaching peace, love, and herb power up in Maine or somewhere."

"What about Mr. Alexis and Lucky?" asked Mollie.

"Mr. Alexis should get a more respectable job. I think he could, with his education," said Jared.

"It doesn't seem that he was really one of them," I added. "He wasn't at Captain Snow's with the rest."

"We have to check on Lucky," Jared went on. "All in all, I think the witches will tone down their activities or hopefully stop them altogether. Victoria Harden won't print a good story, you can be sure of that. Even if we wrote letters to the editor, she probably wouldn't print them. I think Blackwell, Harden, and Smits have learned their lesson. If they used the town meetings and laws to save our town or devised a private land trust, which would have been quicker and easier than going through the town government, they would have been more successful. The way they went about it, being secretive and using witchcraft, only led to them being deceived."

"But what about Allyson?" asked Muffy.

"Is she the teenager from your yacht club?" asked Jared.

"Yes," I answered. "She's the head witch. She was at the club earlier and should still be there. Let's go over. We have to tell Billy about her."

We finished our cones and rode over. Billy and some of the instructors were down on the beach inspecting the rigging on the Sprites. We climbed down the steps to join them.

"Hey, Billy!" called Mollie. "Where's Allyson?"

Billy walked over to meet us. He acted upset. We introduced Jared and filled him in on what had been going on.

"You've got some mystery!" declared Billy. "I can't believe that Allyson was mixed up with that group! Mr. Prince said the police called him last night to tell him what happened. He called Allyson's parents and they drove down from Rhode Island to pick her up just a little while ago."

"She's gone?" asked Mollie in amazement.

"Yeah. They're putting her in a special program for kids who've been in cults. Then they're sending her to a special school in Rhode Island. Ever hear of 'reform school'?"

We shook our heads no.

"Well, it's kind of like jail for kids who get in trouble and have problems. Allyson's parents want her near home, they said. Mr. Prince thought she should go too. She didn't break the law or anything, but what was she doing at Captain Snow's with those crazy adults? It's freaky! Something strange is going on with her. I sure hope she changes, that she wants to change. It would be really sad if she doesn't realize how messed up she is! Her parents promised to get her all the help she needs, but she's the one who has to snap out of it and get back to normal."

Billy sighed and went on, "At least you solved the mystery of Jared's family! Judy's a mystery too. A good kid gone weird, but I guess she's not as weird as Allyson turned out to be. I hope she doesn't get dragged into that black witchcraft too!

I hoped not. Judy had been our friend, even though she was a little odd. She had tried to help us with our mystery. We felt sorry for Billy concerning Allyson and hoped he would recover. What a person to choose as his girlfriend—the teenage leader of a witch's coven! We said good-bye to Billy and pedaled back by the marina. We rode over the bridge, past the lighthouse, and along Main Street to our last stop.

At the library we turned right, up the steep hill of the little lane leading to a row of small houses in back of the library. We stopped at the last one. The lawn was brown from lack of water. Old gym equipment and oil drums stood rusting all over it.

"Who lives here?" asked Louie.

"Lucky Clark," was Jared's reply. There was no response to our knock. A look through the window revealed that the tenant had "vacated the premises," as they say. Lucky was long gone and had taken all the evidence with him! The rooms were bare!

"Well, I guess another one got away," sighed Jared.

"What will we do now?" asked Muffy.

"Let's go home," replied Jared, pushing his bike onto the lane. We followed him back to his parents' house.

When we arrived, Mr. Wells was in the kitchen fixing dinner and Mrs. Wells was reading the mail. We sat in the parlor with her.

"Your mother stopped by to visit, Laura. What a wonderful woman! She's so proud of you. And you all must feel proud of the way you've helped us too!" she remarked.

"We do," said Louie. "But I don't feel right about the rest of it. It's like all the bad guys got away. And the ones still left in town are getting away with it too."

"They did a lot of evil things," said Muffy. "Like making voodoo dolls, ramming Louie's bike with their car and tying him up, locking you and Sally in that barn, and threatening us. It's creepy to think they're still loose! They could come after us again at any time!"

"Oh they wouldn't do that!" said Mrs. Wells. But she should have known better.

"I don't think they will," Jared consoled us. "Their plot has failed. They were deceived by Loggins, who was probably the real leader. I think you kids will be safe. And I've made a decision. I'm moving back. Mom and Dad want me to stay with them." He leaned over and kissed his mother on her forehead. "I'll make up for all the years I was away. This town needs a good, honest lawyer. And I have a former girlfriend who's still single!"

Louie was so shocked that we couldn't help laughing out loud! His Aunt Lydia and Jared were a pair I guess! Mrs. Wells told Jared to invite us for dinner.

"Thank you, but we have another invitation," I said. I told them about Mr. Snow coming to town and inviting us for dinner at the inn. I was beginning to feel the lack of sleep from the night before and from all the excitement. I just wanted to go home to bed, but we had a big evening ahead of us. The other Girls felt the same way too, I'm sure, but what could we do? We thanked Mrs. Wells anyway.

Louie accepted the invitation, though, because he was available. His Aunt Lydia was invited too. We Girls made a plan to meet at Abigail's in the morning, then we'd see Louie at the Clam Bar at one. We wanted to take Mr. Snow to Captain Snow's house in the afternoon. We thanked Jared for all his help and said good-bye.

"I'm glad we don't have to be afraid anymore," said Muffy. "Especially about riding our bikes." It was true. Now that the witches were scattered, we had no one to fear. Muffy headed off to her part of town as Mollie, Abigail, and I rode together down Main Street. On our way past the church, we noticed Reverend Maxon planting something on the side of the parsonage. We rode our bikes up.

"Why, hello!" he called out cheerfully, as we clattered up beside him. "We had quite a night last night, didn't we? I've been over to visit your friend Miss Deighton."

He must have noticed the look on our faces, because he quickly explained, "I heard you and the police mention her name. They telephoned her last night and I gathered from the conversation that she was recovering from an operation and had been bullied by those witches. I thought I should stop by and visit, though she doesn't attend our church.

"Her friend Betty is staying with her. The three of us had tea this afternoon. She showed me—rather I looked around—her garden while she sat in her rocking chair in the kitchen and pointed out the various herbs from there. Lovely woman. So educated and refined. And we have so much in common! Of course she has some ideas I have to reject, but I'm hoping she'll change her views on a number of subjects, once she 'sees the light.'"

We weren't completely sure that we knew what he was talking about, but it sure seemed as if something romantic was going on. I tried to imagine Reverend Maxon and Miss Deighton as a couple, but it was just too weird.

Abigail and Mollie must have felt the same way I did because they were giving me peculiar looks behind the reverend's back.

"Miss Deighton gave me these herbs to plant around the church to keep the evil away. Of course I had to tell her that I don't believe that, but I would accept them as a gift because I do know that these plants are good for tea and they smell wonderful. Oh, by the way, Jerry Mullins returned the missing records. I looked them over out of curiosity. There was no mention of Captain Snow in any of them. Well then, I'll see you on Sunday!" he said to me as he turned back to his work.

"Are we going to be hearing wedding bells?" asked Mollie as we hopped on our bikes and rode down the church driveway.

"Maybe," I laughed as we pedaled down Main Street.

When we got to Abigail's house, I told them, "I'm going to telephone the Inn on the Bay and find out if Mr. Snow's there yet. We have to talk to him privately. And we need to count that money in the treasure box, to make sure it's enough to buy our Eel Grass Palace."

"Maybe he'll give us a good deal on it," said Mollie with a grin.

We could see Abigail's grandmother through the kitchen window, so we said good-bye and Mollie and I rode on. We pedaled through the narrow side streets, behind the lighthouse, to Lowndes River Road, past the marina, the yacht club, and on to my house. Mom was home. I said good-bye to Mollie. We'd all be meeting again soon at the Inn on the Bay.

In the kitchen, Mom was at the table with her feet up on one of the chairs, sipping tea and reading her old novel. She looked up and smiled at me, "Hello, sweetie. I stopped by to see the Wellses this afternoon. They're so thankful to you girls for saving them and finding their son."

"Louie helped find Jared," I told her. "But it does make us feel good that we helped."

When Dad arrived home, I told my parents most of what had happened during the day.

"I can't believe Karl just left town like that!" said Dad, shaking his head. "It looks really suspicious. But maybe Karl was right, maybe the Cape isn't ready for his New Age ideas and it might be just a coincidence that he left."

Yeah, sure! How could my own parents be like that!? Their way of thinking was all wrong. Why couldn't they accept what I was telling them? Karl ran over Louie's bike! He bought my coyote from the coyote shooter to use as a sacrifice! At Allyson's command, he was ready to throw us down an old well! But, no! Since he was a respectable citizen, he must not have done anything wrong! At least he'd left town. There was nothing more we could do about it anyway. We had to have faith that the witches still here wouldn't try to hurt us any more. We could relax and be fun-loving Eel Grass Girls again. Now it was time to get ready for our dinner party!

Chapter Eighty-Two

The Inn on the Bay was just that. It was a grand, old-fashioned hotel situated on top of a bluff and overlooking the bay. My parents and I climbed the brick steps up to the shimmering lobby, which was filled with sparking glass chandeliers. As we entered the lobby, our feet sank into the plush carpet. We then were ushered into the main dining room where Mr. Snow was seated at a long table waiting for us.

He was just as I had imagined: thin, wiry, with a handsome face. His moustache and hair were gray, almost white, and he wore a well-tailored navy blue suit. He rose to meet us when we came into the room, extending his hand to shake ours. Though he smiled, he seemed a little withdrawn.

"Nice to meet you," he said as we introduced ourselves. Just then, Mollie, her parents, and Maxwell the Monster entered the room. Through the glass doors, I could see Muffy and Abigail coming up the stairs. Abigail seemed upset for some reason. The Cortezes and Abigail's grandmother and Uncle Jack followed. As you might imagine, the grownups took over. We four Girls and Maxwell were seated at one end of the table, while the adults were seated nearer to Mr. Snow. Maxwell began kicking Mollie under the table.

"I got a chance to read some of Petunia's day journal," Muffy told us. "It's fascinating. There's even an old map of town she drew herself!"

"I'd like to see that," I said.

"Let's take turns reading it," suggested Mollie.

"I have something important to tell you," whispered Abigail. She started to tell us, but the waiter appeared to take our orders. Our parents were having a great time talking to each other and Mr. Snow. Every once in a while, Mr. Snow would say something to us, trying to include us in the conversation, but it was awkward. We had so much to tell him, but it was private. We might as well wait until tomorrow to talk to him, we decided.

"Cut it out, Maxwell!" hissed Mollie, as he began making spitballs from the cocktail napkin under his Shirley Temple.

I tried to ignore them and enjoy the party. The large room was lined with windows that were framed by flowery curtains and looked out over the bay. We watched the sun set as a waitress lit the candles on each of the tables. Delicate flower arrangements on the crisp white linen tablecloths gave us the feeling of dining in a garden. We had an elegant and fun meal, in spite of Maxwell, but we didn't get to say a word to Mr. Snow! Nothing important, that is.

The dessert table was piled high with sweets and amazing ice sculptures shaped like a swan and a sailboat! We heaped our plates with goodies.

Finally, as coffee was being served to the adults, Mr. Snow leaned over and called down to us from his end of the table, "I would like to thank you girls for solving the mystery of my house. The police were able to locate me here and telephoned to report the goings-on last night. I hope you will give me a tour of the old place. I'm sad to say that I don't even know where my property is."

"Oh, we'll be glad to show you all around," said Mollie.

"We could come by and get you around one-thirty tomorrow afternoon," Muffy added.

"Wear your walking shoes," suggested Abigail.

"Then it's settled," announced Mr. Snow. "We have business to discuss, don't forget!" He winked. We didn't know exactly what he meant, but we could only guess. Maybe he was ready to sell us our Eel Grass Palace!

"If we don't have a plan for tomorrow morning," began Abigail, "Uncle Jack has invited us to go clamming with him."

"Sounds good," said Muffy.

"We'll be over early," Mollie added. She loved to speak for all of us! It could be annoying, but we just accepted it. "I'll swing by in the morning, Laura."

"Don't forget to bring your clamming permits," Abigail reminded us. "And I have something important to tell you."

I wondered what was up with Abigail, but we would find out tomorrow. The four of us were exhausted. We were thankful when our parents didn't keep talking and talking, as parents do. I was very glad to fall into my little bed. This time, though, I took a shower and got into my pajamas.

The next morning Mollie came over before Mom left for work. I was happy that she did because I still didn't feel completely comfortable about being alone. We had momentarily forgotten that there was still a zombie loose!

"Be careful today, girls," warned Mom.

"Why do you say that?" I asked, suspiciously. Was she thinking about the zombie too? No it couldn't be. I had never mentioned him to her!

"I don't know," she said, with a puzzled look. "I don't know why I said that."

A shudder shook my body. Mollie gave me a questioning glance, but said nothing. After Mom left, we rode our bikes over to Abigail's.

"What was your mom talking about?" asked Mollie as we pedaled along.

"Could she mean the zombie? It's still out there, you know."

"Yeah," she sighed. "I know."

Muffy was at Abigail's when we arrived.

"Hey, look!" she called, waving a piece of paper at us.

"What's that?" I asked.

"It's a fax from Doctor Perhonen! He heard about what happened and he's glad that Karl left town. Look here. He says he'll help Mr. Alexis get a new job! He'll be back next summer and see us then."

"Cool!" Mollie exclaimed.

Uncle Jack came out of the house, looking as if he were ready to go on a safari with his khaki shorts, shirt with little tab things on them—epaulets? And a pith helmet, you know, the kind of hat they wear in Africa!

"Hello girls! How are you doing today?" he greeted us cheerfully. We just smiled at him. He looked so eccentric! "Pin your permits to your sweatshirts or hats," he told us. "We don't want any trouble with the shellfish warden!"

He seemed like a nice uncle, the kind who does fun things with you that your parents would never do. Parents are always too busy, but because Uncle Jack didn't have any children and he was on vacation, he had plenty of time to spend with us. Anyway, that's the way it seemed to me.

Abigail was still uneasy about something. She had tried to talk to us last night, but hadn't had a chance. She came over to us and whispered, "I have to tell you what happened." But just then Uncle Jack turned to us and told us to pile into the Land Rover with all the clamming equipment. We drove to the marina. My stomach turned into knots as we approached. It was strange because I knew that Karl was gone and life was back to normal again. Yet I still felt afraid, expecting the evil doctor to appear any moment! But he didn't.

We tumbled out of the car and dragged the rakes and buckets down the dock to the motorboat belonging to Abigail's grammy. We loaded our gear, started the engine, untied the launch, and headed for the channel.

I felt sorry for Abigail. She was really upset, but we couldn't talk. Maybe when we got to the clamming flats, she could tell us. We drove slowly through the channel, past the yacht club, and over to the old lighthouse! I wondered why Uncle Jack had chosen that area, rather than nearer to Womponoy. When we arrived, he anchored the boat in shallow water, and we jumped out. Our feet sank ankle-deep in the soft mud. I wanted to use my hands rather than a rake. It seemed to me that the heavy metal rake would break the thin clam shells too easily. We got to work, but Uncle Jack stayed right with us, so we couldn't talk to Abigail about whatever was bothering her.

Chapter Eighty-Three

"What are you doing?" A woman's voice right behind me!

I spun around to see Sally! Oh, no! What was she doing here? Then I calmed down, a little. We were near her house. It would be natural for her to be there, but I was shocked anyway! I just stared at her with my mouth open. The Girls and Uncle Jack stared too. We all just stood there in the mud. As I looked, I saw that her eyes seemed clear. She didn't seem so frightening.

"Laura Sparrow," she said. "You saved me. Thank you. I want to help you. The bad people are gone. My sister has changed. She is good now. Come to my house." She pointed toward the old lighthouse. I looked at the others, wondering if we should go with her.

"Shall we go to the lighthouse?" I asked. They nodded "yes" and Uncle Jack said, "Sure!" With him to protect us, I supposed that it would be safe to go. I introduced Uncle Jack to Sally. She was a strange woman. I wasn't sure if the witches had made her that way or if it was just her personality. We left our buckets and rakes in the boat and trailed behind Sally through the swaying beach grass.

The old lighthouse needed some paint and fixing. I noticed the peeling paint and sagging trim. I felt butterflies in my stomach as we crossed the porch. Sally opened the door and we entered the cool sitting room where the séance table filled the center. She motioned for us to sit down. While she disappeared into another room, we quickly told Uncle Jack who Sally was and how she fit into our mystery.

Suddenly Sally was back, carrying a pile of books and papers—our books and papers to be exact! Mr. Snow's book, Aunt Sparrow's diary, our notes, and my family tree! I was really relieved! I would never forgive myself if my family tree had been lost! Sally carefully placed them on the table and seated herself. Then as if remembering something, she hurried out of the room again.

"These are all the things her sister stole from us," Abigail whispered to her uncle.

Sally returned with a bag of cookies and some sort of juice. We were afraid to drink the juice, but we ate the cookies because the bag was new and had never been opened.

"Karl hypnotized Gracie and me," said Sally. "Karl is a bad man. He made Gracie a bad woman. We did what he said. She stole your books. She took hair from your houses to make dolls. She tried to hurt you. Gracie was bad.

"Gracie wants to be good now. She forgot everything when she saw the policemen. No bad people came to see her in the hospital. She thought they were her friends. They did not care about her. They used her. The doctors sent her home. Now she is good. I am good. I want to be your friend, Laura Sparrow."

323

I was surprised. Why had she chosen me, of all the Girls, to be her friend?

As if she could read my mind, she continued, "When I was a child, I stayed with old Mrs. Wiggins near your house. I know your house. I knew your father when he was a boy. Come back to see me."

"Would you mind if my mother came, too?" I asked, thinking that Sally might not be able to take care of herself. My mom could get her any help she might need. And Dad could help Sally fix her lighthouse up. He had a group of carpenter friends who volunteered to help the elderly and others make repairs on their homes.

It seemed strange to me that Mrs. Pitts would never be punished for the bad things she had done. Hypnotized or not, she had really appeared to enjoy being nasty to us! Both she and her sister knew right from wrong. Sally could have gone to the police at any time with her information about Karl and the others, but she hadn't—and it was all over now. If the two sisters would never get involved in another evil plot again, that would be enough I supposed.

"Please come back," said Sally. "Bring your mother and father. Take your books." She pointed to the pile on the table. Then she disappeared into a back room and reappeared with a plastic bag. I carefully wrapped up the antique books and papers. We thanked her and left, following the path back to the boat.

"You have some strange friends," remarked Uncle Jack. "An old man from Cincinnati who owns a haunted house. An old lady who owns a haunted lighthouse. An uncle who owns a haunted Land Rover!" he joked.

"The lighthouse isn't haunted," corrected Abigail. "And neither is your Land Rover. In fact, Captain Snow's house is ghost-free as well, thanks to Laura's minister!"

"Correction," Mollie interjected. "Thanks to us!" We all laughed as we recounted our tale of the supernatural exorcism to Uncle Jack. He couldn't help but laugh as well. We finished up our clam digging and headed back to the marina with a bushel of steamers. We wanted to get ready to meet Mr. Snow on time.

Back at Abigail's we rinsed off our feet at the outside shower and then rinsed the rakes and buckets with the garden hose. Uncle Jack took the clams into the kitchen and came out with a tray of lemonade. He sat on the porch with us.

"I'm thinking of staying another two weeks," he confided. "I have my laptop here and can do all my work without going back to the city."

"Is there a way to check my e-mail on your laptop?" asked Muffy. "I e-mailed India yesterday from the computer at the library and I wonder if you could see if I have an answer so I don't have to go back to the library."

"It could take forever to get a reply from India," said Uncle Jack. "But let's give it a try."

He went into the house and came back with his laptop. He set it up on one of the little tables lining the porch. Muffy told Uncle Jack her e-mail address.

"You've got mail," said Uncle Jack, mimicking the computer's voice. Muffy jumped up and down. He opened the e-mail.

"Dear Mora Cortez," it read. By the way, that's Muffy's real name. "We thank you for your inquiry to Douglas Medical Mission. I am Amira Ghandi, a research student at DMM. My current work has been to compile a history of the Mission and I was happy to receive your e-mail regarding the American nurse Petunia Snow. She served at the Mission her entire adult life. She married Doctor Ravi Saleem, an Indian physician, but they had no children. I will send more information about her as soon as I discover it in our archives. Please let me know if I can be of any further assistance to you. Peace be with You, Amira Ghandi."

"Oh my goodness!" exclaimed Abigail. "Petunia ran away to be a nurse in India! How romantic!"

"It wasn't so romantic to escape from her mother the witch!" replied Mollie, the cynic. "And her father who wouldn't do anything about it!"

"I think it's wonderful that you got through," I said to Muffy. "And that they wrote back right away. And that they knew who Petunia was. I'm glad that she got away from her family and was able to fulfill a dream and find someone to marry after Edward died."

"What's this all about?" asked Uncle Jack. We filled him in on Petunia and her family.

"At least we have one happy ending to this mystery," said Muffy, feeling satisfied.

"What about Sally and Mrs. Pitts?" asked Mollie. "They're a happy ending, kind of."

"Is that correct English?" asked Muffy, teasing Mollie, who usually enjoyed correcting our grammar. Mollie ignored her of course.

"And don't forget Jared and the Wellses," added Uncle Jack. "They're a happy ending too!"

"You're right! Time to meet Louie," I announced, noticing Uncle Jack's watch.

"Thank you for letting me check my e-mail," Muffy said to Uncle Jack. "And for taking us clamming." We all thanked him for our outing. If he hadn't taken us over to the old lighthouse beach, I don't know when we would have ever gotten our books and my family tree back from Sally!

"It was my pleasure," he beamed. "It was the most interesting clam dig I've ever experienced!" We laughed, but as the laugh came out of my mouth, I felt guilty. The thought of Sally made me sad. She was different, but she couldn't help it. I determined right then that I would really become her friend. Mom and I would visit her and give her all the help she needed. It was too bad she had allowed her evil sister to influence her, but her life would be better now that the witches were out of business.

Chapter Eighty-Four

The next moment we were on our bikes and pedaling toward the Clam Bar. The books and papers were safely stowed in my backpack. When we arrived, we leaned our bikes next to Louie's brother's bike on the side of the snack shop. To our surprise, Mrs. Pitts was back at work at the counter! She gave us a startled expression, but said nothing. I turned to the Girls. Louie was beside us. As a unit, we approached the counter and gave her our orders, then sat on the grass to wait for our lunch.

Mrs. Pitts called to us when our food was ready. We paid her and couldn't help staring. She stared back, but we didn't know what to say. I knew what she should say because she owed us an apology! She had been really mean and nasty to us! Though she had never been a warm and fuzzy sort of person, she had never been unkind in all the years we had known her at the Clam Bar.

Maybe she truly didn't remember some of her actions and she might not know all that she'd done wrong. I agreed that she had been hypnotized, but most of the time in the past few weeks, she hadn't seemed to be hypnotized at all—she had been just plain evil! She knew the wrong she had done, I was sure of it. I hoped she was sorry too, not just sorry because she could have ended up in jail!

I supposed I should forgive her whether she apologized or not. Holding a grudge would hurt me more than it would hurt her. Karl must have hypnotized her so that she would forget all the important information she knew as soon as she saw a policeman. That way, his secrets would remain safe. He had used her and she knew now that Karl hadn't really been her friend.

We quickly ate our lunch. We told Louie about our dinner with Mr. Snow and how we were supposed to meet him now.

It was a short ride to the Inn on the Bay. When we climbed the brick steps, we saw Mr. Snow waiting for us on the terrace dressed in a white linen suit! We almost fell down the stairs when we saw him! It reminded us of the lawn party at the library! He looked as though he had just stepped out of the past! Was he the ghost of Captain Snow himself? No, I told myself as I quieted my emotions. Of course not! Our mystery had confused my mind! But by the faces of my friends, I wasn't the only one with an imagination.

"He looks like a ghost!" Louie whispered to us as we slowed our pace. But we continued climbing the steep steps. At the top of the stairs, Mr. Snow greeted us warmly. We introduced Louie.

"Good afternoon! The limousine will be here any minute. I thought you could give me a tour of the town before we visit the old house."

At that moment a long black limousine pulled up in front of the inn and we walked down the steps and got in. There was plenty of room. Mollie took the lead and directed the driver. First we drove past the fish pier to Muffy's neighborhood. Then we drove down Seacliff Road, stopping at the home of Mabel and Agnes Weeks. Mr. Snow got out of the car to meet the sisters who happened to be in their garden, admiring their new blossoms. He seemed especially delighted by Agnes. He even seemed to blush! What was going on here? We giggled behind their backs. Before we left, Mr. Snow invited the sisters to join him for dinner that evening. He told them that he would send the limousine over to pick them up at seven. Another romance?

Then we drove through town, past the Wellses' and McLaughlins', to Small Pond and down Pine Street beyond Miss Deighton's. We then passed Mollie's and my house and the yacht club. We rode along the marina to the bridge, where we parked. The limousine was too long to enter the old driveway leading to Captain Snow's.

I was glad that I no longer felt any fear as we approached the house. I guess I had to agree with Muffy, that it hadn't really been a ghost haunting the house. It had been an evil spirit—a spirit who had terrorized us and tricked us, but it was gone now.

Mr. Snow trudged after us up the drive and through the overgrowth of the path. When the old house came into view, he uttered a word I can't repeat.

"So this is it!" he said under his breath. "My, my!" We walked around the house, making a complete circle. Mollie led him across the porch and pushed open the heavy front door. What was this? To our horror, the limp body of a man lay across the middle of the floor!

"What's this?" asked Mr. Snow. We rushed forward and quickly recognized the body as being that of Morton Grounds, the zombie!

"Go tell my driver to call the police—and get an ambulance," Mr. Snow ordered Louie. He raced out of the house in obedience. We just stared at the ragged form. Mollie was the first to move. She felt for his pulse.

"He's alive," she whispered. Abigail's eyes began to fill with tears. She clung to Muffy. Within minutes we heard the sirens. Louie rushed in, panting.

"They're coming!...Can you hear them?...They'll be here any minute!"

Moments later Officer Nick stood in the doorway.

"What's going on here?" he demanded, his hand on his holster. His gaze went from Mr. Snow to Morton Grounds.

"It's a zombie!" Louie blurted out.

"A what?" asked Nick, stepping forward. The familiar faces of the EMS men appeared behind him. The men rushed into the room to set to work on poor Morton.

"It's Morton Grounds," Louie told them. "He didn't fall off the end of the outer bar like they said. Aloma Smits got hold of him and turned him into a zombie in the cedar swamp," he babbled.

"And who are you?" the officer asked Mr. Snow. Mollie made the introductions.

Nick radioed the station and gave a verbal report of the situation. Morton was loaded onto a stretcher and wheeled away.

Mr. Snow asked, "What will you do about the poor chap?"

"We'll check out the kid's story. Morton Grounds drowned last winter, but the guy has to be someone." Officer Nick nodded good-bye to us as he followed the EMS workers out. What did we expect?

"He's not going to do a thing!" stormed Mollie.

"Poor man," muttered Abigail. "I hope he'll be able to recover."

"You mentioned the man was a zombie! What is this all about?" asked Mr. Snow. "More of the mystery?"

"Yes," answered Muffy. "It all revolves around your house. A coven of witches offered their sacrifices and had their meetings here. I guess that's why Morton came here too." Muffy then began to fill him in on some of the details of our mystery.

"Tell me more about the land trust as we finish our tour. It sounds as if it could be a good idea," said Mr. Snow. "I do hope the old fellow comes out of it all right."

"And that Aloma Smits goes to jail for it," added Mollie.

We told him about Karls's plot while we walked around the parlor with its French windows. We'd experienced so much terror here just a few days ago! And even though Morton Grounds had just been found in its midst, it seemed peaceful now, so full of hope.

"Your father is a carpenter, am I right?" Mr. Snow asked me. I nodded. "Then I will hire him to fix up my house! I have been considering moving back here, opening my own inn. I will call it Captain Snow's Inn on the Pond, or something to that effect. What do you say?"

"That's a great idea!" we agreed. It would be wonderful to restore the old house and put it to good use. We took Mr. Snow to the old library and showed him all the books lining the shelves. We were surprised that the books were ship's logs, classic novels, and plays. It was strange that the one book Mollie had grabbed from the shelf had been the book of Mrs. Snow's séances!

After we toured the entire house, we returned to the limousine. We drove back to Yacht Harbor Road toward the field of orange lilies. We again left the limo near the street and walked back to the old barn on foot. We pointed out to Mr. Snow the overgrown bog. When we entered the barn, we showed him the office and told him about the treasure we had found.

"We think that the money was stolen from the shipping company owned by Muffy's great-great-grandfather. We want to use it to buy this piece of land," I explained.

"What on earth do you children want with this old barn?" he asked, giving us a serious look.

"We just like it," said Mollie. I thought we could have been more honest, but we didn't want to give away our secret of the Eel Grass Palace.

"I will deed the land to you," he said. "I've heard that Jared Wells is an excellent lawyer. He can draw up the papers. Then the money can be used as a trust fund to pay for the taxes. You children don't know about taxes yet, but they are pesky expenses that you must pay every year and they keep going up and up until you feel that the more property you own, the poorer you must become!"

That certainly didn't make a lot of sense to us, but we did understand that the Eel Grass Palace was going to be ours! We could have hugged Mr. Snow if he hadn't seemed so formal and stiff. He obviously had a kind heart. He spent quite a while looking at the old tools and cranberry boxes scattered around the barn.

"You should donate all these old tools and whatnot to the Cranberry Museum. I read about it on my flight here to the Cape. Mr. Sparrow can fix up this barn after he finishes my house."

"We don't want it fixed up," protested Mollie.

"At least let him make repairs so it doesn't fall down on your heads!" We all laughed at that. He was right. Dad could make the old building safe for us.

On our way back to the car, Mr. Snow said, "Captain Snow wasn't quite the man I thought he was. He was good, but weak. I hate the thought of his wife being a witch! I wanted you to expose Lowndes & McLaughlin, but the truth is that it was Captain Snow and his family who were in the wrong. I plan to make a lot of changes, changes for the good. I'll begin with the old house. By the way, I need to find a good landscaper."

"We know just the person," said Muffy, pointing to Louie. "Louie and his brother can do it."

"And there's an older man, Slim H., who can do the trimming and clearing," added Abigail. This was the first thing she had said. She still seemed upset about something. We were never alone long enough for her to tell us what it was.

We got back into the limo and drove around by the lighthouse to the Inn on the Bay. Mr. Snow invited us to stay for tea. We gladly accepted. We clambered up the stairs to the inn. A waitress seated us on the wide, shaded terrace. We sank down into the soft, flowery cushions of the bamboo chairs. It was the perfect ending to our mystery. My dad would restore Captain Snow's house for Mr. Snow, we would become the proud owners of the Eel Grass Palace, the wicked witches would no longer practice their black arts (we hoped,) and Karl and Mr. Loggins had left town for good. There were lots of romances growing all around us, blooming like little antique roses. We felt good about it. Mr. Snow turned out to be a real friend.

Our waitress served us little sandwiches and cakes with our tea. They tasted yummy after our afternoon of touring. We finished eating and the tea cups were cleared. We said thank you and good-bye to Mr. Snow. He would be contacting my dad about fixing up the old house. Louie, who had been very silent for the most part, gave Mr. Snow his phone number, and Abigail told him how to contact Slim H. As we were ready to leave, Jared and Louie's Aunt Lydia came out onto the terrace.

"Well, who do we have here?" he asked, stepping up to us. Louie still seemed stunned about Jared and his aunt. He stared at them as if they had two heads each! I introduced them to Mr. Snow. They chatted a little.

"I've been thinking about preserving some of the open land around town," Mr. Snow told Jared. "I have plenty of money, and I can't take it with me, if you know what I mean. Maybe you could help me draw up the papers and we could do what that group of outlaws wanted to do, only we'll do it right. Maybe the Weeks sisters and a few others would want to join in on it with me."

"Great idea!" exclaimed Jared. We thought so too. Then we told Jared about Morton.

"Aloma has to go to jail for that!" exclaimed Louie.

"I can't believe that Aloma would do that!" exclaimed Aunt Lydia.

"She didn't break the law," Mollie stated.

"She did," Jared corrected her. "I found quite a few old laws about witch-craft on the books. They're old, but they're still the law! I know that you kids feel that the 'bad guys got away,' but I promise you that those witches had better not try any of this nonsense again, or they'll have to contend with me! I'll take them to court and I'll make sure they think twice before they sacrifice an animal, put a spell on a neighbor, or make an innocent citizen into a zombie again!"

"Thanks, Jared!" Louie bubbled. He finally snapped out of his shock when he heard the good news of Jared's plan. We thanked him too. Now we could really feel safe again and we had a satisfying ending to our mystery! We happily pedaled toward the lighthouse, but Abigail suddenly pulled over to the side of the road and stopped.

"What's the matter?" asked Muffy.

"I have to tell you something!" said Abigail.

"What?" Mollie showed concern for once, I guess because Abigail looked so scared, or something. I couldn't tell exactly what.

"Remember last night, when you dropped me off at my house, before din-ner? We saw my grandmother in the kitchen, right? So you all left because we all thought she was there, isn't that right?"

"Yes," we replied. Muffy hadn't been there, but Mollie and I had.

"Well, when I got inside, no one was home! I looked all around and called out to Grammy, but no one answered. No one was there!"

"What do you mean?" asked Mollie, frowning.

"I mean Grammy drove up a few minutes later with Uncle Jack. The woman we saw wasn't my grandmother!"

"Then who was she?" I asked.

"That's the point! I don't know! Something strange is going on at my grandmother's house. Some other things have been happening that I can't explain. At first I thought it was just me, but now I think there's a ghost in my house too!"

So began our next Eel Grass Girls mystery. I would tell you what happened, but I think I'll let Abigail tell you the story, in her own words. We call it *The Strange Disappearance of Agatha Buck*.

Get your own Secret Message Kit, that has material for seven different secret codes including the pigpen cipher, plus an invisible ink pen. Visit the Secret Code Breaker Online web site for information on all the Secret Code Breaker products (http://codebreaker.dids.com).

Rachel Nickerson Luna lives and works in New York City where she also volunteers as an assistant Girl Scout leader and teaches French at her daughter's afterschool program. Ms. Luna summers on Cape Cod and serves on the executive board of a local yacht club. She enjoys sailing, rollerblading, and golfing with her husband Armando and daughter Moraiah. In 2002 Ms. Luna won her yacht club's Commodore's Cup and as well as first place in two Daysailor Series.